Lock Down Publications and Ca$h
Presents

SON OF A DOPEFIEND 3

Maxwell's Story

By

RENTA

First Edition 2023

Printed in the United States of America

Lock Down Publications
P.O. Box 944
Stockbridge, GA 30281
www.lockdownpublications.com

Like our page on Facebook: Lock Down Publications
www.facebook.com/lockdownpublications.ldp

Stay Connected with Us!

Text **LOCKDOWN** to 22828 to stay up-to-date with new releases, sneak peaks, contests and more…

Like our page on Facebook:
Lock Down Publications

Join Lock Down Publications/The New Era Reading Group

Visit our website:
www.lockdownpublications.com

Follow us on Instagram:
Lock Down Publications

Email Us: We want to hear from you!

DEDICATION

This book is a salute to who I once was, who I've never been, who I am, and most passionately, to the me I'll become if the reaper doesn't show up to get me before I arrive at the apex of my potential. This one is for you, my friend. Keep ya head screwed on tight and you'll never lose it! As long as you keep your vision on you and yours, you'll only see you and yours...there's no other lane, brodie. You've lived hard and danced in the rain to set your feet on the road to riches, and if you fail here? Shid??? You fail Moose! You fail Helen! You fail Red!! You'll fail everybody that believes in you! You've seen niggas ball for seven summers, only to starve a thousand winters! So what's *your* aim? You live for what you'll die for, but be willing to die for what wants you to live. This road you travel is crooked, and many will disappear, but never forget, my nigga, the greatest piece on the chess board is the King! As long as he's protected, you got you a game to play. Queen may leave...fam may leave...but you can't! *I* can't! Cause we're one, and when you bend, fold or break...so do I, and I'm gonna be real fucked up with you if you do either!

To Myself: Renta
The Jeweler

Chapter 1

Pimpin' Maxwell's Spiel

The room was a mini library. The walls were lined with shelves upon shelves of books, and the outside of the window opened out onto the roof. The only amenity that took up any space was a mahogany desk placed in the center of the room. The tension was as thick as a woman's ass that's had to many butt shots, and as the three men had a standoff in Messiah's study, confusion swirled the atmosphere.

"What the fuck?" The words slipped from Messiah's lips as his eyes bounced from the screen to Pimpin' Maxwell. *How though?* He couldn't believe what he'd seen.

"Ain't this a bitch!" Sunjay spat with murder in his statement. His hand was frozen down by the bulge beneath his shirt, and he lusted for the feel of the steel.

"Yeah," Pimpin' shook his head in resolution. "That is usually what they say when shit turns ugly. Now, you boys chill while I give my spiel," he cautioned while aiming the big .357. Messiah noticed how the barrel was more focused on Sunjay than him. "Messiah, you brought a playa back from being drug head Fred, youngin, and I'll always respect ya game for that, and Sun—" he nodded at Sunjay. "I know you ready to go for that toolie on ya waist, but you boys just give an old-timer his time of glory, and after that?" He shrugged indifferently, before doing what *any* man can do in the thralls of a deadly situation. The man tossed his protection to the floor, and even as Messiah watched it land at their feet, Sunjay was already in motion.

"Pussy ass nigga!" He spat before upping his banga and getting straight to the business. *WAP!* He slapped Pimpin' across the face, knocking blood in the air.

"Sayyy—" Messiah began, but as he stalked over to the fallen man, Sunjay was a vampire for the crimson liquid leaking from the side of the man's head.

"Arrrgh!" Pimpin' cried in pain as he crumbled to the floor. Sunjay, like a shark, was lured to the scent of blood, and once he was standing over his prey, he took aim at his man's top.

"Say goodnight, fool ass boy!" He spazzed as his finger tickled the clit of the pistol.

"Sunjay!" Messiah shouted just as the tool laughed. *BOCA!*

"Fuck wrong with you, nigga!" Sunjay flipped when Messiah slapped his hand and fucked up his shot. The slug punched through the floor, missing Pimpin' Maxwell's noggin by inches, and as Messiah and Sunjay argued, Pimpin' hurriedly scrambled to his hands and knees. He crawled desperately for his gun, and once it was in his clutch, he fought to his feet.

"Negro!" He raged with one hand clutching the steel and the other to his throbbing head. Sunjay watched him out his peripheral, but kept his glare on Messiah. "This hoe ass dude done came up into yo' spot and snatched up your wife and—"

"Shut the fuck up!" Messiah demanded as his glare departed from Sunjay and landed on Pimpin' Maxwell. "Both of y'all!" He eyed his mentor. Blood leaked from the crack in his skull, and he had a head rush from moving so fast. Yet, those two small smudges on his two step was nothing compared to the cracks in his heart. He'd had a hand in breeding both those boys, and to know either could down him in cold blood had his Pimpin' out of wack.

"What, Playboy, what you gonna do with that?" Sunjay challenged with a nod at the nickel plated .357 in Pimpin's hand. "You're a pimp, Blood, not a killa," Sunjay taunted, and Pimpin' chuckled menacingly before Messiah stepped between them. His eyes were hard, and neither man had noticed him slip his own strap off his waist.

"Calm the fuck down, bruh!" He gritted through clinched teeth, his vision reclaiming Sunjay. Sunjay's face balled up in contempt, but when his gaze fell to the pole in Messiah's grip, he tamed the beast in him. "And you—" Messiah's glare captured Pimpin'. Studying the man, Messiah was, and had always been a thinker. *Somebody trying to turn me and Pimpin' against each other! He was with me the day when Justice was snatched up, mane, but whoever did the deed couldn't have anticipated that.* His mental spoke to his heart, but he couldn't figure out *how* that image on the screen showed Pimpin' shooting Rosa? "You know *something*, fam, and either you're gonna spit it out, or these burnas gonna spit bullets. Your choice, Pimp," he offered, and Pimpin' Maxwell's hazel eyes drifted to Sunjay, hurt and temptation of bloodshed a dangerous mixture blending in his gaze. Sunjay merely chuckled, his eyes revealing his lust for that gangsta shit. Pimpin' Maxwell wrestled with the notion of tempting fate but settled on reigning in his emotions before mumbling under his breath and exiting the room. Sunjay thought about giving him the coup de Grâce to the back of the head, but the threat dancing in Messiah's orbs told the tale. *There'd be a blood payment for the sin!* He shook his head in pity at Messiah.

"Your heart gonna get yo' weak ass slumped out here," he foretold.

"Never die alone, playboy." Messiah responded as Pimpin' Maxwell re-entered the room. The man held a towel filled with ice to his head, and the black book in the other.

"I didn't want you to find out like this, Messiah." His admission fed the tension and both Messiah and Sunjay's suspicious visions captured him.

"That's what almost just got yo' stupid ass sent to the upper room, *secrets,* ole man!" Sunjay spat, his trigger finger twitching.

Pimpin' took a seat on the sofa before resting the black book on his lap. "Yeah, sho nuff, slick," he acknowledged. He'd never really trusted Sunjay, but on the strength of knowing the boy's family, he gave him the game so he wouldn't be a lame. Yet, Pimpin' was the streets, and knew a few secrets Sunjay thought he held close to his chest. "But I think we *both* have a few *secrets* that needs to be revealed, ain't that right, Sunjay?" He smirked connivingly.

Sunjay frowned in confusion. "Fuck you talmbout, dude. I—"

"Either you gonna tell 'em or I'm gonna tell him, Pimp. Either or. Nobody leaving this room until all the dirt has returned to the earth," Pimpin' Maxwell cut him off. Turning his eyes to Messiah. He saw the confusion written across his face. "Rewind that tape, pimp buddy, and let's study," He jived with a nod at the plasma screen. Messiah's eyes boomeranged back and forth between the two closest men in his life. *Both of these cats playing foul? Secrets?* He wondered before reluctantly turning and making his way to the screen. Taking the footage back to the top, he glanced back at Pimpin' to figure his aim, and the man nodded for him to touch the play button. The screen came to life and the three men watched Rosa make her way to the door with a smile on her face. When she opened it and the smile slipped away, it seemed as all three men held their breath after the bullet snapped her head back and her killer entered the room.

"Pause it there!" Pimpin' Maxwell requested. "Look at the time stamp in the top left corner, pimp. Now, if I can be in two places at the same time, my Pimpin' would sho nuff be in another dimension, but I know you remember me sitting beside you in that pretty truck you got sitting out front.

So." he shrugged.

"And if you look in the background, you'll see the shadow of someone else the screen didn't catch."

"Nigga that's you on this."

"Naw, sucka, it ain't me!" Pimpin' cut Sunjay's accusation in half. "Now, I admit the playa holds a strange resemblance, but—"

"Wait a minute. Messiah whispered as he stepped closer to the screen. He studied the Pimpin' Maxwell look alike and as soon as it dawned on him, Pimpin' Maxwell chuckled. Messiah's eyes bounced from the screen to Pimpin' and back to the screen as he envisioned, *King*, the man from the party who'd demanded the ransom for Justice's release. He recalled how off balance he was that night. *Justice stared at him perplexed. "Pimpin'? What yuh sayin, pa? Why would Pimpin' Maxwell be involved in dis?" She asked. "Wah going..." her words trailed off as her eyes focused on something behind him. Messiah spun defensively and came face to face with an impeccably dressed man with features so identical to his that it shook him. The man's resemblance to Pimpin' Maxwell was uncanny, but even more so, the resemblance between he and Messiah were frightening! What the fuck! This boy looks like me. Naw, like Pimpin'!* He remembered the night he'd come face to face with the man who'd ran the con on him. Confusion was written all over his face when he returned his sight to his mentor and removing the makeshift ice pack from his head. Pimpin' Maxwell nodded confirmation to an unasked question. Sunjay was as stupefied as a vampire awaking from a centenary's sleep to find how much things had changed.

"Fuck going on, bruh. I'm saying—" he paused to walk over to the screen. "This is *enough* evidence for us to torture this bozo and get sis nem back. What we waiting on, Messiah!" He spat, but Messiah paid him no mind as he and

Pimpin' eye wrestled. Shit got spookier when a storm converged in the older man's eyes. Messiah knew then that life as he knew it would be as funky as a seventies afro! He'd never witnessed Pimpin' relinquish the tight hold on his emotions, so the vision was as abnormal as a man with titties.

"Hold tight, tyke, and let a pimp tell you how the game ain't made for a square, and no matter how ruthless it may be, it can be twice as fair," he jazzed, and as his eyes became unfocused. Messiah watched as the man seemed to fall into an ocean of the past.

***

It was the year of 1978, ya dig—the year the Supreme Court ruled that race could be a factor in the admission to institutions of higher learning! Naw-naw, Pimp; underdig me so you can understand me. I say; it was the year of 1978, twenty four years after Brown vs. Board of Education had changed American history, by making segregation illegal, and further pushing America towards the goal of integration! Brotha man, it was the funky year of 1978, three years after the ending of the war in Nam! Most importantly, youngins, it was the year of 1978–March 14th, and though the sun had risen high and bright, snow had fallen the night before, and covered the ground like a fresh coat of cocaine. I'd just pulled a gorgeous, cherry red Eldorado to the curb of Tif's Diamond Co. in downtown Dallas and killed the ignition. Spring had arrived from between the spread legs of winter, but the chill still clung to the air like reunited lovers and a tight embrace. See...back then, gents, I was just a young bull, swift and swell on my game, and pulling a small pouch from my pocket. I knew I was about to prove that testament. My vision drifted to the passenger's seat. "You hoes know the plan, so stick to the script and we can dip back into the sunset with the leprechaun's gold, ya under dig?" I prepped my hoes. Holly, the Swedish freak in my passenger seat, smiled before flipping down the visor, and applying a fresh coat of cherry lipstick to her thin lips.

"We got ya, daddy, don't stress the small stuff," she assured.

"Hoe," I spat with an appalled expression, as if she'd just asked me to put my lips on her funky pussy. "The only thing a pimp stresses is which colors gators will compliment my slacks to perfection, ya dig?" I jazzed and allowed my vision to lift to the rear view mirror. Sassy, my Russian Jane's grey eyes met mine before she winked her understanding of her role in my movie. I'd thoroughly schooled those bitches to the verb without hitting a curb! I nodded before emptying the contents of the little bag into my empty palm, smiling at the six "simulated" diamonds that rolled onto my flesh. They were gorgeous, and twinkled in their cut, proving that beauty could be held in one's hands. I'd sat on that con for months; long con always needed more attention than short con, because it usually had a bigger pot of gold at the end of the rainbow. "Hand me that briefcase, Sassy. It's time to see if you hoes deserve an Oscar, or a kick in the ass like soccer," I vibed with a chuckle.

***

Minutes Later

"I love it, hon, I absolutely love it!" A middle aged Caucasian dame gushed as she stared down the three carat marquise cut diamond ring on her finger. Her husband smiled knowingly before turning his sights on the sales woman.

"Can I pay in check? Credit?" He inquired. The woman gave him a look of perplexity.

"How about we just charge it to your account with us, Mr. Theodore?" She suggested. Theodore looked stunned. Eyes wide, he dramatically slapped a palm against his forehead.

"Silly me! Yes...yes, please do, Margaret. I totally forgot about the account!" He admitted.

"It's just like you to forget something like that, you old tiger." His wife slapped his arm playfully. Theodore chuckled with a shrug.

"Trivial matters, darling." He downplayed the matter, before lifting a brow to the sales woman.

She smiled, "No problem, sir, just give me a moment—" she was saying when the door opened to the store. All eyes lifted to Sassy and Holly, both dressed expensively, both white women, and both followed by I, a pimp in a cream pinstriped suit. Businessmen recognize bidness, so upon entrance, Theodore's eyes automatically fell to the titanium briefcase hand cuffed to my left wrist. Holly and Sassy were both fashionistas clad in Oscar Delarenta pant suits that were barely visible beneath Holly's faux Russian sable and Sassy's faux fox fur. Both women wore long, hand stitched, silk gloves, adorned with sparkling jewelry on each finger, but it was Holly who stepped forward with an expensive air, before glancing down at her watch.

"Where's the service!" She made a face of impatience, before her eyes lifted to behold the couple. "You'd think they'd break their necks for royalty. Can you believe they'd leave us waiting?" She rolled her eyes dramatically.

"Oh, my God, please forgive me, Ms. Rockefeller. I'm sooo sorry to keep you waiting! Just—just give me a few seconds please!" The sales girl plead with distress on her facial. Holly waved her off, but it was the man's wife who smiled politely.

"They're kind of short on this snowy afternoon, sweety, but their service is just magnificent!" She gushed before closing the gap between them and flashing the six carat mountain on her finger. "And their gems are just to die for!"

Holly gently took the woman's hand by the fingertips, and brought it closer to her eyes, "Yes," she said offhanded. "They're "cute", but I'd went with the baguette cut rather

12

than that marquise if I were you. The marquise is sooo outdated, it gives the ring an ancient appeal. Do better, honey."

"Why I've never!" The woman snatched her hand back in offense before rushing back to her husband's side. He'd just collected their receipt when he turned to frown in disdain as his wife latched onto his arm.

Sassy noticed it and stepped forward with a warm smile. "Please excuse my sister, it's been such a horrid day for us, and we've jet lagged from a flight from Europe," She apologized before slapping Holly's shoulder prissily. "That was just plain rude of you!" She admonished, and I almost burst into laughter when the couples posture relaxed. Money! I'd known that the chump change I "invested" on the costume jewelry at the cheap little boutique, coupled with the cheap, but fancy looking threads would pay off.

Ole Theodore's face softened. "Its quite alright. We just made the trip back from Romania about three days ago, and Lord knows I'm grateful for the speed of our Gulf Stream that shortened the trip by miles and hours!" He lowkey gloated. I smirked. It never ceased to amaze me how the privileged so easily made themselves marks for the con. "That" has to be how the con was invented! A rich mu'fucka had to have revealed how rich they were to a mu'fucka that was tired of being poor. These were my thoughts when Theodore's eyes found me; they fell to the briefcase, before jumping to my vision. Though my skin was tribal dark, and my fluffy afro made a statement, it was just something about my aura that exuded something macknificent!

"And, what business might you indulge in, kind fellow?" He probed; his curiosity was Simon pure. I feigned shock that he would acknowledge a lowly negro as myself.

"Me! Oh, I—I just work for—"

"Martin!" Holly demanded, staring aghast that I'd spoken. "If you value your job, you'd do better not speaking unless me or Cora request it. Especially in reference to the

family affairs." She gave me a glare with the admonishment. I played to that "Martin" character with all I had. Nodding like a scolded child, my eyes fell to the highly polished floor.

"My apologies, Ms. Rockefeller. I'm terribly sorry," I mumbled just loud enough to be heard, and just as I anticipated, Theodore's eyes grew wide at the mention of the name. The Rockefeller's had old money and those in the know, knows that they have a hand in most of all that makes rich folk stay rich! Theodore studied us curiously before fixing his vision on Holly.

"Rockefeller? Well, that's not such a common name, would you happen to be related to the Davison's side? Or—"

"First, good sir, I don't think that's any of your business. We're not aquatinted and—" Holly held up a glove hand to pause him.

"My God, how rude of me." The man remembered his manners and extended a hand. "Theodore, Theodore Bension," he introduced, but Holly merely stared down at his hand as if it were the most filthiest thing she'd ever seen. Theodore's smile became strained as he took the affront on the chin. The Rockefellers had the power to add or subtract from a man's success, and he didn't want to ruffle any feathers. Nodding politely, he and his wife hurriedly made their exit; whispering their feelings no doubt.

The sales woman observed the encounter with apt attention, feeling inferior to the money in the room, and that revealed that my play had its intended effect. I strolled over to the glass display case that encased an assortment of different designs of rings and sat the briefcase atop of it. The sales ladies curiosity was a playa's playground, and it was a pleasure to be the playa the game God had gifted the opportunity to. I popped the latches on the case and as soon as it open sesamied, I spun it to face the woman. Her eyes grew as wide as the skies at the vision of all those Benjamins, and I smiled... knowing there was no way for her to know that though the top layers of each of those stacks of money were authentic. Everything below them were all hype! I'd cut stacks of newspaper into the shape of the almighty dollar and bounded a big face hunnid on top and the bottoms to give the appearance of big money. I'd even dyed the shit to match the real deal!

"I—wha—what might I help you with, sir?" That snow bunny stammered at the sight of all that money. I allowed her to become a prisoner of allure before slamming the top of the briefcase down so hard that the bitch jumped in shock. That's when Holly made her way over.

"It's not what you can help "him" with, but more of what you can help us with." She waved an hand between her and Sassy. "He's." she nodded at me. "Merely our jeweler, who'll inspect the diamonds we want to buy. "Now," she smiled brightly. "We'd like to see a few of your best stones."

The sales woman's eyes searched hers. "You mean actual diamonds?"

"Yes, dear, actual diamonds," Holly assured with a roll of her eyes.

"Well," the sales woman said. "One moment please, I'll go get the manager of the department." That pretty young thang held up a finger before disappearing into the back of the store. At that time, me and my felines could've robbed em' blind, but that would've been a crime, and I ain't ever heard of no pimp that pimped hard from behind bars.

Holly turned to me. " How'd I do, daddy?" Like most feminine creatures, she craved validation. I gave her a stern glare before speaking out the side of my mouth.

"The show ain't ova yet, hoe, until it's time to go! So, tame ya tongue until it's done." I stomped down just as the sales clerk returned with an impeccably dressed middle eastern fella who extended his hand to me for a shake. I glanced at it curiously before turning my questioning gaze to Holly, and she took charge.

"He's just the help. We're the ones you're greeting should be extended to." She nodded from herself to Sassy. The man's vision drifted from me to them.

"Yes—yes, I'm told you and your consorts are looking to purchase some—"

"Martin?" Sassy called to me, cutting dude off with a bourgeois wave of her hand. See, I knew bringing those white women with me on that play was key, cause within the eyes of old money, there was no better stamp of approval back then, than that of a blonde haired blue eyed good ole gal, and so after she'd put the attention back on me, I played the role of a good ole nigger as well as them house niggas did back in the day. Reopening the briefcase, I allowed him to see the stacks of green backs before reclosing the tomb on them dead men before he could study to hard.

"That's a half million dollars, darling and we want to spend it with your store if you carry the gems we're in need of." Holly dangled the bait, and the jackal smiled.

"I think we can accommodate you; it just so happens that we just received a shipment of exquisite stones that may fit your taste," he proposed and ten minutes later, we found ourselves in the back of the store, huddled in a strange room resembling the ones at the banks where safety deposit boxes were stored. Money tended to have that effect on people, and as he pulled out a large shelf from within a large vault, we watched him carry it with care as if it were a new born. Once he rested it on the table before us, I saw why; six perfectly cut gems sat pretty upon a velvet cloth, glistening like small stars under the dim light. I smirked; another reason I'd brought Holly and Sassy along was because that sales lady was none other than Holly's cousin, who'd schooled me of the size and cut of those very stones! All in the name of her choosing fee, pimp. My constitution was prostitution and my Pimpin" went for a fee; never for free, ya dig! The man stared down at the ice with reverence as he spoke his piece. "These are our Kimberly Diamonds from the city of

Kimberly in South Africa. My family mines there and those beautiful stones were cut to exhibit a fabulous clarity. They're five point five carats each of Africa's beauty and they're the only ones of their kind," he passionately revealed as we appreciated the stones the motherland had birthed.

"May I?" I nodded toward them, and the man nodded his consent. I opened the briefcase once more, this time removing a small magnifier before I lifted one of the stones for a closer inspection.

"God," Sassy moaned beside me, and I knew that was cue for the next phase of the play. "I've suddenly taken ill, Sari," she moaned pitifully, and Holly deserved an academy award for the mock concern that splashed onto her face.

"Lord, Carlie May, have you gotten the fever?" She asked before stepping over and placing the back of her gloved hand against her wife in law's forehead. "You're a little warm, sweety. Maybe you should go to the car and lie down until we're finished," she suggested, and though I never took my eye away from the optic device I used to gaze into that beautiful stone, I saw the next phase of my play open up inside my third eye. Just as I pulled the small magnifier away and nodded to that ole fella as Sassy turned to depart. Yet, slipping a small bottle of baby oil from beneath her fur covered sleeve, she squeezed a squirt onto the floor before returning it to its place.

I gave Holly a confirming nod. "These diamonds are free of flaw, Mrs. Rockefeller, and they—"

"Oh my, God!" A loud scream interrupted my flow, and we all jumped with a start as our eyes flew to where Sassy had slipped and fallen.

"Are you okay, Mrs. Rockefeller?" The owner's concern was evident as he rushed over to her, and I wasted no time slipping the sham rocks from the creases between each of my fingers and replacing them with the real ones. The frauds shined and sat just as pretty upon that smooth cloth as the

others did, and when my eyes lifted to Holly's, she went into raw form.

"Carlie May!" She screamed as she raced over to the fallen dame.

"Lord," Sassy moaned apparently dazed as the owner of the store aided her to sit up. "I'm sooo dizzy, I don't know what happened. One moment I was walking and the next," she mumbled before glancing back at the spot she'd supposedly slipped.

"Well I'll be," Holly hissed, mouth agape in mock horror as she gazed down at the spot. "You incompetent imbecile!" She exclaimed before jabbing a finger toward the spot. "You could've put up a wet floor sign or something. Do you not know who our family is!" She raged before kneeling down to help Sassy back to her feet.

"Mrs. Rockefeller, I—that," the owner sputtered with a horrid expression.

"Don't!" Holly demanded with a raised hand as she helped Sassy to her feet. See, the Rockefeller name had heightened the man's fears because of the power it wielded not only in political, but social circles as well. The people had long money within the oil industry, as well as banks, so it was only right that the man that owned the store fear reprisal. "You'll be hearing from our lawyer!" Holly demanded before her glare found me. "Come, Martin, we don't need his stinking diamonds. We'll find another store to do business with," she paused as her eyes fell to the small puddle on the floor. "One that's thoughtful enough to put up wet floor signs!" She demanded before flipping her permed hair over her shoulder real bougie like before heading for the door with Sassy in tow. The owners eyes shot to me, and I chuckled when his vision flickered to the glistening stones. As I passed, I slapped champ on the back and gave him a sad shake of my head.

"Bitches!" I spat before making off with more than I entered with.

Chapter 2

Present Time...
Keisha

"I'm so sorry, Popa, yuh tell 'em mama me ah love her," Keisha cried as she slid from the dead weight of her father. Her eyes were wild as she wobbled to her feet and fought through the storm of emotions that raged within her.

"Mmhh uhh yuuu"! The hysterical cry was muffled by the dirty rag that had been taped inside her captives mouth, and as soon as her eyes fell to the bound woman, Keisha's wild eyes became slits.

"Now yuh see wah yuh made mi do!" She screamed manically, her Patois dialect thickening. Her captives eyes grew as large as the seas in fear as she took in the vision of the lioness of Jamaica. Keisha stood glaring down at her with the deadly shaped knife clutched in her small hand. A thick trail of blood rolled down the blade and fell to the floor just before the captives vision slowly trailed up the now bloody dress the woman wore. Keisha's usually slayed hair was a mess, stray dreadlocks hung wildly about her sweaty face as she glared at the woman.

"Mmmuhh!" The captive cried from behind the tape, and Keisha stormed over and snatched the tape and gag free. The adhesive from the tape snatched skin from her lips and Keisha had no remorse.

Smack! She slapped fire from the woman.

"Her bumbaclot, yeah!" she spat

"Why are you doing this! You used me to get you him! You lied!" The woman cried, and Keisha giggled.

"Jah is a good lover and ya pum pum is nice and sweet, but Jah is de serpent, gyal! Jah ah fuk de gyal man before Jah smile like de batti boi in her gyal face! Now dem gyal made me kill mi Popa!" She spat vehemently before spitting on the floor. Her victim's dirty face was streaked with tears as she wondered *why* she'd gotten involved with the she devil. "Jah will *never* know wah Messiah's dick feels like again." Keisha smirked, madness twinkling in her eyes.

"What the hell are you talking about? I've never even—" she was saying before the ringback tone of a phone gave her pause. Keisha's eyes snapped toward the sound before holding up a finger.

"I'll be right back," she spoke over her shoulder as she headed for her phone. Retrieving it, she returned with a concerned look on her pretty face.

"Wah yuh wan, rude boy?" She answered. Listening, she nodded as if the caller could see her. Whatever was being said, Keisha's eyes watered as they shifted to her slain father. "I av bad news for him, mi father has been murdered. I tink him fun boy bumbaclot Sunjay sent a hit! Mi father is dead, dread! Find him boy Messiah, and de batty boy Sunjay will be with him. Kill *everyone,* but I wan Messiah alive. Don fuck up!" She demanded, already feeling the power of wearing the crown. She disconnected the call before returning her attention to her captive. "Back to you." she smiled before stepping forward with the knife poised.

***

"Pimpin'. Pimpin'." Messiah beckoned while snapping his fingers in front of the man's face. Pimpin' Maxwell snapped to, his eyes refocusing as he came back to the present.

"Huh—wha? Ohh, my fault, young blood. A pimp was reminiscing about my Pimpin' and must've got trapped in the memory." He shook his head.

"Yeah, all that shit, but what *any* of that slick shit gotta do with—" Sunjay paused to wave a hand toward the smart TV. "This bidness right here, nigga?" He spat before tightening his grip on the burna *still* in his hand. "If this ain't you…"

"His name is Junior, and he's someone dear to me and soon will be to you too, Messiah." Pimpin' Maxwell cut him off before glancing to a silent Messiah. "Just give me a second to open yo' eyes to the cruelest trick ever played on a bonafide playa as yaself." He paused as his and Messiah's vision danced. Pimpin' shook his head bitterly, before casting a curiosity into the atmosphere that may have killed the cat, but merely unbalanced the vibe amongst playas. "Lust can defeat love if the moments right, cat daddy, and it's long overdue, for someone to peel the wool from ya eyes, kid."

"Say, playboy, fuck all these riddles. Give it to me how I like my yak… straight, no chase!" Messiah flatlined the cat and mouse game with a dangerous glare.

"Pimpin' chuckled. "No doubt, playa, no doubt," he conceded before falling back into his seat and placing the iced towel back to his head. "You fellas chill while I reveal the tale of how a pimp became a snake, and how the power of *the "P"* became the forbidden fruit one of the classiest dames I've ever encountered, shared within the thralls of dick and pussy." His gaze became distant as a soft smirk curved his lips, and in that moment, the past sucked all three gents back!

Back into the days where the *junkie* monkey rode the fiends backs, and the game was cop, lock, and blow between hoes and Macks! I'm talking, the year of 1978; the middle passage between heroine's ebb, and crack cocaine's awakening! 1978! One of the years turning mothers, fathers, big mamas, cousins, uncles, and aunties into dope fiends!

Chapter 3

1978– Dallas Texas

♫ *"'It was the day of September/ That day I'll always remember/ cause that was the dayyy that my daddy died/ never got a chance to meet him/ never heard nothing but bad thangs about him/ mama I'm depending on youuu, to tell me the truth/ mama just held her head and said; son/ Poppa was a rolling stone/ wherever he laid his hat was his home/ and when he diiiied, all he left was us alone.'"* ♫

The Temptations blared from the speakers as I bobbed my head to the rhythm. As I maneuvered my freshly waxed, new Lincoln Continental down Oakland Boulevard in Sunny South Dallas, I smiled the smile of success, cause that day was sho nuff fine, and the money was made all good! Diamonds sparkled from my pinky to my wrist, and as spring breeze blew through the cracked window, it seemed to dance around my afro before gently caressing the flesh of the four, fly, jazzy and willing dames that occupied my company. Foxy, a red toned, red bone was my bottom hoe that sat pretty in the passenger's seat, and Sassy, Holly, and Myra, my Latin mami, enjoyed the comforts of the big backseat. I was just a young fly champ on the come up, but see, pimp, I've been outchea in these streets since Moby Dick was just a small fish, and Kermit the frog was just a tadpole! And even wayyy back when, before that shark, "Jaws" grew a fin, I was the smooth operator Sade was speaking of in that song she sung, and Poppa was a rolling stone. Wherever he laid his hat was his home and when he diiied, all he left us was alone. Hey mama, is it true what they say? That daddy never worked a day in his life?" All four of my ladies sung, while snapping their fingers and bopping their heads to The Temptations. I nodded along. See, I kept my stable real jazzy; ya dig, and as I watched the world pass from behind a tinted pair of large bubble eyed Aviator shades, I bared witness to prostitution being the constitution! Ho'in was in full effect up and down the boulevard, and though Pimpin' was big bidness, I peeped the slick exchanges of dead presidents for addictions as the pusher man helped the junkies get those funky monkeys off their backs. Heroin had to have been the "eleventh plague" the Bible forgot to mention; The most powerful one that God sent to convince Pharaoh to let his people go. That shit swept from the jungles of Vietnam and Thailand and found land in the ghetto just like the Mayflower did in 1620 at Plymouth Rock! Except for rather than Pharaoh, it was the hood holding niggas hostage, and though the pusher man was able to escape the dirt of the slums, he did so by releasing that plague of monkeys that jumped on a niggas back and rode that mu'fucka like a champion bull rider at a big paying rodeo! Yet, that day of March, I felt real dapper in a sleek silk shirt with a butterfly collar, with its ends tucked down into a fresh, tailored made pair of tan bell bottoms that fell just right down over my platform kicks. That day I had a plan, I'd been slick macking on this pretty young thang that belonged to a fellow pimp with no brain, but the hoe was elusive. See, the game of Pimpin' ain't ever had love in the constitution; just a whole bunch of manipulation and persuasion to motivate a hoe to keep that pussy moving. Yet, even back then, a lot of gents had the game fucked up! They played Pimpin' to the naked eye, but behind closed doors they had hoes believing they were boyfriend and girlfriend. Some real simp shit, ya dig, that never fooled the kid, cause even when I was just chili Pimpin', I could spot the bonafide hoe in most women. See,

Trixy was a bow legged bimbo under the management of Pimpin' Magic Mike, but I knew the sure sucka didn't have a magic bone in his body, and the only reason the hoe was ho'in for his ism was because he was boyfriending the dame. Pimp had the hoe delusional, believing she was cheating if she entertained the next mack's macking, but that's where he was slacking because any sure playa thrives on the power of his game being tested. How you know how far ya game can go if you ain't ever test ya hoe? So, I plotted on daddy, and that day was the day I planned on adding that fine thang to a playa's resume. So, reaching over and muting the music, I set wheels in motion.

"Foxy, you know how to play, and I've already taught you what to say, so show daddy what you made of," I jazzed before pulling the sleek car to the curb, and glancing over my shoulder, back at the others. "I bet not see nan one of these other hoes out here ho'in out ho'in you bitches. Y'all some champ hoes that knows the worth of pussy, so don't short change ya self and make sure my trap right," I motivated with a single clap of my hands, and that's when my ism was tested!

"If I'm good, daddy, can I have a day off?" Holly suggested, and her sister in laws damn near broke their necks when whipping their heads to stare at the disrespectful hoe. They were astonished!

I chuckled. "Sassy, slap that hoe for a pimp, but not hard, we don't want the bitch humping for a buck, looking like she belongs to an abusive relationship," said I. Sassy wasted no time smacking the bitch, so I was just as quick in macking the bitch. "Hoe, ain't no days off in this occupation, and when ya pussy get tired, you betta suck a mean dick to satisfy a tricks kicks, or use ya asshole to get my cash flow. Laziness is a sin cause a lazy hoe can't win, so hump hoe or be a chump hoe and kick rocks, cause it's big Pimpin' over here from my head to my socks," I broke on the hoe before popping my collar. "And just for disrespecting my ism, hoe, you bet not return until my money bursting out ya purse!" I demanded as the ladies slipped out the car. As they shot off in hot pursuit of their next trick, Holly made her way over to my side of the car. I peeped the scene with a gangsta lean and awaited the hoes verbal.

"I'm sorry, daddy, forgive me for –"

"Hoe!" I D.O.A'd her apology before slowly pulling the shades from over my sights and glaring at the dame. "You think I'm a trick or something?"

"Huh," she looked startled. "No daddy, I—I just,"

"You just bout to give me an excuse but dig." I cut her off before flicking the top of my nose. "Never be sorry, hoe, because a sorry hoe is the same as a lazy one, and forgiveness is for God and tricks to give. "Two words, hoe." I held up two fingers. "For." I wiggled a finger. "For that powerful thang between ya legs, a mofo will," I vibed before wiggling the other digit. "Give." I smirked. "Give you diamonds and pearls, and if you know how to use that funky mu'fucka, they'll give you the world. "For", is the reason, and "give" is what they'll do, so never confuse the two, bitch, cause for disrespecting my ism, I'll give you a swift kick in the ass! Forgive that!" I spat before dismissing the lady to her duties and pulling that sedan back into traffic.

***

As the sun beamed down upon the city, and up and down the block, criminal activity ran rampant. Nonetheless, at the car wash on MLK Boulevard, a small cluster of gentlemen stood in a half circle around a sho nuff playas as he shot the jive and gave 'em a spiel they could feel. Red Bone Tyrone's afro was his power, like Sampson in the Bible, and his evening dress was fresh as the spring breeze as he vibes. The men around him loved raw game, and though each was a sho nuff pimp in their own right, not every playa was bred with a golden tongue.

"Talk that shit, pimp. Talk that shit and swallow spit, mack buddy!" Pimpin' Magic Mike encouraged with a boo of his head to Red Bone's groove.

Red Bone was animated with his gestures as he shuck and jived- *"Yeah, pimp, I've broke on pale hoes with pink toes! Hoes from Maine to Ukraine! Russia on down to Liberia! I've pimped white bitches; Persian dames that were mystical, and I done even had some low down rotten hoes that should've been from Germany, cause they were as crooked as that ole Swastika used by Hitler!"* Red Bone Tyrone jazzed as Magic Mike's eyes drifted down the blade. He was just in time to spot Trixy, his number one bread winner get accosted by someone in a big fancy Lincoln. His eyes squinted suspiciously as he tried to cop a view into the unfamiliar machine, but the driver was leaned toward the passenger side, shooting his shot at Trixy. Magic couldn't get a good glimpse. Yet, and in spite of his stalking tendencies, Red Bone Tyrone macked on. *"A hoe gonna be a hoe no matter the love you give her, so with me, she gonna either break bread or break for the hills! Cause if ho'in pays the bills, I'ma slave a hoe until she breaks her heels and everything below the waist she can't feel! My Pimpin' fast like a dash, so if a hoe can't act like a bottle of Heinz Ketchup and catch up, the bitch gonna become a banana and split, cause my "ism" don't stop for no bitch!"*

"Sho ya right, Red Bone. Spit playa!" Sweet Eddie fed the hype, and Red Bone Tyrone wiped himself down.

"Yeah see." He bopped his head before patting his fluffy fro. *"The first nigga a hoe got her game from was a snake, so she can only be a snake bitch! And if her mammy did the same, that means the hoe came out the womb slick and slippery enough to move a sled and the Bible warned us when Joseph was lied on by his master's wife, and even when Herod wanted to kill John the Baptist, but...well, y'all know what Matthew 14 said? For ole John telling Herod it's not solid to fuck, Herodias, his brother's bitch, Herod wanted*

SON OF A DOPEFIEND 3 | RENTA

him dead! And since Herodias knew Herod had that bread, she told her daughter to dance for the sucka, and if it pleased him, demand he give her John's head! That's exactly how it went. Ole Johnny boy lost his head over a bitch...and that's just one funky example of how spooky shit can get! Ya see...it's a cold game between pussy and dick, Pimps, cause though dick stands tall, he never learns to swim... so pussy drowns his stupid ass until he's willing to give all he has to give! Then! Dick turns tender, as pussy hugs him tight, and like a blubbering fool. Dick starts spitting goodnight. Pussy spits in his face, dick becomes a fountain of nut, allowing pussy to win the fight! After it's all over, dick lays down, and pussy thanks him for tricking. Dick becomes an ole soft mu'fucka just awaiting their next tryst of dog chasing the kitten! He falls asleep, never realizing that pussy has come up missing; the funky bitch done ran back, and hid behind the mask of lace panties, just before the bitch she's attached to, comes and pays this Pimpin'!" Red Bone pointed to himself.

"Church!" The crowd applauded the spiel, but Magic Mike's suspicions became his conflictions as he watched his hoe open the passenger's door to the big car. For some strange reason, his pimp alarm was on ten, and his insecurities became dominant. *"Don't no trick drive no car that slick!"* His thoughts reigned supreme, but when he moved to address his hoe, another one blocked his flow.

"Excuse me, daddy, can I have a moment of your time?" The feline purred. She was exotic like the bad bitches of the old, and every playa from the cracked streets of Dallas knew who she belonged to. Silence was instant when she addressed Magic Mike, cause one of the laws instilled into a hoe from the onset of her hoing is to keep her eyes on the ground when in the presence of other pimps glam, but Foxy was a live wire! Her pretty gaze told all with eyes to see, that she was out of pocket, and stepping into a den of playas. That alone was merit for one to intro his ism! In an instant, six of

the eight playas were upon her, surrounding the lady with game, like she was prey trapped within a circle of predators.

"Ya man must be jive, cause not a playa alive would allow you out the hive to roam so aimlessly!" One shot.

"Dig this here, hoe, you out of pocket, and need a boss playa as myself to manage what you can't see, and to transform you into what you wouldn't otherwise be, and that's a bonafide winner!" Another jazzed, and so on and so on, but Foxy never broke her stride, nor removed her eyes from Pimpin' Magic Mike. She recognized his insecurities as he watched Trixy slide into the glossy, stinkin' Lincoln, and at that moment, she reflected on the game Pimpin' Maxwell had injected into her brain before she came. "A boss bitch oozes seduction and steals so much of a man's thoughts, that she obtains the control of them! Play with them, molest them, and most of all, seduce them into all that "you" want them to see, and the lame will become all you want him to be! I need you to work this sucka until I got his dame on a one way train out his stable," he schooled, and seeing that the quest was accomplished, Foxy smirked. Pimpin' Magic Mike's gaze drifted from the sleek continental that was sliding down the street and captured the PYT that strolled before him pigeon toed. Breaking away from the crowd of aggressive men, Foxy paused before ole Mikey. Her name fit her to perfection—her flesh was smooth as Malaysian silk and glowed with a reddish tint like that of a red fox's fur. Her naturally curly hair was cut into a cute bob, and though the woman was exotic in beauty, it was more of the hot pink, spandex shorts that cut up into the crease of her paradise that gave birth to the man's lust. That, coupled with the hot pink halter top that cut off mid stomach, and showed of her flat tummy was a pool of sex appeal that any man would love to dive into. Magic Mike and Red Bone Tyrone's vision fell to the hot pink, heels she wore, and "Bad Bitch!" was their mutual thoughts. Yet whereas Magic Mike became a victim to her seductions, Red Bone's suspicions brought a smirk to

his lips. He was a street nigga "first", and a certified pimp after! At that moment, it dawned on him! Moments earlier, he'd peep Trixy sliding into Pimpin's new machine, and as he studied the web being woven, he chuckled at Pimpin' Maxwell's winning hand. Mentally saluting his mack brotha's game of enticement, Red Bone's smirk widened when Magic Mike's hand slipped into his pocket and came out with a nice bank roll.

"Hoe, you know my flow fa sho, and ain't a dame alive that's stepped into my circumference that ain't paying to be blessed by Magic. Since you outta pocket, I know you're ready to drop that simp and jump with a real pimp!" He jazzed with a pop of his collar, and Foxy nodded her acknowledgment.

"Sho nuff, daddy. I'm tired of Pimpin' Maxwell's heavy hand, and I wanna know if you've got any room in ya stable for a thoroughbred bitch like me?" She spoke the best words to a pimp, and Magic Mike felt like he'd just won pimp of the year. Bopping over to the pretty young thang, he used the roll of money to trail down the crevices between her juicy D-cup breast, before lifting it to his nose and inhaling.

"Um umph! Hoe money is fa sho money!" Said he, before slipping the bankroll back into his pocket. He appeared intoxicated from the aroma of hoism exuding from her, and knew he'd hurt the game for knocking her from Pimpin'.

"You choosing up, may be, but my Pimpin' ain't ever been free." He knew she understood his request for her choosing fee. Foxy smiled seductively, spotting more desire aflame in his gaze than stomp down, and when her gaze danced over to the studious eyes of Red Bone Tyrone, she knew her ruse was being captured within the lenses of a sho nuff playa, that would never fall head over heels for the sake of sheek thrills. Yet, it was the sneaky smirk on his face that revealed to her that not only was he onto her, but her performance would be a reflection of her man's macking, so? She made sure to show that pussy was big bidness to her!

"Can we—" she paused to glance around at the others that admired Pimpin' and hoing at its finest. "Let's go somewhere more private so I can give you my choosing fee, love. What I brought as a contribution is only meant for yo' eyes, honey," she revealed. "I—" she tried, but the raised palm from dude paused her.

"Hoe!" Pimpin' Magic Mike spat before stomping a gator against the stained street. "Peep it, all us gents in the same bidness," he jazzed with a wave toward his brothas with the same hustle. "Pimpin' don't gossip, and Pimpin' don't leak it, so if you choosing up, hoe, you betta do so in front of the world cause Pimpin' ain't no secret!" He jazzed with a roll of his shoulders and a quick flick of the tip of his nose. Foxy allowed the tip of her tongue to moisten her lips before her vision returned to the playa before her. Her gaze briefly fell to his alligator skinned shoes before slowly taking a journey up his tailored slacks and pausing on the slight bulge in his pants; the moment was turning him on. A soft smile curved her full lips as she shrugged indifferently before stepping into his personal space and doing the unthinkable!

"Sayyy, baby, what's the haps with lady!" A short pimp with a lisp demanded, appalled when Foxy unbuttoned Magic Mike's trousers and massaged his little man. Magic Mike was knocked off his pivot by her boldness, and it took him fast.

"Hoe!" He demanded, but a bonafide hoe can recognize the sucka in a man no matter his projections. His dick hardened within her caress even though his verbal contradicted his body language.

"Kinda games you tryna—" he tried, but as quick as a wink, Foxy had dropped to her hunches and his dick trapped within her warm mouth as the sucka's slacks fell to his ankles, revealing his silk boxers.

"Say, Pimp, what type of strange activity you engaging in!" Shorty Mack, a pimp from East Dallas exclaimed. Some were repulsed at the vision, a few applauded Pimpin' getting chose and getting topped on the stroll, but Red Bone shook his head in shame, knowing the pimp had lost his aim to another playa's game.

"Shit!" Pimpin' Magic Mike gritted in pleasure as Foxy showed why Pimpin' and frivolous pleasure don't coincide.

***

Pimpin' Maxwell

The big Lincoln coasted through the city of Dallas, floating down the street as Johnnie Taylor created a playa's vibe for me and the sweet thang in my passenger seat.

"Where ya been, all of my liiife/Tell me where you been hiding/ I've been looking for someone like youuuu, that I can share my life with/ How'd you get out of my dreams. Tell me, how'd Heaven lose youuu."

JT sung that "good love", as I bobbed my head and molested the wood grained wheel. The joint between my lips was filled with that Colombian gold, and the potent ganja had me right. Pulling to the light on MLK, I gazed over at baby love. I could tell she was impressed by my finess but was reconsidering her decision on sliding into the whip with a pimp, and feeling my gaze capturing her, lil baby verbalized that fact.

"Now, Maxwell, I know you ain't scoop me up to take me on a trip through the city in yo' big fancy car," she spoke before reaching over and playing a pimp like a sucka. Massaging my thigh, she smiled seductively and I chuckled, encouraging the hoe to be a hoe. See, I'd learned young that a woman is a very perceptive creature, and they're trained from Barbie dolls how to seduce. I understood that my reaction would lead the lady to fall deeper into her hoism. Needless to say, Trixy leaned over and her vulgar massage slid between my thighs until she held the portion of me that had the power to reveal to her if I was more sucka than playa. Dick has no brain, nor loyalty, so my nature rose against my will. *"Baby,"* Trixy purred like a jungle cat. The good smoke had me feeling good as I admired the lady, I mean the bitch was a replica of Pam Greer, afro and all! *"You've been wanting to sample this pussy for a long time, daddy, and for just fifty measly bucks, you can have me for an hour,"* she enticed my mite as I drove through the light, and turned into the parking lot of a cheap hotel.

"Fifty for an hour, huh?" I smirked with an exhale of ganja smoke. Johnnie serenaded the ambiance of the moment as my vision drifted to mama. *" 'This time we got a good love/ This time we got something special/ This time we gone do it, do it, put our minds to it/ Until we get it riiight/ Though I've had my share of heartaches, baby."* I sung as Trixy nodded confirmation. I shook my head pityingly.

"Hoe, fifty punk ass dollars, plus ten dicks in ya pussy, equals five hundred measly bucks! A stripper makes mo' than that and all the bitch do is flash her titties and make her ass clap for lames with a lil too much change," I shot over my shoulder before pushing the door open and slipping out the sleek machine, but before closing the door, I left the dame with a quick jewel to help her shine bright as a light. *"Hoe, you have a goldmine between ya thighs, and if you not fuckin for pleasure, you gotta be fuckin for compensation, but compensation means a mu'fucka paying you for what you're giving them."* I paused to give the clueless bimbo a gander of disgust. *"And if fifty funky ass dollars is all that pussy worth to you then you're highway robbing "yourself", cause you giving a John what makes you woman. What may come out of what he's giving you may cost "you" more than the price you laid down for in the first place!"* I spat before slamming the door on the shocked expression on her face. *"Wake up, hoe, you been sleep walking on the yellow brick road where clicking those pretty heels won't lead you home,"* I jazzed before going to "invest" in a room that would be the transformation chamber for the bitch!

***

"Pimpin' done lost his motha-fucking mind!" Shorty Mack shouted.

"Naw, naw, Pimp, Pimpin' stone cold bad. He just knocked ole Pimpin' Maxwell for his bottom hoe, and had the bitch gobble him on the blade for the world to see!" Jew-L, a Mack from way back refuted with an envious shake of his head as he watched Pimpin' Magic Mike get topped. Hearing the praise of his fellow pimps, Magic Mike fed the hype and tossed his head back in pleasure before gripping the back of Foxy's head and pumping in and out of her mouth. Cars slid down the boulevard, and as pedestrians strolled pass, all had a surprised expression or shocked reaction. Though it was the norm for crazy shit to transpire on that strip of land where South Dallas thrived, it never ceased to amaze Red Bone Tyrone when the life he lived became poetry in motion. Though all with eyes to see were held captive by the display of shaming the game, Red Bone's vision paid attention to the jewel they were missing! Magic Mike went rigid as his and Foxy's hand became as swift as a pick pocket when it dropped to the bunched pair of slacks around the pimps ankles. Magic Mike was oblivious to the act, and by the time his eyes rolled backward, Foxy's swift hand was just slipping from behind the waist band of her shorts. She'd did her do, all while swallowing his jism, and the bitch was so bad, she hadn't let a drop escape her wet imprisonment. The man had went flaccid and tender, and she was sucking him back to life but he stopped her.

"Gotdamn, you soul sucka!" Pimpin' Magic Mike exclaimed before pushing her away. "What you tryna do, hoe, suck the Pimpin' outta me?" He chuckled before pulling his pants up and getting himself decent. "Now, hoe, hit my mitt and make it quick!" He vibed with an extended palm. His requesting choosing fee was big time in the eyes of a few of his comrades; to see the hoe swallow jism, then pay his

ism was for sure Pimpin', and as Foxy erected herself and wiped her mouth with the back of her hand, she smiled.

"I got you daddy," she purred before slipping her hand down into her shorts. Seeing this, the crowd, save for Red Bone Tyrone, went wild!

"Pimpin' on a roll! Ain't no better smell than money fresh out the pussy hole!" Jew-L exclaimed before turning to Shorty Mack and twinkling his fingers as if he were sprinkling him.

***

Pimpin' Maxwell

As soon as we were safe in the room, Trixy wasted no time stripping down to nothing but flesh. I'd taken a seat in an old, cushioned chair beside the bed. Crossing my legs at the ankle before leaning back in the seat, I studied perfect imperfection. Trixy was a stone cold bad bitch, from the curly afro on her head on down to the manicured lawn between her legs. Lady's tits were the size of grapefruits and her caramel thighs bulged from shapely hips as she stood bow legged for a pimp to behold. Trixy erotically massaged her sandy red areola's as she stared at me from eyes at half-mast.

"Aren't you gonna get undressed, love, so mama can—"

"Hoe, the name of the game is Pimpin'!" I cut that jazz she was blowing. "And love ain't got nothing to do with it, so save the pet names for the tricks, and talk to a pimp with the correct mannerisms," I scolded, and though she rolled her eyes, Trixy never lost the art of her seduction.

"I'm sorry, daddy," she purred before running a wet tongue over her lips.

"Come here," I demanded, and watched her sashay over to me until she was so close that if I so desired, I could reach out and pet her kitten. Uncrossing my legs, I pointed to the floor. "Kneel before a playa, sweet baby."

A frown of impatience eased onto her pretty facial before Trixy placed a hand on her shapely hip. "Look, I ain't got all day, Pimpin' Maxwell, so," she sassed as a suspicious twinkle came to life in her gaze. "Did you bring me here to let me please you, or trick me here to mack me?"

I chuckled while digging into my pocket and coming out with a knot of dead faces so fat I had to struggle to free it. Peeling about fifteen hundred away, I caught the disrespectful bitch off guard when I balled the bills one by one. "Bitch," I spoke with no emotion before pointing at the floor again. "Get on ya knees," I reiterated. Money has always had a way of making mu'fuckas do some of the craziest things to possess it, and seeing Benjamin's face printed across all those green backs, Trixy was willing to let a pimp shit in her mouth and she'd lie and say it tasted like steak! Falling to her knees before me, the woman wasted no time reaching for the zipper of my slacks, and as soon as she had my nature free, I slapped her hand away.

"Ouch!" She cried, startled.

"First off, bitch." It was time to get her mind off "my" bread and get it on some sho nuff hoin! Taking all fifteen crumbled hundred dollar bills into my mitt, I drew my hand back just enough to have a bit of sting before I smacked the dame with twenty nine more fifties than she usually charges for an hour! The money fell around her like green snowballs.

"Ahhh," she cried out in more shock than pain.

"Never question a pimp, hoe. I ain't ever tricked my time, money, or efforts; especially on a bitch I have to lie to!" I spat.

"Why the hell you slap me, Maxwell!" Trixy demanded with a glare so hot it would've cooked me if it had the power to.

Again, I chuckled, but this time I gathered as much spit as I could in my mouth before leaning forward and spitting in the gal's face.

"What the," she cried, hands shooting to wipe the saliva from her prettiness.

"Bitch, the slap was for touching my dick without permission," I revealed as Trixy scrambled on hands and knees to her clothes. I watched with a smirk on my face as she used her red maxi dress to dry her face.

"You funky—" she began before the rest of her verbal died in her throat at the stomp down reflecting within my gaze. "Why'd you do me like that, Maxwell?" She murmured, finally giving me a peek at the soft side of her.

"I believe I answered why I put the big paw on you, and I spit in ya glamour for misaddressing me. My name is "Pimpin'" Maxwell, hoe. Pimpin' the profession, and Maxwell what my mama called me when I came out her pussy and she had to wake up and smell the coffee. "Pimpin'" Maxwell, doll, don't forget the Pimpin'," I schooled before I ruled. Jabbing a finger toward the floor before me, I reigned like a boss, ya dig. "Now, front and center, and don't make me repeat myself." I left no room for argument, and though I paid it no mind, my dick was free and as strong as Superman as Trixy glared at me. I chuckled as I began to thumb through the block of loot in my hands. Psychology is the deepest part of Pimpin', and when that woman's vision fell to the bread, I witnessed the internal battle between emotions and the love of money. That alone revealed she valued it more than she did her self-respect, and that's what convinced me that she'd be a stomp down go getter! From that shadowed corner, I watched Trixy climb to her feet, but as soon as she took a step, I held up a palm.

"Uh-uh." I paused her. "The same way you got over there, find ya way back to where you should've never left," I ruled, and though at that moment, something broke in her, lady complied. Her eyes submerged as she returned to her hands and knees, but this time, rather than the seduction of a feline, love crawled to me with a posture of a woman that had the world on her shoulders. I watched her until she

reclaimed her position, on her knees between my legs, and when she gazed up at me, something dawned on my Pimpin'! I shook my head as I saw the truth hiding just behind her gaze. That bitch wasn't a bonafide hoe as she portrayed! She was merely a bitch in love with the wrong nigga, and willing to do it all to prove to him that she was all he needed. A lone tear dropped from her left eye, and not wanting me to see her weakness, Trixy quickly wiped it away. Determination bled into her gaze and strangled the vulnerability, but when a storm came, rain doesn't just turn off on demand. Two tears fell from her right eye, and before she could erase them, I leaned forward and used a hundred dollar bill to wipe it away. Her emotions had my dick as hard as Calculus. It was just something about breaking a bitch that turnt me on. So, gazing down upon my project, I decided it was time to spin my web. Without breaking eye contact, I wrapped that same hundred dollars around my Johnson before I began to slowly stroke myself.

"You say it's fifty for an hour, so I'm gonna give you thirty of em."

"Max—" she paused to correct herself. "I mean, Pimpin' Maxwell, I have—"

"Shiiish." I shushed the bitch as I stroked my muscle. "You ain't ever made this much bread in one day, and all I want you to do is open ya ears and mind to this live shit I'm trying to spill on you." I smiled as a confused expression tainted her beauty.

"So," she whispered as her eyes fell to my pumping hand before lifting back to my gaze. "You don't want me to do—"

"Naw." I cut her off. "I don't want no pussy, head, nothing physical. I just told you what I want, and that's nonnegotiable." My pace quickened. Trixy's face was inches from my pumping muscle and when her vision fell to it, she impulsively licked her lips.

"Why you hoin', baby doll? What makes you sell that pretty snatch between yo' legs?" I quizzed, and without taking her eyes away from my dick, she gave me the truth.

"Cau—cause, I love my man, and I'll do "whatever" to prove that to him."

"So, selling pussy is an expression of love?"

"No." Trixy's answer was firm as her eyes studied me. *"It's merely a sacrifice for love."*

I nodded my agreement. *"But what love sacrificing for you? See, pretty baby, love starts in the mind."* I paused to tap a finger to my temple. *"The dangerous part is, love has a strange way of altering the psych, and the psych is…"* My words drifted as Trixy reached towards my length.

"Ouch!" She cried out when I slapped her hand. Yanking it back with a start, the trick had the nerve to glare at me. I merely chuckled before resuming my stroke.

"Let me tell you why love had the power to turn the psych into the worse imbalance a mu'fucka has ever experienced," I offered before pumping faster, desire burning while I lusted on the future of the lady humping to get my trap right.

***

Foxy slipped a fat roll of money from inside her shorts and the crowd's eyes grew large as humanly possible at the sight of that much mula within the grips of the feminine creature. Pimpin' Magic Mike's mouth fell open in shock as he salivated, but his awed expression quickly melted into one of stern disapproval when Foxy didn't hand the money over. Instead, she gazed down at the bankroll in thought, before a sudden expression of resolution firmed her facial.

"On second thought," she begun before pulling a few bills from the stack and extending them to him. *"Imma just stay with Pimpin' Maxwell's heavy hand, honey. A little discipline won't hurt, and I'd rather stand with a man whose*

not so giving with his tally whacker." Her words sparked a fuse.

"Say it ain't so, pimp. This hoe going down in the hoe hall of fame," Shorty Mack exclaimed, laughing hard at the wild expression on Magic Mike's face, and before long, all in the proximity of the scene contracted the contagious fit of laughter.

"Pimp in distress!" Jew-L laughed hard when Pimpin' Magic Mike snatched the money from the hoe's mitt and moved to relieve her of the rest, but seeing his intent, Foxy turned and fled with her bread.

"Funky, bitch!" Magic spat before his murderous glare shot to the laughing men. "Fuck you bozos laughing at? Name one pimp you ever heard of that got "paid" just for letting another pimp's hoe eat his Johnson?" He regained his ism before popping his collar and counting the few bills she'd given him; it was a merely thirty bucks.

"Sayyy," said Jew-L as he tamed his goofy. "I ain't think 'bout it like that, Mike. Sho ya right, ya game tight!" His praise returned and extinguished the sting of laughter as Magic Mike's words took root within the minds of the rest. Slow but surely, they all begun to nod their agreement.

"Pimp hard, main man, ya game too large not to have a game plan! Pimpin' ain't never been for a sucka, ya dig. So, next time you see Pimpin' Maxwell, you be sure to flash that cash you got from his hoe's ass!" Suede Wade, big Pimpin' from the northern region of the city, encouraged before wiping Magic Mike down. In the midst of it all, Red Bone sat back in the cut, just awaiting the conclusion of the display of game he'd just witnessed. His vision drifted down the stroll to where Foxy had just pulled open the passenger's door to a trick's car, just as Pimpin' Magic reached in his pocket for his bankroll so he could add the thirty to it. At that moment, his facial went through metamorphosis as he dug inside his left pocket. Confusion was the first phase, and when he patted his other pocket to see if he were tripping, the second

facial phase was one of shock! His vision shot up just in time to capture Foxy sliding into the safety of the trick's ride, but before she was fully in, she waved at him and that's when the third facial expression arrived. Rage!

"Bitch done played a pimp," he mumbled before taking off in full pursuit of the prostitute! "Bitch Ima kill you!" He raged as he ran, and Red Bone Tyrone doubled over in laughter. The other pimps stared dumbfounded as they stared from the pimp running and yelling blasphemies behind a fleeing car, to Red Bone Tyrone crying with laughter. Red Bone had never seen a hoe suck a man's dick, steal his money, and pay him a percentage of his own bread! Foxy was a sho nuff, certified hoe!

"Bitchyoucumguzzlingbimbo!" Pimpin' Magic Mike's curses drifted down the street in a mesh of words as he pumped his arms as fast as he could in his pursuit, and though the car had slipped into the distance, he didn't lose hope. Until he slipped and went airborne! The startled look on his face was priceless as he crashed to the asphalt in a heap. "Awww!" He cried. "A pimp done bust his ass and this funky hoe done beat me for my cash!" He cried in defeat.

***

Pimpin' Maxwell

Trixy pouted, her bottom lip poked out and little beads of sweat beaded her forehead and nose as her eye's continued to drift from my saluting dick to my sweaty face. By then, I'd pulled my slacks down until they bunched around my ankles, and my button down was open to reveal my flexing chest. My stomach clenched tight; jacking off and controlling my nut was a task, but I had a statement to make.

"See, the psych is a frame of mind, ya dig…and…thaatsss," I gritted as I pumped. Sweat glistening all over my exposed body as I preached my gospel to the congregation of her mental and spiritual. "Psyching" you

out is what mu'fuckas call encouragement when you don't feel like doing shit. When you climb out the bed in the a.m. to go to work, or even when you have to convince yourself to exercise when you're not feeling it, you "have" to "psych" yourself out!" I grunted. Trixy's eyes did a slow walk from my face, down my chest and stomach, and didn't slow their stroll until they captured what the sleek freak wanted to behold. Precum leaked from my nature as it stood tall, and that lady may not have been a natural "whore", but "all" women has some natural "hoe" in em; it just takes the right nigga, with the right game and timing to seduce it out of them. It was no playing in what I was saying as I eyed Trixy, gritting as my pump became ferocious. And feeling that demon screaming from my nut sack, I growled upon its arrival.

"Arrrugh!" My explosion was thick and flowed like a fountain of life. Trixy's mouth fell open in awe as her eyes grew wide in shock of my spurts, and reaching to touch me, her finger tips paused just out of reach of my flesh before she snatched her hand back. I smirked. She'd taken heed of the lesson on touching a pimp without my consent, and only after my rigidness eased and ceased it's spit, did I really lay it on the bitch. "Don't ever psych yourself into believing sacrificing yo' pussy for a nigga that finds more value in the money you give him than he does what you're using to get that money is love. See, that's why people use to scream "psychhh" after they'd played a joke on mu'fuckas! It's a joke, and any nigga that loves the money more than he does yo' pussy is sho nuff turning you into a human ATM machine! The money can disappear at any given moment, but as long as you got pussy between ya legs, "you" have the potential to make a boss playa piles of money." I nodded down to baby love. "The same money he should "reinvest" into his investment, ya dig?" I nodded to the dame to let her know she was the investment. Removing my sticky hand, I allowed my limp Johnson to fall back between my legs, and coated

41

with my release, the hundred I'd used to stroke myself with, stuck to me. "Boss up, mama, cause you sellin' yaself cheap for a creep."

Tears welled in her eyes. "He—he told me he loved me. I—I never wanted to do this, but I have two little girls to tend to Pimpin' Maxwell, and" she sobbed. "He—he said he'd take care of us; he told me I was his woman!" Trixy cried before dropping her head in shame.

I laughed inwardly at the hoe. This bitch's mama should have had sympathy for her, cause Pimpin' pimped hard, pimp, and being young, fly, and stomp down, I was hard on a hoe! Reaching down, I placed my semen drenched hand beneath her chin, lifting her head until she was gazing up into my hard eyes. My love juice shined across her chin as I realized a broken woman is a playa's greatest gift, cause he can rebuild the bitch into "whatever" he chose. I used my thumb to smear my nut over lady's full lips, I knew I was about to build me a certified hooker! Smiling, I macked, "First off, "never" lower ya head unless you feel the playa's game you belong to is inferior to the playa you're standing before. Secondly," I held up two fingers. "A boss bitch knows "no nigga" can take care of "hers", he can only "motivate" you to be the woman of "his" dreams, and when the word woman is broken down to its lowest common denominator, it becomes an acronym! W—o—man! "W" for "without", the "o" stands for "oneness", and when those two words are added before the acronym, "M.A.N," which stands for Man Ain't nothing, this word breaks down to: without. oneness. man. ain't. nothing! Oneness meaning being "one" with woman. "That's" why woman was created! So man would be complete!" I schooled as I ran my thumb down her lips. "Without man, woman wouldn't exist, and without woman, man could never multiply, oneness! The Bible says God created woman from a man's side, to stand "beside" a man, and I need you to choose "my side", cause daddyo whose management you're under can't "manage" what you're *"meant" to be. Management, love, feel me?" I jazzed, and with tears rolling down her pretty face, Trixy studied my Pimpin'.*

"He'll kill me if," she began before I slipped my finger into her mouth.

"Physical death is nothing in comparison to the "living" dead, and every day you sacrifice this pussy for a sucka, you die a bit more. You gonna either choose, be confused, or pay the cost. The first letters are the only difference between the words loss and boss, and I refuse to take the "L" rather than the "B" cause you're confused by default!" I broke on the hoe as Trixy sucked my fingers clean. Pulling them free of her mouth, I let her speak.

"What will be the difference between you and Pimpin' Magic. I need to know my choice won't be in vain," she questioned Pimpin'.

"Hoe, ain't no difference in Pimpin', just management!" I vibed before leaning back in the chair. "But Pimpin' ain't ever been forced, so make your choice, and make it quick!" I demanded, my demeanor suddenly aggressive. "And if you choose the winning team, you'll be awarded like a winning bitch," I added before retrieving the seventy five hundred dollars I'd placed beside me. Trixy's gander fell from my facial to the dag wood, and then to my messy lower self before it returned to my uninterested gaze that was fixated on my money.

"Okay," was an entire sentence, and when she whispered it, my gaze lifted to capture her.

"Okay what, Trixy? There's four letters between "o" and "k", and that's too many in betweens for a pimp to fight through!"

Trixy sat up straighter. "Okay, I'm with you, Pimpin' Maxwell, just "please" don't do me dirty," she sniveled as I peeled the soiled money off my masculinity.

"Sweet baby, I'm way too clean to do you dirty, but come here and let me reward you for making the best decision of

ya life," I offered and watched as though she was confused, she obeyed. Leaning forward, Trixy gazed up at me curiously, and I nodded down at my Johnson.

"Clean a pimp with ya tongue and lips," I instructed, and shocked, lady took me into her hands. As she began to lick away my earlier explosion, she sucked my nuts, licked my length clean, and made sure to suck my juice from my pubic hairs. My nature hardened in her grasp. "Swallow my sustenance, love, because this is the only way to get it in ya womb." I smiled before stopping her. Trixy's lips popped when she popped my flesh out her mouth, and after I slipped from my seat, I took her fast. I was completely out of my clothes in a flash and had slipped the condom I kept for times like that over my strength. In seconds, I had sweet baby on all fours, ass hanging off the edge of the bed before sliding behind her. Her lower lips were already damp so I wasted no time in slipping into her cave with a powerful stroke.

"Ooohh, Pimpin'" she cried when my thick ten inches busted her open.

"The only time you'll get daddy's dick is when you deserve it, mama."

"Ahh! Ah! Ahhhumm!" Trixy cried, unable to speak. She nodded vigorously in response as her hands balled up that blue blanket. I'd already conquered her mentally, and the physical of any person was the easiest for man or woman to master. Her walls oozed around me as I began to punish her. "It's—it's too bi—big, ohh it hurts soo—ooo good!" She cried before attempting to crawl away, but I gripped her hips. Pretty soon, she'd adjusted around me as I made circles in that ocean, and I navigated through her waters like Amerigo Vespucci did the ocean to explore distant lands.

"Pimpin'! Pimpin'! Hard-e-r, Pimpin'!" She was wild with desire and like the snap of my fingers, I slipped out of her unexpectedly. "Oooo myyy G-o-d!" She cried. And by the time she spun to see why I'd stopped before she could reach the finish line, I was half way into my pants! "Wha—

what happened; why you stop?" She cried in horror when seeing I was almost dressed. "Did—did I do something wrong?" She inquired. Slipping my shirt on and stuffing my bank back into my pocket, I smirked.

"We just shared something beautiful, mama, but we can't consummate our union like this." I nodded between us with a crest fallen expression, and Trixy scrambled from the bed as fast as light.

Making her way before me, her eyes were desperate. "What you talkin' bout, daddy, like this?"

I shook my head. "You still don't get it, do you?"

"Get what, Pimpin' Maxwell. Stop talkin' in riddles and just give it to me straight!" The chick demanded.

I ran a hand slowly down the side of her face. "Listen slow so I don't take you fast, pretty lady. I just gave you a gem of the game. I just brought myself to climax without your aid. I wanted you to see that dick and pussy don't need each other to be pleased, but a "trick" psychs themselves into believing that they need either to enjoy the fruits of ecstasy." I chuckled. "It's your seduction that will lead you to be able to bring a trick to climax without being touched; a pimp pimps and a hoe hoes, it's the name of the game. "Yet, "we" can never be until you pay the fee and let ya ex-boss know you're under new management." I jeweled before stepping around her, and as I headed for the door. Trixy did just as I expected her to.

"Pimpin'!" She screamed, and I paused before glancing back at her; Trixy was racing to collect the fifteen hundred balled up dollars, and once she had them, she hurried over to me. "Here, baby." she extended them. I glared down at them before my gaze lifted to the funky bitch.

"Bitch, you must take my Pimpin' as a game, but you better wise up before ya face crashes into an open palm!" I spat.

"But—but I"

"Ain't no buts, hoe. Ya butt on ya backside!" I growled, but in the time it takes a baby to wink, I switched my game from a stiff hand to a playa's vibe. I reached behind lady and squeezed that ass. "Tonight is the night of the playa's ball, baby, and that chump will have you there as sure as ya mama care. If you're truly bout me, choose up proper." I advised as my eyes fell to the money in her grip. Lord knows how tempted I was to snatch my shit back, but Pimpin' is ten percent physical and ninety percent mental, so I stilled my urge. Kissing Trixy on her forehead, I turned for the door. "Bring that chump change "and" something to top it, and we're gonna make it a night to remember," I informed before making my exit.

Chapter 4

Sunny South Dallas
The Playa's Ball

The moon had arrived upon the wings of night, and that reflection of the sun sat pretty against the black canopy of the dark sky. Beneath its powerful glow, the city of Dallas came to life like a vampire after the sun retires for the day, and club, "Playa's Ball", was the place to be. Outside, the strip of Oakland was lined with exotic and luxury automobiles, and it was a fashion show! Every ten years, the cities of Atlanta, Chicago, Oakland, and Dallas rotated the city the venue would be held in, and that year of 1978 was Dallas's time to shine. The Playa's Ball was an invite only affair, and the irony of it being held at a club fashioned from it notoriety only added to its allure! The entrance to the club had a long red carpet rolled out, extending to the curb where the valet stood to greet the movers and shakers of the world of Pimpin' and hoing. There was a crowd of jolly folk outside the club, and parking lot Pimpin' was in full effect for those that only fantasize of entering the rendezvous. Though many were dressed to impress, faking the funk to appear as if they were part of the culture, many were there with cameras, cause the Playa's Ball was a sight to see! The scent of ganja wafted in the air as the crowd outside turned up, and as hustlas and killers mingled amongst sack chasers and sneak freaks, Pimpin' arrived! "'She say she want my pimp juice/Yes she do/ She do.'" Bumped from inside a midnight black, 1976 Cadillac El dog as it pulled up to the curb of the club. The sleek machine was a vert, and with its top back and windows down, all with vision got a gander of Pimpin'. In the driver's seat and passenger's seat were two Red Bone jazzy felines, and in the backseat, Red Bone Tyrone sat crooked. The night had a cold breeze drifting through it, but one couldn't tell by the scantily dressed ladies and groovy vibe of the crowd.

Pimpin' Red Bone Tyrone was known all throughout Dallas and at least thirty of the fifty states for his Pimpin' and keeping a stable of nothing other than red bone, and caramel skinned freaks, and though he had at least fifteen hoes under his gators, that night he'd only stepped out with a few of his top choice. The valet hurried to open the passenger's door of the fine car, and out slid a five foot ten stallion with skin the hue of Egypt's sands, and a long flowing mane of curly hair that cascaded down her back. Yet, it wasn't the bitches beauty that caused the uproar and the cameras to start flashing! It was the fire red, latex catsuit that had its ass cheeks cut out, and the plastic devils horns on her head that did it to em, and the five foot eleven Jezebel that slid from the driver's seat wore an identical outfit, except where her wife in law was a slender tender, she was a thick miss with an ass that could balance a glass. She sashayed to the back of the long car and pulled the door open,

"Girrrl, that's Red Bone, that pimp from Oak Cliff. I heard he got a big dick!" A lady announced to her friends.

"I heard he pissed on one of his girls in broad day just cause she was "fifty cents" short on his trap!" Another chimed from the crowd.

"Uh-uhhh, bitch!" Naysayers from the crowd fed his infamy as Red Bone slipped from the plush backseat, clad in fire red, silk pajamas, complete with a pair of forest green with the red strip Gucci slippers. The man's long hair was freshly permed and hung down to his shoulders, and as he *gazed out at his admirers, he placed a retro smoker's pipe between his teeth and puffed a cloud of soft smoke from it. Though his attire was different from the many other pimps that arrived before him, playa was fresh as spring and dripped with more ice than the artic. From his earlobes, neck, and wrist, gold and diamonds sparkled and when he reached into the car for something the people couldn't see, they all knew it would speak of his Pimpin'. Stepping back, there was something strange in the man's hands, and when he stepped around the car, the crowd went wild!*

"This negro done it, Brotha man! Pimp hard, pimp!" A hyped man praised from somewhere in the crowd. Red Bone merely sucked smoke from the pipe without paying the crowd much attention as his two hoes took their positions beside him, before interlocking their arms through his. Yet, it was the diamond leash he held in his right hand that had spectators in an uproar. The leash was about six foot long and attached to the diamond collar around Mini's neck. Mini, a midget with skin the hue of honey, smiled brightly as she led the procession. The custom made, latex catsuit she wore was identical to that of her wife-in-laws, except it was black. The lady was built like most midgets, but her ass and titties were full grown.

"That nigga sho nuff power!" A brotha from the crowd praised as a nickel silver, 1976 Rolls Royce eased to the curb where Red Bone's Lac had just vacated. The windows were so dark there was no seeing inside, but all in the know knew the playa that went by the name, Too Choice Royce! He was an albino skinned pimp from Milwaukee that had been slaying hoe strolls since Popeye first learnt about spinach, and before Abraham Lincoln's face was on pennies! Just behind the silver Rolls, a teal blue one pulled up, and the passenger's doors opened on both cars simultaneously, the crowd awed at the scene before them. Two long legged blondes slipped from the cars in "nothing" but cocaine white dyed mink coats, that were tailored to stop mid-thigh. Their

heels were six inch stilettos and making their way to the rear doors of the foreigns, they opened them for their occupants. White woman after white woman filed out the cars until there were nine long legged, thick, slim, and even chubby Caucasian felines standing on the curb in matching cocaine white ensembles. Heels and mid-thigh minks! There legs and cleavage were on full display and as one of the beauties made their way to the still open rear door of the second car, she extended her hand. From the darkness of its confines, a pale hand took hers, followed by an ejection of playaism. Top Choice slipped from the backseat and got chose for his pose. Draped in vintage, the man wore a cocaine white three piece suit, with a blood red tie that whispered to the matching reptile skinned shoes on his feet. Yet, the cocaine white rabbit he held lovingly in the crook of his arm was ideal to the nine snow bunnies in his stable, and as the entourage made their way toward the entrance of the club, a beautiful chocolate skinned diva broke from the crowd and rushed over to him.

"Top Choice, baby. I've been waiting all my life to get down with ya program, and, baby, I swear I'll sell pussy, ass, and even my mama's house to make you the happiest nigga on earth if you let me in!" She professed as two bouncers headed for her.

Top Choice Royce studied queen with contempt in his gaze. "Bitch, everybody city to city, and state to state knows Top Choice don't believe in black slavery! I'm into white bitches, and I'll jump over black hoes by the million, just to make "one" white hoe bow down to my Pimpin'!" He jazzed as the bouncers pulled the lady away kicking and screaming.

"Fuck you, Top Choice. You ain't shit but a trick baby! Ya mama should've shit you out right after she found out she was having you!" She screamed. Top Choice chuckled as he absently stroked the fur of the rabbit.

Turning his eyes to the nine ladies, he nodded toward the club. "Proceed, ladies, Pimpin' don't wait for nobody, not even Father Time," he jived with a dance of his shoulders.

"Fuck around and get left behind trying to procrastinate on my dime."

***

The club was posh, the dècor a white and burgundy color scheme. At the front of the room, a large stage was there for anyone with the talent to grace it and that night, many would find their way upon it. The vibe was set for playas, and besides the pimps and hoes present, there mingled some of the slickest con men and woman from around the world! The playa hosting the venue had turnt the club into a playa's paradise, and though some shot pool, others had turnt pool tables into dice tables as they shot the cubes atop of them. There were small tables spread out throughout the room and each were covered with silk red cloths, with an ice bucket stationed in the middle, and chilling bottle of the best buried in ice. Each playa had name plates that displayed their name, and as Johnnie Taylor sung, "These last two dollars/ I'm not gonna lose/ These last two dollars/ I'm not gonna lose/ Got one for the bus fare/ The other one for the jukebox, I'm gonna hear me some blues/ Lady at the casino'"

Pimpin' Magic Mike sat fresh in a turtle colored tux, white Versace loafers, white bow tie, and a snow white fedora with a turtle green hat band. The floor length fur he wore was as white as Hitler's skin and around him sat three of his baddest bitches. Trixy was glamorous in a turtle hued halter top and matching mini that barely covered her ass, and as she sipped champagne, nodding her head to the music, she weighed her options. Magic Mike was a sho nuff playa, but he'd lied to her, and one lie equaled a foundation of lies, so she now questioned his stance not only as a pimp, but as a man! "Why" would a certified playa have to lie to a woman to get what he wants instead of testing the truth of his game to see how far it got him? She wondered as her eyes scanned the place for Pimpin' Maxwell. Not too far from where she sat *allowing her eyes to become reckless, Black Diamond, the wife of a hustler stood pretty in a sleek mini dress made of velvet that stopped mid-thigh and it's charcoal black texture blew a kiss to the black, calf high leather boots she wore. Black Diamond's hair was styled in a sexy finger wave and as she fought off the vultures shooting their shot, she rolled her eyes at the vision of Cedric, her husband, that found more interest in the gamble than he did her. The man had promised the night would be theirs, but like always, he'd fallen victim to the call of his addiction. "If poppa was a rolling stone, then mama had to stay at home," he jazzed as he shook the dice up to his ear. "I ain't scared of six and eight, cause I don't do the bar, just straight make!" He shouted before releasing the cubes. They tumbled and rolled before one fell on three, and the other flipped over the green surface on the pool table until it came to a stop on five. "Hit dice!" He boasted before scooping up his money. Red Bone chuckled. Cedric was a known dice shooter, and only his closest allies knew he shot the crooks with crooks. The others had a feeling that he played with a slick hand, but none were slick enough to catch him being slick. As he chuckled at the stacks he was raking in off the suckas, a disturbance behind him caused all with eyes to take a peek.*

"Ole Pimpin' Maxwell, see ya showed up late, pimp buddy. I thought ya done tapped out and bowed down to my Pimpin' being more superior." Sir Brandone, a bonafide pimp out of West Dallas, popped his collar. Pepto Bismol pink suit, and Now-n-Later red crocodile skinned shoes, the man looked like the spokesperson for Valentine's Day, and most known by those in the know, he'd won the pimp of the year award two years in a row. Yet, Pimpin' Maxwell knew the man didn't deserve the title and lusted on snatching it from him. He smirked crookedly as he entered the room as if he'd already won the title, and the lizard skinned three piece suit he wore was a testament to his air. It was royal blue, with a pair of sky blue lizard skins on his feet to offset the color

scheme. The sky blue died fur hat on his head matched the silk, baby blue shirt beneath the suit coat, and around his neck hung a thick gold rope, with a Diamond encrusted plate that read—"Max"...

"Listen creep, let's get one thing straight," Pimpin' smirked before gazing at the Rollie on his wrist. Diamonds glistened, and mu'fuckas paid attention as the man's vision returned to Sir Brandone. "The only time Pimpin' can be late is if he left money to wait or he let his hoe miss out on a million dollar date! Sure sucka, I ain't behind time, you're just so busy watching the clock that you can't see what time it really is! Time waits for Pimpin', pimp, Pimpin' don't wait for time, cause by the time the rooster crowd at sunrise, the fox done already made off with the chicken for dinner." The man danced his shoulders before flicking the tip of his nose.

Sir Brandone's laugh was high pitched as he waved a diamond encrusted fist toward him. "Yeah, pimp, I hear that jive, but you sho not gone best me without ya hoes by ya side."

Pimpin' Maxwell chuckled before deading all convo and heading for the table with his namesake imprinted on the card atop of it, and with that, the festivities began. The music died and a debonair dressed playa took the stage.

"Aight, ladies and gents, pimps and hoes, hustlas and macks." His voice was deep, but smooth as stainless steel. Raising a golden goblet with the word, "Bishop", embellished in diamonds across it, all present knew the playas legacy in the game of Pimpin' and hoin'. "This is a toast to the tenth anniversary of this beautiful event, but most of all, it's a toast to hoe money, cause we all know," he paused to wipe down the lime green three piece suit he wore, and before he could complete his spiel, the entire room shouted, "Hoe money is fa sho money!" Laughter filled the room as some held up a glass and others a bottle in toast of the life.

"Sho ya right!" The playa on stage acknowledged before taking a sip from his goblet. The room followed suit as he, who the world knew as Bishop, spoke his piece. " Tonight is a grand night, it's a night where playas from all over the world can come to congregate and congratulate, and most of all, it's not only a night where a pimp can be awarded for being top notch in the trade, but it's also the spot of where stomp down hoe can be recognized for being the hardest working hoe on the blade!" He announced to the roar of the crowd.

"Sho ya right, pimp. Show ya might!" Someone praised.

"Ain't no hoe alive done humped for a buck harder than me!" A hoe from a back table exclaimed, and "Smack!" The sound of the palm against cheek echoed throughout the room.

"Hoe, you may be the hardest hoe to ever walk humanities roads, but surely you know my pimp hand strong. Don't speak until you're told!" Sir Brandone scolded the woman who'd spoken. Again, laughter reverberated throughout the room.

"Pimp, pimp, pimp hard!" Don nodded his acknowledgement. "Now as y'all know, we do two awards; Pimp of the Year, and Hoe of the Year."

The applause was foundation shaking! The Bishop smiled as he raised a palm to calm the room, and as soon as the peace was restored, he signaled a jazzy, chocolate doll to the stage. In nothing but bikini bottoms and heels, she strutted onto the stage before handing the Bishop a stack of what seemed to be greeting cards, and before she departed, the Bishop extended his hand and lady planted a juicy kiss on the big diamond ring on his pinky.

"Without further ado." He returned his attention to the crowd before glancing down to read the cards. "Awww shit!" He laughed. "I see this year will be a bit difficult, because for the first time in pimp history, we have ties!" His revelation rocked the room.

"Oh, hell naw, ain't no ties in Pimpin'. Bishop, kinda monkey bidness is that!" Sir Brandone spat.

The Bishop held up a diamond encrusted hand. "Hold up a sec, pimp, and keep ya emo's in check. Remember these jewels so you won't be fooled, cat daddy. It ain't no such thing as the coldest pimp in another dimension, and I've seen a hoe use her pussy to get a playa millions, but just when I thought I've seen it all, the Pimp God shows me I ain't seen shit!" His vibe was felt by all. The Bishop took another swallow from his cup before hitting it slightly toward Sir Brandone. "This is just where playas catch a vibe, cat daddy, so let's see what the cards say," he suggested before glancing down at the first card, and after reading it, he chuckled. "Yeah, this shit real groovy, baby," The Bishop mumbled more to himself than the crowd. "The first category we'll give an award to is the hardest hoe on the stroll!" The felines went wild, as the men raised their drinks in acknowledgement of their hoe being "that" hoe. A drumroll emitted from the speakers as the Bishop lifted his glass. "The hardest hoe on the stroll goes to..." he chuckled at the anticipating expressions on everyone's faces. "Foxy, Pimpin' Maxwell's gal." The crowd went wild, save for Magic Mike. The sour look on his face was a story in itself, and it took everything in him not to shame his game and react to being played. All eyes shot to Pimpin' Maxwell's table, giving him a strange gander for showing up homeless, but he rose and headed to the stage as if it were "his" name that had been called.

"Don't tell me, Pimp, pimp down! I ain't ever seen a sho nuff playa that's hoeless, Pimpin' Maxwell. It done got so bad you stepping up to accept ya hoe's reward," Magic Mike taunted the laughter of the crowd. Pimpin' Maxwell chuckled, but slid onto the stage undaunted as if he hadn't heard a thing! He and the Bishop showed each other love before Pimpin' whispered something in the man's ear that made him chuckle.

"Sho ya right, playa, keep ya game tight!" The Bishop handed Pimpin' the card before nodding to his lady that stood beside the stage with the reward. Queen, again, sashayed onto the stage, titties bare, and swinging her hair as she handed a gift bag filled with an assortment of feminine trinkets.

"Right on, Pimpin'. Congratulations, you the first pimp to ever receive the hoe of the year award! Y'all give ol' Maxwell a nice round of applause!" Pimpin' Magic Mike shouted before clapping hard. The only other person to engage him was Sir Brandone, but Trixy rolled her eyes as Pimpin' Maxwell tilted the brim of his hat at their table as he passed, heading for his own.

The Bishop chuckled." I've been knowing that brotha since he was just a tyke riding his bike, but I tell ya, Pimp ain't ever been Joe from Cokamo or a square from Delaware! Pimpin' keeps his game tight!" He praised the pimp. "Now." He flipped the next card and his chuckle was a call to curiosity. "Now, this will knock you mu'fucka's off ya feet, so ladies and gents, pimps and hoes, hold on to ya seats, cause this here category is for Pimp of the Year and for the first time we got a tie!" He declared with a stomp of his foot and a dance of his shoulders. Red Bone Tyrone popped his collar; he just knew it was him. Magic Mike had already rose from his seat already knowing his name would be called, and Sir Brandone chuckled, his hoes already kissing his cheek and ring in congratulations. The drumroll built the anticipation...Every pimp present drooled for the moment of their game being recognized.

"And the two mu'fucka's to be chosen for their "P" issss..." The Bishop toyed with the crowd.

"Come on, Bishop the don, quit playing with these chumps and let me take my place on that there stage," Sir Brandone jived.

The Bishop nodded his assent while wetting his tongue with whatever liquor he had in the golden goblet. "Aight

aight!" He laughed. "The honors goes to, Top Choice Royce and Pimpin' Maxwell!" He declared, and though both men were top shelf playas, the hate and envy was thick just below the halfhearted applause and fake praise. Both men smiled big as they made their way to the stage, and once there, they embraced like playas.

"It's a pleasure to share this accolade with a bonafide mack buddy," Top Choice saluted, making sure to keep the rabbit in his other arm safe.

"Sho ya right, cat daddy. Pimpin' ain't easy, but you make it look like a tyke can ride this bike, Playa." Pimpin' acknowledged, but the Bishop smiled before clearing his throat, and breaking up their moment.

"Now dig, I know you chumps didn't think it would be that easy." He caused both men's eyes to snap to him. He chuckled before snapping his fingers. "Ain't no friends in this here life, Pimp. It's a dirty game and ain't for no lame!" He declared just as two men carried a table onto the stage before two chairs were positioned on both sides. All eyes drifted to the table before ricocheting back to the host. The Bishop nodded toward the side of the stage, and when all eyes drifted, they captured what he'd just gifted. A pale skinned diva, five foot eight in stature, a natural red head from her head to her pubes, and the bitches nakedness allowed all to see that she was as thick as can be!

"Y'all meet Sleeping Beauty!" The Bishop introduced as lady stalked onto the stage as naked as Eve. The white woman's eyes were exotic green like that of a tigress, and as her hips swayed, every mu'fucka with eyes could see the hoe in her. Bishop chuckled. "I once got fifty large out this hoe's pussy. I'll cry to ya before I lie to ya. The hoe is sho nuff made for a boss, and this here the deal…" He paused as the woman took a seat at the table. Lady flipped her fiery red mane over her left shoulder before crossing her legs as if she weren't sitting there newborn naked. "To break the tie, each of you playas will get a shot at this Caucasian persuasion,

and whichever one knocks the hoe, not only takes the title, but also a thoroughbred hoe!" Bishop revealed before lifting his glass in a toast. Everyone knew the snow bunnies were Top Choice's game of choice, and as his fingers absently stroked the fur of the white rabbit he cradled in the crook of his arm, he smirked.

"Let the show begin." He chuckled before hurrying to the seat, and glancing back at Pimpin'. "Hope you don't mind me going first, pimp, and while you're standing there, you may as well take notes, cause that's as close as yo "P" will get to my new lady." He nodded toward the red head. Bishop and Pimpin' Maxwell's eyes clashed with a mutual recognition; the Bishop had "just" said... There's no friends in the game of Pimpin'!

***

Outside the Playa's Ball was a vibe all in its own! Weed smoke wafted on the air as the felines were pursued, and the playas were chose for their pose. Al Green's melody floated from open car windows, and afros were seen from as far as the eyes could see as soul brothas enjoyed the company of the soul sistas. Though it was late in the city, the people partied as if it were midday. Only three years had passed since the Vietnam war was buried, but the monsters it had left in its wake were arguably more life snatching than the actual war! Heroine was big business, and though the people partied that night in South Dallas, the opioid monster was ever present within their midst.

"Check it out, cat daddy," someone shouted and pointed to the curb of Club Playas Ball. Murmuring grew into wonder as a sleek, midnight black Lincoln Continental eased to the curb. The valet made quick time rushing over to it and pulling the passengers door open, and when a peep toe heel slid onto the concrete, attached to a sexy, freshly waxed leg. The crowd's attention was held captive. Simultaneously, the *other three doors opened on the machine, and as if choreographed, simultaneously, four bad bitches slipped from the inside! All four women were dolled up, makeup flawless, and hair slayed, but it was their attire that fucked the world up! Wearing cheerleader outfits with a different letter printed across their individual shirts, and with pom-poms in each hand, the group of women headed for the entrance of the club.*

***

Inside the club, it was as quiet as an empty cathedral as all eyes and ears turned into the vibe on the stage. The lights had dimmed to darkness, and the only light source was the spotlight focused on the stage. Top Choice Royce sat with his leg crossed at the ankle as he gently ran his fingers over the soft fur of the rabbit in his lap, and as the red head sat silently appraising him, she smiled encouragingly and it was the gas to feed Top Choice's macking.

"You see something cute or funny about my Pimpin', hoe?" He spat and the smile slipped from lady's lips.

"No, I'm just curious to what you have to say, daddy."

"Oh, so you think what I'm about to say is funny? Cute?"

"Noooo. Top Choice, that's not what I'm sayin. I—"

"So, what you saying, Sleepin' Beauty; that is what they call you, right? Sleepin' Beauty?"

Lady giggled while nodding her confirmation. "Yes, that's what Bishop calls me, and—"

"Bitch, how can beauty be sleep if sleep can't tell if it's beautiful or not? What, while sleeping you see beauty in ya dreams?" Top Choice's tone was neutral, but his mackin' was beautiful. "And if you're sleep walking through beauty, you gotta be calling the Bishop a rapist, cause for a nigga to get that much cash out ya ass while you're sleep, you had to been raped! You calling one of the livest playas to ever take Pimpin' state to state a rapist?" His question was loaded and

all eyes shot to Bishop, who chuckled before sipping from his cup. It was all love with him. He'd seen Pimpin' pimp high, and Pimpin' pimp low, and one thing he'd learned along the blurred lines of mackin' was never intervene when a pimp mackin' a hoe. Sleepin' Beauty's mouth moved, but no words emitted as she stumbled over a safe response.

"I—no!" She finally found her voice. "I don't even know "why" he calls me that."

"Cause you're sleep walking through life, love, but listen," Top Choice's tone became as gentle as a summers breeze. "I'm here to wake you up." He whispered before slipping from his seat and making his was over to where the Caucasian woman sat, and with tender eyes, he extended the rabbit to her. Sleepin' Beauty's gaze revealed her hesitancy. She couldn't seem to fathom how he went from being rough as tree bark, to being as soft as baby hair. "Forgive my brash handling, but I just—" the man actually sniveled as his eyes watered. Sleepin' Beauty was taken aback by the authenticity of the storm converging in his eyes, but just beyond the table, Pimpin' Maxwell's and the Bishop's eyes clashed within a big bang theory of kindred respect.

"I just will hate to see you fall into the hands of a brute like Pimpin' Maxwell, and—"

"Saaayy, jive turkey," Pimpin' Maxwell warned while taking a step toward them, but Bishop placed a hand on his shoulder to stop him. Whispering so that only he could hear, "All's fair in the game of cop, lock, and blow, daddy, even if dirty mackin' is a low blow. Chill for a spiel and you'll get a chance to turn Sleeping Beauty into, Beauty Awaken!" He quieted the storm and Top Choice took full advantage of the moment.

A lone tear dripped slow from his left eye. "See!" He cried. "The man can't even tame his emotions to allow a man as myself to get an honest try at your heart." A strong sob escaped him as he hurriedly placed the rabbit in her lap and turnt to walk away. "You know what, I give up! You win,

Maxwell!" He declared before taking two steps away, knowing that even if she didn't want to follow, it would be impulsive for her to give his rabbit back.

"Hey!" Sleeping Beauty cried before exploding from her seat and doing exactly what he'd anticipated. Top Choice, with his back to her, smiled triumphantly at Pimpin' Maxwell, who glared. He wasn't feeling being a pawn in another man's game.

"Top Choice," Sleeping Beauty called from behind him, but Top Choice kept his back to her.

"What you want, Beauty? You already have me looking like a sucka in front of these people!" He sniveled with his head down in shame. Sleeping Beauty's vision ricocheted to Pimpin' Maxwell, and then back to the man who had made her a trophy within the battle of boss game. The Bishop merely shrugged; there would be no help for the damsel in distress, only her decision as a woman would be her savior. Her eyes slowly drifted back to the man who'd showed his vulnerability.

"No, you're not a fool, Top Choice, and in fact, I think you're my choice." Her words made Top Choice stiffen, before he slowly turned to face her. A "false" expression of new life fell over his face as he studied her.

"Don't give me hope, mama, only to snatch it away like a tigeress playin' with her food. I'm a broken man, doll, and I can't be mended if you just keep on breaking me."

"No," she said before taking a step toward him. Her eyes were studious as her mental attempted to untangle the web he'd spun. Please, Lord, don't let this be some type of pimps deception. She silently prayed as she absently stroked the fur of the animal she held close to her naked body. "Top Choice, I choose—"

"Before you sell ya soul for a lame bitch's role in a cornballs movie, why don't you tell ole Top "wrong" choice to tell ya the truth?" Pimpin' Maxwell splashed some dirty mackin' in the mix, and when Sleeping Beauty's eyes shot to

him, "his" drifted to Top Choice Royce. "Why ya ain't tell the Jane that the only reason ya mackin done turnt actin is because you tryna hide "the real" reason ya entire stable is "Caucasian persuasion." He chuckled when Beauty's eyes became suspicious. Top Choice feigned confusion.

"Hell you talmbout, creep. You lost, so beat ya feet!" He demanded with a glare, but already knew the game was fair.

Pimpin' Maxwell chuckled while stepping forward; massaging the diamond medallion with the word "Max", emblematized across it in gold. "Yeah, playa, you know just what I'm spitting, and just so she gets the memo." He nodded to the white women. "Let me open her sleeping eyes, so she no longer sleep walking through this fairytale you tryna manifest."

Top Choice peeped game in his sleep, and talked shit and swallowed spit before he brushed his teeth; so seeing Pimpin's intentions, he held up a hand. "Nigga, you ain't talm bout nothing."

"Hold up, Pimp, you hand ya chance. Now let a boss mack do my dance!" Pimpin' bulldogged the convo. "Why you ain't tell the lady the only reason you only allow snow bunnies into ya stable is cause ya mammy was raped by a white trick, and that's why ya flesh so ivory? Tell the Ms. that out of revenge, you don't whore your own race, cause you want all "white" bitches to feel how ya mammy felt that night that pale skinned devil impregnated her wit ya." Pimpin' glared with "false" anger. The web he spun was as make believe as the story of the wolf huffing and puffing and blowing down the houses of the three little pigs, "but"...the seed was planted! Apprehension was born upon the face of their trophy, and that's all he needed to see. "May I?" He asked but took the rabbit before she could refute. Handing it back to Top Choice, he smirked, "Silly wabbit, tricks are for kids, and my game too big!" He whispered before returning his focus to the white woman standing naked in a place oceans away from the Garden of Eden. Pimpin' smiled *assuringly, before waving a hand toward the abandoned table. "Shall we, love, I believe it's my turn to have ya ear."*

***

Down the street from the club, in a dark alley just off a street dubbed, "Park Row", a steel oil drum had a roaring fire burning within its depths, and just beyond the flames reach, two lonely souls were lost within their down home blues. Doll Face, a once beautiful queen, who traded beauty for the sake of being a fiend, sat on an old milk crate, her eyes staring dreamily down at the needle in her arm. She flinched just a bit when easing her thumb down on the plunger of the syringe, but as her vein filled with the shot of "Heroin," she sucked in a sharp breath. Doll Face was Pimpin' Maxwell's first love, but him choosing "the life" over their union, coupled with the woes of life, had led to her addiction. "Goddd!" She cried in ecstasy as the boy crashed into her blood stream. Images of her fall from grace danced in her mind, causing her eyes to water. Many nights had been spent with her lost beneath the kiss of the moons light, and this particular night was no different. In a dingy muscle shirt and a pair of stained bell bottoms, the lady braved the chill of the night. Leaning against a chain linked fence that had seen better days. Doll Face let her head fall back in dirty bliss. Life was as cold as the arctic, but if only for that moment, heroin's midnight train took her away from the breath of Jack Frost. Her legs were wide as she gazed up into the blackness of the sky; the moon resembled a beautiful pearl, and with a quiet river dripping from her eyes, Doll Face reached up to touch it. As high as Jupiter, lady's finger grasped for that moon, while only mere feet away, a bum in tattered clothes, and with a head of matted, nappy hair, stood just beyond the burn of the fire. His dark skin was stained with dirt from days and nights of sleeping on the cold treacherous streets of the crooked "D", and as he gazed into the roaring fire, he began to speak his blues.

"Love don't love nobody, and nobody loves love! I've seen a grown man introduce a young gal to grown woman problems, and with these ole eyes, I done seen an ole cougar use a young bull as a mirror to her confidence. "Mirror mirror on the wall, whose the prettiest of them all?" They ask, and though the mirror never answers, the need to feel beautiful is insanity trapped within a woman's vanity. Ya, see, love can be a low down... "dirrrty" mothafucka, that don't give a damn bout "me"! "You"! And it sho don't give a damn about being "clean." The bum shouted, his voice echoing throughout the night. His dirty face was lined with age, a face made old by the woes of the world, and splaying his arms as if he were crucified to midair, the man shouted into the flames. "Money gone, love gone, ohhhh it's a low down dirty shame! Ohhhh, the troubles of the world; the ills of the ghetto, where even God plays a low down dirty game! Everybody cries, but whose crying for the ole bum in the alley, or the lady pushing the basket filled with the only possessions she owns?! And though grandmama had me in church erry Sundy monein, God still let her face every woe beneath the heavens!" His truths were simon pure, and as Doll Face rode the wave of that funky hurricane, tears melted down her face. Yet, that bum had his own blues to sing.

"The preacher use to be a pimp, and before she became sanctified, his wife was his bottom hoe! And and church is a fashion show, that got me wondering if grandma use to sit on the front pew, to give that ole preacher a peek beneath her dress on the low! Yeah, I remember them days he'd come to dinner... and when it was time for dessert, I was sent to play, while granny praised God with her legs spread, and pastor used his penis to turn the Holy Ghost into a sinner! Yes, sir...I was raised wayyy down in the jungle deep! Where Tarzan ran into the jungle and stepped on a sanctified

gorilla's feet! That sanctified gorilla said, "Tarzan, if you don't get ya funky ass of my feet, I'ma slap ya slick ass wayyy back to the Caucasus Mountains, where ya people sent you from, to come and snatch the fruit off me and my peoples family tree!" Tarzan said, "You ugly monkey, you and Toby gone get y'all black asses on this here ship, and we're gonna skip the middle passage and go straight to a faraway land, where the monkeys are tamed by the whip!" That ole sanctified gorilla roared his roar, "Tarzan...ole Tarzan, you ain't shit! See, I know the secrets of the ages, the ways of the sages, and the black man has finally seen the white woman's tits! Yous a slick, blue eyed devil and teach a lying ass history! So, I ain't getting' on ya funky ass boat. You funky mothafuckas just gonna have to come get me!" Said he, before slapping Tarzan so quick and fast that, that white man spun the other way, and that sanctified gorilla gave 'em a swift kick in the ass!

"Ouch! Screamed ole Tarzan, just before that monkey dashed, and as Tarzan cried in agony, he rubbed the burn from his aching ass. "Ohhh, you ugly gorilla, just for that, me and my folk gonna flood the hood with dope. Then, we're gonna feed you black sons ah bitches swine! We're gonna place a blindfold over the eyes of the Statue of Liberty, and make her blind! All this, before the Bush's' help us bring dope into the country, and y'all gonna meet Uncle Sam! We're gonna kill JFK's nigger loving ass, and Nixon helps end Nam! Reagan gonna show you how to hustle, and money's gonna double, but in the end, you'll know you kicked the wrong mothafucka!" The bum concluded as his vision drifted to where Doll Face sat, nodding into heroin's waters. She absently scratched at her arms as that monkey rode her back, and that ol bum shook his head in pity, "When a change gone come?" he whispered.

***

Pimpin' had moved his chair to the side of the table where Beauty sat, and studying her posture, he knew the woman was conflicted.

"You okay, beautiful?" His voice was melodramatic as their eyes met. A few yards away, but cool within the dimness of the stage, Bishop and Top Choice parlayed as they observed. Top Choice was heated he'd been too slow with his counter to Pimpin' Maxwell's game, but Bishop was merely curious how the younger pimp would unravel the game Top Choice had wrapped lady in.

Sleeping Beauty nodded. "Yeah, I'm okay, just don't see how that scum bag could lie so good!" She spat.

Pimpin' chuckled before rubbing his hand over her bare thigh. "Don't fault him, Ms. Lady. Even a lie can become the truth if the one being lied to can see the possibilities within it. Plus, everybody lies, mama, you just gotta be woman enough to determine if "the reason" they're lying is worth you understanding."

"There's no reason to lie." the woman rolled her eyes.

Pimpin' smiled. "Depends on what's at stake," he said, and Sleepin' Beauty's eyes appraised him.

"Do "you" lie?"

"I have." Pimpin' knew with what just transpired. His game was under a deeper scrutiny than the suckas before him. "I will." He told the truth, knowing that it wouldn't set him free, but it would give his game a different appearance.

Beauty flinched from his honesty, and as ironic as it was, his truth cracked her distrust of him. "Why?" She wanted to know.

Pimpin' waved the question off. "You ever heard of King Kong?" His question puzzled her, but she nodded nonetheless, and it was all Pimpin' needed to show his ass. "See, when those white people went onto that island, they hadn't expected that pale skinned "beauty" to fall for that dark skinned "beast". See, sweet thang." Pimpin's slick fingers slid over queen's right thigh and impulsively she spread her legs. Pimpin' Maxwell chuckled; bonafide hoe! He thought. "See, the spiel of King Kong is really the story of the beauty and the beast in disguise; a beautiful white woman falling for a dark skinned "man"! See, when that ivory fleshed white woman stumbled across King Kong, he was still in his "beast" state, and it fucked ole Kong up to find something so exciting as a white woman. So he macked her and unblind folded the dame to the truth of the black man, ya dig." Pimpin's hand drifted tantalizingly slow up her smooth skin, and as her green gander danced with his hazel one, a soft whimper escaped from her. "She saw that she'd been deceived by the ones she once believed, and the black man was only an animal because that's what the jungle demanded us to be! Africa! Yet, this story of King Kong is a pure examples of opposites attracting, cause though his entire life, ole Kong faces off with the ugly, until that woman exposed him to the sunset, to beauty!"

"Pimpin'?" Sleeping Beauty moaned as the man's hand found the X that marked the spot.

"See, just like every other black man that was stolen from our land, when King Kong was brought to the unUnited States of America, he wasn't used to the concrete jungle, so he fucked shit up! All that man ever wanted was to be understood, and though he could've reigned supreme against his enemies, just like most of all the other greats, his demise came from his love for a bitch! Beauty! So..."

"Pimp-in Max—wellll!" Sleeping Beauty moaned as he spread her clam and massaged her pearl.

"Will you be the cause of a pimps fall?" His question was psychological because it made her the pursuer and his game the pursued. Sleeping Beauty could only shake her head "no" as she gasped. Pimpin' Maxwell licked his lips. "See, sweet baby, a woman is forty percent physical," he vibed as he quickened his pace. Lady's hand fell to the edge of the table, gripping it with all she had as her eyes drifted closed. "No!" Pimpin' slowed his massage with the demand. "Look

at me when I talk to you, bitch." His vulgarity intertwined with pleasure fed the freak in her, and when Sleeping Beauty forced her eyes, it was war! A war between obedience and her body! "If ya take ya eyes away, pretty baby, I'll disappear like a dream, and allow you to exist within the nightmare of the man that almost just stole your heart with a lie." He threatened while his fingers manipulated her "physical".

"Faster!" Beauty demanded, forcing her eyes not to roll in ecstasy...

Pimpin's fingers rotated upon her clit like a circle of fire, and she trembled. "A woman is ten percent impulsive." He chuckled before suddenly removing his hand, just when lady was standing at the edge of her explosion!

"Uhh—ahh—nooo—what? Why?" She was flustered while "impulsively" reaching to pull his hand back to her. "Wha—what's wrong? Why you stop?" In a sudden turn of events, Pimpin' Maxwell's vibe switched like Mr. Hyde becoming Dr. Jekyll.

"Bitch, you calling me a trick?!" He demanded with a disgusted look.

"Huh?" Sleepin Beauty was puzzled, and with her pussy still dripping." she glared. "Is this another trick or something?"

"Bitch, money ain't the only way to trick; a sucka can pay with his fingers, time, or dick! The other fifty percent of a bitch is all mental, so until you choose up proper, you can just think about the possibilities of what I can do to that pool of lies between ya thighs." He pimped before slipping from his chair. "So, hurry up and make ya decision, hoe, because if there is two things I hate," he held up a finger. "One is a hoe trying to play me like I'm King Kong and got the mind of an ape, and two," he held up two fingers. "Is layin an entrée of game before a hoe and her picking over the details instead of cleaning her plate!" He vibed, and in that instant, *there was a ruckus at the entrance to the club that stole everyone's attention.*

"Give me a "P"!" A woman's voice shouted, and in chorus, she was echoed by a collage of femininity.

"PPPP, you got yo "P", you got yo "P"!" They cheered, and the entire club stared toward the sound in bewilderment.

"Give me an "I"!" There was the lead woman again, and that's when Foxy bent the corner shaking her pom-poms and dancing real raunchy!

"I—you got yo' "I", you got yo' "I"!" Behind her came Holly, Sassy, and Myta, Pimpin' Maxwell's girls. The lights flashed on and as the girl's shook their pom-poms and danced their way to the stage. Pimpin' Maxwell popped his collar before exiting the stage.

"Give me a "M"!" Foxy cheered, adjusting a small backpack on her back.

"M—you got yo "M", you got yo "M"!" The cheer was so funky that not only did the other three women do their part, but also every other woman in that club.

"Give me a "P"!" Screamed Foxy, and before you knew it, the room became a pep rally!

"P—you got yo "P", you got yo "P"!" They cheered as Pimpin's four women turnt their backs to the crowd, and standing side by side, they did it to em!

"P!" Foxy shouted before flipping her skirt up and bending over touching her toes. The letter P was painted across her ass cheeks in black.

"I!" Screamed Sassy, repeating Foxy's display to reveal and "I" painted across her ass in hot pink.

"M!" Shouted Holly, and across her round rump, the letter "M" was scrawled in lime green.

"P!" Sung Myta, and the orange paint across her gluteus max formed a "P" on one cheek and an "I-N" on the other. She swayed her tanned glutes back and forth so the crowd could see, and when Pimpin' Maxwell made his way before all that ass, he chuckled. His stable was able and surely

capable, and they knew what they were doing! Legs spread, just below all that ass their coochie lips pouted for all to see, and Pimpin' smacked Foxy's ass so hard it echoed throughout the room.

"Pimp hard, Pimp, it ain't a playa alive ain't feeling ya vibe!" Bishop saluted with a lift of his golden goblet. Pimpin' Maxwell chuckled with a tilt of his mink hat.

"Sho ya right, playa," he jazzed before pointing at the ass on display.

"Pimpin' but not cause Pimpin' is the occupation, but because Pimpin' is the name, and," he pointed to himself. "And I pimp to the mothafuckin'" Again he paused, but this time to lift the gold and diamond piece dangling from his necklace. "Max!" He jived with a stomp of his gator. "Pimpin' Max, and the "well" stands for where a bitch can drop my trap in before "wishing" that the good lawd created a replica of a playa like me so she could hoe for my reflection!"

"Preach!" Red Bone Tyrone was the first to "amen" his ism.

"Church!" Others had to give it up, but Pimpin' ignored the SUCKAS.

"Attention!" He demanded and his ladies up righted themselves before turning to face the crowd. "Foxy Lady," he called.

"Yes, daddy?" Foxy stepped forward.

"Show these good people why you won hoe of the year three years in a row, baby doll."

Foxy smiled before tossing her pom-poms and making her way over to Pimpin' Magic Mike's table. The man glared up at her, the urge to slap fire from her was at the tip of his fingertips, but he knew that would stain his playaism, and even more, he knew the sin would lead Pimpin' Maxwell to "have" to be the hand of God. So, he merely smirked while wondering the hoes intent. Foxy paused before Trixy.

"You got something for my daddy, don't you?" She smirked seductively.

"Hoe, I don't know what type of slick—" Magic Mike begun, but his words died when Sassy, Holly, and Myta stepped forward, each woman brandishing a box cutter. Pimpin' Maxwell stepped forward just as Holly pointed the blade at Magic.

"Don't act up, sucka," she warned.

Pimpin' gave her a tap on the ass. "Foxy, time is money, and money don't got time," he jazzed. There was an empty chair beside Trixy and Foxy propped her foot upon the seat in a Captain Morgan pose. Yet, it was Pimpin' Maxwell that spoke,

"Now is the time to choose, lose, or be confused, and confusion ain't ever been a winner. Lose ain't a full sentence, and when you choose; success or failure can be found in whichever side you step to," he told Trixy.

"Pimpin' Maxwell, now I done seen plenty parts of the game, but kidnapping a hoe at knife point is beneath even—"

"See, Pimp," Pimpin' deaded Magic Mike's spiel. The man had a sheen of sweat on his face, and as he lifted his bottle of champagne, Pimpin' Maxwell could see the hate in his eyes. "See, you and a few of these scumbags laughed at my steelo when I entered hoeless, but a real boss playa would've peeped it, that I had a secret. Yet," he chuckled. "Since you were blind, my hoe Foxy will bless you with "my" envision." He jived with a nod to Foxy, and the woman bunched the skirt up around her waist to reveal raw pussy with an "x" shape being the only form of pubic hair to be seen. Trixy frowned and was about to give her a real deal ass beating but—

"You ready to make the right choice, love?" Pimpin' asked before nodding to Foxy's waxed snatch. "If so, put my dough where it go and plant a kiss on the "x" that marks the spot." Trixy's vision lifted to him before drifting to Pimpin' Magic Mike, who guzzled from the bottle before glaring at

her, but when she slipped from the chair and onto her knees, the man shot to his feet!

"Bitch you bet not—"

"Now that's a bit barbaric, don't you think, pimp?" Pimpin' chuckled as Holly, Myta and Sassy fanned out around Magic Mike. "Choose up hoe," Pimpin' told Trixy, and the lady wasted no time reaching under her skirt and pulling a nice roll of money from her panties. Pimpin' Maxwell frowned in contempt; he knew it was the money he'd given her.

"Bitch, I know you ain't gonna disrespect my—"

"Honey," Trixy cut him off with one word and a five six goddess slipped from the chair behind her and without being told, went to her knees before pulling a knot out her own bra. Trixy gave Pimpin' a smile, "I brought you company, daddy," she told him before leaning forward and planting a nice juicy kiss against the x of hair on Foxy's pelvis. Muah! Honey followed suit, and when Foxy spread her feminine folds, Trixy pushed the money inside. Honey went to follow, but Foxy stopped her.

"Uh-uhh, baby, this here may be as fat as a bat, but it can't fit all that!" Laughter exploded throughout the room, but to Pimpin' Magic Mike's ears, "he" was the object of humor. To his chump sight, fingers were being pointed at him as his brethren laughed, and disregarding Pimpin', all the sucka came out of dude. He lunged at the closet bitch to him.

***

You low down, dirty motha—" Pimpin' Magic Mike had screamed as he and his ladies were removed from the venue for suckaism. Moments later, the venue had went on as if it hadn't been disturbed, and Pimpin' Maxwell had been crowned Pimp of the Year. He was on top of the world, having captured not one, not two, but "three" new freaks to add to his stable was sho nuff one for the books!

Pimps, playas, and hustlas made their way to his table to rub shoulders with his ism and each of his seven women had pride radiating from their gazes as they too were saluted for their part. Holly and Sleepin Beauty sat so close to each other one would think they were conjoined, and Pimpin' wondered if they would become secret lovers. Counting the trap he'd been bestowed by Honey and Trixy, his mental was flying as realization dawned to a strange thought that had plagued him ever since he'd stepped onto that stage and allowed his game to be tested. Thirty three hundred was the grand total, eighteen hundred more than the fifteen he'd "invested" into Trixy.

Chuckling as he pocketed his bankroll, Pimpin' allowed his vision to take an expedition around the club and it was alone at the bar, where his eyes captured the only weakness he'd ever had in his young life besides Doll Face. Black Diamond sat gazing down into a glass of whatever she was partaking of, and when Pimpin' Maxwell's eyes went on the hunt for her man, they found him at one of the pool tables shooting the crooks. Pimpin' chuckled before rising from his seat, his vision falling to his ladies.

"You ladies go and mingle. It's plenty sure suckas up in this mu'fucka that wouldn't mind sharing their night with a sho nuff freak in cheerleader's uniform."

"Beauty," he called, noting that her and Holly were still as close as vagina lips as they shared a glass of bubbly, and at that moment, he knew he was about to shock the underworld twice that night.

"You come with me, sweet thang, I never believed Sleeping Beauty was actually sleep. I think the bitch was playing lame to wrap the right nigga in some good game. It ain't that much sleeping in the world!" He chuckled.

***

Black Diamond had felt his eyes on her. His gaze had burned her as it always did. Before her and Cedric had fallen in love, her and Pimpin' had written a few chapters to an incomplete book, and she knew she was his weakness. Smiling sadly, she lifted the glass of Alizé to her lips and finished it, subconsciously allowing her mind to wonder of what could've been. Would Pimpin' had become Pimpin' or would she kept him an honest man? She giggled at the thought. "Hell, I couldn't even keep Cedric's ass honest!" She thought as she heard her husband shout.

"Hit dice!"

***

Top Choice Royce was choppin' on a rogue hoe when Pimpin' Maxwell entered his circumference, but rather than pause his drip, he allowed his fellow pimp to get sprinkled with a bit.

"Yeah, hoe, I see ya dashed with a bit of class, but you may need to slow ya hearing down if I'm talking to fast," he jazzed.

The white woman he was macking rolled her eyes while bouncing her leg impatiently, and though she was glamorous in a red sequin dress and red come fuck me heels, Top Choice knew she wasn't shit beyond sex appeal. Sucking her teeth, lady's baby blues captured him. "Why you always rhyme when you speak?"

Top Choice frowned before wiping himself down. "Bitch, why you ain't ask Jesus why he speaks in riddles, or ask Aesop why he writes fables? A pimp rhymes cause it adds to the allure, and fascination is the companion of the imagination, and since you're asking," he paused to look her up and down. "You're a rogue hoe. That's playing in a treacherous game. It don't take shit for a vet bitch to lay on her ass and sell pussy, but it takes a special typa woman to adhere to a boss playa's guidance. You may know how to fuck, but—"

"I think he's waiting on you." The lady interrupted him with a nod to Pimpin'. Top Choice wanted to check the hoe for the lack of tact, but he too was curious of Pimpin' Maxwell's approach. His eyes drifted to the man and within that split second, the dame he'd been choppin' on made a hasty escape!

"Dammit, Pimpin'!" Top Choice spat in frustration. "That's the second bimbo you done cost me tonight, mack buddy. Your arrivals getting kinda expensive, cat daddy." He slipped from his seat, diamonds dancing on his fingers and neck.

Pimpin' chuckled before extending his pinky. "My apologies, Pimp friend of mine, you know it's all love, and in fact, that's why I'm interrupting ya flow." He revealed as Top Choice linked pinkies for a playas shake as his orbs drifted from Pimpin' and captured Beauty. The confusion on her face was identical to his and both their visions met with the image of Pimpin' Maxwell.

"What's this strange language you speaking, daddy-o. You speak to a hoe in riddles, and the only time "I've" ever had any hoe in me, is when I was giving my Johnson to the opposite sex without a fee." Top Choice flicked the tip of his nose. "So, tell me, why you got ya Eve out chere naked amongst serpents?"

"Sho ya right, daddy, and I wouldn't approach a top notch playa as ya self with nothing less than some boss game to chop, so dig." Pimpin' placed a gentle hand to Sleeping Beauty's back and led her closer. "I'm here to return what's rightfully yours."

"Huh?" Said Top Choice Royce.

"What!" Sleeping Beauty demanded as her and Top Choice's visions met, and when their eyes shot back to Pimpin' Maxwell, it was only to find him departing.

"Pimpin'?" Top Choice called to him, but Pimpin' Maxwell let it slide off his back. He allowed his gators to carry him to a part of his life that once had him ready to square up, and as he strolled, his and the Bishop's eyes clashed. The man had taken up a corner and was choppin' game with another known playa known as Yellow Shoe, and when a knowing smile curved the Bishop's lips, Pimpin' knew his decision made him stupendous! See, Pimpin's first indication that shit was funky was when the Bishop revealed that he'd made fifty out of Beauty's pussy hole, and Pimpin' Maxwell couldn't grasp for the life of him "why" a bonafide playa would "give away" such a goldmine! The second and most awakening warning before destruction was when the Bishop told the truth! "Now dig, I know you chumps didn't think it would be that easy and... "Ain't no friends in this here life, Pimp. It's a dirty game and ain't for no lame!" Were his exact words when Pimpin' and Top Choice were congratulating each other on tying for pimp of the year. That was what woke Pimpin' Maxwell to the swift game of "why" Bishop called the woman Sleeping Beauty! The hoe was nothing more than the mole Bishop was sending into another playa's stable to "recruit!" She would get close to the other hoes and sway 'em over to the Bishop's team. The beauty that caught a playa sleeping on his game; hence Sleeping Beauty! Pimpin' Maxwell touched the brim of his hat when the Bishop lifted his golden goblet. Game don't peep game, it meets game and greets game, and while some playas never learn, the true playa prospered off their blunders.

***

"Evening, beautiful, ya man should be dragged into the city's square and flogged for leaving you unattended, looking so pretty." His voice reached her before the vision of him did, and Black's heartbeat sped up. Pimpin' Maxwell made his way to the bar and ordered himself a double and

something "neat" for her. She blushed before giving him a gorgeous smile.

"Now, Maxwell Davenport," she addressed him by his government. "You know better to address me with that slick mess. I'm not one of those little naive girls you have doing Lord knows what for you." She admonished "teasingly."

Pimpin' Maxwell gave her a wounded expression before placing a hand over his heart. "Now, Eddie Ruth," he returned the favor of addressing her by her government name. "It has to be a sin how you treat me; cause God in Heaven knows I'd never place you in a category, only on a pedestal where you belong." Though his words sounded like jazz, they both knew he meant every word, and it did something to Black's heart that surpassed the explainable. They both respected their space and being that Pimpin' Maxwell and Cedric were long time friends, they'd vowed many moons ago that whatever chemistry was between them would have to lie dormant. Their drinks arrived and Black busied herself with hers as Pimpin' downed both of his one after the other. Slamming the second glass down, he growled from the liquors burn. "I see the ole boy ain't changed a bit." He chuckled as both his and Black's eyes trailed to the pool tables. Cedric had a pile of money beside him and was shaking the dice up by his head.

"Hot sex on the beach makes the night complete, and I can jump that six, cause six holes is just enough for one dick!" He put his mojo on the dice before letting them roll. "Hit dice!"

Black Diamond shook her head at her man. She loved him to death, but his gambling irked her last nerve! "I've been telling this man I've been ready to leave for an hour now, and he steady!" She mumbled to herself.

Pimpin' chuckled before glancing down at the presidential on his wrist, "Well," he began before his eyes lifted toward where his ladies had sat, and smirked to see the table vacated. Hoe money was sure money! When his vision *drifted toward the pool tables, he could tell Ceddy boy wasn't planning to take his leave anytime soon. "I'm 'bout to blow this joint myself, love, if you want me to, I can drop you where you wanna be," he offered when his eyes returned to Black. She glanced over at Cedric before smirking at Pimpin' Maxwell.*

"I don't know, Maxwell. I don't wanna offend none of ya women. Lord knows I'm—"

"Being disrespectful. That's what he knows you're doing." Pimpin' cut her off before waving a hand toward the pool tables. "Now go and tell ole Ced I'm taking you home." He suggested and after a few moments of studying, Black smiled before slipping from her seat and shaking her head at him.

"Still the same ole demanding Maxwell; cute," she whispered before patting his jawline, and doing as he suggested. As she departed his company, she could feel his gaze searing her backside, and though it wasn't "intentional", a woman's seduction was "impulsive" when she knew she was being observed. Black Diamond's hips swayed with her strut, and Pimpin's eyes fell to the jiggle of her ass until she reached Cedric and whispered something in his ear. Cedric was so lost within the gamble that he barely acknowledged her with a nod of his head and a quick kiss on the cheek. Pimpin' watched as his old friend held out the dice for his wife to blow on for good luck, and after she'd done so, Black Diamond left him to his vice. With an exhale of short breath, Pimpin' Maxwell's vision captured her like the lens of a camera. The velvet dress and boots fit her attitude perfectly, and as she headed for him, Pimpin's gut told him the night was just getting started.

***

15 Minutes Later

" 'I was born by the river/ In a little tent/ Ohhh, and just like that river, I've been running ever since/ It's been a looong time coming, but I know change gon' come"

Sam Cooke sung as the big Continental floated through the dark streets of Dallas, Texas. It was also dark inside the car, save for the occasional illumination of the street lights they passed, and as Pimpin' maneuvered the wood grain expertly with one hand, he reflected on the night. He knew Magic Mike would be sour, and it would be in his best interest to keep the big eye on the chump, and when the thought of the slick move ole Bishop had tried to pull, he chuckled, drawing Black Diamond's attention from the passenger seat.

"What's so funny?" She wanted to know, as her pretty eyes drifted to him.

Shaking his head, Pimpin' Maxwell chuckled. "It's nothing, beautiful. Nothing worth disturbing your peace with. Looked like you were in deep thought over there?" His observation came out more like a question. Black hugged herself and rubbed her arms as if she were cold, before returning her gaze to the passing scenery out the window. Notin this, Pimpin' adjusted the heat for her.

"Maxwell?" She murmured before turning away from the passing city lights.

Pimpin' Maxwell's eyes flickered to her, before returning to the road, "Yeah, Eddie Ruth?"

"Do you ever?" Her words hung on the air as she watched tiny drops of rain begin to pepper the window. "Do you ever think of how things use to be; I mean…" she seemed to contemplate her next words. "When we were kids? Before me and Ced; you and Doll?" Sam Cooke's melody was the only disturbance of the peace as Pimpin' considered her question. He and black had grown up down the street from each other; played house, doctor, and hunching games together. They'd come in the Jim Crow era; born in 1954,

the year segregation took a turn in black folk's favor. He and Black had come just in time for the 1957, Civil Rights Act, where Dwight Eisenhower signed into law for the creation of the Civil Rights Commission! They were six years old in 1960, when four black college students from Greensboro, North Carolina refused to move from a lunch counter after being denied service. The same year, the birth control pill was approved by the FDA. Black Diamond and Pimpin' Maxwell had crushed on each other way back in 1962, when James Meredith became the first black student at the University of Mississippi. They'd lived through the 1963, Children's march, that was dubbed by Week Magazine as "The Children's Crusade." All this while the people in charge of U.S. foreign policy being on the Rockefeller payroll! These two individuals had experienced a lifetime together, yet, Pimpin' Maxwell knew she wasn't speaking on the harsh conditions they'd weathered. He knew she spoke in reference to what once was but could never be again.

"I have," He answered truthfully. "But, so much has changed, Eddie Ruth, and so much will continue to change."

Black Diamond smiled ruefully, nodding in agreement. "Yes, and I love my man, but you wouldn't deny a girl her memories, Maxwell Davenport, now would you?" She smiled as soft drops of morning mist drizzled against the window. The sleek car glided down Deuce Deuce Beckley real nice and smooth as Pimpin' smirked, and allowed his orbs to trail to her.

"Naw, queen, I'd never do such a thing, especially when that girl's memories are so intertwined with my own," he whispered, and at that moment he wasn't pimp of the year, nor did he think of the man they'd just left at the club. At that moment, he was just Maxwell Davenport, the boy trapped inside the man, and as if the universe gave a nod to their chemistry, the song on the radio changed to one he and she had first did the nasty to many moons ago.

"'First of all, I'd like to say good evening and we're so pleased that so many of you could come out and share in all the love and all the happiness we have in store for you. We want you to have a real good time, cause that's just what we have in mind. Is that alright with you?'" Betty Wright's, Tonight Is The Night, intro came on and Black Diamond's face lit up as she gave Pimpin' a mischievous smirk. "Now, this is a time that I composted, and it's called, Tonight Is The Night," Betty said, and Black reached over and turned up the volume.

"Heyyy! I know you remember this, Maxwell. This is our song!" She gushed, and Pimpin' couldn't tame the strange feeling that blossomed in his stomach. Betty took them both down memory lane.

"'You see, it's a story of a young girl, making love for the very—first—time! Now, when I finally got a melody, I took it home, and I played it for my mother…now I gotta tell you a little bit about my mother. You see, I come from one of those pretty large families, and I'm the baby of the family, and you never grow old to yo' mother!" Betty Wright set the vibe, just as—

"I'm not ready to go home, Maxwell Davenport. Turn there!" Black said out of the blue and pointed. Pimpin's eyes shot to her in confusion before he jerked the wheel at the last minute.

"Goddammit, Eddie Ruth!" He swore before easing the car off Beckley and into the empty parking lot of Beckley's Recreation Center. Parking the car, his confused glare shot to her as he threw the car in park. Betty talked: "I'll never forget the way she looked at me when I played it for her. She said; uh, I like the music, you know, baby, the melody…it's really nice, *but I know you not gonna sang that song*! But we eased it right on by, yes we did, and it became one of my biggest records too!'" She exclaimed.

Pimpin' Maxwell was the one to break their stare off. "Now why would you wait 'til the last minute, woman, and even more, why would you wanna be dropped off here?" He asked, bewildered, and to his astonishment, Black Diamond's eyes became slits in the darkness of the car. Yet, with a soft smile, she begun to sing along with Betty Wright.

"'Tonight is the night/ That youuu, make me a woman/ Mmmm/ You said you'll be gentle with me/ And I hope you will/ Mmm/ I'm nervous"— she sung before pushing the car door open and slipping out into the chilled drizzle. "Come on, Maxwell Davenport," she called from over her shoulder, and left Pimpin' Maxwell just as confused as he'd been a moment ago. He sat for a moment gazing out the windshield, before cursing and killing the lights. He slipped from the car, not too happy about getting his fancy threads wet.

"Now, Eddie Ruth," he began, once he'd made it to the back of the car where she was. But? Whatever he'd intended to say, died a slow death in his throat as he watched poetry in motion. Black Diamond, in a beautiful velvet dress, danced in the night, with no regard for the soft rain that was about to ruin her finger waved hairstyle. She spun in a dizzying circle, before coming to a stop, facing him.

"'And I'm trembling/ Waiting for youu, to walk in/ I'm trying hard to relax/ But I...just can't keep still!" She sung along, and without his consent, Pimpin's mental carried him back to that night he'd snuck over while Black's mama was at work. That song was what she'd played. Coming back to the present, Pimpin' Maxwell flinched in surprise at how close she'd snuck up to him; she was so close they were breathing each other's breath. "I can hear your car door slamming/ I wanna play big girl and put on a sexy smile/ But I know so little about what love is/ I just can't help actin like a child/ You're knocking on my door and your ringing my bell/ Hope you're not impatient after waiting so very long/ A whole year I put you off with my silly hang ups/ And we're both old enough to know right from wrong/ Tonight is the night," she sung low; her breath a mixture of liquor and

mint. Smiling seductively, Black Diamond ran a hand down the side of his face.

"Woman?" He croaked. "What you—"

"I remember how tender you were that night, Maxwell, as if you'd thought I'd break," she cut him off. Drops of rain fell upon them as they stood beneath a pale moon and as he gazed down into her eyes, Pimpin' Maxwell didn't know if it were tears or rain rolling down the woman's chocolate face. "You said you'd be gentle with me," she whispered as her eyes searched his, and he could tell that she was no longer singing the song. Beautiful! Was the only word that came to his mind as his vision captured her.

"Eddie Ruth, we need—"

"You remember when things were so simple; when love really meant something, Maxwell? You remember when Ms. Carla Thomas caught us kissing after school?" She cut him off. Pimpin' Maxwell's memory was on auto, even though he'd hardened his heart since those days. He nodded his remembrance.

"Yea, Eddie Ruth, I remember, but—"

"You were so crazy about me back then, could never miss the chance to kiss me or put ya hand on my butt wit yo' mannish self!" She giggled, before gently slapping his chest.

"What you doing, Eddie Ruth? This isn't—" is as far as he got before her lips touched his...softly...sensually.

"But what if my mama should come home early and catch us doing what we're doing/ Not only will I never live it down, but my whole family relationship, it'll all be ruined/ But we've gone a little bit too far now, ohh, to turn around," she sung before her hand went to his. Uncertainty danced in their gaze, but when Black Diamond lead him to the backseat of that car, their chemistry was as sure as a victim pointing out a suspect!

***

Present Time—2010

"Nine months later," Pimpin' shrugged his shoulders before tossing the now soggy towel to the floor. "Ya old lady, Messiah, was laid up in Parkland Hospital, giving birth, but he paused as his vision captured the dropped jawed expression on Messiah's and Sunjay's faces. Pimpin' lifted a palm with a sad shake of his head. "There's more," he revealed, before scooting to the edge of the sofa and resting his elbows on his knees. "Ole Cedric was absent as usual; out of town on one of his great conning missions, but I was there! Watching as not only "you" popped out, Messiah, but at the last minute, and even to those doctors surprise, so did another child!" His revelation almost floored Messiah. He stumbled before backing up until his back touched the wall, and sliding down its surface, he sat on the floor. Messiah's grip on the gun in his hand was dangerous as he stared death toward Pimpin' Maxwell.

"So, what you telling me is I have a twin, or some shit?"

Pimpin' nodded confirmation. "Yeah, his name is Junior."

"But—" Messiah shook his head in confusion. "How?"

Pimpin' chuckled, knowing shit had gotten funky like a donkey. "When you and Junior came out, your eyes were dark, but his…" he shook his head sadly. "We're identical to mine. There was no way we'd be able to convince ole Cedric that that was his boy. I mean," he paused and lifted his hands palms up. "It was a one night affair. We never intended to hurt the man. Ya mama loved him and I respected—"

"Don't!" Messiah cut him off with a glare. "Fuck she love him or you respect him and y'all crossed 'em? That's the funniest love and respect I've ever seen, and if that's what love looks like, I'd rather go blind!" He gritted.

"So." he shrugged. "Fuck y'all keep this secret? Where this so called twin been all this time, fam?"

Pimpin's head fell in shame. "We felt it was better to play it out, and to protect Cedric from the heartbreak, since he already knew Black was with child. We sent Junior to live with my sister in Houston."

"And let me guess the rest," Messiah growled before rushing back to his feet. "Y'all pawned me off to him so he believed in a fairytale, huh? Y'all some—"

"Messiah," Sunjay whispered, but Messiah was on a roll.

Rushing over to Pimpin' Maxwell, he aimed the tool at the OG's noggin. "Nigga, you lying! You not my mothafuck—"

"Messiah!" Sunjay demanded more forcibly and Messiah's eyes shot to him with murder playing in his gaze.

"Fuck you want, nigga? Can't you—" he spazzed but his gangsta fizzled at the fear dancing within his boy's eyes. "Wha—" he began as his vision trailed to the object of Sunjay's fascination, and when his eyes found the TV monitor, his heart fell to his feet. Three Jeep's pulled up to his spot and even if the big artillery they clutched weren't evidence enough, the twelve dread heads that poured out the trucks told the tale of who'd sent the killers. They scattered in different directions like roaches when the lights came on, and to Messiah's horror, a lone dread walked up to the front door. He was a tall muscle bound cat with long dreads dyed blonde at their tips. Wearing an all-black, one piece Dickie suit, the Jamaican lifted the business end of a monstrous sawed off Mossberg pump action to the door, and— *BOOYAH!* He squeezed the trigger and the buckshot damn near knocked the door off the hinges. *BooYah! BooYah!* He fired twice more and where the door once stood, was now a cave mouth! Hellafied way to announce one's arrival; and with his head tilting to the left, and his dreads falling across his scarred face, JonJa smirked up at the camera in the corner of the porch.

"Say, Blood!" Sunjay shouted. "I know you got some shit to get the bidness done, huh? This shit ain't gone cut it." He nodded to the burna in his hand. Messiah snapped out of his shock before rushing over to the bookcase and reaching up to the fifth shelf of books and grasping a leather bound addition with the words *Art Of War,* on its spine.

"Negro!" Sunjay roared. "We 'bout to get stepped on and you trying to read a mu'fuckin book on war?" He spat in utter shock, but when Messiah pulled on the book, a mechanical sound emitted from the book shelf, Sunjay took a step back in amazement. "Fuck is—" he begun until Messiah slid the bookcase back to reveal an arsenal of weapons. Sunjay and Pimpin' stood frozen in place as Messiah snatched a bulletproof vest out and strapped it on before tucking his pistol onto his waist and pulling an SKS down from the gun rack. Snapping a banana in place, he spun to see what the hell was taking the boys so long to strap up, but it was the crashing in of the back door that snapped them into action. Sunjay tucked his fire before rushing forward and snatching up a Keltech with a double drum, and Pimpin' settled for a smooth Ruger SR9. Now armed with two pistols, he spun to see what their next move was, and that's when the devil smirked. *The power went out!*

Chapter 6

The big house was as dark as a demon's soul as the thrill of the hunt fed the energy in the air. Pimpin' Maxwell's hand's perspired as he clutched his pistol and licking his lips nervously. He fixated his eyes on Messiah.

"What now, youngin, when…" He paused when Messiah put a finger to his lips.

"Shiish!" He hushed him, before rushing to the door and gently closing it. He held his verbal as he rushed over to the window and snatched the blinds down. The noise was loud, but pushing the window open, he was on auto pilot. The nights breeze invaded the room like a cold spirit, and as the glow of the moon followed it in. Messiah turnt to face his fam, "Listen, we have to split up. It's harder to hit targets that's moving and spread out than it is to hit one's sitting still and in a bunch," he acknowledged and didn't have to tell Pimpin' twice. He headed for the window, but paused when he remembered they were on the second floor.

"Say, Pimp, we're two stories off the ground, baby, can't we…"

"Negro?" Messiah cut him off with a look of disbelief. "You rather risk a bullet to yo' dome than a ten foot jump?" He asked irritably.

"Son," He paused to correct himself when Messiah glared. "I mean, Messiah, you know a pimp hate heights, and I've gotten too old to be…" His words trailed at the sound of hurried footsteps rushing up the stairs.

"Ya slow moving, Star. Yuh ah let mi ah find ya scared!" One of the dreads chidded his brethren.

"Scared! Wer him batty boi, him dead mon!" Came a response.

"Mi bust him boi head first. Yuh nah huh put de first blood clat bullet in him melon, rude boi!" Yet, another man swore, and when Pimpin' scampered out the window with no further arguments, Sunjay would've laughed if that gangsta business wasn't surging through his veins. While captured within the pale glow of the moon, he and Messiah's eyes locked. It had been years since they'd stood side by side in war.

"Nigga, fuck you looking like you waiting on me to hug or kiss you or something? Get outta here, I got ya back!" He declared, his grip on the pipe confident. Messiah frowned, " Nigga this not the time to play super gangsta! Let's go!" He demanded. Sunjay pushed him toward the window. "Dawg, get the fuck outta here. I'm right behind you!" Messiah wanted to argue, but knowing the depth of Sunjay's stubbornness, he merely relented with a shake of the head.

His hands were on the windows ledge when he froze with a strange expression on his face, and as Sunjay studied him with a perplexed look, Messiah turnt and rushed back in the room.

"Fuck you doing, Blood!" Sunjay whispered harshly, and Messiah snatched the black book off the couch before rushing back to the window. All Sunjay could do was shake his head, "Blood, you the only cat I know that thinks of a book when the devil lurking."

Messiah laughed before climbing out onto the roof, and as soon as Sunjay was sure he was good, he smirked wickedly at the sound of quickly approaching steps. He could hear doors being kicked in throughout the house, and the opps Patois dialect only fed the hunger of his demon. He briefly reflected how back in the 90's, the Jamaicans had come to the Triple D and tried to strong arm the game, but quickly learned why the Trinity River stank of decomposition. Murder was the way of life in Dallas/ Ft. Worth, and just as movement was heard on the other side of that door, Sunjay's smirk became that of a madman!

"Kick de door, let's—" was all the uninvited guest could say before Sunjay let the stick breathe. Flashes illuminated the darkness like the flash of a camera in a dark room as he finger popped the Keltech. Sunjay's expression was a mask of pure evil as he spun in a half arch so his bullets could tear through as many as possible. Cries of agony echoed just above the rapid fire, as .223's punched through the plaster. And only after the gun clicked empty did he end his finger fuck. As smoke wafted in the air, Sunjay impulsively massaged his swollen dick. It had risen during his moment of fire, and thrill had him on the verge of climax.

"Awww shit! Yesss sirrr!" He shouted gleefully before tossing the weapon and rushing over to the exposed cache of Messiah's weapons. "That shit made my dick hard, Blood, on OG Juvenile!" He saluted before yanking a Beretta ARx 160 assault rifle from the rack and locking the magazine. He snatched a second clip down and put it in his back pocket before slamming the book shelf back in place. Spinning the mouth of that dragon toward the door, Sunjay didn't need to rock dreadlocks to be a rude boy; hailing from the slums of Oak Cliff, Texas made niggas rude by nature, and though he didn't hear any movement on the other side of the door? *Bttttah! Bttttah!* He let the dragon breathe fire…*just in case!* "Fuck tucking tail out windows, I'm going out how I came in—" he chuckled. "Harder than a mu'fucka!" He whispered a line from Jeezy as he silently made his way to the shredded door. And as soon as he put his hand on the knob, the door fell off the hinges. Caught off guard, Sunjay jumped in surprise. "Hell?" He hissed before shaking his head at himself. The door fell outward, and with the mouth of the rifle aimed and ready to spit, he stepped into the darkness of the hallway. It took him a second to register two things, but once his vision was one with the darkness, the first thing he noticed was the twisted bodies bathed in their own blood.

"One, two", he counted and when his vision fell to the ruined door, the second thing he realized was that he was standing on it, and it was laying atop a third body. The scent of blood rode the air as Sunjay's eyes lifted to find a fourth dread head attempting to crawl to safety. A long smear of blood trailed behind the crawling man, and Sunjay relaxed the stick against his leg before slipping his FN off his waist. The darkness of the hallway was eerie, but the silence was bliss as he stalked his prey, eyes alert as he tiptoed until he stood over the wounded man. Sensing his presence, the dread head paused to glance up and though fear blossomed in his gaze, dude murdered it quickly.

"Yuh ah dead mon pussy clat bumbaclat! Mi brethren will—" *BOCA!* Fire flashed from the tool in Sunjay's hand when he rocked homie to sleep, and the impact of the bullet knocked a few dreads loose with a mist of blood.

"Or them pussies will meet you at the crossroads; tell Juvie I say wud up." Sunjay chuckled before listening to the night. As silent as a whisper, he crept forward, placing the hot pistol in his pocket so he'd be able to work efficiently with the big gun. Yet, only if he wouldn't have become so trusting of lady fate, he would've felt when a shadow slipped behind him, clutching a beautiful, triggerless pump. JonJa's face was hidden behind his wild dreads as he smirked evilly, and just as he aimed the Mossberg, an exhale of breath escaped one of his slain men. It was a small sound, but predators could hear a moth piss! Sunjay froze, and when the hair on the back of his neck rose, he knew he'd become food.

"Yuh die fa de blood of mi brethren, batty boi!" JonJa screamed at the top of his lungs, and with the face of an African warrior at battle, he jerked back on the pump. *BOOYOW!* Fire escaped the pipe and when the buckshots punctured Sunjay's back, they ate away everything in their way. A gust of breath escaped from between his lips, as Sunjay flew forward from the heat opening him up.

***

Two dreads stood patrol in front of the house, one smoking a cigarette, and the other leaning against the side of one of the trucks. Both men clutched assault rifles, and both were trained to go.

"Wha bean, mi youth?" The one leaning against the truck asked just as his phone rung. The rude boi smoking the cancer stick paced back and forth, eyes alert as he exhaled a long stream of smoke.

"Yuh hear dem der shots!"

His brethren nodded his acknowledgment without taking his eyes from the screen. "It's what we ah come for, Star. Ya murder dem dere bumbaclat fa de blood of our yard," He spoke off handedly.

"Yeah, but don ya—" the other men began before movement behind him deaded all convo and he spun just in time to see Pimpin' Maxwell step from around the truck with his hands held high in surrender.

"Don't shoot, I ain't got nothing to do with this. You gents have the upper hand, main man, and I ain't ready for dem pearly gates," he announced.

"Him! Ya talk like pussy clat fuck boi asking fa ah mercy. Yuh ah get none!" Cigarette smoker spat vehemently as his grip tightened on his weapon. "Dead mon, him boi!" He gritted as his finger coiled around the finger.

"Wait!" Pimpin' shouted in alarm. His hands trembled as he held them above his head. "You're here for Messiah, right? Well...I know where you can find him. I'll tell y'all, *but* I gotta be spared. Just let me leave with my life, man," he bargained, and the two goons gave each other a quick glance before the cigarette smoker, with wild dreads tied so they stood straight up on the top of his head, smirked evilly.

Retuning his eyes to Pimpin', he nodded his agreement. "Cool, Star, but yuh play games and mi and mi brethren whack ya quick, Jah!" He agreed before taking a step closer to Pimpin' Maxwell. "Wer de bumbaclat boi der hide?" He growled, knowing damn well he'd murder Maxwell once he gave them Messiah. Pimpin' Maxwell must've sensed it, for his entire body trembled in fear as he hesitantly pointed behind them.

"Th—there he is, right there." His claim brought confusion, but then one of the dreads slowly turnt to peek.

"There him bumbaclat!" He cried just as chaos was born. He dove for the door of the Jeep, just as Pimpin' dove for cover, but cigarette smoker became the sacrifice. *TuTuTuTu!* A spray of hot lead cut through his back and knocked his internals out his stomach and chest. The man's face was a mask of agony as his fingers involuntarily squeezed the trigger on his weapon and sent a wild volley of hollows in an arch. Stumbling sideways as he fought to stay standing, the dread attempted to face off with his killer, but fate was a treacherous lover. Messiah walked him down. *TuTuTu!* The fire escaped the mouth of that pipe, and briefly illuminated his murderous face. *TuTuTuTuTu!* He showed no mercy as the scorching balls of fire cut the opp in half. Not far away, the dread that dove into the jeep, scurried across the seat in an attempt at climbing out the other side, and sneaking Messiah from his blind side. Yet, as soon as his head popped out the passenger's side to scope the scene.

"Peek-a-boooo!" Pimpin' Maxwell sung. *BOCA! BOCA!* Two shots erased dude's face.

Hearing the shots, Messiah wondered who'd the reaper just visit, but even as he came to the conclusion that Pimpin' was the only psycho enough to use two pistols in a war zone, he heard the soft crunch of grass. His eyes widened as he tried to spin and face off with the unseen, but— *CRACK!* A blow to the back of the head turned off his lights.

Chapter 7

10AM Next Morning

"Amen! Hallelujah...Lawd, have mercy!" Someone praised from the massive congregation.

"Preach, Pastor!" An elderly woman exclaimed while rocking back and forth in her seat as she fanned herself. Inspiring Body Of Christ Church is a mega church located on the south side in Dallas, Texas. It has five thousand seats and over fifteen thousand members, which of each placed a dollar into the collection plate, would generate the establishment twenty thousand every Sunday morning. Pastor Rickie Rush was as energetic as usual as he delivered a powerful message, and the church was on fire with the spirit.

"And, ya see...ya see," He paused to wipe sweat from his brow. "It's said that Ja-cobb," he sung in that southern pastor's way. "Wrestled with God! Well, I tell you, congregation, that not only Jacob, but I-I-I," he *sung* preached while pointing to himself. "I say—I say, you, you, and youuu too have wrestled with the Lord himself!" He pointed out at the crowd, jabbing a finger out at different members of the church. A woman shot from her seat, stomping her feet dramatically as she clapped.

"Tell it like it is, Pastor Rush. Tell—it—like—it—isss!" She shook her head as if she couldn't believe how anointed the man was.

"I say—, if you've *ever* fell on hard times and said to God, Lord!" He paused for effect.

"Say it, preacher, lawd have mercy!" An older man shouted.

The preacher chuckled before pausing center stage, just right of the pulpit. "If you've ever said to God, *God I need you!* If you ever second guessed his timin'! If you've *almost* given up! I sayyy!" The pastor sung passionately. "If you ever prayed and prayed, until ya prayers became a tearful plea, then *you.*" he pointed to a young man in the front pew. "And you." He pointed to a middle aged woman further back, and finally he begun to point theatrically at different individuals. "And you, you, and you have wrestled with God, and God has said *let me go. For it is daybreak,* and that's merely him saying to you; *look, child, you've made it another day!*" Pastor shouted before stomping the ground. "Can we have some church up in here this mawning!"

"Lorrrd! Jees-uss! Yes, Jesus!" The woman that had jumped from her seat began to tremble as if she were having a seizure. As she begun to speak in tongues, another woman rushed over and began to fan her.

"The spirit is in this place; let it have ya, Sista Pat. Let the Lawd have his way!" She encouraged.

"Amen; yes sir, amen! Now brothas and sistas, I have a very special treat for y'all this good Sunday," the pastor announced as he made his way back to the pulpit. "I have a guest Deacon whose had his share of wrestles with God, and he's here today, to give his testimony! So y'all give a warm welcome to a man I know from waayyy back! I'm talking about a man I've known since coaching him at Skyline High School! Deacon Robert Matthews, everybody!" He waved a hand to the side of the stage, where an impeccably dressed brotha was coming from. The crowd gave him a warm welcome, and as the man made his way toward the Pastor with his hand extended for a shake, someone deep in the crowd wanted him dead. That same someone had shown up to that Sunday service, *not* to praise the Lord, but to ask God for a blessing of blood...Deacon, Robert Matthews, was once known to the streets, as Blow, had an enemy that prayed to God for his death.

***

Messiah's eyes cracked open, and an instant headache caused him to force them back closed. As his head swam, and his mind ran wild, he subconsciously registered he was tied to a chair. His wrist and ankles were bound tight, but his mental was as free as Broncos running wild on an open plain. Flashes of the past few hours began to snap into place with a collage of images. *JonJa and another dread arguing about his death date; JonJa wanting to execute him...but the other man being adamant about someone wanting him alive.* He vaguely recalled being snatched up and bound before being tossed roughly in the back of one of the many jeeps, and then *blackness!*

"Yuh ah stand down, JonJa. Mi papa is dead, and no one knows the ins and outs of de business like me. I—"

"De men respect *me,* and Gator raised *me* to run de business," JonJa growled, his tone deadly. "And *I* say him fun boi be ah dead!" He spat as his vision flickered to Messiah, who kept his eyes shut so they'd think he was still out of it. His heart pounded in his chest. He recognized JonJa's and Keisha's voices, but he couldn't understand what they meant by Gator is dead? He didn't *want* to understand. He knew JonJa had wanted him dead for years, but Gator's rule kept a leash on the man's crooked intent. Now, it was up, and his only chance of survival depended on who won the power struggle between he and Keisha. They stood merely feet apart...the lion versus the lioness, their stares homicidal.

"I won't stand fa it. Mi family won't take de orda from one without de blood in him veins," Keisha spat snidely.

JonJa smirked wickedly before his vision fell to the slain body of the man who'd groomed him, and slowly making his way over to the corpse, he knelt down to examine the death wounds.

"De cuts run deep, deep like *betrayal,*" he whispered as he smirked. "Yuh av a lot of blood calling from de dress yuh ah wear," he spoke absently.

"Mi held him in him last breaths," Keisha lied. "Wha yuh ah sayin', JonJa?" She glared.

Reaching down and running his fingers through the slice across Gator's throat, JonJa brought them to his eyes, studying their bloody tips as if the crimson liquid would speak to him. When his vision lifted to capture Keisha's, his eyes told a tale of suspicion, intermingled with a bit of malice, and with a sinister chuckle. The man ran the tips of his bloodied fingers down his tongue. Sucking them clean, JonJa rose and allowed his eyes to take in the ten or so dreads standing around the room. Most were blood relatives of Keisha's, and the ferity reflecting within their gazes left no doubt whose side they'd ride for. Ignoring Keisha's question,

"Dread, Baptiste, Lion!" He called to the three dreads he'd crawled from the slums of Kingston with, and all three slid beside him like Navy Seals. Keisha smirked. She'd hidden the knife she murdered her father with and when JonJa's eyes fell to the baby Glock she clutched in her soft hand, he knew it was being held by the same hand that delivered the death blow to his mentor. He shook his head amazed at the icicles that *had* to have hung from the lady's heart for her to snatch life from her own father.

JonJa spat on the floor as he registered the anxious expressions on the faces of those not standing beside him; one false move would call to the God of murder. "We cut de head off de snake back in the yard, yuh know," he spat.

Keisha smiled mischievously.

JonJa glared, "So much blood on yuh dress?"

"Yuh still have yours, JonJa. Maybe mi ah help ya lose it, hmm?" She smirked with the words.

Again, JonJa's eyes fell to Gator's corpse before he spat on the ground. When his orbs returned to the black widow, their state spoke of evil to come. JonJa smirked before snapping his fingers and turning for his exit. Dread, Baptiste, and Lion shared looks of regret with their brethren that somehow, now stood behind enemy lines, but Dread being JonJa's younger brother, his loyalty was in stone.

"This must end here, sister. We are from de yard! Jamaicans til—"

"Be ah careful of de side yuh ah choosing, mi youth. There will be no mercy fa de mad mon who opposes mi rule!" She spat, cutting him off without losing the smile on her pretty face. "Queen Nanny watches mi steps." She added, and the mention of the dead warrior Queen of the Blue Mountains in Jamaica, caused Dread's eyes to widen fearfully. He knew the ancient was said to be a practitioner of *obeah ancient African magic.*

"Dread! Lion! Baptiste!" JonJa's beckon drew the line in which all three men would have to choose their side of. *No straddling would be tolerated!* Dread nodded to Keisha before his vision fell to Gator's stiffening form. He kissed his knuckle in respect, but he and JonJa are blood brothers, and in Jamaica, treason was attended to swiftly. Brutally! He turnt and made his exit, and after knocking a fist to his chest to express his love, Baptiste followed suit. Yet, Lion seemed unsure as his eyes fell upon Gator, the man who'd brought him to America.

"We are family, Keisha, and a family divided cannot stand," he whispered as his vision lifted to behold her. Before she could speak, his attention drifted to a light skinned rude boy with dreadlocks so long they fell to his waist. Blue was his half-brother who'd came down from Little Haiti in Florida to thug with him.

"Don do dis, Brotha," Blue plead. He loved his brother, but Keisha was his blood cousin.

Lion lifted his assault rifle over his head like the head of a decapitated enemy. "Live long, Brotha!" Were his departing words as he turnt to choose his side of the line. When he'd gone, Keisha smirked.

"Kill de mon, all of he. Bring mi JonJa's head let he ah be de example," she demanded.

***

"As my good friend has stated, I'm Deacon Matthews, and I've had my share of troubles y'all. Ya see...I say, I sayyy. I've haaadd, my share of troubles y'all!" He shouted into the microphone.

"Amen!" Someone shouted.

"Let the spirit have its way, Deacon. God is good!" A brotha encouraged.

"All the time!" Another fed the energy.

"God is good!" A multitude of the audience shouted. Deacon Matthews chuckled before stomping across the wide stage.

"I see we got us some God in the church this Sunday mornin'!" His words were fuel and the shouts and praises of the congregation should've been pleasing to God's ears. The Deacon chuckled.

"See, I have a testimony, brothas and sistas. A testimony I ain't to proud of, but ya see!" The man shouted passionately into the microphone, and spun to give the crowd a powerful stare. Spreading his free arm out like that of a giant bird in mid soar, he spoke from the gut. "But that's what a testimony is, ain't it? A test that makes ya moan!" His play on the crowd got a rise out of the congregation.

"Hallelujah, Deacon!" A man shouted.

"Yes! Yes! Yesss!" A woman agreed, and Deacon Matthews loved it.

"I say, a testimony is a *personal* story of your wrestle with God!" He fed off the pastors earlier sermon. "And I've wrestled with my belief in God! I've wrestled with God's timing! I say, I say, I've wrestled with *how* God has answered a prayer! I'vvve— He jumped up and down dramatically as he shouted his message. "I've, wrestled with God!"

"Amen, Deacon!" The church praised.

"Lawwwd! Lawd the anointed is in this place!" The church cried.

"Have church! You better preach, Deacon!" The church encouraged.

Deacon Matthews fanned himself. "Brothas and sistas of IBOC, I've been a prisoner to vice! I've been a prisoner to the streets! I've been a prisoner to love, and I'vvv—" he sung. "I say, I've been a prisoner to one of the State of Texas's penitentiaries! But now!" He declared with a jab of his finger toward the ground. "But noww!" He cried. Sweat peppering his face as he lifted his face toward the ceiling. "Lord, they don't wanna have no church in here this mawning!"

"You betta have some church in here, Deacon! Lord the spirit has grabbed a hold of me!" A middle aged sista cried before her hands shot in the air, trembling with the Holy Spirit. She began to speak in tongues before suddenly, and in four inch heels, breaking out in a full sprint down the aisle!

"Yes, sir! Yes, sir!" Someone shouted.

Seeing this, Deacon Matthews made his way to the pulpit, and placed the mic in its cradle, before pointing out at the woman who the ushers had on the ground. She shook as if she was having a seizure as the Holy Spirit surged through her, and the ushers prayed while fanning her.

"It's what's *inside* of us that releases us from what imprisons us! It's what's *inside* of a person that gives them the strength, like Jacob had while he wrestled with God in the form of man. Turn to Genesis 32, verse twenty-four, if you would, brothas and sistas of the congregation," he suggested before opening his own Bible. "Twenty-four through twenty-eight. Now, Pastor Rush already touched on a few things, but I wanna touch on this brief section in the passage of verse twenty-eight; for it states, *your name won't be Jacob any longer, but Israel, because you have struggled with God "and" with men and have prevailed!"*

Now we know that the name *Jacob* means *trickster,* so I see this as a metaphor that God used to say that this man had lived and shed his old ways! For it says that he'd struggled with God and with man and prevailed! So, this wrestle *had* to be something *spiritual!* How many of you," Deacon Matthews pointed out at the congregation. "Can say you've wrestled with the *timing* of God, as well as with the ways of man? How many of you can say there were times you felt the almighty wasn't moving fast enough! How many of you done loved a man or woman, but that man or woman's love was based more off of benefit than matters of the heart? Don't be shy, lift ya hands high!" He encouraged, and as every hand in that church rose. There was a woman dressed in a black dress, her dry hair pulled back in a neat bun, and her cheeks sunken from many nights of crack cocaine being her companion, sitting in the very back. Tears baptized her experienced eyes as she held her hand high, and as she gazed up at the man behind the pulpit, she'd remembered the day he'd set the wheels in motion that lead her to become a dope fiend. Black Diamond's heart was as cold as the arctic as she marveled at Deacon Matthews; the man she once knew as *Blow. God may have forgiven you mu'fucka, but it ain't that much forgiveness in the world!* She thought before smiling.

"Hallelujah! Praise God!" She shouted, with revenge in her heart.

***

Keisha had dismissed her shooters, having them to carry out her father's corpse along with them, and when it was just her and her captive alone in that basement, she smiled at him. Messiah's head dropped low, his chin touching his chest. Blood had leaked from the wound in the back of his head and dried around his neck, and side of his face, but even in his most unkempt state, the man was handsome to her. Keisha, still clutching the gun in her small hand, made her way over to him.

"Messiah," she called, but Messiah held his ruse. Keisha inched her dress up a bit, before going to her knees before him, and resting the pistol on the ground. Lady studied the man she'd lusted for since the first time she'd laid eyes upon him. It was just something about the way Messiah bossed up that reminded her of—*well*—her father! Keisha ran a tender hand up his thigh, the texture of his slacks smooth against her palm.

"There will be changes, Babi. We can be together with no worry now." Her hand had paused at the buckle of his belt. "Messiah?" She purred as her eyes lifted to study his face. His eyes were closed, but his mental was open like a woman's legs while giving birth.

When his buckle was undone, pants unbuttoned and pulled open at the zipper, he wanted to spazz out, but decided to play it out until he figured out how to *mack* his way out the spider's web. He stiffened when his masculinity was freed, and soft kisses were planted sporadically over its landscape. Keisha kissed and licked his flesh as if it were the sweetest candy she'd ever partaken of, smiling seductively when blood surged through it; transforming his flaccidness into a hardened weakness! She ran her tongue from the base of his dick and slowly up the thick vein on the underside of it until she captured the swollen head between her lips. Her tongue played with his piss slit as her lips hugged him and her head bobbed. Messiah's cock tasted delicious to her. Releasing his mushroomed head, Keisha opened her mouth wide like the freak she was, and began to stab herself in the throat with the man's blade. In an freakish attempt at swallowing him whole, she forced her head down into his lap, allowing his inches to slip passed her tonsils. Her mouth was so wet that as she swallowed him, her saliva leaked out the sides of it. Gagging noises echoed throughout the room before she finally came up for air and giggled at the mess she made. Her spit had turned Messiah's lap into a wetland, and with it dripping down her chin, snot escaping her nose from choking, and her eyes bloodshot, Keisha looked a hot mess. But appearance was the last thing in her mind as she gripped Messiah's hardened flesh with both hands and began to jack him in a feverish pace.

"Yuh ah will cum fa mi! Yuh ah pretty dick ain't yuh…ah yas yuh isss!"…she cooed to the dick. She kissed the dick. She forgot the dick was a bomb, and with her tongue and hands she helped it to detonate—*explosion!* Thick, white milk erupted from him, and that Jamaican woman lapped it up like a thirsty cat before a bowl of warm milk. Messiah's body was tense, and as Keisha suckled him, her eyes lifted to find his pouring down upon her. His facial was absent of emotion, but his gaze was hateful. Still, she cleaned him with her lips and tongue, amazed at even after his ecstasy had shot from his body, his dick still stood mighty and strong. *Smop!* Her lips popped as she popped him free of her mouth. Keisha planted a wet kiss upon the swollen head before releasing him and climbing to her feet. Messiah said nothing, only glared at her. Her burgundy dyed dreads had fallen about her face and though the cream colored dress she wore had her father's blood smeared across it, the way it hugged her frame was sinful!

"Him boy awaken," she murmured as her hands trailed down her body. Messiah said nothing. Smiling softly, Keisha shimmed the hem of the dress up over her hips, it rose above the black thong concealing her paradise, and stopped only when it bunched around her small waist. She stood before him naked from the waist down; save for the thin material of her panties. The rude gal became pure seduction as she reached down and pulled her thong to the side to reveal the ravine between her legs that made her female; her pussy was bald, except for a triangular patch of small curls on her pelvic that was freshly manicured. Holding her thong to the side with one hand and massaging herself with the other, Keisha moaned like a kitten. Messiah had heard the earlier standoff, and wondered if the bitch could be so cold as to slaughter her own father, and then have the gall to cum? *Cold as a polar bears paws!* He concluded as he watched the woman's fingers gyrate against her clit.

"Mmmmahhh," she moaned, absently biting her bottom lip as her chinky eyes drifted shut in pleasure.

"Yo' father loved you." Messiah finally broke his silence.

"Him ah love de power. Him ah love de money." Her dialogue trailed off as her soft lips parted in ecstasy. Lady stood bowlegged as she created music against her piano key. "Oooh"...the melody escaping from her lips was an erotic call of a freak, and when her eyelids fluttered open, there was a sadness in her gaze that deserved its own tale. Her left leg and thigh trembled as pleasure warred with self-restraint and just when he thought she'd carry herself over the ledge of raptures peak, Keisha gritted her teeth.

"Mmmmmuahhh!" She hummed as her fingers slipped away in mid-massage. A thick trail of lava leaked from her volcano, and raced down her thick thigh, but seemingly obvious to the purr of her pussy *cat,* lady made her way over to Messiah. "Mi Papa was a gud mon, but," said she, before straddling him. "His love ah av nothing ta do fa mi," she told him before easing down on him, *slowly* drowning his head. "Him ah loved mi mama him ah seen in him little gal." Her words brought a frown of perplexity to Messiah's face. *Fuck this psycho bitch talmbout!* He wondered as her pussy squeezed him...inch...by...inch! *Gulp!* Her lower lips ate him with a wet bite. Keisha growled passionately as she wrapped her arms around Messiah's neck. Back and forth, forth and back, she rocked on him. Messiah wanted to throw her off but knew his attempt would be fruitless. To make matters worse, he was only a man; a man of temptable flesh. That wet wet was exclusive! It was an exclave that enslaved his resistance. Messiah willed his body to not become a victim, but just like a captive with Stockholm Syndrome, his body betrayed him for the feelings she was feeding it.

"You're a sick bitch, Keisha," he gritted against the pleasure.

"Did yuh know mi dearest father raped mi at de ripe age of fifteen? He ah took mi pum pum fa he self." Her revelation rocked Messiah's foundation, knocking the portraits of love and respect he held for Gator off the walls of his mind.

"Wha—what!" Was all he could manage, as Keisha rode him like a rollercoaster.

"It's...all...betta...now," she fought to speak. Arms around his neck, she rocked her pum pum back and forth, causing Messiah's knife to slice through her fruit. Her juices pooled around him as she studied him. Messiah's face was void of emotion, but inside, his thoughts were a storm. Justice. Karma. Black Diamond. All the stress of his life had robbed him of feeling, so at that moment he chose to give into the only feeling that was a momentary escape from the rest; *pleasure!*

"Faster!" He spat, eyes ablaze with something wild. Keisha's eyes widened in surprise at the demand, but was happy to oblige.

"Um! Um! Um! Umph! Umph! Ahh! Ahhhhh!" She grunted. The sound of her ass cheeks slapping against his lap created erotica, and as captor fucked captive, their woes created an explosion. "Mess—iah, mi—ah mi pum pum ah ready to—toooo—oo," she whined as she buried her face in the crook of his neck and bit down on its tender flesh.

"Grrrrr!" Messiah growled through clenched teeth, and as Keisha's hips picked up the pace...her and Messiah exploded; her hurricane smashing head on into his typhoon.

Chapter 8

Hours Later

Their faces shined with a beautiful luster as they tried to catch their breaths. Keisha rested her forehead against his, while running her hands down his jaws lovingly as her nectar oozed into his lap, but Messiah wasn't on the vibe.

"Look, I'm ready for the next phase, Ms. Did you bring me here to fuck me before turning out my lights or what's the bidness?" He murmured. Keisha laughed softly before planting a gentle kiss on his bald head, and only after his flaccidness slipped from within her, did she rise from his lap. The lioness pulled her dress down proper, and though she smiled, her eyes became a look that Messiah fell into the tale of. Keisha's orbs trailed to the blood stained spot where her father had just laid, and soft storm converged in her gaze. Trailing from that dark puddle where the blood whispered of treason, her vision fell to the dark stains smeared across her dress, and finally—her eyes rose to behold her captive. She was lost. Merely a young gangstress with a thirst for a power that was too powerful for soft hands to hold on to. Keisha gazed at Messiah as Messiah studied Keisha; it was a poetic stand-off, where the black widow could change her story. Yet, Keisha knew the outcome of letting Messiah live, just as she knew the loss of his death, and as if indecision was a swift jab to the chin, she slightly jumped.

"Okay," she whispered before hastily exiting the musty room. Messiah was as lost as a car with no GPS, but fate

quickly found him. The door to the room reopened, and a man with short, nappy hair, and a fucked up attitude entered with a gun in one hand; and a gift in the other.

That was hours ago, and the last step before he found himself where he wound up; *the hospital!* The man had cut him loose. "Go!" Was his only demand before he shoved the small gift wrapped package in Messiah's hands.

"Well, Mr. Ridge, nine stitches, and this prescription is for your pain killers. You're good to go!" The physician smiled, his voice snapping Messiah into present. Gazing up to find himself sitting on the edge of a hospital bed, with the doctor standing before him with a clipboard, it only took him a moment to remember stumbling into the emergency room to get the laceration on the back of his head looked at.

"So," he began before slipping off the bed to stand. "I can dip?"

"Excuse me?" The white man asked with a perplexed expression.

Messiah chuckled. "Can I *leave*, Doc?"

"Ahh, yes, yes. Just don't forget to stop by to pick up your prescription." The physician reminded him and moments later, Messiah exited the elevator on the first floor of the hospital. The waiting area in the emergency room was mostly empty, save for a few people; three of them being his fam. Paradise, Pimpin' Maxwell, and Dream. Paradise was there because she'd driven him, but Messiah didn't understand how the other two found him. His eyes flickered to Paradise with question marks reflecting from his gaze, but it was Pimpin' who rose from his seat to address him. First thing Messiah registered was the black book the man extended to him and the disheveled appearance of his mentor. He knew the night had been rough for them, but as he accepted the book of his life, it was the glassy shine in Pimpin's gaze that told the tale. The man was as high as a satellite in space! When their eyes connected, the OG rubbed a hand down his five o'clock shadow self-consciously.

"Paradise let me know the haps, so I pulled up in class, baby." He chuckled at his own sarcasm. Messiah only held his stare for a moment before deciding it wasn't the time to address the man's weakness. Instead, his eyes found Dream, and a frown eased onto his face at what he saw. The usually composed woman's eyes were bloodshot from crying, and it looked as if she hadn't slept in *years!*

Fuck wrong wit sis? He wondered. "Say, I'm good, sis. It's gonna take more than a knock against my top to rock my socks," he jazzed with a chuckle, but Dream merely shook her head as her eyes watered.

"No, it's not you, bro, it's Sunjay." Her words were like a splash of cold water to the face. In the thralls of his own self-preservation, he'd forgotten all about his brother from another mother.

"Bruh, this ain't no time to play hero! Let's go!" He remembered telling Sunjay.

"Mane, I'm right behind you, nigga. We can't climb out that small ass window at the same time! Go, bruh!" Sunjay's response echoed throughout the space in his head as Messiah's orbs shot to Pimpin' in alarm. The old man could only drop his head to hide his own turmoil.

"Where the hell is Sunjay, Pimpin'?" He asked but seeing that the man refused to meet his gaze, Messiah's vision boomeranged back to Dream. "Fuck going on, Dream, What happened to—"

"Nigga!" Dream spat, cutting him off as she shot from her seat, and before he knew what happened, she'd slapped fire from him. "Bitch, *you,* happened to him! Every time he fucks wit *you, anybody* that messes with *you,* evil happens to them! Now, look!" Dream screamed as she glared murderously at him. She stood rigidly before him, fist balled at her sides, and ready to go to war behind her words. Paradise stepped closer. Messiah's eyes revealed the urge to release the animal in him, but as he rubbed his jaw, he deflated.

"What?" He mumbled before stumbling to the nearest chair, and as if all energy abandoned him, Messiah melted into it in exasperation. "Happened to Sunjay? Huh?" He mumbled as his vision blurred with water. He quickly used his palms to clear them before they could liquify down his face. The lady's words had done it to him, because he was thinking the same thing. Paradise on the other hand wasn't feeling it.

"Bitch, you better—"

"Paradise!" Messiah cut her off and when her eyes cut to him, he gave her a sad shake of the head. "She," he whispered, and biting his face in his hands, Messiah's heart cracked.

"She's right, baby girl." He ran his hands down his face. Eyes bloodshot and empty, he stared at the floor. "Everybody I love gets a crooked hand. Maybe, I'm just bad luck," he spoke more to himself than to them.

"Messiah," Dream began, sighing heavily. Hugging herself, the regret was evident on her face, "I'm—I'm sorry," She mumbled as rain fell from her eyes. "It's just—"

"Is he dead?" Messiah cut through her apology.

"Wha—I mean, *who?* Is who dead!" Her mouth fell open as an expression of shock engulfed her face. Messiah's red eyes lifted to behold her.

"Sunjay. Is he—"

"No!" She spoke a little too loud, as if the mere thought was absurd! "No, he was shot in the back, but—"

"Mr. Ridge, there you are!" Someone exclaimed. All eyes deviated to find Coffe, one of Parklands Registered Nurses, rushing toward them. Messiah shot from his seat, thinking something had gone wrong with Black.

God, I know me and you don't see eye to eye, but, my nigga, don't play with me when it comes to my T-Jones. I'll wig out for real! He thought as Coffe rushed over to him. Trying to catch her breath, her eyes left him, and briefly took in the others, briefly pausing on Pimpin' before returning to Messiah.

"Umm, can I have a moment with you, please? It's quite urgent." She asked.

Messiah frowned, "Naw, you can speak freely. This my family. What's the business, Coffee? Is everything good with my—"

"No, Messiah," she cut him off, with a sad shake of her head. "No, everything isn't okay! Your mother has esca— I mean, disappeared. She been gone six days now, and we've been trying to contact you for just that long. Haven't you gotten any of our messages? Her tone held a bit of a snap to it, and the revelation knocked the wind from Messiah's lungs. His mouth fell open in shock. *Six days! Fuck?* He thought before taking a step toward her.

Coffe watched as the expression of shock melted, and one of rage took its place.

"Bitch, fuck you mean she *disappeared?* How can a woman with a rotten brain just up and disappear? Tell me, Ashley Lawson, *how* my Queen, who can barely remember her own name, let alone, her own son, remember her way out this big ass hospital? Huh?" He gritted. Veins throbbed in his neck as he was ready to erupt. Coffe's eyes widened in alarm, though she had a jones for him and yearned to be blessed by his *ism*, at that moment, Messiah's gangsterisms overrode his playaisms and shook her foundation.

"I—I don't know how she did it, Messiah. When we got to her room, she'd—"

"Bullshit!" Messiah demanded, and in two long strides he was up close and personal. "The average nigga would sue this mu'fucka for malpractice or negligence, but *me!*" He jabbed a finger against his chest. "I'm a whole different animal, love, and if I don't get some answers as to where my T-Jones at, this emergency room won't be needed, cause there's no resurrection for the dead!" He declared. Coffe's mouth fell open in surprise.

"Messiah, what do you mean? I…" she faltered with a disbelieving shake of her head. Messiah's *"G"* couldn't be ignored. "Why are you threatening *me? I* had nothing to—ahhh!" She cried when Messiah snatched her by the arm and began pulling her toward the elevators.

"Come on, bitch!" He growled.

"Whe—where are we going? Let me gooo, Messiah!" She cried, *feebly* resisting his force. Nonetheless, they boarded the first available elevator, and as soon as the doors hissed closed, Messiah flung her away from him. Coffe slammed into the wall of the elevator, barely keeping her balance as she stumbled. Rage blossomed within her as she caught her balance, and spinning to face Messiah, her eyes reflected an internal fire.

"Negro, if you—*ever*—" she spat, but paused when her eyes captured the storm converging in his orbs. Messiah pinched the bridge of his nose in frustration, and the twin droplets of eye water that dripped from both windows to his soul, murdered the glare Coffe was giving him, and gave birth to a look of concern. His pain made her heart tender, for she knew how deeply he adored his mother. "Messiah, she'll be—"

"Listen, fam—" He cut her off. "Don't mistake this shit—" He pointed to the rivers his tears had become. "For *weakness,* cause this is the pain of a crocodile, Coffe, and crocodiles cry for one or two reasons! The tears of a playa comes at a high cost, and the price of mine can only be paid in blood. So—" He paused to wipe away the trails of his diamonds. "You're gonna take me to see my nigga SunJay, and then…" He glared up at her. "You're gonna make me understand *why* you've disappointed me before I've given you the opportunity to make me happy?"

***

110

Black Diamond had returned to Tutt's home because it was the last place anyone would look for her. The earlier church sermon had moved her, but even more, it had proved to her that change is the only constant. Blow was no longer Blow, but a reverend! A man washed in the spirit, yet, even as she reflected, Black Diamond envisioned him washed in blood instead. Still in her Sunday's best, she sat at the edge of the couch, staring in wonder at the metal stem she stuffed her escape down into. Messiah's last read from the black book had revived many jagged pieces of her memory, and though she was still corroding inside, her heart was fixated upon the retribution owed to her and the handsome man she now knew without a doubt—her son!

"Black Diamond, girrrl?" Tutts called to her from the other side of the sofa, where she licked her lips in anticipation. Her eyes were drawn to the crack pipe as if she were a vampire, and it, a throbbing vein in the neck of a victim. "You gonna put a flame to that, or let me do it? Girl, I ain't got high all day!" Her thirst was shameless, but Black merely studied the pipe; the thief she'd traded vows with. The same thief she'd given her all to, watching it become greedy, and continue to take and take, even when she didn't want to give any more. A look of disgust eased onto her face as her vision lifted to capture her younger friend. Tutts was a thirty-five year old beauty, hidden behind the face and body of a fifty year old "rock" star. Crack had given her an old face, and as Black extended the pipe to her, she wondered which was the steeper price, crack robbing her heart or crack robbing Tutts of her beauty? Nonetheless, Tutts was oblivious to Black's internal chaos as she lit the tip of the thief. Her jaws caved in with her inhale and after she pulled the stem away, she smacked her lips as if savoring the smoke. Eyes bulging and repeatedly licking her lips, Tutts extended the pipe to Black, who with no further ado, replicated the smoking technique Tutts had just demonstrated. Save for the extracurricular. Tutts exhaled a thick cloud of smoke before her bugged eyes shifted to the woman who'd been her idol since she'd met her. Black exhaled a mushroom of tainted smoke as her vision fell to the long dress she'd worn to the house of the Lord.

"You sho looking pretty and all, Black Diamond. I bet you turned that house of worship into a den of sinners this Sunday mornin'." Tutts acknowledged with a giggle as she accepted the instrument of her addiction back from Black.

"Tutts—" The older woman's call was a wisp upon the air, so soft that Tutts didn't hear her. "Tutts?" Black called again, and with lungs filled with crack smoke, the younger woman's eyes lifted to behold her.

"Hmm?" She hummed.

Blacks expression was one of confliction as her eyes fell to the stained carpet in thought. "How'd *you* wind up like this, baby girl? You were so beautiful and filled with promise. Wha—" she paused, wrestling with her words. "What happened to *us?* I—I mean, I know what happened to *me*, but somewhere in the back of my mind, my memories of what lead to," she glanced around in disgust, before waving a hand around the room. "This!" She spat the word as if it were a vile taste. Tutts exhaled a fluffy cloud of putrid smoke before chuckling bitterly, and when her eyes completed their assessment of the woman across from her, she shook her head in disbelief.

"So, it's true? Your memory has gone?" She asked in wonder.

Black's eyes found her before nodding confirmation. "A lot of it. I mean, I've recaptured a lot, but there's a—" she spread her hands wide in measure. "A big island of things left blank an island filled with beautiful flowers, but trapped in the middle of a vast, Black Sea. I remember my name, Tutts. I remember selling my twat. Hell, I now remember I have a son, and a few things, but…" Her words drifted as her glossy orbs watered.

"You can't remember *everything*. The most important!" Tutts concluded, and Black studied her. Tutts smiled a sad smile before repositioning herself on the couch and tucking her feet beneath her. Patting her head to silence the itch beneath the dingy scarf on her head, again, she shook her head in disbelief. "Black Diamond, I can't tell you much about your journey *before* we met, but I can refresh ya memory on the happenings of the journey *after* the handsome *storm, Messiah,* blew into my world."

Her smile held a hint of promiscuity, and self-consciously she cupped her now sagging breast. "Yeah, Black Diamond, I was a bad bitch back then, wasn't I? We both were," she spoke in a whisper as her eyes became cloudy. "Well," said she. "Decisions are the story of a woman's life, Black, and rather good or bad, the decisions a girl makes will lead her to the outcome of those decisions. For me." Tutts shook her head sadly, as her mind carried her back into the year *1995,* when the game was too fast for a lame, and a playa known as Messiah had upgraded her prostitution to the highest pinnacle. "Here's your memories, Black Diamond. A portion of how much ho'in started me to smoking," she whispered before she began speaking life back into Black's memories.

***

"How'd this happen? Come on, fam, I told you," Messiah whispered more to himself than seeking an answer from anyone in the room. His eyes were saturated as the digested SunJay's condition, heavily sedated, the man lay with IVs in his arm and a zigzag of twenty-five staples in his head.

"We didn't think he'd make it. He'd flatlined on us three times during the second surgery," Coffe's voice was low as she shook her head. Sadness radiated from her gaze; she just couldn't understand why her people were so set on taking each other's lives. "He took a pretty nasty shot to the back from a high powered rifle..." She paused as her gaze traveled to Messiah. "The doctors shocked themselves to have saved him. What I don't get, Messiah…" When her words trailed, though it was a battle, Messiah pulled his stare away from his man, and fixed her with the windows to his soul. Coffe crossed her arms beneath her breast, and gave him a look that was a mixture of disgust and curiosity. "Why do you brothas seem so *attracted* to death?" Her question seemed to offend him, and the frustration on his face was the evidence. Yet, rather than spazzing, the man turnt and trudged over to the two chairs in the room. And after plopping down into the seat, as if just registering his appearance, he frowned at his wrinkled and ruined attire.

Exhaling a hard whoosh of breath, he tossed the thick book he'd been carrying, and it landed with a smack against the tiled floor; *Attracted* to death?" He mumbled as his vision lifted to Sunjay's sleeping form. *I told this dumb ass dude not to play hero, and now look at 'em. Playing super negro got bro on bed rest!* He gritted his teeth at the thought, vaguely noting when Coffe retrieved the book of his life from the floor.

"Yes, Messiah, *attracted* to death, I mean—" she shrugged before making her way to the chair beside him and taking a seat. "How can you not be? *Everything* you've experienced in the streets, leads to either death or jail, and jail is merely death by another name," she offered her perspective, and Messiah glanced at her as if seeing her for the first time.

"*Everything* leads to death, Coffee. Some things merely prolong the trip."

"Yes, which leads to the exact question posed with different words." Coffe shrugged before resting the black book in her lap, and gently running a hand down its cover. "So, why are most black men of this generation so *in a hurry* to reach the *promised* destination? The ultimate destination that every one human being is promised?"

Messiah exhaled while rubbing a hand over his bald head. "I'm from the ghetto, lady. My story is filled with death and crooked times," he revealed before slouching down in his seat, and resting his head against the back of it. He allowed his eyes to drift shut. "You don't know me, Coffee. You're attracted to the *allure*, but don't understand that we're raised from different scriptures from a totally different bible," he whispered; suddenly feeling exhausted.

Coffe allowed a bitter laugh to follow his proclamation. "You'll never know the depth of similitude we share, because your conjectures leads you to believe that being street savvy make you omniscient." She shook her head pityingly.

"Wow?" Messiah spoke the first word to his mind. Chucking, he bumped her knee with his. " So, you just gonna go geeky on the kid, huh?" He smirked, yet, Coffe's gaze never deserted the object of her fascination.

"You carry this book everywhere." Her vision finally made the trip to him. "It's merely my postulation that's there's *something* dear within it that you hunger for?" Her statement converted to a question.

"Postulation?" Messiah laughed. "It's just my *postulation,*" he mimicked in a scholarly, girlish timbre. "Fuck?" He lifted a questioning brow.

"*Assumption,* postulate means, assumption; or guess. Yet, context clues should have…"

"What? Told me that your postulations of me is based off of me being from the slums?" He cut her off with a sneaky smirk. "Well, my *postulations.* " He paused to air quote. "Are that the inposse of you being a sho nuff bread winner for a playa as myself, will never exceed the definition of potential, because your pussy demands more from my dick than my stance as a bonafide pimp demands from the sho nuff hoe in you." He spoke these words with such lactation that Coffe didn't know if he'd just complimented or insulted her. Her lips parted in shock, but Messiah lifted a calming hand.

"Don't take it as me being insolent, love, but you know my gators stay tied as tight as the pussy on a female mite, and *insolent* means overly rude or audaciously disrespectful. And, inposse is *Medieval Latin, meaning...* "

"Yes, I know it means having potential, but not in actuality. But?" Coffe sliced through his verbal, with an offended expression. "Did you just call me *a hoe!*" She spat, and for the first time since he'd met the woman, Messiah noted the educated underlay to the dialogue.

"What's your alma mater, Coffe?"

"TWU, apropos; what does that have to do with you calling me a..."

"Don't you have a nice brotha that drives a Benz? The same brotha that brings you lunch every day?" Messiah inquired with a knowing smirk. Studying the shocked expression on her face, he internally appreciated her beauty. The baby blue scrubs she wore hugged her thick frame, and naturally pretty, her pie shaped face needed no cosmetics. As her naturally long lashed eye lids fell low in a glare, Messiah smirked.

"Yes," Coffe snapped with a roll with of her eyes. "I have someone that I'm seeing, but that is irrelevant to –"

"Just humor me," Messiah cut her off with a challenging gander. "Complete honesty, Ms. Lady, lies are a waste of a meaningful convo. Dig?" He paused to sit up straight in his seat. "You just admitted to having a fella you share time with, so allow me to ask you this?" He reached over and took her hand into his. "*When* we get the right moment, will you give me that pussy?" The question was psychological. The word; *when,* played on the fantasies he knew she had of them, and to deny, would turn *when,* into *never!* Messiah allowed his orbs to tell her just that, *but* it was *the way* he'd laid it before her that caused her lower self to moisten while she fiddled with the impulse of cussing him out. Her caramel cheeks flamed red in a blush as she pulled her hand free from his.

"I just told you I have a—"

"Answer me." Messiah's demand was bossy, and left no room for *BS*. Coffe studied him; unsure of her answer, but—

"*Maybe,* Messiah, maybe copulation is a possibility , but—"

"No, *buts,* mama, ya butt is on ya backside and please," he cut her off with a lifted palm, and an irritated look. "Please, let's slice the fancy words out this movie we're trying to create. Now listen, hoe." He paused to allow her shock to reach its apex, and just as he'd anticipated, Coffe attempted to rise from her seat.

"Nigga, you got me messed up! You will not—"

"See." Messiah reached over, stretching an arm before her to prevent her from progressing. "*This* is the reason I've never fed upon the lush I've seen trapped inside those pretty eyes of yours. See, it's *always* the shit we don't understand that intrigues us. Coffe, I'm a mack, a man that aides women in *hustling* themselves, and you *know* that, cause my *ism* has awakened your hoe alarm on many occasions."

"There you—"

"If you just pause, I'll give you a cause." He glared at her, and after a moment of eye wrestling, Coffe plopped back down into her seat.

"Whatever!" She rolled her eyes.

"Coffe," Messiah called, before falling back into his seat, and exhaling a powerful breath. "We have no similitudes; your world and my world are galaxies apart, sweetheart. See, me calling you a hoe only offends you because you lie to *self,* and since I won't allow you to do the same with me, you're forced to see your own reflection. Yet, what's a hoe to you, Coffe?" He questioned, and Coffe pouted with a roll of her eyes. "That was a question." He pushed.

"And I'm grown, I don't have to answer."

"Yeah, real grown answer." Messiah chuckled. Coffe smacked her lips.

"A hoe is a woman that's loose; a woman with no morals," she relented. Messiah nodded his agreement before crossing his arms over his chest and closing his eyes.

"Yes, *but* a hoe is also a woman that has a nigga, but will fuck another, merely because the time is right. Attraction was present, or because she's too weak to be faithful. Anytime a female is spoken for but spends more time seeking the attention, affections or association of *per* man versus *her* man, it's hoish! Do *you* fit *any* of the criterions, Ms. Coffe?" He whispered, and though his eyes remained closed, the smirk on his face screamed *checkmate.*

"I. Am. Not. A. Hoe!" Coffe jabbed a finger into the cover of the book with each word as she glared at him.

Messiah's lids cracked open before his gaze captured her, "The truth often gets shunned for a lie. Yet, since we've established that there can never be anything between us, let's move forward."

"Excuse me? I—I never said there can't be any," Coffe tried.

"Of course you did."

"No, I didn't, nor did I imply it."

"No, you didn't, cause what you said, you didn't mean? Or you did mean, but didn't mean what you said?"

"Huh? I—I mean, I meant what I said, but how you took it, I didn't mean."

"So mean what you say, because didn't already did, and that's the only way it can come past tense."

"What! I—what the." She was flustered and lost within his web. Shaking her head in frustration, Coffe chose to ignore his extracurricular. And allowing her vision to return to the black book in her lap, she ran a soft hand over its leather cover. "Whatever you say, Messiah." Her time held a tinge of sadness. "But, as I said earlier, there's *something* in this book you're either looking for, or feel will lead you *somewhere?*" It came out as if she were inquiring. She could feel the power emitting from the book, and as she allowed it to encase her, Messiahs eyes drifted back shut.

"There is," he mumbled.

"I don't mean to pry, but..."

"Then don't."

"What?"

"You just said you don't mean to pry, so...don't." He clarified, and for a moment, silence became dominant. Messiah had almost drifted into a much needed slumber, but lady's silence anchored him to consciousness. Cracking his blood shots, he found her gazing at him.

"You're a handsome brotha, Messiah, and I want to get to know you."

"I'm already married to two people, Coffe."

"That's polygamy; bigamy, which is a crime."

"Only in the eyes of the cultureless; in this land where a feminine Statue of Liberty holds a torch toward a rotten apple. Yet, I live by the laws of the jungle, where a predator can do whatever he desires as long as he can defend it." Messiah smirked.

Coffe considered it for a mere moment before curiosity embraced her, "Who are the two women you're married to?"

"Justice and *my game.*"

Coffe smacked her lips, "Yeah, Justice and *your game* sounds like synonyms."

"Huh?" Messiah asked, with a peculiar expression. And in that instant, an icy chill slid down his spine. Studying her suspiciously, he noted the nervousness in her expression. Coffe shook her head in an attempt at downplaying.

"It's nothing, just my silly mind playing trick—"

"Tell me," Messiah cut her off, his eyes now alert.

Coffe studied him. "Let's make a deal?" She proposed, and Messiah glared.

"A deal?"

"Yes, I tell you my thoughts, and you let me read a few pages of her journal." Her proposition was simple, but even as Messiah nodded his agreement, he was uncertain.

"Only." He held up two fingers as their eyes danced. "Under two conditions." He cast his stipulations, and with a raised brow. Coffe shrugged indifferently.

"Okay?"

Messiah nodded. "You have to be undiluted when speaking your piece." He dropped a finger. "And the second one is when you read from that book, you gotta read it aloud."

"Okay." She agreed, without having to consider. And taking a quick breath, she honored his first request. "Messiah, the night you brought Karma in, I'd told you she'd said some *strange* things about her mother. As soon as her words left her lips, Messiah's mental snatched him back to the night he'd held his daughter in that exact hospital.

"Daddy, are you mad at mami?" She'd asked as he'd held her. Messiah smiled down at her.

"And why would I be mad at mami, baby!" He'd asked.

"For being mean to me."

"She'd said her mother was being mean to her," Coffe's voice puked him back to the present, and something crazy inched a bit closer to the front of his mind. Oblivious to the darkening of his eyes, Coffe continued. "She'd also said her mother told her not to hate her, and to be good." Her next revaluation shocked Messiah so powerfully that he flinched.

"Wha—she—what?" He flustered, and for the first time in years, he'd been off his Pimpin'. *Fuck? Is this hoe playing funny games? Why would Justice tell our seed that? Why this lady now telling me?* His thoughts ran wild and seeing them written all over his face, Coffe hated his turmoil. Messiah blinked, and as if she was unworthy of seeing his weaknesses, his face went blank! Unreadable!

"That could mean *anything,* and *when* was this said? Karma is only five. Justice may have just said that to calm

120

her worries," He rationalized. Coffe gave him a *yeah riiight,* expression before choosing her words wisely.

"That's a possibility." She shrugged, with a faux smile, but Messiah saw the doubt within her gaze. Meeting it head on, he chuckled the moment away.

"Why you looking like that?"

"Like?"

"Like you pitying the fool?"

"Messiah?" She smiled sadly. "A fool needs no pity. He needs sense, and *that* you have plenty of! Yet, I do pity the heart."

Messiah nodded with a smirk and returned his head to the back of his chair. His eyes drifted shut and it seemed as if all the energy had been sucked from him. "Read to me, Coffee. Read the words a dope fiend inscribed to her son as she fell from grace," he mumbled just before sleep snatched him under. Coffe was uncertain of what to do, but after a few seconds of studying Messiah's handsomeness, she exhaled softly. She didn't know the conclusion of his journey, but the man's story had truly won her over.

"Our stories have so many commonalities, Messiah Ridge, so many." She whispered before cracking the book of Messiah's life, and being a woman of her word, she began to read aloud...

Chapter 9

Messiah's Journey

Entry 9: *My Joy, today has been a trying one, but nobody ever said being a stomp down bitch would be easy. My old bones are starting to ache, and boyyy...crack cocaine has turnt out to be a low down, rotten sumabitch! But enough about my little ole woes, let me give you a jewel that'll grow ya game. See, as of late, I've watched your macking surpass that of your peers. And though it admirable, you "must" practice humility. "Always" remain humble before the eyes of grand men with destructive pride, Messiah. Yes, baby, I heard of your exploits, and the game you displayed with knocking that ole gal, Tutts, from that sucka was legendary! Yet! Let me school you before the game abuses you. Messiah, the most prominent aspect of Pimpin' and hoin', and "the art" of "building" a sho nuff boss bitch, is the "psych!" The mental! "Everythang" about the game is "psych"ological, and if you can get a bitch to see it in her mind, she'll become it in her heart! See, one of the coldest lies man has ever believed is that only women can be pimped! Son, women are the biggest pimps! They seduce men just as men mack women, so it only comes down to the will of persuasion! The ability of "psyching" one into believing in "your" vision of the mission will make you one of the hardest niggas to have pissed standing up! Now, Messiah, the word; "psych", with an "E" added can change the "concept" of the entire word. "Psyche" can mean either spirit or soul, and without the soul of the sho nuff playas from the past surging through its veins, the game and all that thrives within it would be doomed! Amen? Yet, no matter if the word psych is spelt with, or without the "e", the word still speaks of the mind! So, let me tell you a quick tale to keep you swell, baby. See, in Greek Mythology, Psyche was a beautiful dame that was said to turn heads wherever her peel toe heels lead her. The bitch was so bad that even Aphrodite, the baddest bitch to have slayed the day and night became jealous.*

It's even said that Aphrodite became so envious of this girls beauty that this Goddess of Love enlisted the services of her son, Cupid. See, baby, Cupid aka, Eros, was the God of Love, but is also "sexual" yearning and desire! So, when Aphrodite ordered him to pull up on Psyche, and make her fall in love with the ugliest mu'fucka around, Ole Cupid slides up on the same without a sound. He aims his arrow for the grandest shot ever took...

But just when he's about to let loose; Psyche glances, and this God of Love and desire shoot's himself in the foot!

Playboy tries to keep it playa, but when he sees how jazzy lady is, he falls in love with his own tricks and in love with the fantasy. He dips without fulfilling his mother's request.

Aphrodite's hate for this woman deepens, and though niggas still salivate at her beauty and star at her booty, Psyche is cursed so no man falls in love with her. So when Psyche two sisters gets married, their parents get worried that they've angered some God. They decide to seek the advice of one of the Apollo's oracles to see how Psyche's life will spin. This oracle tells them that Psyche is destined to marry the boogeyman and there is no way to prevent the girl from sipping from this fountain. What does these parents do? To get the cheat off their family, they sacrifice their youngest daughter to a mountain!

To await this monster that will beat... mistreat... despise... and pound her! But the game was good to little miss thang, cause that's exactly where Zephyr, the west wind, found her!

He lifts her gently, and carries her to a glorious field of flowers, where she gapes awestruck up at a majestic palace; but somehow she's confused and can't remember how she found it! She enters to find a gorgeous layout of splendid amenities, only to hear voices telling her it's all hers! That night, Psyche is treated to a feast.

And after all the wining and dining, she retires to her chambers to sleep. Within the darkness of the room, her husband approaches; his eyes digesting her fine ass, but since it was so dark, Psych couldn't notice.

He tells her that he loves her, but she should "never" attempt to see what he looks like, and she agrees. Yet, over time, she becomes lonely cause her husband only comes home at night, and no other human she sees. So, though her husband was against her allowing anyone into their palace, she puts that pussy on him and changes his mind...and agrees to allow her sister to visit just that one time! When her sister shows, Psyche tells her about the great palace and her wonderful husband, but the sister is convinced that her sister has lost her mind. Cause what Psyche sees as a wonderful palace; is merely a field of flowers and nothing else; so the sister tells her, "Psyche, you've lost yo goddamn mind! There's no palace here, and how can you be married to a man you've never seen yourself? What you should do is fuck him so good that he falls asleep. Then, light a candle on the sneak! Psyche argues, but her sister tells her that this invisible husband is really the monster of "insanity!" She tells her to just come home!

"No, sister, this is a palace, not a field of flowers, can't you see it?" Her conviction was strong, but her sister was adamant, and leaves only after Psyche promises to do exactly as she asked when her husband comes home. So, that night she does just that, and finds that all along, her husband has been Cupid, and she's blown away by his playerisms and feels stupid. She is in awe that she doesn't notice a drip of wax drip from her candle and burn his skin, and when Cupid *wakes to find her staring down at him, he's furious! He leaves ole Psyche, promising she'll never see him again. The beautiful palace vanishes and the lady finds herself alone in the fields of flowers her sister once described. And though the rest of the story ends with Psyche traveling ally the way to hell to find Cupid; going through some shit, but finally they reunite and live freely. My point is this. All this shit was in Psyche's mind! That's why her sisters couldn't see what she saw, cause within one's mind, one can create a palace within a deserted land! The psyche, son! The mind! And since Psyche was a bitch, that means every man has a piece of that bitch in them and that's what a man's emotions are! They derive from his psyche! My point is, Messiah, you have to be very cautious how you caress one's psych, cause though; with an "e" added, it becomes mental, psych with an "o" added will lead that person to become a psycho! A mu'fucka that will ruin your game because you've abused their psyche! Tame that bitch at all times, baby.*

-Mama-

***

The Past—1995

Bang! Bang! Bang! Bang! Sunjay pounded on the door; barely taming the urge to kick it in. Yet, out of respect for Murda's G-lady, he tamed it. Beneath the nights sky, he and Messiah clutched the type of heat that could turn the chilled night into a biting sensation, and that's exactly what they intended to do!

"Nigga, fuck?" Murda was in the midst of saying before both men took aim. Messiah was a nano second away from squeezing when Sunjay lowered his tool and stepped in his aim.

"Say, fool ass dude, you almost got yo shit pushed back!" Messiah raged while quickly decreasing the pressure on the trigger. Sunjay ignored him. He knew Messiah and Murda

had never rocked like that, so it wouldn't be nothing for Messiah to rock him to sleep. Though he'd noted the burna Murda clutched, his gangsterisms were on ten as he big cheated his way into the apartment, head on a swivel just in case fuck shit was lurking.

"Watch out, Blood. Fuck you bum rushin' my G-lady spot in the a.m. for?" Murda demanded before stiff arming Sunjay attempt to venture any further.

"Blood, fuck what you talmbout? Where yo buster ass twin at, and if you lie, I swear on the "Nine" one of us gonna get stretched!" Sunjay seethed.

That gangsta business eased into Murda's eyes and posture. "Nigga, first off, my shit clap too! And secondly, fuck you looking for my brotha for!" He spat, with his clutch tightening around the iron. Sunjay gritted his teeth as they eye wrestled. He was so fried that he contemplated cooking Murda's noodles right there, but their bond was too thick.

"Dawg," he gritted before his eyes flickered toward the back of the apartment. Though it was dark, he'd spent his pup days running in and out of that spot, so he knew the layout. "That nigga ran up in my big mama's spot, and—"

"Bullshit!" Murda cut him off. "Y'all may not see eye to eye, but bro wouldn't—"

"Tony?" Both men froze when Ms. Dorothy stepped from the back room. Concern was evident on her face. "Who ya talkin' to, boy, and why ya got my door…" Her words trailed off for a second, and Sunjay hurriedly hid his tool behind his back. "Sunjay? Messiah? Is that y'all? Why y'all standing in the door in the dark? She inquired.

"Hey, Ms. Dorothy!" They greeted simultaneously, and that's when her gaze became suspicious. Studying the three men she'd had a hand in raising, her spirit became troubled. "Come on in and close that door, Messiah, you knows how Ms. Dorothy is about her air, honey." Her southern accent was thick.

SON OF A DOPEFIEND 3 | RENTA

"Naw, Ms. Dorothy, we were just leaving..." Sunjay
saved the bar, and Ms. Dorothy experienced eyes took in his
posture. Though he smiled, it was the way he stood with his
hands behind his back that heightened her suspicions. Her
gaze shifted from him, touched Bam, and found Messiah.
She'd always seen something special in that one, and as her
intuition troubled her soul, her vision returned to Sunjay.

*"Okay, baby, well, I knows ya not just gonna leave
without givin' an old woman a hug?"* She smiled lovingly,
and Sunjay went rigid in alarm. The burna was hidden
behind his legs, and when the moment became tense, he
exhaled in relief when he felt the tool taken from his grip.

*"Give Ms. Dorothy some love, bruh, so we can smash
out."* Messiah patted Sunjay's back to let him know he had
him. Sunjay made his way to do just that, and Messiah
quickly tucked his and Sunjay's weapons. When his eyes
lifted, he and Murda's gaze collided, and for the millionth
time, Messiah couldn't shake the feeling of the man having
eyes of a serpent. He'd never really fucked with the twins,
and Bam Bam's sins only fed the enmity between them. As
Sunjay hugged the leader woman, Messiah formed a gun
with his fingers and mockingly pulled the trigger.

Bang! Bang! He mouthed, and Murda smirked his
sentiments.

*"Ms. Dorothy, where's Bam Bam's crazy ass, I mean;
butt."* Sunjay quickly corrected himself. Ms. Dorothy
laughed as Messiah made his way in and over to her for an
embrace. She pulled him in, but her words were for Sunjay.

*"Chile, I ain't seen that heathen since this mornin', and
if you see 'em out there in dem streets, you tell him he betta
have God with 'em when he carries his narrow behind back
in here; ya hear."* She released him before he and Sunjay
headed for their exits, and as soon as they were gone, she
had Murda to lock the door. Afterwards, she turned to her
grandson with evil in her glare. *"Bam Bam, bring yo' ass out
here, and I'm talkin' right! Now!"* She seethed. From the

127

back of the apartment, Bam Bam entered the living room, and as soon as Ms. Dorothy noted the massive pistol in his grip, she shook her head in disgust. This boy has been rotten as old milk since he was old enough to stand up and tinkle by himself, but he's my baby! She thought protectively. "Now, I don't know what ya done did to dem there two boys, but—"

"I ain't did nothin' to them niggas, G-lady. They just—" Bam tried, but...

"Stop!" Ms. Dorothy spat with a lifted hand. "Negro, I wiped yo shitty ass, and changed ya pamper when you was just a cooing fool. Ya daddy came from between these old legs, and I've let him and y'all get away with everythang beneath the sun, but one thing I won't let ya do is lie to my face! You lie to the police, negro, not ya family!" She fumed, and for a second, the three of them merely stared at one another. Murda knew his twin was guilty, but of what, he wasn't sure. Bam dropped his head; he was never good at lying to his grandmother.

"Mann, G-lady, I—"

"Aht!" She cut him off with a wave of her hand. I don't wanna hear it. Now, I love you two boys, but you two are my flesh and blood, so all I'll say is, all four of yous done grew up together. There should never be a time I see a hate as strong as the one I just seen in those boys eyes," she acknowledged, and when her eyes drifted to Murda, he already knew what she'd say. "Tony," she addressed him by his government. "Blood is thicker than mud, never forget that, baby. What I just seen in those boy's eyes was pure evil, and you bet not let nan evil come to ya brotha. Wrong or right, you stand beside him and fight," she spoke with passion, and Murda nodded his understanding.

"Yes, ma'am, I'm always my brotha's keeper," he vowed.

Chapter 10

Next Day
The day was humid, the sun was out, but hidden behind big white clouds. The stroll of Harry Hines was pregnant with crooked activity. Prostitution ran rampant up and down the blade, and where Motor Street intersects is where more than pussy is sold. A small fleet of glossed Cadillacs, Lincolns, and a Benz or two we're sitting and looking pretty, as pimps and playas balled and parlayed. Pimpin' Maxwell sat on the hood of his freshly waxed sedan just peeping the scene with a playa's lean as his cohorts surrounded a disheveled dressed man. Six pimps stared admirably as the bum tap danced with a prance that should've been too fast for his bones, and without warning, he leaped into the air, and clicked his heels together in conclusion of his show. The crowd applauded him, and as he bowed theatrically. He smirked as if that day he'd just gotten his groove back,

"The game bless you gents, but rather than idle praise, I'd rather ya bless my mitts," he jived. Pimpin' chuckled at the dingy man; the fella was clad in a dingy bucket hat, a long, stained bathrobe, and to compliment his dress, all he wore beneath the robe was a pair of dirty old boxers and a pair of yellow rain boots! Taking off the hat, he held it out for the spectators of his game to spare him some change and that they did. All knew the fallen playa by his old pimp moniker; Suade Wade, and though he'd fallen off his ism long ago, his peers still toasted his contribution to the game.

Quickly, the old hat was filled with loose change and a few dollar bills, and Suade Wade smiled a stained smile in appreciation. In the midst, and gist of it all, a smooth, feel green machine slid into the parking lot and that captured the attention of all Pimpin'. The Kag eased backwards into the parking space, and even with the windows up, the bass rumbled from its confines.

Do or Die talked that shit, and as swift as a butterfly's dance, Red Bone Tyrone slid over to where Pimpin' Maxwell parlayed.

"Say, P, ain't that ya boy?" The question was rhetorical, and the conniving smirk on the man's face let Pimpin' know that all puns were intended.

Chuckling, he nodded his answer while admiring the fruits of his protégés labor. "I always knew ya had it in ya tyke, keep ya game tight!" He thought as the driver's side of the passenger's side doors swung open.

♫ Do you wanna riiide, in the backseat of a caddy/ Choppin it up with do or die. The music flowed from within as two sets of smooth legs appeared. Tutts made her appearance first and if she was merely a preview to whatever else was to slip from the foreign, then it was sure to be a spectacle. Diva's hair was slayed and her face was made, but it was the see through cat suit she wore that whispered vulgarities to the imaginations of all with eyes. Naked beneath it, lady's titties, kitty, and all that ass was on display for all to see, but only the ones with deep pockets would be able to surpass the mere act of a lustful stare.

Messiah had upgraded her and as Liberty slipped from the passenger's seat, she became a motion picture. Hair braided back into three thick braids, and though her chunky eyes were hidden behind a large pair of designer shades. She peeped the dropped jaw expression of admirers when they took in her freak apparel. She wore nothing but a stretched muscle shirt that barely stretched to cover the bottom of her pelvis. Just as bare as her wife-in-law, Liberty's lower lips hung just below the thin material of the muscle shirt she'd spent days stretching. The bottom of her plump little butt cheeks peeked from its hem and when one's visual rose to behold the way her C-cups sat up behind it, the way her chocolate chip nipples imprinted the shirt exposed her shape.

"Aww shit, P, junior pimp got his "P" turnt up to the tenth degree!" One of the six pimps shouted, and as they watched Tutts make her way to the rear door of the sedan. The way they sway of her hips held their captive, gave credence to the man's statement. She pulled the rear door open, and a soft cloud of smoke rose from inside, but Tutts seemed oblivious to it. Turning on her four inch heels, she made her way to the nose of the car, and after securing the driver's side door, Liberty joined her.

"Girl, how I look? You don't think it's too "revealing" do you!" She smirked a nasty girl's smirk before rubbing her hands seductively down her body. Tutts vision fell from the lady's head to glittery pumps on her feet before recapturing her face.

"You're letting it "all" hang out, bitch, but a trick won't resist; that's for sure." She giggled. Liberty bathed her lashes, loving the way the humid air self against her exposed paradise.

"And I?" Purred Tutts, before striking a slut's pose.

Liberty took her hand, and holding it over her head, she helped her wife-in-law do a slow spin to give a full view of what it do. From behind the see through material, her chocolate assets were a lot to digest, but nakedness gave all with eyes to see, what they could partake of for a small fee. When she faced her again, Tutts stuck her tongue between her teeth and smiled hoishly. Liberty licked her lips seductively, and only a short distance away, Pimpin' Sweet Eddie gritted his teeth at the vision of the bitch Messiah had knocked him for. Yet, Liberty pulled her close, and slipped her tongue into Tutts' mouth. The praise of his fellow pimps *did it to him. Tutts and Liberty put on a show before making their way down the stroll to go make daddy's money.*

"Goddammit man, Pimpin' got his freaks doing thangs that's hard to explain!" A pimp known as Fat Pat exclaimed while groping himself.

Sweet Eddie spat on the ground. "Mane, that sucka ain't talm bout shit. All his game came from—"

"Hate doesn't suit you, my boy. Let's keep it playa." Pimpin' MAXWELL cut into the man's blasphemies, and got a few chuckles from their brethren. Sweet Eddie's glare shot to him just as Pimpin' slid off the hood of his whip.

"Hate!" Sweet Eddie spat as if the mere notion was alien to his ism, and again, he spat on the asphalt. "Hate is for the bitter, and the only thang bitter bout Sweet Pimpin' Eddie is my memories of being broke!" He stomped a Now-n-Later gator to the ground.

Pimpin' Maxwell and Red Bone Tyrone's vision clashed before they both burst into laughter. Bitter people, had a bitter aura, and Sweet Eddie's was as bitter as stale beer.

He glared at the two men, contemplating if they'd think the sight of the .38 special hidden at the small of his back would be so hilarious, but before he could rationalize the irrational, a silver bullet hued, Rolls Royce silver spur; two years before its release, slid into the lot. Mimicking Messiah's backwards park, the beautiful car eased in beside the Jaguar, and idle with the sounds of Atlantic star beating low from its sound system.

All eyes captured the sleep machine, wondering who the top notch playa could be that sat behind tint, and without much ado, the driver's door swung open. From inside the St. James red interior, slipped out one of the hardest playas Dallas, Texas has ever spit from between her legs. Yellow Shoe was a certified pimp that had taken his game from coast to coast and made his name synonyms with Pimpin' like slut and a hoe. He was real dapper in a cognac colored two piece, with a fresh pair of bitter scotch hues lizard skins on his feet that blew a kiss to the rest of his ensemble. Yet, it was the matching Fedora, with the butterscotch hued feather and silk ribbon around it that sparked the drip into the movie he was making. Yellow Shoe paused for the cause, allowing his orbs to take in his surroundings, before they settled on the valeted Jag. Messiah reclined in the backseat, with his fresh pair of Air Max 95's kicked up on the window sill and having heard the word on the young up and coming playa, Yellow Shoe decided to bless him with his presence.

He made his way over to the rear door on the driver's side and tapped a diamond ring encrusted knuckle against the window. Messiah glanced up at him before nodding towards the door as if you say, "It's unlocked." Pimpin' Yellow Shoe slid in and upon taking his seat, he admired the interior of the car; it was created with a playa in mind. And, when his vision drifted to Messiah, he got a peek at how times had changed since he'd enter the game of management of prostitution. Messiah kicked back like a real mack, in a pair of black leather shorts, and shirtless. Yet, it was his jewelry, that spoke volumes.

Around his neck were the "original" Cuban link, overlapping the thick Rolex necklace, and both were weighed down by heavy, diamond encrusted medallions. On all ten of his fingers he wore different styled rings, and to cap off his drip, his gold framed Versace glasses broadcasted the dime sized Medusa heads on both sides of their frames.

"What ya know good, young blood, I'm Yel"— He began but was interrupted.

"Pimpin' Yella Shoe; yeah, I know ya bio, daddy, I'm—"

"Messiah, the new golden child from what I hear." Yellow Shoe smirked, revealing to youngin that he too has his ear to the pavement. Messiah's hair was cut into an Oak Cliff shag, with an intricate design cut into it, and for the life of him, Yellow Shoe couldn't understand how the days of perms and Shirley Temple curls, the pimps of old use to rock, had

become extinct. Feeling the OG's appraisement, Messiah peeped him through the clear lens of his Saces.

"And to what do I owe this meeting of macks, OG?" He probed and Yellow Shoe chuckled. His eyes drifted toward the windshield, where he could see the group of playas congregating and conversing, and when he spotted his old playa partner, Pimpin' Maxwell, his vision returned to Messiah. He traced his thin goatee with his thumb and pointer finger as he spoke.

"I ran into a pimp friend of mine that told me you're a gifted gent that he holds dear to his heart. He asked if we were to ever rub shoulders, for me to drop a jewel or two in ya lap."

Messiah studied him, but after a moment he chuckled and rested his head against the soft leather of the backseat. Yellow Shoe watched youngin bring the half smoked blunt to his lips and suck the spirit from it, and when he responded, a snake of smoke rode his words.

"As you can see, I ain't got too much room for jewels," he capped before wiping himself down and flashing the face of his plain Jane Rollie.

Yellow Shoe chuckled. "Today's youth." He shook his head with the mumble.

Messiah frowned, taking no offense to dudes choice of words, "OG, I'm cool like a breeze on the pep talk, and I—"

"Think quick when I'm talking slick, gent, cause it's good in the way I spit, ya dig?" Yellow Shoe cut him off with a lifted palm to give him pause.

"If you was as swift as you claim, you woulda never forfeited ya first stable to the next playa." He went for blood and awaited for the cut to take affect. Messiah didn't disappoint. He moved so fast Yellow Shoe blinked in surprise at the sight of the burna Messiah had snatched off his waist and rested on his lap. The indirect was somehow direct, but Yellow Shoe was a sho nuff pimp. He excelled in the lane of mind finessing. The act proved that Messiah was still tender *about blowing his stable to Pimpin' Maxwell, and not to mention, too easy to surrender to emotion.*

"I think you need to excuse ya self, OG, before we get blood on that pretty suit," he growled, but the older pimp wasn't moved.

Pimpin' Yellow Shoe's gaze fell to the nickel plated Glock before recapturing Messiah's. "You wanna know what your generation lacks that could take their game to the top of the mountain?" He proposed, and Messiah contemplated knocking his noodles out the slick hat on his head.

"Naw, what I wanna know is why you still parked in my shit?"

"I'll let you know after you catch this drip I'm tryin' to coat ya with, and please," Yellow Shoe waved a dismissive hand at the steel resting upon the man's lap. "Put that thang away. It has no room amongst playas while choppin' game, cat daddy."

And maybe it was how he said it, or maybe it was merely the vibe oozing from the older man's ism, in the end. Messiah chuckled before slipping the burna back onto his waist.

Yellow Show laughed inwardly. Who won the war? The man whom came with his emotions on fire, or the man whom made him feel silly for allowing such a fire to ignite in the first place? He thought before waving a jeweled hand toward the windshield where a clear view of Pimpin' Maxwell stood amongst the extracurricular.

"The man has a soft spot for ya in his heart, and the gem he dropped on you by knocking you for those dames was priceless, but you were too young to see it."

Messiah took a deep pull from the shrinking blunt. " That nigga a stone cold snake. He didn't "knock" me for shit but my work I kept at his spot. The hoes," he spoke as he exhaled a long stream of corn smoke. "He "snuck" me for."

"Ahhh, snuck you for em, huh?" Yellow Shoe chuckled with a nod of his head. "I see—"

"What you see, OG? Clue a young nigga in so I don't keep wondering aimlessly through lame man's land without a clue."

"I see that just like most young gents that entered this here life of ours, you got the game fucked up." Yellow Shoe's *lack of sensitivity almost brought on a reenactment of the moment they'd just surpassed, but his next words were the calm to that gangsta shit.*

"See, me, Maxwell, and ya ole man Cedric use to be as tight as pussy on a female lice. Now Ceddy boy," he chuckled *in remembrance of the slain con man. "That was a playa after my own heart."*

"You ain't got no heart, Yellow Shoe. Nan nigga or bitch in "this" way of life does," Messiah spat, and took one last *drag from the swisher before flicking it out the window.*

Yellow Shoe cut a hand through the air.

"See, lil daddy, all that jive you kicking is a fools rhetoric. Shit mu'fuckas heard on TV or in one of these "tasteless" rap songs that's out now. Nigga, I ain't met a man or bitch alive that ain't have a heart they feel. It's your definition of the heart that's corrupted." He jeweled, and as blitz as a *stoner, Messiah reclined and soaked up the game. Yellow Shoe tapped a hand against his chest for emphasis. " To hide ya feelings is truly a talent, but it's the heart you put into this here game that's gonna keep you swell and eating well. Cop, lock, and blow? I ain't never met no bonafide pimp that ain't lost no hoe! Ya dig?"* The man's tone had become *passionate. "When you cop a hoe, you betta work that bitch until that pussy ain't got no mo' grip, cause if ya game ain't outta space enough to "lock the hoe", you gonna "blow the hoe" to another pimp! Ya game "is" ya heart, play buddy, and every time you give a feline a sip of it, you give her a piece of ya heart. So, if you ever lose her, the "only" thang that's gonna keep ya pride in tact is how you used her, and if you failed to "use" the hoe, you deserve to lose the hoe; and that's a fact, Jack!"* Yellow Shoe was in raw form, and

Messiah was feeling it. He nodded his head in understanding as Yellow Shoe took the hat from his head and pointed toward youngin'. "Messiah, what Pimpin' did "for" you was priceless! "That's" what you call "real" love, daddy."

That brought a frown to Messiah's face. "How, Yellow Shoe? Pimpin' is like my pops, my main man, and he snuck—"

"Negro, ain't no such thing as "sneaking" a nigga for no hoe! A nigga can't tell yo bitch nothing special, and nothing she ain't ever heard before! So, if she leaves you for him, "she" wanted to do that! "Attraction" did that! That hoe wasn't loyal to you, Pimpin' was!"

"Huh? Bruh, you trippin'." Messiah laughed.

Yellow Shoe didn't. "Which one of em left you!"

"Huh?"

"Nigga, you heard me twice the first time," Yellow Shoe spat.

Messiah thought for only a moment, and when his silence became to profound, Yellow Shoe "forced" truth into the convo.

"Them funky pussy hoes did. That's who. And who put you on game bout their departure? I'm "positive" it was my main man, Pimpin', that made the hoes keep it a kilo with you and tell you they'd rechose...right?" He smirked.

Messiah frowned as his vision drifted to capture Pimpin' standing out there laughing at Sweet Eddie. He'd never really thought about it that way, and when his vision reclaimed his company, Yellow Shoe chuckled. Messiah rubbed a hand over his wavy hair.

"That's" what the gem is, Messiah. Can't you see the man was teaching you! Ain't no such thang as loyalty in the life of the streets! No matter if your Pimpin' and hoin', trappin' or robbin', or just scamming. There is no loyalty when you're living wrong, son." Yellow Shoe put his hat back on. "There's no loyalty in the game cause the spoils are too beautiful to let go of. When a person gets a taste of real money, there's nothing more they care about. When their time is up, and jail

or the grave is in their futures, the first things they think of is "not" family or love, it's the spoils, Messiah. "That's" why snitchin' and fuck shit runs rampant. It's cause mu'fuckas don't wanna lose the spoils, even when the war has already been lost, and there's no surrender." He jeweled before slipping out the car and stretching.

Messiah watched the man nod toward Pimpin' Maxwell, and after they shared a moment that didn't need any verbal, Yellow Shoe made his way to his driver's seat of his own car, and slid in.

🎵 Drifting on the memories/ There's no place I'd rather be, than with yoouuuu/ lovin youuu— 🎵

The Isley's drifted from the inside as he started the ignition and pulled off. All eyes ogled the Royce as it slip cater corner to where Messiah sat with his door open, and only when Messiah caught the hint and slipped out into the sunshine, did the passenger's window ease down. Messiah made his way over and leaned into the window, but when his vision fell upon the jazzy feline in the passenger's seat, he almost jumped back in surprise. He'd assumed Yellow Shoe had shown up dolo, but the dame, obviously mixed with negroid and caucasoid blood, sitting and looking pretty proved otherwise.

"Y'all give the champ a warm greetin'." Yellow Shoe smiled.

"Y'all?" Messiah wondered aloud, but before he could wrap his mental around the implicature, Yellow Shoe's request was met with obedience.

"Heyyy, Messiah!" A chorus of femininity greeted him. Messiah's eyes grew wide in shock as he looked passed the dime in the passenger's seat, and captured forty cent in the backseat. A Latina, two yellas, and an Asian persuasion were on deck, and to Messiah's utter amazement, one of the beautiful yellow skinned diva's in the middle, lifted her legs. Her wife-in-laws on both sides, grabbed a leg and held them open as lady scrunched her skirt up around her waist. She *was pantiless, and with her bald flower on display, she spread her pedals. In the midst of, the beauty in the passenger's seat flashed Messiah her D-cups before lifting her left one and sucking its flesh. Messiah's johnson throbbed before he hurriedly diverted his attention to Yellow Shoe.*

"You's a mu'fucka, Playboy, but it was a pleasure to rub elbows with ya," he slick praised, and the older pimp chuckled.

"Sure ya right, but before I dip, allow me to give you some muscle to keep ya game tight," he jazzed before waving a hand toward his lady friends. "Never forget this diamond, cat daddy, cause it's gonna help ya shine and live fine," he jived before dropping a bit of game in Messiah's mind. "One hoe is too close to no hoe, and two hoes ain't too far away! Get ya hoe game up and take it on the road. True Pimpin' is city to city, and state to state. It should be a crime if you can find a time one of ya lady's ain't got a date! Put ya game in another lane, daddy-o. Amarillo, Texas has one of the longest hoe strolls in the states, but Detroit, Milwaukee, and Oakland, California are sho nuff aims you should try ya game," he suggested before tipping his hat to the youngin and unmuting the bass on his stereo. Messiah caught the hint, and just before the car eased out the lot, the chick that had flashed him with her tits, gave him a seductive wink.

♫ *You know that I'm living/ for the love of youuuu/ I rather be living/ for the love of youuu* ♫ *The Isleys serenaded as the Rolls dipped into traffic.*

Chapter 11

Gator's massive, yet, beautiful estate never ceases to amaze Sunjay. Every time he stepped onto the property, the only constant was his thoughts of one day making it "that" big. Though heavily guarded by menacing dread heads brandishing the type of artillery that could turn a house to ruble, the opulence was still grand, and as he was lead down the highly polished hall, Sunjay allowed his vision to be a glutton of the beauty surrounding him. Marble statues the size of giants were sporadically placed, and though there were many paintings depicting historical moments in the reggae country, it was the giant portrait of the late, great Bob Marley. The artist had a light hand, and the portrait was so lifelike, that Sunjay almost expected the man to reach out and hand him the joint he was depicted smoking in the framed work.

As the muscled rude boy lead him down the south wing of the house, he spotted beautiful, vibrant plants of an exotic species, and though Sunjay loved the hood he repped, it was just "something" about the life his orbs were capturing that made him almost ashamed of the bricks he hailed from. Along their trek, they'd passed rooms, but one particular became a thief of his attention. The room was finely decorated, but more so, it was a beauty of a different kind that made him glad not to be blind. "Keisha!" Her name echoed throughout the corners of his mind. The girl was so *entranced with whatever she was doing that she didn't notice he'd slipped into the room until it was too late.*

"Huua!" She jumped with a start. Sucking in a sharp breath, she glared at him. "Wah Gwen, boi, ya ah not allowed here, ya know," she fumed with her patois dialect thick.

"What?" Sunjay frowned, not really understanding her, but rather than give her his attention, his vision had again been stolen. This time by a beauty more captivating than that of sex appeal. There, resting before her on a red velvet cloth were three flawless, five carat stones, and each revealed "why" certain gems were dubbed "precious!" Keisha hurriedly covered them.

"Ya ah go far from mi, batti boi!" She spat, and for some strange reason, her feistiness turned him on. Sunjay smirked to let her know exactly that, and if it weren't for the interruption, he would have got verbal. Yet, the game god wasn't feeling generous.

"Wah ya ah do, Star, de boss man is dis way," a raspy voices laced with a Jamaican dialect came from behind him. Sunjay winked at Keisha, and just before he turnt to follow his escort, he found humor in the chocolate beauty's roll of the eyes.

"No more detours, hmm, boi. Next time me ah lose ya head fa de act, yea," the dread head gritted with his clutch familiar on the banana clip equipped stick, and with a nod of his head, the man turnt on his heels for the exit. Sunjay gave Keisha one last gander before chuckling and following the fellow.

***

One hoe is too close to no hoe, and two hoes ain't far away! Get ya hoe game up and take ya show on the road. True Pimpin' is city to city, state to state, is should be a crime if you can find a time one of ya ladies ain't got a date! Put ya game in another lane, daddy-o! One hoe is too close to no hoe, and two hoes ain't far away! One hoe is too close to no hoe, and two hoes ain't far away! One hoe is too close to no hoe, and two hoes ain't far away!

Pimpin' Yellow Shoe's gems bounced around in Messiah's head like a handful of coins being thrown against a brick wall. Since their convo, he'd driven aimlessly through the city, "fantasizing" of slaying hoe stroll within the likes of cities of Detroit, Michigan...Oakland, California! Amarillo, Texas? The Mill in Wisconsin? The strip in Las Vegas? He'd never stepped a foot out of Dallas/Ft. Worth, let alone dreamed of slipping out the Lone Star State. Yet, here was a legend of a man, pulling his coat to the idea that the real check is secured out of bounds. Messiah's mental was a mad zone as he maneuvered the machine through the city's best bush. In the nineties, a strand of ganja known as corn, was considered exotic, and at that moment, Messiah was loving its company. When he slid the Jag through the entrance of the bricks, the projects were lit as usual, and he gazed out in wonder at how his folks had become institutionalized by the ghetto. It seemed absurd to him how the ghetto had become synonymous with home, and even more so, how he himself felt safer and found his solace within the slums.

As he pulled into the parking space, he reflected on something he'd once read. The word ghetto was the name of an island near Venice in Italy, where Jews were "forced" to live in the 16th century. "An island!" Just as his hood was an island of poverty, surrounded by a sea of shit that detested it. Slipping from the whip with the blunt dangling from between his lips, Messiah allowed his vision to soak in his surroundings and just when he spotted someone dead to his heart.

"Heyyy Messiah!" A group of four girl's greeted as they passed. He nodded his acknowledgment as he took them in. Porsha, Tweety, Kayla, and Monica were all young women he'd watched fall into the deceptive hands of lady

"promiscuity", whom taught them the secret of pussy, weed, and alcohol being kryptonite to all street niggas. On that humid afternoon in the Jects, all four girls wore either daisy dukes or cut off shorts with revealing halter tops, but it was Porsha, "the fastest of the group," that stopped and struck a pose. Standing as if she were bow legged, she placed her hands on her small waist, and Messiah took her in. Her dookie braids were fresh, and the pink and white Guess short set she wore hugged her body like it missed her. The girl feverishly chewed a wad of bubble gum and blowing a large bubble, she eyed Messiah as if he were a meal. Messiah wondered when the large inflation would pop, and when it did, Porsha returned to her "expert" chewing, Messiah made his way to the curb where she stood. Thotism oozed from the girl's essence like the fragrance of exotic perfume and he knew she wanted the dick. He pulled the blunt from his lips.

"Sup, mama, I see you still too hot to trot." He smirked, glad to see his homegirl.

Porsha smacked her lips. "And I see ya chocolate ass still fine. I'm sayin' tho. 'Siah, when you gonna let a bitch get some dick?" She snaked her neck real sassy-like.

Messiah chucked as his vision swallowed her. At five foot even, the girl was chocolate and thicker than a Snicker. Her pink shorts cut up into her feminancy and hugged her thighs, and after his orbs fell to the crisp white high top Filas on her feet, they returned to her lustful gaze.

"What about ya girl Justice?" He toyed with her.

"What about her? She's way in Houston with "her man." I spent the summer with em. I told you she givin' up her coochie and errythang to that nigga." She laughed at the quick flash of hurt that vanished just as quick as it had arrived. "Ugh!" She made a face. "Messiah, the girl has been gone "years", it's time to get you a big girl and stop playing." She flirted, but she mustn't have received the memo. The friendly banter suddenly died a slow death as

143

SON OF A DOPEFIEND 3 | RENTA

something she couldn't describe begin to ooze from
Messiah's aura, and he laid down the law.

"Bitch, if you ain't talkin' bout flat backin' to pay my
mackin, what you talm bout?"

"Huh? Wha—" she tried, flustered, but Messiah had
slipped into his mode. Stepping up into her personal, he
palmed her round glutes.

"Dig this flavor, Jezebel, if a hoe ain't freakin' I ain't
speaking! Cause the only word a bitch's cunt can say to me,
is "cum"...telling me to cum get my cock suckin' gwop from
between her stanking twat!" He jazzed before flicking his
nose and fixing lady with a questioning gaze. Not only
Porsha's, but the eyes of her friends took in the man child's
ism, and as if she were an explorer discovering uncharted
land, Porsha's mouth fell open in shock. Now that she'd
thought of it, she recalled the whispers of Messiah trying his
hand in Pimpin', but his absence from the hood had deprived
her of separating fact from fiction.

"Get up with the kid when ya pussy decides to spit more
than bodily fluids, lil baby. I can upgrade ya grade from and
"E" for effort, to a "double B" for Boss Bitch." Messiah
broke on her; live and direct before allowing his Air Max to
carry him beyond her presence. But? Just before he traveled
too far away, Porsha had one more card to play.

"Heard y'all been looking for Bam Bam," she wagered
as she turnt to face him. Messiah froze mid stride but didn't
turn to face her.

"Don't play ya self, Porsha. If you know where that boy—"

"Meet me at my apartment tonight and I'll tell you." She
cut him off before relinking with her girls. Messiah finally
turnt to face her, and eyed her suspiciously.

"Say—"

"Tonight, Messiah, be there," she retorted before the
group sashayed away, giggling.

Messiah shook his head before making his way over to the
nigga he didn't have to wear his mask around. Lil Zetti sat

on a green electric box, taking it all in, and when Messiah made it to him, he lit up.

"What's popping, Blood? You crazy!" He laughed with a shake of his head before gazing out at the group of girls. They were just bending the corner, and when he returned his attention to Messiah, he had an expression on his face that said. "Nigga, somethin' wrong with you!"

"What's the haps, lil one, and what I tell you about that gang banging shit?" Messiah took a seat beside him.

"Mannn, Sunjay say he gonna put me on set when I—"

"Shut up, fam, you sound like a lame!" Messiah spat before slapping him on the back of the head.

"Say, fool, watch out!" The boy protested with an evil growl. Messiah paid no mind to him as he sucked the spirit from the half smoked Optimo. Ever since he'd met the youngin, he'd developed a soft spot for him, and tried to lead him down a different path than he and Sunjay. Yet, Sunjay was hell bent on making him a gangsta.

"Let me hit the dope, dawg." Lil Zetti reached for the stick, and Messiah obliged. Passing it to him, his eyes fell to the baby nine and dope sack the boy had in his lap, and though he'd seen little man on deck like that before, it always saddened him. The ills of the ghetto, where the young are grown!

"Why you always kickin' that anti-gang stuff, big homie? Sunjay loves the "9", why you don't?" Lil Zetti's line of questioning burglarized his thoughts.

Messiah gazed out at the jungle the called home. The Butta Beans apartments were run down and a low down dirty shame. Little girls ran wild, some as young as thirteen were pregnant by niggas their daddy's age! Dope fiends were everywhere, and kids played football, barefoot as if the shards of glass, and discarded drug paraphernalia knew better than to bother their exposed flesh.

"Lil Zetti, Sunjay is family, and I love guy like we came out the same pussy, but homie's philosophies and ways of

doin' things aren't always the best. Bro is the type of fella that lives by the next niggas standards, you dig what I'm saying, lil man?" He asked uncertainly. And only after taking a big boy pull from the corn did Lil Zetti nod his understanding.

He held the smoke in his young lungs as long as he could until the pressure snatched a coughing fit from him. Messiah laughed and wanted to ask if the boy was good but knew the question would be rhetorical. Lil Zetti was a seed of the bricks, and they got introduced to brown people shit way before they could understand that they were too young to know it.

Composing himself, Lil Zetti gave the dope a brief gander before again nodding his understanding. "Yeah, big bruh, you're saying he a follower." His answer was so raw that Messiah's eyes shot to him in surprise before he burst into laughter. He'd attempted to skirt around the "uncut" version of his view of his mans, but at times he forgot Lil Zetti was more Zetti than lil, and hailed from the same trenches that he himself crawled from. As he accepted the stick back, he nodded his agreement.

"Yeah, Lil Zetti, bro is more a follower than leader." He confirmed. "He's a good nigga, but Sunjay will follow a trend versus setting his own." He opened up before glancing at the youngin. "Like this gang shit he got you screamin'. Niggas round this bitch screaming blood and crip, but don't even know nothin' about that shit. 4'9 and 457 blood is Oak Cliff sets, "but" let me ask you something, lil nigga. Where'd they come from? Who started 'em?" He quizzed and watched as a puzzled expression eased onto the boy's face. Messiah chuckled when he shrugged, his ignorance, and after downing the rest of stick, he tossed the stub.

"See what I'm talm 'bout, lil one? Bro, 457 is out the Bay Area just as how and 415 Piru, and 4'9 is out the lane as well, so I'm askin', Lil Zetti, how and why would a nigga wanna rep another nigga's hood? Niggas ain't even been to

Cali, let alone these hoods, but they're reppin' them harder than their own blocks! Fuck a nigga gonna rep LA, Compton, and San Diego blocks way in another state!" His frustration was evident in his tone, and Lil Zetti seemed to think on it for a moment before shrugging his indifference.

"I don't know, dawg, but let me ask you something," he proposed. Messiahs vision left him and fell to the strap and drugs in his lap.

"Only if you'll answer a question for me?" He wagered.

"Sup, big homie?"

"Why you hustling? You're thirteen, Zetti, you 'pose to be in school playing somebody's sports and fuckin' on them lil females?" Messiah felt like a hypocrite; he had done the exact same when he was little man's age, but he wanted to know where Zetti's head was at. Eyes glassy from the high, Lil Zetti gazed down at the felonies in his lap.

"Messiah, I ain't been to school in a year. Nigga, I got tired of being laughed at for wearing the same clothes and having holes in my kicks. My mama a dope fiend, big homie. That bitch don't give a damn 'bout me or my—"

"Watch yo mouth, bruh. Don't ever—" Messiah seethed before slipping off the generator and standing before the boy. "Ever disrespect ya T-lady like that again!"

"Mann, my mama—"

"I don't give a fuck bout her addiction, Lil Zetti!" He cut her off with a heated glare. "That woman pushed you out her womb, and fed, and clothed you when nobody else would. Where ya daddy at?"

"Fuck my daddy, dawg. I don't know that nigga, and fuck you too, Messiah!" Lil Zetti spat before snatching the metal off his lap and jumping off the box. He was so fried that he didn't register his dope sack falling to the ground, and as he and Messiah faced off. He hoped he didn't have to "man down" one of the only men who'd helped put something warm in his belly. Messiah eyed him from behind the lenses of his Versaces; seeing deeper than animosity emitting from

him. He knew the ills of the slums had a way of cracking a mu'fuckas heart, and at that moment, he wondered how a people, "black people", that weathered times when all they had was the love of the community? How could it corrode to the culture of fathers becoming rolling stones, and mothers sacrificing it all for so little?

Messiah smiled a sad smile before squatting down, noticing though he wasn't aiming the tool at him, Lil Zetti's grip tightened on the metal in anticipation. Messiah ignored him as he retrieved the sandwich bag, studying its contents and remembering the times when he was hugging the crooked corners of the hood. Lil Zetti had a half ounce of hard cut up into different sized stones and as Messiah extended it to him. The boys mug eased into a gaze too old for a boy so young.

"If I don't get out here and get it, me and Tweet gonna starve, Messiah. My sister got two kids by P-Bo, and he don't even come around no more!" He shrugged. "What else can I do?" He accepted his sack as Messiah stood and diverted his attention out at the concrete football game being played.

"Never pull up steel on a nigga and not use it, lil daddy. You give 'em a chance to regroup and checkmate you at a later time," he spoke over his shoulder as he made his way back to the car.

"Messiah?" Lil Zetti called, but Messiah didn't turn around. Lil Zetti quickly tucked his burna before hurrying after him, and by the time he caught up, Messiah was slipping into the driver's seat. When the car started and Messiah eased it out without even a glance in his direction. Lil Zetti dropped his head, cursing himself for his earlier reaction. Man! Now Messiah don't want me around, I'm always fuckin up, man! His thoughts were turbulent.

"Sup, lil dude, you gonna get in or stand out there looking like a cry baby?" Messiah's voice caused his head to snap up, and a big smile eased onto the boy's face. Though the cold of the ghetto had pushed him into the reality of

adulthood before his time, Lil Zetti was still the epitome of adolescence. He tried to put his "G" back up as he bopped to the passenger's side and hopped in. Messiah chuckled as he navigated the foreign out the apartments. But just as he turnt up the knock and let Do or Die have it, he glanced over at Lil Zetti, "Say what you was gonna ask me earlier?"

Lil Zetti's look was one of confusion until he remembered. "Oh, I was just wondering why you don't ever wanna get wit none of the freaks in the hood, especially Porsha. That girl fine!" He exclaimed as he eyed Messiah.

Messiah smirked at he molested the grain. " Listen, lil daddy, and listen with ya ears "and" eyes, cause I'm about to sprinkle ya senses. A hoe will be a hoe today, tomorrow, and next week, so "why" be in a rush to freak when you can charge that hoe a fee?" The game he spit was official, but Lil Zetti nodded not because he truly understood, but more because it sounded exotic to his young ears. Messiah was hip to this fact, and desired to elaborate.

"How you think I get my lucci, Lil Zetti? How you think I keep my bank tight?" He inquired and without much consideration, Lil Zetti answered.

"Hustling! Sunjay say you get yo money off the blade or somethin' like that. I just figured you sold work like the rest of us. What's the blade anyway? Like a razor or something?"

Messiah laughed with a shake of his head. "Naw, lil bro, the blade is another name for the "hoe stroll." It's a strip where women get paid for sex." He broke it down to its lowest common denominator, and Lil Zetti frowned.

"So, you sell work where they sell sex?"

"Naw, negro." Messiah burst into a fit of laughter. "Naw, I'm like some of those women's daddy. I "help" them manage their money. They go get it and give it to me, and I tend to everythang else. "That's" what I'm telling you." He paused to turn down Overton before crossing Sunnyvale.

"Porsha, and most of these lil girls she runs with make pretty "trophies", but poor whores. They're too lazy for a

playa as myself to entertain. They only want dick and some shoes, whereas I want money and a vet bitch that can get me plenty of it. Your dick can either derange a bitch or motivate her to be the best you need her to be. And a deranged hoe can only bring strange problems, whereas a motivated hoe can only bring a playa fame and dollars!" He jeweled with a flick of the tip of his nose, "Fuck a bitch with "your mind" and you'll get more out her pussy than a baby and child support, lil daddy." He chuckled as Lil Zetti soaked it up with an expression on his face that said, I've never thought about it like that!

***

The same dread head Sunjay'd followed in was the same one he'd followed on his way out. Except, on his way out, he now drudged with an army duffel bag stuffed with neatly compressed blocks. The plug hadn't understood why Messiah hadn't shown up, and preferring to do business with, as he'd put it, "the thinker" of the two, Gator "reluctantly" handed over the six bricks. When people constantly compared he and Messiah and they constantly made Messiah out to be the king, and he the prince, it fucked with Sunjay's two step. So, he was low key hot as he was led toward his exit but wasn't so distracted by emotion that he didn't pause upon coming upon the room he'd spotted the sexy little Jamaican girl in earlier. He had a jones for Keisha and when his vision captured her screwing the top onto a golden urn before placing it back onto the mantle above a huge fireplace, he licked his lips in lust.

Almost as if she'd felt his gaze, Keisha spun with a suspicious gaze in her eyes, and when she found Sunjay on the lurk, molten vulgarities arrived on the top of her tongue, but when Sunjay was pushed from behind, she swallowed whatever she was tempted to spew as a smirk eased onto her face. Dread, a young shooter from Haiti was the pusher, and she knew the Haitian was infatuated with murder, but the look Sunjay gave him made Keisha wonder if the young American was bout that shit.

"Move!" Dread demanded with a kit of his mini 14 toward the exit. Sunjay's glare never wavered, almost as if he had no fear for death.

"Keep ya hands to ya self, potna. Where I'm from, we get our licks back, huh." He smirked.

"Go!" was Dread's only demand, but they all noted his finger twist around the trigger. Sunjay nodded his recognition before his gaze shifted to Keisha. She rolled her eyes when he winked, but little did she know, the wink had nothing to do with his attraction. Sunjay headed for the exit, but his mental was rotating with possibilities—

"Smooth but risky! I bet the old man keeps his diamonds inside that urn! Bet he ain't expect his daughter to lead a crook to the X that marks the spot!" He thought with a chuckle.

Chapter 12

Hours Later

The business had been concluded, and Messiah and Sunjay found themselves sitting on the sofa in Porsha's living room. The apartment was tidy and the furniture was top of the line as far as project living was concerned. Beige leather sofas, and glass coffee tables were evidence that the girl either had a mean pussy game, or she had a secret job; and Messiah knew the latter wasn't even a consideration. He and Sunjay sat on either side of the sofa, and from Sunjay's nonchalance, Messiah concluded that he had been there a time or two. He'd heard Sunjay and Porsha had been fucking on each other, and when he chuckled, it beckoned Sunjay's attention.

"Sup? Nigga, what's so comical?" He asked, gazing out from a cloud of weed smoke. Messiah studied him with mock suspicion, coupled with a knowing chuckle.

"Nigga, quit faking the funk. You and Porsha been getting booty on the L."

A slight frown eased on Sunjay's mask; his first mind was to deny! Porsha was as fine as wine and had more curves than a country road, but she had an unsavory reputation. "Most" of the hood claimed to had either smashed or experienced her dick suckers, and though he knew niggas lied on their dicks, he was in tune with the cliché. "When it's five or more? It ain't a lie no more!" A lot of truth can be found in a little bit of lies, yet; he shrugged indifferently. Messiah was his main man.

"Yeah, I cut the bitch, Blood, and that snappa gets an "A" plus!" He bragged, and they dapped while sharing a laugh.

"She "walks" like she got that come back kid!" Messiah admitted.

Sunjay nodded his confirmation, "Yeah, and she's been trying to put that pussy on you since we were still huggin' them corners," he spoke public knowledge before trying to pass the joint he was blowing. Messiah shooed him away.

"I'm good." He waved him away. "On both." He added, and Sunjay shrugged.

"Mo' for me." He laughed before hittin' the dope with a deep drag. "You already know that's why she called you over here, nigga, she trying to put in that split!" He laughed at the strange expression Messiah gave. He'd always known Porsha wanted more than his friendship, but on top of his respect for Justice making it a "no no", his Pimpin' quieted the call of his dick head.

"I'm good, homie, I—"

"Damn, bruh, why "errythang" gotta "always" be 'bout you! For once, stop being selfish, blood! If this hoe know where this mark, Bam, tucking his tail at, let's get it out her by "any" means!" Sunjay spat, and Messiah reared back in surprise.

"Nigga, I want this boy's head just as bad as you, for what he done to G-lady, but that's yo' problem. Sunjay, you talk too much! If you wouldn't have been yappin' to whoever you been yappin' to, nobody would've known where you kept ya fetti! I been told you about them twins, but you always gotta play with fire, fam, and when you get toasted, you want errybody else to jump in the toaster wit you!" He seethed, his glare matching his man's. "Niggas like bitches, they talk to much!" He spat.

Sunjay's body language spoke that gangsta shit. "Messiah." he chuckled sinisterly. "You know I'll beat yo ass, blood, so be conscious!"

Messiah's face balled up. "Sunjay, you a shooter, but I'll flush you from the shoulders, nigga. On God!"

Sunjay was rising to the occasion when Messiah threw a curve ball. "And, I ain't gonna tell you no mo' about puttin' that gangsta shit in Lil Zetti head. Damn, Sunjay, you can't fuck up everybody's life, bruh! Somebody" gotta be off limits to the bullshit!" He demanded, and Sunjay plopped back down in his seat.

"Yeah, that's what I thought. You ain't talm about catching that square!" He smirked, "And Lil Zetti? It's in his blood. He's destined to be a dawg."

"What y'all talking about?" Porsha saved the bar because Messiah was tea kettle hot! She frowned in confusion at the hostility in his glare, but as soon as their glares took her in in totality, a wicked smirk eased onto Sunjay's face. He gripped his johnson, but Messiah's mind was different.

"Mane, I may need to lay the law down on miss, cause if she can understand that prostitution is the constitution, I can make her a star!" He thought, not aroused by her hoe appeal.

"Well?" Porsha lifted an arched brow while standing sassy-like. Her left leg was cocked out and her hands on her shapely hips like women do when they're slick trying to show off their shape or posing for a picture. The black spandex shorts made it evident that she was pantiless, and her nipples pressing against the fabric of her gray sports bra, whispered to the fact of her either being cold, or turned on.

"Girl, get out of grown folks business," Sunjay said with a laugh, and Porsha rolled her eyes.

"Boy, "everybody" in here grown, and why you even here, Sunjay? Ain't nobody invited you, right, Messiah?" She turnt to him with a flirtatious smile before strutting over and *plopping down between them. Sunjay was lowkey offended but hid it behind a chuckle and a time of the joint. Slipping from his seat, he headed for the kitchen.*

"Wrong!" He humored her before disappearing around the corner. When he returned, he held three cups and a bottle of E&J that Porsha kept on deck. Reclaiming his seat, he lined the cups up and poured a generous amount in each before retrieving his.

"My bro invited me, and if it weren't for me, "he" wouldn't have come, so you may need to pipe down and show some appreciation for a playa." He lowered the volume on her self-assuredness, and with a smack of her lips, the girl reached for her own cup.

"Is that so, Messiah? Did this bullshitter have to "force" you here?" She gazed to him before taking a sip from her drink. Messiah chuckled, and though he wasn't a fan of liquor at that time, he obliged "himself".

"Porsha, where the boy Bam Bam at? Stop playing with me, mama?" He wanted to skip all the appetizing and get to the main course. Porsha watched him take a deep swallow of the yak before she did the same. Sunjay smirked as he watched it all unfold. Damn, this bitch thick thick! He thought of the last time he'd sliced lady, but Porsha's attention was taken. She smirked before turning to Sunjay and snatching the joint from his fingertips, but before he could protest, she'd returned her focus to Messiah. She sucked the soul from it, not knowing the joint was a mo', "ganja laced with cocaine." Her lungs instantly rejected the foreign smoke and Sunjay had to pat her back to help her breathe easier.

"Easy, lil mama, I told you to stay out of grown folks business." He chuckled as she stared at the half smoked joint.

"What the hell is that, Sunjay? It tastes funny!" She whined before taking a gulp from her drink, but just to prove she fit in the "grown" category. She took a more cautious

drag from the dope before passing it back to him. The high envelopes her without delay, and the power of it sliced through the cord of her inhibitions and allowed the freak in her to walk free. Again, she rolled her eyes at Sunjay before returning her attention to Messiah, "So, what's up, daddy? You gonna give a bitch some of that dick, or what?" She licked her lips as if the question alone was tasty.

Messiahs first impulse was to lay down his Pimpin', but one glance at Sunjay let him know that wasn't the time, and to stick to the script. He chuckled before downing the rest of the liquor.

"Porsha, how long have we known each other?" He asked after resting his cup on the table. He'd give one last shot at preventing the unthinkable!

"Huh? What does that have to—" Porsha began, but paused to slap Sunjay's hand away for the third time. "Stoppp, boyyy!" She whined, but now the men noted the erotic purr just beyond the demand. Sunjay knew the dope was on her ass, and ignoring her, he rubbed his hand down her thigh. The caress was like pleasure fire against her flesh; the drugs coupled with the liquor was like a three way call! Narcotics called to her brain, who then gave a ring to her clit, and as her orbs became smokey, Porsha ease dropped on their convo.

"Look, 'Siah, this what's up. You want something and I want something—" she began before reaching down massaging his thigh. "I promise as soon as I make this dick spit, I'll lead you right to that hoe ass nigga," she bargained and though he studied her with disgust in his irises. Messiah could see Sunjay being dramatic as he silently encouraged him to get his dick wet. Messiah gritted his teeth and before he could attempt to Mack the info out of her, Porsha had his johnson out and in her mouth. Though he was a playa through and through, he was still just a man, and Porsha's work was official!

"Damn, girl,!" He gritted as pleasure and the effects of the liquor collided. His kids drifted shit as he lay back and exchanged his ism for thrill.

"Umm amm youuu," Porsha mumbled around a mouth filled with muscle. The sound of rustling clothes caused Messiah's lids to flutter open in suspicion, and seeing Sunjay slip lady's shorts down, he already knew the deal. *Chooo choooo! It ain't no fun if the homie can't have none!* And with that in mind, a mischievous smirk eased onto his face.

Smop! Porsha's lips smacked when she popped him out her mouth.

"Uh uh, Sunjay, this not what's happening." She glanced back, but even as she said it, she was tooting it up. Messiah wanted to laugh. The girl still held his inches in her grip, stroking him as she faked the funk. She was a freak, and Messiah knew the girl's *"act"* was more for his benefit than it was for her fucking the clique.

"Porsha?" He called, and she turnt to give him mock irritation.

"Whaaat!" She whined.

Messiah chose action over the verbal. He gripped a fistful of her braids and lead her mouth back to the business.

"Mmmmahh!" She moaned as Sunjay stood behind her, and crashed into that pussy. Her lip service became sloppy with each pound he gave her and Messiah began to fuck her mouth in response. *Fuck it!* He thought. *Ain't the first time me and bro bro have trained a freak.*

Chapter 13

12 AM

The night was as calm as it would get in the Butta Beans Apartments. Though loud music pumped from numerous different places, car systems, open doors of certain apartments. It was Friday night, and most of the hood inhabitants were out on the town. Save for the hustlers and roguish seeds of the ghetto that hugged its corners and breeze ways. Most of the streets lights had been knocked out, leaving the rundown buildings in shadow a, but being on Overton Avenue, the action was ever present as if the sun was still beaming down.

At that moment, a candy purple box Chevy eased to the curb at the back of the complex, the twenty three inch triple gold D's it squatted on twinkled beneath the canopy of the dark sky, and within is spacious confines, the twins sat ace duece, bopping their heads to UGK's "Front Back Side to Side". Bam Bam rode passenger, mind twisted back from the liquor and Kush smoke he'd been indulging. He and Murda were celebrating their birthday that night but had started as soon as their eyes cracked open.

"Say, Bleed," Murda began before muting the music until only the bass rattled the trunk. "You out her wilding. You 'pose to be on ghost mode after what you did to Blood, but you strutting round this bitch like you the terminator or something! Like yo dope bulletproof or something!"

"Nigga!" Bam Bam growled before snatching two semi autos off his waist. Both guns were bulky and equipped with extendos. "I ain't ducking nan fool, Blood. My tools talk too. Fuck Sunjay "and" Messiah pussy ass! On 457, if one of them niggas want it, I'm gonna feed 'em the whole clip!" He declared before his blood hits swung to his twin. "What's bracking, nigga? Let me find out these niggas got you shaking in ya boots?"

"Bruh, you got me wrong. I'm just sayin, shit ain't sweet!" Murda spat, offended that his "G" had been questioned.

On the late night after Sunjay had stormed their G-lady's spot, Bam Bam had confided in him how he'd struck oil at Ms. Betty's crib, and though Murda wasn't feeling it, they were twins, and he'd go down in a blazing glory of fire for his...wrong or right, hot lead or fight! He shook his head disdainfully, Bam Bam didn't seem to give a damn about life, let alone the cons of his decisions. The man just didn't understand that when blood tainted the waters, sharks had no concept of innocence! Their grandmother, kids, "anything" that brings them happiness could get it.

"Look, Blood, all I'm saying is, after tonight, move wiser. Our iron claps for sho, but we can't be foolish enough to think Sunjay ain't with it. He came up in these same trenches we did, and that nigga Messiah's slick ass won't hesitate to squeeze if that's what the bidness is. Let's get this money and thug, but tonight, we fuck up the bity on our blood day, bet?" He chopped before extending his fist for some dap. Bam Bam sucked his teeth in irritation. These niggas got bro spooked, dawg! He thought before obliging him with some love.

"No doubt, five, but look, I know Sunjay ya mans and what not, but if he jumps out some monkey shit, I'ma peel his cap back, on Blood! I ain't running from "nobody"!" He swore.

Murda pulled the keys from the ignition before glancing back at the man who'd slipped out the same pussy as he, and seeing the, "give no fucks", reflecting from his gaze made Murda chuckle with an amazed shake of his head. "On Fo' Nine, King, sometimes I'on even believe we came out the same split!" He laughed before pushing his door open and slipping out into the night. Bam Bam followed suit before heading for their grandmother's.

"Murda, watch out now, young balla, dig this here!" The voice belonged to a dope fiend the hood knew as Smokin' Joe. Though the night wasn't as live as it usually was, nights in the bricks are like a constant block party. Young and old thots run wild, sucking and fucking their way into the hearts of sponsors and future baby daddies and the male seeds of the ghetto statues on their thug, doing something of everything to put coins in their piggy banks.

That night was a twin of the many before it, but being Friday and the word being out that the twins were having a birthday bash at Club Blue, most of the inhabitants from that slum were already at the turn up site. Murda's hand had inched to the burna on his waist until he saw that it was Smokin' Joe rushing toward him with something black in his hands. Murda's hand relaxed it's clutch as he laughter at the approaching man. Smoking Joe still sported the Jheri curl, and though his was as dry as his crusted lips and ashy elbows, he rocked it as if it were juiced up with glycerin or Soul Glo!

"Boyyy!" He proclaimed in his most impressive Flava Flav impression. "Everybody been tryna get this thang up off me, but I say I says, naw naw. Mama, this for my main man with the game plan, Murda!" Smoking Joe claimed with a "piano" smile; the type of smile where there was a missing tooth after each intact one. Murda's eyes fell to the object in the man's hands and he had to fight to tame the laughter climbing up his throat.

"Is that an Atari, Smokin' Joe!"

"Nigga, hell yeah! And look—" The fiend exclaimed before thrusting the game box into Murda's hands. "Hold *this real quick, playa, I know you gonna love this!" He spoke excitedly. Murda frowned as he inspected the machine, shaking his head, though he was not surprised. The lip that was used to enclose the game cartridge was missing, and when Smokin' Joe pulled something from under his shirt, Murda couldn't hold it any longer. He exploded in laughter! Smokin' Joe extended a joy stick to him with a mischievous smirk. "And I got this too!" He tried to hand it to Murda, but the man was laughing too hard to accept. The joy stick with the long cord was too comical to him.*

"Get the fuck. Fuck outta here, Joe, where you—" he tried but his laughter overrode his ability to speak. Only when he grasped for self control, did he try again. "Where'd you steal that shit from, OG?" He chuckled. Smokin' Joe, clad in a white tee shirt so stained that it had turnt beige, and a pair of navy blue Dickie pants, looked appalled at such a question.

"A true gentleman never tells his secrets, playa. Now, looks here, all I'm asking is five hunnid and—"

"Five hunnid!" Murda roared; all laughter extinguished. "These hoes so old they may only cost two dollars, brand new!" He demanded.

"Nigga, "that's" why I say five hunnid! Young ass boy, can't you "appreciate" a "classic" when you see one!"

Murda laughed. "Get this shit, Smokin' Joe, before I have to kick yo' ass," he said as he tried to hand the game back, but the smoker knew he'd went too far.

"Aiight, aiight, damn!" He sucked his teeth, "You young niggas have no respect for a playa's hustle. Look." he licked his chaffed lips. "Just let me get a dub, and you can have all this shit!" He bargained while shoving the controller into Murda's hands. Knowing there is no winning a debate with a fiend, Murda merely shook his head in amusement. From five hunnid to a twenty dollar piece of crack! He chuckled at the thought before deciding to support the man's hustle. He

sat the mercy on the ground before digging in his pocket for the compensation, and that's when it dawned on him.

"Sayyy, Joe, fuck the rest of the game at?" He inquired, and an expression of confusion eased onto the other man's face.

"The rest of it! Negro, that's the whole thang!"

"Mane, Smokin' Joe, how the hell I'mma hook it up to the TV without the adapters? And where's the games at?"

"Aww, see, I-I didn't think you needed all that, when I stole it from my sisters—" was as far as he'd explained before the night erupted into chaos.

"Ttttah! Ttttah. That stick talked. And Murda's vision was just in time. Boca! Boca! Boca! Boca! Boca! He saw his brother firing both tools Yosemite Sam style at a figure dressed in all black, save for a red bandanna covering the bottom of his face. Sunjay! Bam Bam thought— and the way he worked the assault rifle he was firing, proved that he was hungry to get his man's. The fire fight illuminated the night like a camera flashes in a dark room and by the time Murda joined the fray, his twin was in trouble.

Boca! Boca! Boca! Boca! Bam Bam fired both guns, the fire leaping from their muzzles casting his facial in brief light, but the opp's artillery was macho man to his puny man.

Ttttah! Ttttah! The volleys of lead cut through the air, whistling towards him, and self-preservation saved his life.

"Damn!" He cried out before throwing himself to the ground just as hot lead sliced through the brick of the building behind him. Yet, luck was never held long in the hands of street fellows, the hitman recognized the tactic and smirked as he leveled the choppers mouth toward the ground, but just before he was able to send .223's to eat his man's face.

Boom! Boom! Boom! Boom! Murda got busy with the forty he clutched. The other shooter seemed to accept his losses, and though he swung the pipe toward Murda, he backed away as he fired. Murda ducked and used his car for cover, and just as the shooting begun, it ceased! The silence after a shootout is eerie, it's as if someone flipped a switch and turned off all sound, and it was within the silence of the lambs that Murda noticed Smokin' Joe sliding from "beneath" the car.

"Nigga, fuck you get "under" the car?" Murda laughed nervously before taking a quick peek to see if the coast was clear. He gritted his teeth in anger before erecting himself. Somebody just tried to dirt us! He thought vehemently. His vision quickly swept the area as his heartbeat calmed its gallop, and not seeing his brother cut into pieces gave him peace. His eyes gritted to Smokin' Joe. Just as the men climbed to his feet, trembling from the fear of the near death experience, Murda's eyes fell to the wet spot that had spread across the front of the man's pants and chuckled.

"Nigga, you pissed yaself!"

"Yeah! Smokin' Joe cried before reaching back and holding the back of pants. "And I done shit at the same time. Them mothafuckas trying to kill us cause that Natari, man. June bug nem mad and—"

"Oh shit!" Murda exclaimed before dipping low and aiming his tool.

Smoking Joe's last theft would be committed that day, and the same with his last breath.

Btttahh! A spray of .223's cut him up from the back. Another shooter had snuck up with I'll intent, and though Smokin' Joe wasn't a part of the plan, when the reaper wanted his man, he had no remorse for the extra souls he snatched in order to get him. Murda stayed low as he raced for refuge. All the while, he let his metal back from over his shoulder; taking blind shots, but when death is on one's heels, drilling with something that spits thirty rounds per burst, blind shots just may save the bar!"

***

Bam Bam burst into their grandmothers apartment like a mad man and hurriedly slammed the door locked behind him. He'd saw his brother escape the reapers kiss by using their car as a shield, so he took comfort in his survival. Yet, noid, Bam Bam peeked out the peephole to ensure he hadn't been followed before tucking one of his guns back in his waist. He leaned forward and rested his forehead against the cool surface of the door as he fought to catch his breath, and that's when a cold smooch was planted against the back of his cranium.

"Surpriiise!" Evil greeted. Bam Bam went rigid at the feel of the metal, and for the first time since he'd entered the apartment, did he register how dark it was. "Let me get this off of you, playa," the man suggested before plucking the pistol from his left hand.

"Now, turn yo bitch ass around, busta, and if you go for that tool you just put on yo' waist, I'mma put ya face on the wall," the gunman swore before the barrel left the back of Bam's head.

"Fuck!" Bam Bam swore, sick to his stomach about getting caught slipping. He knew the voice, and knew shit was about to get stupid, but within the thralls of a life of death situation, one always gave self false hope! Bam Bam turned slowly to face a man he'd just swore to his brother he'd smoke. The man wore all black like the other shooter, and if he'd opted for a red flag to cover his face rather than the black ski mask, Bam Bam would've sworn on a thousand bibles that the man knew some sort of sorcery. Bam's mouth fell opening at the sight before him.

There were three shooters on deck. All wore the colors of the reapers attire, and all but the one closest to him brandished a stick. Yet, though he'd registered all this, it was the sight of Latoya, his BM, and his G-lady, both bound and gagged, sitting, trembling on the couch. All the lights were off, but the room aglow with the flickering of lights of what seemed to be a sixty candles positioned around the room, and on the dining room table sat a large birthday cake with at least twenty of the flickering sticks of wax.

"Happy bloody day, homie, ain't you gonna blow out ya candles?" The goon who'd met him at the door smirked, the jewelry in his mouth twinkling beneath the dance of the candles flames.

"This ain't got nothing to do with them, nigga!" Bam Bam gritted, his eyes taking in the tear trails racing down the faces of his two ladies, and it was then that he noticed the cone shaped birthday hats on their heads. Bam Bam's blood cooked, but when his forest gaze captured the masked man, the goon merely smiled before pointing to his own party hat.

"It's a gangsta's party, homie, but me and my folks didn't receive our invites, so." He shrugged with a mischievous smirk. "We came to show some love." He chuckled.

"Fuck you "and" yo love, nigga. You "always" been pussy to me. I told Murda you was a—"

"A good nigga, right? That's what you bout to say, huh?" The goon cut him off with a contemptuous smile, but his eyes revealed a threat of malice. The man had always wanted blood between them, and though he was getting money nowadays, Bam Bam could now see in dudes eyes what his brother had warned him about only moments ago in that car.

"Let them go, and let's keep the streets in the streets, nigga. My G-lady innocent, and you can see my bitch pregnant. Let em—"

"Shut yo pussy ass up, playa! I ain't tryna hear that rap you trying to kick! Where was all that sentimental ass shit when you ran up in my granny's spot? Huh, bitch!" Ski mask roared like a manic lion before stepping close to him with a madness dancing in his irises that Bam Bam hadn't recognized until that moment.

"Homie, I ain't the one who ran up in Ms. Bet—"

WAP! Before he could complete his deceit, the intruder slapped him across the face with the iron. Bam Bam crumbled to a knee with a wounded growl as his hand shot to the split the metal had cut into his face. Blood escaped from between his fingers and leaked down his face as he glared up at the masked man, but the man was unbothered.

"At least if you gonna "play" gangsta, do it to the end, fooly. Don't do gangsta shit, but turn pussy when gangsta shit returns for its lick back! So?" He smiled down at Bam. "I'm gonna deal you a better hand than you dealt me and mine," he said before making his way over to the cake on the table. "Come fuck with me." He suggested, but when Bam Bam didn't move, or respond, the goon chuckled. His eyes drifted to one of his shooters and as if communicating with their minds; the man positioned himself in front of the two bound ladies and aimed something with a drum attached to it.

"Mmmmmmmm!" Ms. Dorothy mumbled from behind her gag.

"Ahmaah!" Latoya cried from behind hers, and the tears cascading down their faces cracked Bam Bam's heart. And though he "overstood" the threat, he still contemplated going for the fire on his hip. Be patient, blood, wait for your moment! His mental whispered to his instincts. With that, he climbed to his feet and joined dude at the table. The leader nodded at the cake.

"It's you B-day; make a wish and blow out the candles, birthday boy." He smiled connivingly, but when Bam Bam merely stood staring at the two tiered, German chocolate cake, the man bristled. "Make a mu'fuckin wish and blow out the candles or watch ya peeps get shredded by them .223's!" He growled.

Bam Bam's eyes saturated with angry tears. German chocolate? Only his G-lady knew it was he and Murda's favorite cake. Knowing this, reflecting on the birthday hats, it wasn't hard to seduce that Ms. Dorothy and Latoya were planning to surprise him and his brother. With that, Bam Bam's vision trailed from the cake to the goon, and finally to his girls. Ms. Dorothy's eyes leaked tears, but just beyond their baptism, was a hardness he knew too well. She'd want him to forfeit "her" life and fight to the end! "I ain't raise no cowards, boy, you fight and fight until you can't fight no more!" She'd say. Latoya was his bitch! His rida! She sat with terror radiant in her eyes, and when his eyes fell to her swollen belly, he wondered if the seed she carried would be a boy or girl.

"I won't say it again!" The goon hissed, and the shooter aiming the stick at his family tightened his grip. Bam Bam gritted his teeth before returning his gaze to the cake. "Make a wish, gangsta." The goon encouraged, and though he'd never admit it, Bam Bam did just that, before leaning down and blowing out eight of the candles.

"All of em, pussy!" The HNIC demanded, and Bam Bam appeased him. As he blew out the last candle on the cake, he smiled at the thought of his wish. He'd wished that God gave him the chance to blow dude's brains out the ski mask. "Now—" The gunman said before saying something that fuck Bam Bam's mental. "Lil bro, step out the way. I can't let you keep scaring Ms. Dorothy and this pregnant lady," he ordered, and the man aiming the assault rifle did exactly that. The lead goon stepped over to Bam Bam and to his astonishment, draped an arm over his shoulder. Bam went rigid when he felt the muzzle of the pistol jab him in the side, but when the man lead him to the spot, the other shooter had just stood, he frowned as his eyes locked into his grandmother's. The intruder slipped his arm away, and when he slipped behind him and the tip of his gun kissed the back of his head. Bam Bam almost melted into a puddle. "They bout to murk me right her in front of my folks."

His thoughts were muddy waters and a lone tear dropped from his left eye. "Fuck it! At least they'll be good." Resolution closed the door of God granting him that wish! "Pull that burna off ya waist, play boy, and if you get stupid,

'I'mma put ya thoughts in Ms. Dorothy's lap." His tormentor's request twisted his thoughts.

"Huh?" He asked in confusion.

"Pull ya strap off ya hip, bruh. Ya heard me!" The man sounded irate, and it wasn't until Bam Bam did as instructed that it dawned on him. *He wants me to do myself in front of...damn!* He thought, but when his eyes fell to the bulge in his gals stomach, then trailed to the Queen who'd raised him, he knew he'd have to be the sacrificial lamb.

"Pweeee oooo!" Ms. Dorothy cried from behind her gag as he lifted the bangs and put it on his temple.

"Fuck you doing, clown!" The mask man demanded before slapping the gun away. *"Naw naw, I don't want you to whack yourself. I'm giving you a chance to live!"*

His words piqued Bam Bam's curiosity. *"Fuck you talm 'bout dude. If it's time to die, let's get it over with!"* He spat with his nerves shot from almost squeezing on himself.

"See, I'm a good nigga, fam. I'm so much of a good dude, I'm gonna let you choose, and you got fifteen seconds, sucka," The man told him before digging the barrel deeper into the back of his skull. *"One, two, three, four, five—"* Dude began his count, and Bam Bam's mental became an open field, allowing his thoughts to run free like the mustangs.

Hell naw, I'd rather do me! Think, blood, think? Do something! He thought as he considered trying his captors but he knew the hand he was dealt was stacked against him, and if he didn't make a choice, it was a chance they'd all die. *Mannn! This some hoe...ass...shit!* He thought.

"Eleven, twelve—" The man counted, but paused in confusion as Bam Bam begun bouncing on his toes. His eyes became wild as they bounced from Ms. Dorothy to Latoya. *Granny? Latoya? Granny? My seed?* His mind was a maze.

"Ot meeee!" Latoya cried from behind her gag as she rocked as best she could.

"Ooooommmm ord," Ms. Dorothy cried, sitting as still as a statue; with twin rivers dripping from her orbs.

SON OF A DOPEFIEND 3 | RENTA

"Fourteen," the gunman counted. "Fiftee—"

Boca! The explosion on Bam Bam's pistol was reminiscent of King Kong's roar, and his tormentor chuckled at his choice.

Chapter 14

Two Days Later— 10 AM
"Daddy, daddy, wake up!"
"Girl, he must be sick. He ain't never slept like this."
Just beyond the fog of his slumber, Messiah registered the voices of his girls, but it took him a moment to swim to consciousness. When his eyes fluttered open to the power of sunlight pouring in through the sheer curtains covering his bedroom window, he groaned before snapping them back shut.

His thoughts were murky, and as the events the night before flooded his thinking cap, he vaguely recalled how he'd made it home. When his eyes reopened, he blinked up at the ceiling, allowing his vision to adjust to the light. Home! He thought. Home being the four bedroom, two bath adobe he'd copped out in Desoto Texas. It wasn't as major as he fantasized of living, but at eighteen, and getting his ciabatta from the pavement, he deserved a pat on the back.

He was still staring at the ceiling when something landed on his stomach, and when he glanced down at the stack of money, he recalled dropping Liberty and Tutts on the blade to get paid. At that moment, both women laid on side of him. Both looked fresh like they'd just showered. Liberty wore nothing at all, but Tutts's nakedness was covered in a very short, silk robe that she wore open to display all her glory. He wanted to fuck her and he knew he could go raw because they were healthy!

"Damn, Daddy, you must've had a hell of a night. You ain't ever snored." Tutts giggled, and for a moment, Messiah was snaked by her beauty. Both women could've had any man they craved, but beyond him macking them, they chose to sell pussy. As bad as he wanted to believe that it was his game that made them happy to do it all to keep his piggy bank on bulge, he was playa enough to know that true macking was never forced! Ten percent cohersed, forty percent game, but most importantly, it was fifty percent of what he wanted the hoe to do so anyway, and just needed the incentive.

With that in mind, Messiah sat up and begun to count Liberty's pussy count. She smirked in anticipation as he licked his lips, knowing she'd doubled the fifteen hundred trap night he required.

"Thirty five dead men for that backing?" He smirked at her, and to further reward her acclaim, her eyes were blessed to behold how her contribution aroused his Pimpin'. Messiah's strength rose beneath the bale blue satin sheet that covered his lower half, and her tongue seductively moistened her full lips as her chinky eyes became a smoldering fire. Messiah made in principality to deprive them of his dick until they did something to prove worthy of his nut. He'd cut Liberty many times for her services to his Pimpin', and she found his dick game to be an aphrodisiac. She'd even raved about it to Tutts, and the chocolate diva lusted for her chance to freak him to his peak. She watched as he tossed the sheet back to reveal his moment of weakness, and her mouth watered. *Damn, this nigga got a pretty...ass...dick!* Tutts' thoughts became vulgar.

"Liberty, you want some of this shit?" He asked, and Liberty seductively bit her bottom lip as her gaze beheld his swell.

"Umm hmm, yes, Daddy," she purred, and Messiah nodded towards his lap. He wasn't stressing a condom. His dames strapped up with their Johns. Raw was his alone!

"Kiss him for me. Show me why mu'fuckas paying you so much." He placed Pimpin' to the side, as lady crawled over and swallowed him. As her head began to bob, Messiah's gaze found Tutts' beautiful chocolate, thick...and ready for him to slay that fire between her legs.

"You got something for me or do yo' hoin go out of fashion? I know your pretty ass ain't let this bitch out grind you?" He manipulated, knowing that a little rivalry only motivated her to wanna out do her wife in law. And it never failed! A dark fire ignited within her irises before she nodded and pulled a dope boy knot out the pocket of her robe.

Messiah took it and counted out. *"Nine hundred"* dollars! His eyes shot to her before returning to the dirty money. He flipped it over with a "strange" expression on his face before recounting as if he'd missed a few bills. Not! His recount resulted in the same total, and when his vision recaptured hers, the disgust was prominent. Liberty's head bobbed quicker. Her head game was sloppy and it was a battle for Messiah to ignore her expertise, but before he relinquished self-control, he needed to lay it down. The man used one hand to grab a fistful of Liberty's hair. He was sho nuff a playa, but still just a man; and she was turning his lap into a pool! Pushing her head down on his seven and a half inches, he held her there to pause her. *"Assault with a deadly weapon,"* before politely handing the money back to Tutts.

"Here's ya lil loot back, doll. I need you to do me a favor." He smiled, but his eyes told a different tale. Tutts knew he'd frown upon the short trap, but she felt she deserved a reprieve.

"Daddy, I—" she tried.

"Will you? Do me a favor? I mean?" He cut her off, and she froze with her mouth opened. He waited. Liberty breathed through her nose as she suckled him.

Tutts deflated and nodded a meek yes.

Messiah reached over and massaged her kitten. She almost melted. *"I want you to take that money, and pay yo cab fee back to Harry Hines, and when you see that weak ass nigga Sweet Eddie, pay his weak ass to take you off my hands."*

His favor was mean and obscene, and Tutts' eyes grew large in disbelief. The man's request was simple, but it was the exact simplicity that made it so powerful! Heartless! She watched as he removed his hand from Liberty's head, before lying back, and interlocking his fingers behind his head like a boss playa. Liberty reached between her legs and begun playing with herself while attempting to suck all the playaism he had from that small hole in his nature.

Messiah watched her for a moment before looking at Tutts. "Never forget this line, cause ain't no slacking on mine! You may be a sho nuff bad bitch...you may can suck and fuck a trick until he cursed Jesus on his good Sunday...and Lord knows you're sure nuff fine! But?" He gritted as Liberty gripped the base of his muscle, stroking him feverishly as she turned his lower head to a popsicle.

"Mmmmah! Smop! Muah! Muah! Mmmaah!" She hummed, kissed, and sucked. Messiah's vision fell to her as she pleased him, but his words were for Tutts.

"Yes...Jesus knows he created you as fine as wine; without a blemish in ya shine, but I'm a playa that lives by the motto: "if she don't mind, she ain't mine!" He dripped on her, before giving her the decency of his gaze. "And you treating me like you have to still be under a sucka's delusion if you think you can chump change me, and I just take it on the chin like a champ. Bitch make ya presence scarce," he demanded as his toes curled. Liberty blowed him with fervor before.

Smop! She pooped his flesh out his mouth. Stroking him, she smirked mischievously.

"Don't be so hard on her, daddy. "I'm your bottom bitch, and when a bitch workin," she paused to suck his head into her warm mouth before releasing him once more. "When a bitch workin from the bottom. The only other way she can

173

take you is to the top of ya game! Every bitch don't got that power in em'. I—"

"Shut up, bitch, and use them pretty lips for something more than the verbal!" Messiah demanded, and she smirked before getting back to her work.

"Jealous bitch!" Tutts spat with a roll of her eyes before fixing Messiah with her gaze. "Baby, I—"

"Bitch, babies shit and piss on themselves, and get their milk from the titty! How I'mma sho nuff playa that shit on niggas, piss champagne, and get my milk from the same place Moses lead his folks! The lane of the milk and honey! Where if a bitch ain't hoin, I ain't going."

"I'm sorry, Daddy. I—"

"Was just leaving?" Right?" He drew the line and tears came to her eyes. Tutts had fallen in love with him and knew he was a rare fella. The game he invested in his girls was priceless, and when any woman partakes of a dose of raw game that elevates them. They become junkies of the fountain it pours from! So, as she slipped from the bed, robe open to show her perky breast and juicy peach; she vowed to upstage her wife-in-law and knock her for her seat on the throne.

Tutts paused at the door and gazed back at the great show. Liberty had Messiah's nuts in her mouth as she jacked him off. Yet, Messiah's half-mast gaze was fixated on Tutts.

"That measly money that bitch gave you is nothing compared to what I got for you, Messiah! I'm a vet bitch, and if you would just listen, you'd be rich by next week!" Her words tickled his mental and did CPR to his curiosity. Yet, euphoria was stronger than curiosity, and Liberty was proof! Squeezing his balls gently, she stroked his length and bobbed her head on his mushroom as fast as she could.

"Got—damn—it!" He gritted as body and soul separated and a demon shot from his piss hole. Liberty drank him greedily until his fountain oozed empty. Planting a kiss on his nature, she rose and stuck her tongue out.

174

*"See?" She flickered it like a snake. "All gone, daddy!"
She bragged with a freak's smile.*

*Messiah chuckled before rising and pulling her beneath
him, laying her on her stomach before slapping her ass. He
reigned supreme.*

*"Assume the position," he demanded, and she faced
down ass upped him. The vision alone got Messiah back
strong, and without further ado, he gripped her waist and
sunk dick until her feminine lips kissed his nuts.*

*"Ahhhuuu!" She moaned as he began to crash into her.
Squeezing her right ass cheek, he became a madman in that
pussy.*

"Oouuuuu! Ouu! Oooo!" Liberty moaned. "Dad-dyyyy!"

*"Shut up, bitch, and take this dick!" Messiah growled,
right stroking her and punishing her walls. When he was sure
his stroke was official, his gaze lifted to behold Tutts.*

*"Talk, bitch, or walk bitch. I know you see how I'm trying
to break this hoe's back!" He gritted. Tutts eyes swallowed
his stroke and her island became saturated.*

*"Tonight, I need you to dress in yo best suit, daddy. I'm
gonna give you a reason to fuck me into a coma before
putting "that" "princess" on ice. Only a "Queen" bitch
deserves dick like that." She vowed, and even while he
punished the kitty, he studied her.*

*"One shot." He paused before lifting himself into the
push-up position. Liberty's knees were spread to the max, ass
tooted, and when Messiah began making circles inside her,
she began to wound her hips.*

"Do—it—baby!" She cried. "Fuck...this-sss pus-sssy!"

*"Shut up bitch!" He demanded before digging,
attempting to touch her womb. Liberty moaned before
balling the sheet and biting her bottom lip. Messiah's orbs
reflected a wilderness as he captured Tutts within his gaze.*

*"One shot at redemption, T—T—Tutts!" He sputtered as
his pace quickened.*

"Zad-ddyyy!" Liberty couldn't tame it.

Tutts nodded her acceptance. "That's all I need, Papi, and I'll show you. Besides—" she smirked at the way Liberty's eyes rolled to the back of her head. The girl's teeth was bare and it was evident she was about to cum. Tutts shook her head, " You need a bitch to take that dick like a big girl. She nodded at Liberty. "She ain't it."

"Fuuuuck youuuu—bi-tch!" Liberty stuttered just before her damn broke in an explosion of cum. "I'm cum—cum—mmming! I—I—I"— she cried in ecstasy, and when Tutts clit tingled, she made her exit.

***

BOCA! Bam Bam fired, and though the hole in Latoya's chest was small, the spray of blood that exploded from her back and stained the couch was evidence of a nasty exit wound. Her mouth fell open in a silent scream as realization sucked her under. *Her baby's father had chosen her to be the sacrifice!* And even before he hit her up twice more, her last breath was on the precipice of death valley.

BOCA! The third was a charm. She fell forward, but before he could witness her death land, Bam Bam was already in motion. *Fuck it!* He concluded as he moved as fast as he could, in attempt to swing his tool towards the goon closest to him. He knew the reaper wouldn't spare him, so he figured he may as well take one opp with him. But? *Boom!* The bullet blew the side of his top open. Finito! He crumbled crookedly to the floor. And just as he landed, one of the other shooters wasted no time; he scooped up Bam Bam's pistol and in the same fluent motion took aim at Ms. Dorothy.

Boca! The shot went wild when the lead goon smacked the gun away. His comrades eyes went wild in the eye holes of the ski mask.

"Let her live with the torment," the head shooter ordered and that's when the sounds of sirens permeated the air. The men made for a hasty exit, but not before one of them snatched up the birthday cake!

Moments later, Murda burst through the door, out of breath, and not expecting to find a murder scene. But when he turnt and beheld the carnage, his eyes went wild, and he vomited. Falling to his knees in torment, he cried hard! His twin, his other fifty percent was gone! Yet, it was while on his knees, crawling towards his slain brother that he heard the muffled sounds coming from his grandmother. Shocked, he scrambled to his feet and over to her, only to notice her making strange jerking movements. Her eyes were wild pleading! Murda sobbed as he peeled the tape from over her lips as tender as he could, and as soon as she could speak, the first and last word she spoke was *Mes-si-ah!* Then, Ms. Dorothy had a massive heart attack right there beneath the glow of numerous flickering flames of candles. And as Murda hugged her and begged her not to die on him, he noted she wore a birthday hat. The many candles made for an early birthday *candle light* service, and one he'd never forget!

"Murda! Murda? You're scaring me, baby. Say something!" Meesha, Murda's gal's voice punctured the walls of his high, and he slowly came back to the present. He blinked, mind slow as he tried to recall where he was. For the past two days, all he'd done was try to numb the pain! Gin and juice had become his escape, and as he glanced down at the Sherm stick that had left him stuck, frozen in place and staring off into space. He was numb.

"Why the hell do you niggas smoke that shit? Ugh!" Meesha, a five foot even, ghetto princess rolled her eyes at him. Short and as thick as a brick, the girl was ugly, but had some of the best twat in the spot, and it had hooked Murda.

After he'd found his family slain, and his G-lady had taken her last breath in his arms, the police had burst in to find him saturated in blood, and drowning in his tears. Murda felt empty! And in an act of, fuck it, he'd tried Gorilla Piss for the first time; loved it! Fry, Gorilla piss, Dip, Sherm, or

Whack were just a few names the users dubbed the substance Formaldehyde!" An aldehyde used in fertilizers, but mostly it's used to make embalming fluids. Made popular in the late eighties in California, it became the drug of choice for gang members and one that's not afraid to tempt fate. And wishing it's power stole his ability to think...to feel...Murda had inhaled three Sherms to the face that morning, and that, combined with liquor was a scientifically bad combination.

As Meesha shook her head at him, his mind flipped backward. Oblivious to the fact, she rolled her eyes before heading for the kitchen. She planned to cook for them and her child.

"I don't know what you done got yo roguish ass into, but you bet not bring no mess to my apartment, Murda. I'm on Section 8, and if you fuck up my kids food stamps, I'mma beat yo ass! You got niggas running up in yo house and—" She was just ranting and ranting as she rummaged through the kitchen. With four kids, at the age of twenty, she was on every form of government assistance known to the ghetto. Murda sat staring out the window, a Glock nine with two extra clips rested in his lap as he gazed out at the happenings in the hood. Though his family had been man downed only two days ago, the hood went on.

"Niggas done killed Ms. Dorothy and Bam and it's a shame!" Meesha was still babbling as she began breakfast. "Since you've been here, all you do is sit at that window, with that damn gun like somebody coming for you!" She spat, shaking her head in disdain. "I'm glad I didn't send Maria to Ms. Dorothy's, I—" she was saying when Murda went stiff.

His eyes became suspicious as they slowly fell to the stained carpet of the living room. There were red Kool-Aid stains tainting it, but in his mind, they were blood!

"I'm glad I sent Messiah to kill Ms. Dorothy!" He heard Meesha say, and as if on autopilot, he snatched the tool off his lap and followed the blood stains to the kitchen, where

Meesha stood cracking eggs over a skillet. When she saw him, her eyes fell to the banga before lifting the wildness of his glare.

"Murda?" She spoke cautiously, but to his ears, she was taunting him. Murder! Murder! He heard; versus, Murda, his name. His face morphed into a madman's expression.

"Bitch, you what! So, you sent Messiah, huh!" He screamed at the top of his lungs and before Meesha knew it, he fired a shot.

Boom! The slug went wild, but chaos as born. Meesha impulsively squeezed the eggs she held. Yellow yolk slime squeezed between her fingers as she screamed.

"Wha—NO! What are you talking about? Messiah?" She didn't understand that the Sherm was twisting everything she said. Her saying I'm glad I didn't send Maria to Ms. Dorothy, echoed in Murda's head as I'm glad I sent Messiah" to kill Ms. Dorothy! And though it was a known fact that Ms. Dorothy ran a temp daycare, and Maria, Meesha's five year old daughter, usually went there after school. Murda's mental was fried!

"Murda?" Meesha cried as the man took a step toward her. "Murder!" Is how it registered in his mind. Meesha knew she was in trouble, and it was nobody there but her, Murda, and Maria, who stayed home with the chicken pox.

"Mama?" Maria called from somewhere in the apartment.

"Maria, stay in the room, baby!" Meesha shouted, but "Messiah", stay in the room, baby!" Is what Murda heard.

"Oh, you got that nigga waiting in the room, bitch! Huh?" Spittle flew from his mouth. Meesha's eyes went wild in confusion.

"Wha"— she tried, but—whap! The butt of the strap cracked her top.

"Ahhh!" She exhaled before crumbling to the floor unconscious. The formaldehyde was merciless. He began to see his twin laying in his own blood, and he fell to his knees beside Meesha. Pulling her head into his lap, he rocked her.

"Damn, Blood, wake up…wake up, dawg. G-lady had a heart attack and—"

When Meesha began to come to, she moaned in agony, causing him to pause and glance down.

"Whoa, shit!" He cried before reading back. Meesha's face had become Ms. Dorothy's.

"Heyyy, baby, how ya doing!" His grandmother smiled a bloody smile.

Then, shit got twisted! Her smiling head sprouted horns before the face became a demon's.

"Yous a lil bitch, nigga. You let them niggas step on yo peeps and they still breathing?" He growled, and Murda began to pistol whoop him until his face was nothing more than a bloody mess. Blood was everywhere, and when the sounds of the footsteps came from just beyond the kitchen. Murda knew Messiah and his squad had come to finish him. He leapt to his feet, and just when Messiah bent the corner, army crawling with a burna clutched in his hands, Murda wasted no time getting busy!

Boom! Boom! Boom! He fired down at him, flipping him back.

"Y'all cant fuck wit me, bitch! Teflon Don shit! Come onnn!" He raged, spit flying everywhere, but that's when something snapped in his mind. For a moment, he was coherent, and what he saw screamed to his common sense. Run! And that he did; leaving behind a dead woman and child. Who he thought was Messiah, was merely, Maria, Meesha's five year old daughter, and the gun he'd seen was nothing more than a teddy bear.

***

The day was sweltering hot, but the city was "outside!" Messiah had just dropped "a book" to his mama in the gritty Grove, and with the sixteen bands he'd been paid bundled in a brown paper bag, and resting on his backseat, he made

SON OF A DOPEFIEND 3 | RENTA

sure to tip slow through the cracked streets. It was the 90's, and the murder rate of Dallas/Ft. Worth was at an all time high. Ft. Worth was now the murder capital, and with Dallas having always been a wicked city, the crime rate had the laws on edge.

Coming down Buckner and heading for Military Parkway, Messiah kept a close eye on the rear view mirror. Though he wasn't sure, his street senses were telling him he was being trailed. He'd seen the same black Crown Vic dipping in and out of traffic since he'd slid passed the Walmart fifteen minutes earlier and though it would fall back two to three cars, it never turnt or allowed more than that to clog the distance between them.

Messiah eased his burna into his lap as he turned towards Jim Miller Road, and watching his pursuers in the rear view, he smirked when they did the same. " Aight, niggas wanna tempt fate, huh?" He whispered to himself before chuckling sinisterly. One kill doesn't make one a killer, but after one's second or third body, they've crossed over into the realm of a stepper, and murder becomes something that's a part of the business.

So, as Messiah eased the Jag to the side of the road and threw on his hazards, his first mind was to lead talk, and allow his bullets to convince whoever was on the lurk, that shit wasn't sweet. But as he jumped out, strap in his clutch, the black Crown Vic had an ace in the hole that trumped the sixteen shot Glock he held.

Whirrp! The sound of the siren activated before the red lights in the grill revealed who his pursuers were. "The police!"

"Fuck!" He spat before hurriedly jumping back inside the car. Survival becoming primitive as he reached for the gear shift. "These hoes gotta catch me!" He whispered to himself, but just when he was shifting to drive, the back door swung open, and someone slid into the backseat.

"Woahhh, Cowboy, where ya in a rush to?" The familiar voice froze the blood in Messiah's veins.

"Fuck!" He spat before slamming a palm on the steering wheel. Low down and dirty, Dallas, Texas's Detective Spinx, smirked knowingly as his eyes fell to the brown paper bag beside him on the backseat.

"Fucked is more like it, homeboy." He chuckled before reaching for the bag of money. "Well, well, well, if it ain't my boy Messiah, the hardest, up and coming pimp in the game! Courtesy of none other than ole Maxwell Davenport; a vet." Spinx chuckled while opening the bag. His eyes grew wide in mock surprise. " What we have here, my boy? Looks like money." He laughed. "Drug money, May I add."

With no way to prolong the inevitable, Messiah reclined his seat before speaking. "What you want, Spinx? Don't you have some unsolved murder to solve? You are a homicide detective, right?" The question was rhetorical.

Detective Spinx chuckled. "Now, that I am, Messiah, and very good at it, if I may say so myself. Which leads me to you, a murderer!" He spat. "Oh, and I've just switched over to narcotics."

Messiah laughed with a denying shake of his head. "Nice try, but wrong guy, playboy. I'm into management, Detective, of seeing how far bitch's pussy can push me. Murder?" He smiled as his vision connected with the dirty cops in the rear view. "That bidness too messy for a pretty nigga like—"

"So, you and ya boy's aren't responsible for that nice work in the Beans, huh?" Detective Spinx smirked, cutting him off. "Damn, ole Sunjay getting soft on me. I could've bet my badge that he'd done the boy, Tadis Little, and the other two vics a few days ago." He chuckled.

Messiah didn't.

"So, you're telling me that that wasn't y'all, huh? Well, what about this?" The detective extracted a bundle of money from the bag and brought it up to his nose. "What about the kilo of crack you just sold to Marquist Williams, down on

Peavy? Hmm?" He smirked triumphantly when the shock on Messiah's face revealed the tale. Detective Spinx took a deep sniff of the green backs, and without taking his eyes off the rear view, he pocketed the money.

"Let's cut to the chase, shall we?" The smile vanished, and his eyes revealed the depth of rottenness tainting his spirit. "I know Sunjay gave you my message, and since you boys ain't come see me, I've decided to make my presence known," he spoke, and before Messiah could respond, the cop had shot forward and his arm snaked around his neck.

Instantly applying pressure, Spinx made sure to hold tight. "From now on, you lil niggas splitting all that dough three ways! Thirty percent tax, nigga, and it's to be paid weekly!" He hissed as Messiah gagged.

When clawing at the man's python tight forearm didn't work, Messiah used the gun, trying to aim at any part of the man, but seeing the attempt, detective Spinx used his free hand to take hold of his wrist. The gun was rendered useless! Spinx chuckled menacingly, and just before the younger man blacked out, he released him. Messiah fell forward, gasping for air.

"I—mma—kil—kill you, fool! He raged.

"You, you do that, lil nigga, and you're going down for life! You kill an officer of the law, and you'll have every sumabitch with a badge on your heels, and I know you too smart to make such a rookie mistake. Sunjay?" The cop shrugged. "Maybe, but you, Messiah, you're a student of the old school gangstas. Next Friday, I'll be expecting my first payment, and if you little punks try me, I'll began to trickle the evidence I have to the DA. Don't fuck with me!" He spat before slipping out the car. "Oh." he smirked when he leaned back into the car and retrieved the bag of money. "I planned to only keep a few dollars, but since you're gonna kill me and all." he chuckled before ending harassment.

Messiah's irises contained a roaring fire as he watched the dark skinned, bald headed cop slip into his car and ease it away. Yet, just before he drove pass, the Crown Vic eased to a stop beside him. The passengers window eased down and Detective Spinx allowed their eyes to tango for just a moment.

"This can be a beautiful union, son. Think about it. A get out of jail free pass, and the number one homicide detective in Dallas in your pocket. Just think of the possibilities!" He chuckled, and just before he drove off, he left Messiah with something to think about. "Tell ole Pimpin' MAXWELL I send my love. We had a wonderful relationship. Maybe you need to umm," he paused, and placed a finger to his temple as if in deep thought. Then, snapping his fingers. "Yeah, that's what the playas say; maybe you need to rub shoulders with the old man. He'll lead ya right." He saluted before slipping back into traffic.

***

"Well, baby, that's the last of it—" Jojo, Justice's father confirmed uncertainly.

Justice could see the turbulence in his eyes and she smiled. "Yuh worry too much, daddy. I'll visit home so much yuh won't know I've moved." She assured, her Trinidadian tongue loose. Her parents had driven her down from Houston and helped her move into her new apartment in Lancaster, Texas, just outside of the Triple D, and though Leah, her mother wasn't feeling her child moving so far away, she understood. Yet, Jojo was heart heavy, and just couldn't grasp the fact that his baby was no longer a baby.

"Yea, I know, baby, I know." He nodded while looking around the room. "We will be waiting." He faked a smile before glancing down at his watch. "Well, we can help yuh unpack and decorate if yuh whan, or we can stay de—"

"No—" Leah cut him off with a giggle. "We can't, Joseph. We need to leave de gyal be and get back on de road. Plus," she had to fight not to laugh at the pitiful look on her

husband's face. She knew out of their three children, the man was protective of their middle child. Jojo for all his strengths, was weak in terms of Justice, and with a sad smile, he nodded his agreement.

"Yea right; ya know." He whispered before pulling Justice in for a hug. "Mannn, yuh grow too fast! First, yuh sister, and now you. You girls making an old man out of me," he said before planting a kiss against her forehead.

"Daddy, I'm eighteen, I'll be okay. Yuh just take care of mammy and Bobo, I'll be home before yuh know," Justice assured, and only after another tight hug and kiss did Jojo, with misty eyes, make his exit.

Leah smiled. "He go cry in de truck yuh know."

Justice eyes watered, but she giggled. "I know, mammy, I know."

"I will miss yuh, Justice, and," she paused to pull her child in for a hug. "Just ah know, a mother knows."

"Knows?" Justice inquired as they separated, and Leah took her child's face in her hands. Her eyes were searching as she smiled knowingly.

"Us island women have been cursed to love our men with deep love. See, daughter, love is like a ghost that yuh can actually see! Feel! A strange ghost that can play invisible even when it's not invisible at all. Love is argumentative, it'll always pull you back to de one it wants, just to argue with yuh mind of this being where yuh needs to be. Even if it hurts a little." She nodded, as if her words were as much for her than they were for Justice. Her hands fell away and though her orbs misted. Leah smiled. "Find de boy and let yuh love argue it's point. The beautiful thing about love arguments is that they awaken the love of another, and makes it listen." Leah allowed a tear to escape before turning to leave, but pausing at the door, she spoke over her shoulder. "Love only fails when it's possessors walks away."

Chapter 15

8:30PM

After Messiah had made it home, he'd showered and jumped fresh. It Tutts' words help true, he knew he'd have to be at his best in the events of any test.

"Ya looking real dapper, boy, where you going?" Black Diamond's voice drew his eyes to her. His mother stood in the threshold of the bedroom, admiring his sauce. Messiah wore a black, silk button up. It's ends tucked into the waist of some fire red, Karl Kani slacks, and the black suede Versace loafers he wore with no socks. Yet, it was the red bandana he wore tide sideways on his head, along with the red suspenders with the hood clamps that did it to em. He was clap doctor clean; his jewelry game was mean, and as he smiled at the first woman he'd ever loved, he gave her a peek of the VVS stones glistening at the bottom of his mouth.

"Shiid," he shrugged. "I don't know, mama, but this hoe Tutts bet not be playing with my game or I'mma send her back to from which she came; on Daddy's grave!" He swore, and Black shook her head. Like father, like son, she thought in memory of how swift her late husband used to be. As she admired her seed, pride blossomed within her chest. "He's gonna be a star!" She thought, but even within her admiration, she detected turmoil just below his handsomeness.

"Yeah, but what's really on ya mind?" She probed, as she leaned against the door sill. Messiah's smiled waned;

knowing she knew him better than he knew himself. Black crossed her arms over her chest, waiting.

"Ma, have you ever just got tired of the life?"

Black's eyebrow rose curiously. "Everyday, why?"

Messiah exhaled a strong breath. "I mean; I love the money, and the hoes. They're cool as a breeze, but the game is dirty and ain't no respect no more."

"I see," Black's tone was thoughtful. "Messiah, this life has never been clean, so it's filth should never surprise you. You were taught since nine years old, to never shoot clean dice at a game where everyone else is shooting the crooks. So?" She shrugged, not understanding his plight.

Messiah nodded. "Fa sho, Queen. It's just..." His words trailed off. He wanted to tell her that there was so much more to life than the streets, but instead, "This pussy boy, Spinx, pulled me over on some extortion shit, and the nigga claims to have something on me and Sunjay," he fumed.

"Does he?" Black asked, but the expression on Messiah's face was evidence even before he nodded confirmation. Black's eyes fell to the floor in thought, and only returned to her son after the sound of a car horn blared from outside.

They exited the room and together, they made their way to the front door, and when Messiah pulled it open, his sight beheld something that complimented his playaism. A cocaine white, stretch limo sat idle at the curb, and when the driver stepped out and around the back; he held the door open.

"Sir?" He inquired.

Messiah and Black's eyes met in awe before Mesiah smirked. "Yea, wud up?" He was all hood.

The Caucasian man smiled. "I was told to escort you to the function tonight; my name is Jeff, and I'm at your services on behalf of Mr. Don O'Riley." The man spoke with an English dialect.

"Don O'Riley?" Messiah whispered; confused but Black Diamond helped him find his way out of nativity.

"Boyyy!" She exclaimed in shock. "The O'Riley's own most of the property in downtown Dallas, and I heard the baby girl is some sort of rich artist or somethin'," she informed, with awe in her tone.

The ills of the game forgotten, Messiah flicked invisible lint from his shoulders. "Well?" He smirked connivingly. "That pussy trap strikes again!" He chuckled before making his way toward the car.

All the while, Black's mental became an asylum of worry. "Spinx pulled over on some extortion shit, and the nigga claims to have somethin' on me and Sunjay." Messiah's words played within her mental. She shook her head as worry grew arms like an octopus and sores throughout her internal. "You be careful, baby. That rotten mu'fucka Spinx is the pig that put the squeeze on ya daddy back in the day," she whispered while watching her son slip into the backseat of the limo. "Ya real daddy," she added with a bitter smile; knowing Messiah would never learn the truth.

***

9:40PM

Lil Zetti stepped off the Dart bus on Bonneview and Highland Hills Drive and headed for the Pinks; the 'Jects! Highland Hills is a thick vein running through the slums of Oak Cliff and being one of the most hated hoods out the city, it's notoriety was made concrete in the 90's. Just like any other drug-infested, gang related hood throughout Dallas-Ft. Worth, Highland Hills was pregnant with every type of hook and crook known to the gutter. And as Lil Zetti made his way behind enemy lines, he knew to keep his head on swivel. Though his older cousin C-Bo was a stepper from those breeze ways, and was much respected, a lot of younger seeds of that section of land wasn't felling Zetti's visits.

The world was Crip crazy in the 90's; *everyone* wanted to either be Hoova or Sixty! The crips ruled the streets, and in

Dallas, niggas repped either Baby Cash's or SDJ's 7's, Ru Circle, or Webb's Chapel. But even when Crips held the numbers, that's exactly what made 212 Fish Trap in the wicked West, 415 East Dallas, 44 in the South, 4Nine King and 457 in the Cliff so infamous. They were the minority, but repped like Sparta's 300. Yet, Lil Zetti wasn't moving through waters where blood was welcomed. So, after C-Bo had reached out to him, knowing Lil Zetti would let him shop for the low, Lil Zetti should've respected the land.

Like most Oak Cliff niggas, the youngins' arrogance was loud! Clad in a red and white color scheme, his fit was disrespectful to that section of jungle. The red KC hat he rocked matched the red and white classics on his feet, and the fire red backpack he wore on his back was stuffed with the nine and a baby C-Bo had asked for. The glares from the hood's inhabitants made Zetti tap the butt of the steel on his waist; he wasn't amongst his Dumu/Piru brethren; he was out of bounds in 357 and 247 Crips territory. To make it worse, he'd been warned to not fly his flag, so as soon as his feet hit the pavement, he became the main attraction! It's something *wild* about a gangsta from another hood that didn't give a fuck about rules or regulations; niggas want him dead; but their felines wanted the dick!

"Heyyy, Lil Zetti!" A group of young ladies purred as he passed, and though he smirked with a nod, *Messiah* had instilled in him: Business first!

Niggas' faces were balled up at the sight of him, but Lil Zetti was bred by gangstas, and felt his links to *his* hood made him bulletproof.

As he made it to the entrance of the complex, a group of hoodlum thugs mugged him.

"What that C like, cuz?" A long haired gangsta greeted with a menacing glower.

Lil Zetti's hand fell to the ass of his burna; heart pounding as he eyed dude. The crowd noted the move and the tension thickened. "Nine life here, Blood. What that B like?" Zetti's retort would've made Sunjay proud, but Sunjay was absent, and there's no trophy for bravado.

All hands went for their metal, but the long-haired goon lifted a calming hand. "At ease, cuz. This C-Bo's cousin." He chuckled, and though his comrades lusted to bust Lil Zetti's head, they tamed their gangsterisms.

Lil Zetti's gut warned him to turn and dip, but pride robs men of common sense; and seeing he'd gotten a pass, with his hand down by his fire, he diddy-booped toward C-Bo's apartment. The gun on his waist made him feel invincible, and that's what did it for him!

Making it to his destination, he brushed the incident off and knocked on the door. "Pussy ass niggas know they ain't built for how the hood comin' 'bout me. Sunjay n'em will paint this hoe red!" He talked that talk, and just as the door was being unbolted, the dice he'd rolled by ignoring his gut, fell on snake eyes.

"What's crackin', Tomato Head! Crip on mine, Loc!" Someone shouted from behind him.

BOCA! A hot slug followed the proclamation and punched through the backpack and Lil Zetti's back. His blood splashed against the door as it made its exit.

"Ahhh!" He sucked in a sharp breath. Fire ignited throughout his anatomy, and even as his knees buckled, the shooter was squeezing to finish him.

BOCA! The second shot pinched him face-first into the door. *BOCA!* The third took him down at the same time the door opened. C-Bo rushed out before pausing at his little cousin's twisted body at his feet; then the craziest shit happened.

As his eyes lifted to the shooter, the remaining troops that had stood in front of the complex earlier arrived. "Say, Loc, you niggas was just 'pose to take him down, not kill 'em!" He spat.

The long-haired goon reached down and pulled the backpack from Lil Zetti's back. "Damn, cuz, can't you see he's *down*?" He chuckled at his own joke.

C-Bo gave Zetti one last gander before yelling over his shoulder into the apartment, "Kay Kay, don't open the door for nobody! Call Bug and tell him to hurry over here and clean up this blood before the laws show up!" He instructed his gal, before stepping out. "You niggas move this nigga away from my spot, then meet us over at Jr's pad!" He ordered before he and the long-haired fellow disappeared into the labyrinth of the bricks.

For nine and a half ounces of cocaine, C-Bo bit his family's hand. Blood is thicker than water, but water is the strongest force in the world!

***

10:25PM
The clicking of champagne glasses and mirthful laughter intermingled throughout the room as sophisticatedly dressed art connoisseurs chattered over fine art. Downtown Dallas was aglow; red and white LED lights romanticized the skyline against the darkness of the sky. The limo had chauffeured Messiah to a posh penthouse just north of the beautiful sky scrapers, and the 4,500 square foot condo was a gorgeous place for the function he'd been deposited at. The place had been converted for the night, into an open space art gallery, and as the mostly Caucasian, some middle Eastern, and a trickle of Afro Americans mingled about, Messiah stood out like a monster trapped within a fairytale. His attire was in complete opposition of the soft elegance surrounding him, and for the first time in his life, he noted witness to the difference between people with money versus those with wealth!

As he stood, admiring a painting depicting a charcoal silhouette, captured in dance against a black background.

He wondered how one could deem such as art. While surrounding him, the other guests stared, awe-struck at what he found simple to be strange. The art was everywhere, and seeing the other guest rotated from painting to painting, Messiah merely mimicked them; faking interest. Servers balancing trays of cocktails and chilled hors d'oeuvres on their palms became his refuge when he realized they were free. He'd never partaken of wine, and only had heard of Martini in James Bond flicks; nonetheless—Messiah had downed three of the cocktails and was on his fourth. Tipsy was an understatement!

"Would you like and hors d'oeuvres, sir?" He was accosted by a waiter balancing a tray of tooth picked morsels of food.

Messiah nodded his sentimental. "Appreciate this, my nigga. This shindig y'all kickin' is real groovy; ya dig," he complimented, and the man smiled a strange smile. That's when Messiah noticed his eyes—eyes so blue they glowed! Taking in the man's entirety, a chill danced down Messiah's gut; it was something off about the man's aura that contradicted the caterer's uniform he wore.

"Excuse me?" The pale skin man asked with amusement in his eyes.

"Yall's lil' party." Messiah waved a hand around the room. "It's funky, cat daddy, but not my type of two step."

His response caused the man's face to turn beet red; appalled when Messiah plucked six of the hors d'oeuvres from the tray.

"Y'all trippin' wit' this food though. How a nigga gonna get full off this shit?" Messiah asked before sucking pieces of sheepshead and cheese off three of the toothpicks. He smacked as he savored the taste and almost burst into laughter when the waiter high tailed it far away from him.

"There you are!" A familiar voice gushed.

And to his amazement; Messiah's vision feasted upon prostitution stuffed into a skintight, purple column gown, with the matching Monolo Blahnik boots on her feet. Tutts' hair was freshly permed and cascaded over her shoulder, and if he didn't know she was a bonofide hoe, he'd sworn on his soul she was a model. Mouth agape, his eyes drifted to the man whose arm she held, and digested him with a gander. Polished European, tweed jacket over a black dress shirt tucked into black slacks; the man's plain Jane screamed money even before Tutts made the formalities.

"Don, this is my younger brother I was telling you about, Milton. And Milton, this is the man behind the event." She smiled big, but it was her eyes that spoke silent secrets.

Brother! Who the fuck is Milton? Messiah wondered, but the game was first nature to playas and he got hip without a slip when Don O'Riley extended his hand.

"A pleasure, son. I've heard a lot about you!" His voice was rich.

Son? Messiah laughed inwardly as their hands connected for a shake. "All good things I hope," he responded.

Don smiled broadly. "Let me be the first to congratulate you, graduate. Accepted to one of the country's most prestigious institutions of higher learning? I must say." He chuckled. "Accolades are due," he was saying when Messiah's eyes shot to Tutts before boomeranging back.

"No doubt, my nig—" He caught himself. "Thank you. I mean; appreciate the—"

"Don!" He was interrupted by a gleeful shout, and when his eyes captured Beauty, it was hell for him to tame the lust in his gaze. "I've looked all over for you, dear." She poked her lip out in a playful pout.

Don smiled lovingly at the beautiful woman. "Kate!" Love was evident in his exclaim, and they embraced before Kate kissed him on both cheeks.

After doing the same with Tutts, Kate turned her sights on Messiah. "And who might this handsome gentleman be?" She inquired with a dazzling smile.

"Oh, how rude of me," Don began before gently touching her arm. "This is Milton, Kylee's younger brother. And Milton, this is my sister, Kate O'Riley." He made the intros. "This is her exhibit, and most of the art is her work."

"Interesting," Kate whispered, watching as Messiah downed the rest of his drink.

Seeing the chemistry in their vibes, Tutts smirked mischievously at Messiah before squeezing Don's arm. "Honey, why don't we leave these two, and you show me this famed sculpture you've raved about," she suggested, and after one last look to his sister, Don agreed.

After they'd departed, Messiah held Kate captive within his appraisement; the woman was a five-foot nine gift! Her head was a mass of blonde, permed straight hair, parted down the middle and accented with black tones. Skin tanned perfectly, and her lithe body was wrapped within a sexy wrap-around dress that showed off the beautiful shape of her D-cups. Messiah placed the remainder of the hors d'oeuvres into his empty glass. He'd finally understood that it wasn't Don O'Riley that was the catch, but Kate that Tutts was feeding him.

He smiled before Turing to a massive painting of a pale skinned woman standing nude in a vibrant garden. "So, you're an artist?" He asked, and when Kate joined him, she smiled.

"So they say, but this?" She ran her fingertips over the canvas. "Unfortunately, I'm not responsible, nor am I such a talent," she whispered, a hint of awe in her tone. "This is a Michelangelo original. Don't you just live the artistic touch of his brush? So, elegant and sexy." It sounded as if she'd cum at any moment.

Messiah's eyes bounced from the painting to her. "You say Michelangelo original? You tal'm 'bout Mike that owns the tire shop on Sanger? I didn't know that boy paints!" He chuckled and Kate frowned.

194

"Wha-what!" She sputtered, aghast by his ignorance. "No-no, I'm speaking of Michelangelo Buonarroti, the Italian sculptor and painter that not only did this beautiful piece—" she waved at the painting. "But also, the sculptor of David, and he's also the creative genius that painted the ceiling of the Sistine Chapel in the Vatican." She educated.

"Oh." Messiah felt lame. Yet, he knew it was the liquor that fogged his game. "Look, ma," he began before handing his glass to a passing server. "On the cool, I don't know shit about Michelangelo, Da Caprio, nor the ceiling at no sister church in Webb Chapel, I'm just—"

"No, not web chapel; the Sistine Chapel, in Rome Italy." She corrected.

"Yea, all that. What I'm sayin' is, I'm just a child of the ghetto that's never experienced nothing like this." He waved a hand in a sweeping arch. "But, I do know beauty." He added with a smile. "And even trapped within the perfect picture, this woman, nor the painting, holds a candle to what's before me." His game was on, and Kate was taken aback by it.

From surprise to a blush, her expression transformed until her smile became worth the effort. "Umm..." She seemed speechless as she placed a hand to her chest. "Thank you." She giggled before her vision recaptured the painting. "Wish I was worth as much." She laughed a bit, but those words were what piqued Messiah's curiosity.

"I don't understand. Worth as much? Love, you're priceless!"

Again, Kate blushed, but didn't allow her vision to stray from the canvas. "What's worth more, Milton? Something priceless, or something worth millions? Which would you desire to possess?" She asked in a whisper, and Messiah's eyes shot to the painting.

Millions, his mind screamed, but before he could answer, Kate took his arm, and gently pulled him down the wall of art.

"Come, handsome, let me show you sixty million dollars, and then…" She smiled with mischief in her eyes. *"Then you can enlighten me on why your gaze keeps falling to my tits."*

***

Lil Zetti had been dumped on Highland Hills Drive and left for dead, but somebody had to be praying for him 'cause that's where he was found, barely breathing. He was rushed to the nearest emergency room and green lighted into surgery. One of the nurses on shift recognized him, and that's how Sunjay and Ms. Betty found themselves there, awaiting the boy's fate.

Sunjay paced the tiled floor, his thoughts homicidal, but Ms. Betty sat in one of the hard chairs in the waiting area, reading her Bible while praying that the good Lord saved her baby. Lil Zetti was as dear to her as Messiah and Sunjay, and she'd raised him most of his life.

"Sunjay, will ya stop all that pacin'? I know ya worried, chile, and if worrying could change anythang, I'd worry wit ya, but worrying don't change a thang." She admonished lightly.

Just when Sunjay paused to respond, the elevator door dinged open, and a doctor in blood spiked scrubs stepped off. His expression was morose as he approached. As Sunjay helped Ms. Betty out her seat, his mind concluded what the man's sullenness meant.

"Are you the family of Zetti Jackson?" He asked

"Yes, we are, doctor. Is he okay?" Ms. Betty probed, but the look on the man's face was answer enough. *"Lord, have mercy,"* Ms. Betty murmured as her hand went to her chest.

"I'm sorry, ma'am. I'm so sorry to have to tell you this, but Mr. Jackson is…"

***

There was a private rooftop for the penthouse, and that's where Messiah and Kate found themselves; in the air of the night and standing beneath a star filled sky. Both nursed glasses of their pleasures, but while Kate admired the constellation of Orion, Messiah's mental had little dollar signs spinning like a tornado. Kate had showed him four paintings— two "bottowed" from the Vatican, where "the Pope" calls home, and the other two from England, where a very rich admirer of hers allowed his 20-million-dollar art to travel across the Atlantic to her hands. Combined, all four works of art were worth—

"Sixty million dollars, Milton. Not too bad, huh?" Kate's voice was low as she took a sip of her wine.

Messiah downed his before glancing at her.

"These paintings will be here, under heavy guard, for three days. Lots of money in here."

"Especially for some paintings I—"

"Not just some paintings, but a Michelangelo original, two Vermeer classics, and a Rembrandt. The Michelangelo alone is worth ten million." She smiled. "Yet, Milton, you never answered my question."

Messiah studied her, wondering the best way to implement his Pimpin'. He'd never faced such a challenge as a spoiled white girl. She didn't need him. She'd seen more and possessed more than he could use to entice her with. He knew the hoe stroll would never be her reality, but he knew she was attracted to him. "What to do, pimp, when Pimpin' has to be quiet, 'cause Pimpin' needs a disguise," he asked self before giving Kate his most charming smile. "Which question, love? The one of worth, or the one about your tits?"

That got a giggle from her before she swallowed the rest of her drink. "Um?" She smiled. "Let's start with the one of worth."

"I think something that's priceless is worth more than millions."

"But which would you prefer, Milton? Millions? Or something priceless?"

Messiah thought on it for a moment; his vision lifting to capture the crescent moon blowing above their heads. *"I'd prefer millions."* His answer caused her mouth to drop.

"Why, babe? money can't buy you everything. Money is—"

"Nothing to someone that's always had it, but everything to a mu'fucka that's only dreamed about its power. See, only a rich mu'fucka would say money can't buy everything, but if asked would they exchange all their money for what they say they can't buy, what do you think would be their choice?" His question was flawless. *"What can't money buy, Kate?"*

Kate scoffed before her cheeks reddened. *"Love! Money can't buy love, and I can't speak for anyone else, but I'd give every dime I have for it!"*

"You're a liar, Kate, and a liar is the worst kind of person. Money can buy anything, including love! Rather circumstantial love or genuine love, you get the same out of both in the end, and you'd never give up a dime for love! Why?" He spat before stepping so deep into her space that if he'd pucker, their lips would touch. *"You're just a spoiled girl, afraid to venture out on her own. You've been so pacified that just the thought of losing the power of the dollar frightens you."* He smirked before running the back and of his hand down the side of her face. *"A paradox, Katie,"* he whispered.

As soon as the name slipped from his lips, Kate flinched. Tears sprang to her orbs and she began to tremble. Unbeknownst to Messiah, Katie was her government name that only her grandmother, whom she loved more than breath, used to call her. Her deceased grandmother! She spazzed before glaring at him through teary eyes. *"You— have—no—idea—what I—I—I've been through!"* She *sputtered as a lone tear fell from her eye. "Nor do you know me. I don't depend on anyone. I'm self-sufficient."*

"Maybe." Messiah chuckled. "Maybe not. But what I do know is you have a fascination with the color of my skin, but—" He paused to study her. "This is just a wild guess, but I bet your parents would disown you if you was to bring me home, huh?" He smiled, and the look on her face was evidence enough. "Yet, since your brother is a man, they can overlook it. On second thought—" Messiah snapped his fingers as if he'd suddenly had a thought. "There is something money can't buy." He contradicted his early statement. Turning to head back into the penthouse, Messiah smirked.

Kate cried silently as she studied his back. "You're a piece of shit, ya know?" she told him.

"Yea, I know," he spoke over his shoulder. "And you're just a slave to your fear of the unknown, but the one thing money can't buy is a rewind button for better decisions," said he, before making his exit.

***

"Lord," Ms. Betty exclaimed as soon as she set eyes on Lil Zetti's condition. Her hand lifted to her mouth in despair, and the doctor's words continued to play in her mind.

"I'm sorry, ma'am. I'm sorry to have to tell you this. Mr. Jackson is now stable but was shot in the back with a high-powered gun, and the bullet shattered the T-11 vertebrae in his spine. He'll never walk again. It's a wonder he's even alive." The words played like a sick mantra within her old mind, and uninvited tears soaked her eyes.

"Oh, chile, what ya done got ya self into?" She whispered.

Sunjay stood leaning against the wall, his vision fixated on the IVs and tubes running in and out of Lil Zetti's body. "Nigga, naw, what's gonna happen is you gonna get bruh's

199

melon cracked, and when you do, yo heart gonna split 'cause you gonna know it was you that fed him those bullets by default!" Messiah's words sliced through him. Guilt is a parasite, and it gluttons on the conscious of the solid when they're in the wrong, and Sunjay felt it as Ms. Betty prayed.

"Lord Jesus, in ya name we call for the healing of this child. Make a liar out of these physicians, Jesus. Jesus—"

"Fuck Jesus!" He spat vehemently, and paused Ms. Betty's convo with her Lord.

In a flash, the woman made it before him, and before he knew it, there was a sting at the side of his face. She'd slapped fire from him. "Negro, don't ever let me hear ya curse the Lord, again! Ever! Ya hear me, Sunjay! This?" She pointed at Zetti's sedated form. "Ain't the work of the good Lord, it's the work of the devil! Them dog gone streets you heathens care so much for." She hissed, and then— all the night seemed to escape from her like air from a hole in a tire. Ms. Betty sagged; her experienced eyes melting into soft streams down her weathered but beautiful face. Turning from him, she slowly made her way over to Lil Zetti, and ran a hand over the side of his face. "Sunjay, the devil is always busy, chile, and let me tell ya somethin'. When a man dives into a fire, he'll never know which flame burnt the most or burnt the life out of him." She whispered as her old heart ached. She'd lived seventy summers, and it bothered her spirit to live through a time white folks killed and handicapped her people, to seeing her people do the same to themselves. Ms. Betty rested a hand over Zetti's chest, merely taking comfort from the feel of his heartbeat. "God don't make no mistakes, Sunjay, and though he's a merciful God, his love is mysterious. Sometimes he has to allow disorder to come about so he can make some order," she prophesied, and though the hospital room was dim, Sunjay noticed the sad shake of her head. "Don't make him bring disorder into your world in order to get yo' attention, Sunjay, 'cause in my day, I've seen him humble some of the biggest and baddest sons of—" she was saying, but allowed her words to die off into the silence when she heard the door click shut.

Sunjay had made his exit.

Ms. Betty took a seat in the chair besides Lil Zetti's bed, and placing her hands on her lap, the old woman began to sing to him. She hummed the old church hymn Wade in the Water as her old eyes continued their slow leaks. She knew her grandson was the cause of Lil Zetti's affliction, and even more, she knew God was gonna bring disorder into Sunjay's world in order to get some order. "Wade in the water. God's gonna trouble the water..." she sung softly.

Chapter 16

Next Day— 10AM

When the door opened, Messiah smirked at the woman before him. Candy, the Puerto Rican beauty had aged better than cognac, and at forty one years old, was as jazzy as a sweet melody blown from Satchmo's trumpet.

When her eyes took him in, they ignited with recognition; then burned with confirmation. She always knew Messiah would be a boss. "Measiah?" She purred before seductively licking her lips.

Messiah chuckled. "Ole, Candy, just as sweet to the vision as you were when I was just chili Pimpin'. But save the sexy ganders for ya John's, hoe, 'cause my game is now in another dimension." He broke on the hoe, and though he hadn't slept a wink since he left the shindig, he popped the collar of his dress shirt as if he hadn't worn it the night before. "Now, go tell Pimpin' a playa on deck. And Candy?" He stopped her as she turns to go do his bidding.

Candy's nether region moistened as she fixated him with her gaze, and Measiah knew then that he was chose for his pose.

Flashing her a glimpse of the diamonds on his button teeth, he set it in stone. "Hoe, if I catch you recklessly eye ballin' again, I'ma arrest yo' hoism and place you under new management." He jammed before he scrammed. Messiah hadn't returned home since he left the day before. His mental was pregnant with the con, and all he could think about was,

"How can I knock this bitch for a few of those millions? Three days? That's how long she say those paintings will be there? Under heavy guard? Three days? Shid, if Jesus could die and resurrect in 72 hours, I know I can come up with something slick to play a bitch," he whispered to himself.

***

Pimpin' Maxwell was a certified playa that had taken his game to another plain, yet behind his love for his profession, his next love was mental stimulation. He loved to spend his mornings reading, and that's exactly what he was doing when Candy escorted Messiah into his study. Ever since he'd put Yella Shoe onto him, he'd been expecting the visit.

Messiah stepped in, Dapper Dan clean, and when he set his eyes on his mentor, he gave a nod of appreciation to the burgundy smoking jacket Pimpin' wore over the golden hued, silk pajamas. Sitting behind a massive oak desk, the man was pressure!

"Candy," Pimpin' called to Candy, who stood in the threshold of the door, staring as if she were witnessing Jesus's return.

She jumped at the mention of her name. "Yes, Daddy?"

"What's your purpose in this world, honey?" Pimpin' inquired, and she frowned in confusion.

"Huh?"

"Your purpose, hoe, you know. The reason you breathe, eat, and take shits?" Pimpin' Maxwell rested the book upon the desk before steepling his fingers.

Candy shrugged. She'd never considered the question. "Pimpin', all I know is hoin, Daddy. My life revolves around pleasing you."

"So?" Pimpin' Maxwell leaned back in his chair before fingering his pencil thin goatee. "Why are you still standing here amongst two gents, rather than serving yuh purpose in life? Bitch, you can rest on ya own dime, but not on mine.

*Properly excuse ya self before you properly confuse ya self."
His demand was made with a graceful tone.*

*Candy's eyes momentarily flickered to Messiah before she
departed and Pimpin' chuckled.*

*"The older a hoe gets, the more I realize they begin to
view us as husbands rather than pimps. Time creates
familiarity, and familiarity gives birth to mistakes! Never let
a hoe get so lax in familiarity that she begins to see you for
anything other than what you are, Cat Daddy— a stomp
down playa! Now." He interlocked his fingers behind his
head as he captured Messiah in his gaze. "What does an old
playa owe the pleasure of ya presence, daddy-o?"*

*Messiah took a seat in one of the two chairs on his side of
the desk, before crossing his leg at the ankle. "It's been a
minute, OG, but I see time only ages ya physical, and not ya
mental." He jazzed with a smile.*

*"Sho' ya right, tyke, but I'm sure our time is too precious
to waste with the baseline, so kick it to me fresh, like a baby
suckin' milk from the breast." Pimpin' studied him, and
Messiah nodded in agreement.*

*"Look, Pimpin', you're like a pops to me, but that shit you
pulled with them hoes was Amish, and—"*

"That's the—"

*"Hold up, bruh, let me finish." Messiah re-hogged the
dialogue before holding up a calming palm. "When you
knocked me, I felt like you did some hoe shit, 'cause I
would've never rocked you like that, but when me and Yella
Shoe chopped game, he opened my top to the laws of the
land." He shrugged indifferently. "Though a hoe may be
taught, she can still be bought, and if a playa can smile when
he cop or lock a hoe, he gotta smile when he blows her."*

*Pimpin' Maxwell smiled bright. "That's law, Mack
Daddy, and with my ears to the streets, the pavement told me
yo gators have been tied tight so you don't trip over the same
game twice." He chuckled before leaning forward and*

placing his palms on the desk. "Yet, let's chop. Ain't that why you're here? To chop game and pick my brain?"

Messiah's expression revealed his surprise. "How-how'd you know?"

Pimpin' laughed. "What else could've brought you here? So how 'bout we get to it; shall we," he suggested, and that they did.

***

YANNNNN! The motor cycle's engine sounded like a roaring thunder cat as Sunjay pushed the powerful machine to its fullest potential down Walton Walker Freeway. The morning was still a new born, but he was already twisted off of Hennessy. No helmet or other safety gear, Sunjay felt like a dangerous bird, plunging through thin air as the wind blew dangerously around him. Lil Zetti's plight had his heart crooked. "It's my fault my lil mans fucked up like this, mane!" His guilt had become a monster, and as he dipped in and out of traffic, he had no fear of the reaper.

He'd spent all the night before in the trenches searching for answers, and it was Tweety, Lil Zetti's older sister, that placed him on his current crash course. "Last me and Zetti talked, he was catchin' the Dart to Highland Hills to holla at C-Bo's punk ass! I told him not to trust that hoe ass nigga!" She'd screamed when he'd given her the news.

Sunjay dipped off Loop 12, hit Bonneview, and zoomed through the Cliff, gritting his teeth at the thought of the The Pinks, The Whites, Browns, and Greens. All were projects in Highland Hills, and names like Big Jack, Rod Ri, Tat Dow, and Black Rat were synonyms with those projects. When Sunjay slid onto Highland Hills Drive, a few natives of those corners were oblivious to the storms speeding into their section, but the revving of the powerful bike drew down their attention.

There was a young couple standing out on the sidewalk in front of the Pinks when Sunjay skidded the bike to a stop before them. Twan was a young wild Loc that was making his bones throughout the city, and as he stood behind his lady friend, armed wrapped around her waist in affection, he was caught down bad when Sunjay jumped off the bike. Twan's cohorts fled; abandonment.

"Bae?" His girl cried in shock and fear when Sunjay upped his burna. "Wait, I—" she began as he took aim.

"Shut up, bitch!" He spazzed, the liquor in his veins hydrating the madman in him.

The girl's mouth opened and closed, but she'd became mute.

Sunjay smirked sinisterly, noticing her trying to pull free from Twan's embrace, but dude held tight. "Where that boy C-Bo at?" Sunjay got to the point.

"Who?" Twan feigned ignorance, but Sunjay was out his body at that point.

Chuckling, his eyes clouded with evil before BOCA! He squeezed the trigger.

Twan jumped as the slug knocked his girl's noggin back, causing her to headbutt him as her soul made its exit. Her body sagged in his embrace before he allowed her to crumble to the concrete, and impulsively his hands shot up in alarm when Sunjay trained that fire on him. "Wait-aiight!" He shouted, switching from foot to foot nervously. "Look, cuz, I—"

"Bitch, do I look like a crab! Respect my mind, Blood! Fuck that boy C-Bo at?" Sunjay demanded, noticing the animals of the ghetto emerge from their buildings at the sound of the gunshot.

Twan noted it too, and seeing reinforcements, his nuts swelled. "Nigga, suck my dick!" He put on for all eyes to see, and Sunjay knew he'd lost his moment.

Cracking a crooked smile, he shrugged. "You got nuts, huh?" He chuckled before, as fast as a striking snake, he lowered his aim and fired. BOCA! The slug tore through where Twan's zipper would've been if he wouldn't have been sagging.

The boy folded, hands shooting to his crotch in agony. "Arrrgh! Hoe...ass—" He was gritting when Sunjay's aim spotted it's target.

"And since you don't use this mu'fucka, you don't need it!" He shouted, spittle flying from his mouth. BOCA! The next ball of fire knocked Twan's brains out.

***

After Messiah revealed his dilemma, Pimpin' Maxwell sat back in thought. Millions! Heavy security! His mind reeled with the possibilities.

"Three days, ya say?" He asked.

"Two now," Messiah answered almost miserably.

Pimpin' Maxwell chuckled. "Well, son," he began with a sad shake of his head. "Every con can't be laid. The con is a slick play, Messiah, not a quick one. Even short cons take a lil time, play boy, so if you ask me, I suggest ya let this one go." He gave regrettable advice, and Messiah cringed.

"Millions and the affections of a trust fund bitch that's too lame to resist a playa's game? Come on, Pimpin', it gotta be a way I can play and get away!" He held fast, and seeing the desperation in the man, Pimpin' shook his head in dismay before rising from his seat and stepping around the desk.

Leaning against its edge, he crossed his arms over his chest. "Dig this here, Mack Buddy. Let me pour you a glass of fresh thoughts so you can think like the best boss. This here, Pimp, is the parable by a playa friend of mine. The tortoise and the hare," he introduced, and Messiah soaked it up.

***

Red Bird Mall was jumping, and on that breezy morning, it drew a nice crowd. Porsha and Justice were doing early shopping for Foxy Brown's concert that was jumping in a week at club GiGi's, and both sides knew they had to be on point for Foxy's vibe.

"Girrrl, and Tweet's fast ass was fuckin Toyah's man, and Itty Bitty told me that Toyah and them hoes from East Dallas bumpin' their gums about catchin' Tweet slippin'. And—" Porsha was the gossip of the city, but Justice's mind was elsewhere.

Lifting a cute pair of short shorts from the rack, she examined them, visualizing them with the halter, the thick tube socks, and Jordan 9's she'd just bought.

"Justice? Justice, do you hear me, girl?" Porsha noticed her silence.

"Girl, yes, I was thinking about—"

"Messiah!" Porsha cut her off, and with a dramatic roll of her eyes, she placed a hand on her hip. "Look, Jus, I know you and him used to have a thang, but that is a hoe! Girl, since him and Sunjay started getting money with them Jamaicans, they've been like the Goodwill of dick; givin' it out to any bitch who'd take it! That nigga even tried to fuck me, but I checked that shit!"

"And you just, what? Didn't fuck him? And he's getting money? Come on now, Porsh, I've known you my whole life!" Justice giggled.

Porsha didn't. "Ugh." She gave Justice the stank face. "I know you not callin' me no hoe?"

Justice looked her up and down, lowkey hurt that Messiah would try to fuck her bestie. "Umm." She smiled. "Yes, I am, and you know you've been a boo Joe since back in the day, Porsha. Don't front." She laughed at the look on her girl's face, not knowing Porsha wasn't merely a hoe, but a snake as well!

***

It was a warm day in the forest, and the tortoise sat sunning beneath the kiss of the sun when the hare approached with a challenge.

"Hey there, turtle. Mighty fine day we have here, playa. How about a race!" He called but the tortoise declined.

"What ya know good, hare? Yea, this day is mighty fine, and as much as you enjoy a good race, I'd rather appreciate the day."

The hare frowned. "Aww, come on, fella. I know yo slow ass ain't gonna let lil ole me scare ya." He was ever the show off, and when a group of lady birds and bees cheered him on, that ole graceful rabbit stuck his chest out in pride.

On the sideline, the tortoise's son watched expectantly, as a female rabbit batted her eyes at that arrogant hare; and seeing the shame in his son's eyes, the tortoise rose slowly. "You know what, you low down dirty hare!" He exclaimed. "I'll accept your challenge under one condition!" He wagered, and the hare grinned in triumph!

"Name it, sucka!" He demanded.

"If I win, you have to give me your lucky rabbit's foot, and if I lose, I have to give you my protective shell, so that I may be eaten by predators! And—" The tortoise stretched his old legs. "Since you chose the challenge, I choose the grounds," he proposed, and after they shook on it, it was in stone.

As the tortoise sat stretching, his son crawled up to him. "Father, father. Why'd you accept the race, knowing the hare is much too fast!" He cried.

The tortoise smiled assuredly. "Dear son, life has never been a race! Those that run fast only enjoy the speed of *missing* what one whom takes his time to appreciate. Fret not, my boy, 'cause a man in a rush may beat one that paces himself, but his rushing is a sure thing he'll make mistakes!"

He comforted, and moments later, he and the hare were at the starting blocks.

The land was surrounded in vegetation and dense undergrowth, but a slim trail cut through it. All the animals cheered the two, and the fox did the honors.

"On your marks…get set…GO!" He shouted, and the race began.

The hare took off in powerful hops, while the tortoise made slow progress. Minutes into the race, they'd left the spectators behind, and the hare was making quick work of the poor turtle, and as if the Gods had turned against him, the tortoise fell on hard luck!

"RRRRoar!" The hungry growl of a beast sounded from the bush, and before he knew what hit him, he was snatched up in the jaws of a hungry lion. The beast with its wild mane crunched down on him with its razor sharp teeth, but no matter how hard he chewed, and no matter which side he tried, he just couldn't crack through the tortoise shell.

"Hey, lion!" The tortoise called from inside the shell, and the lion paused his vicious chew. "Listen, play boy, you can bite and you can chew, but no matter what you do, you'll never get through." The tortoise swore, and the lion growled before biting down with all its mighty. To no avail. "Can't you hear me, you spineless beast; you gotta be a coward to be picking on a turtle like me!" The tortoise taunted, and finally the beast spit him out. From inside his shell, the tortoise cast his play. "Listen, damn fool, if you're that hungry, I can lead you to a meal, but only if you're willing to make a deal!"

The lion considered it for a moment, but his stomach made the decision for him. "Speak, tortoise, and what you say better be sweet, or I'ma chew and I'ma chew on your green ass 'til I chip my teeth!" He growled.

"Fair enough!" The tortoise bargained. "I know where a juicy hare hops, so fattened and sweet, and only if you let me go, will I tell you where, but if you continue fuckin' with me, you're going to crack your teeth. All I'm asking for is his rabbit foot, and we'll both have a good day. Mr. Lion?" He proposed and that lions stomach sealed the deal even before the beast gave a confirming nod.

So, as the story concludes…moments later, the tortoise crossed the finish line with the hare's lucky rabbit's foot, and his son beamed unbelievably.

"Pop! Pop, how'd you beat the hare?" He wanted to know.

The tortoise smirked. "See, son, that's neither here nor there, but just know that all game is fair." He jeweled. "Now." He smirked. "Do ya pop a favor and go inside ya shell, 'cause in just a moment, there'll be hell!" He prophesied, and almost instantly, a loud roar emitted and the lion exploded from the brush.

In seconds, he'd made quick work of the birds, bees, and the female rabbit. After his feast, that ole lion chuckled, seeing the fox had fled and the tortoises had gone into their shells. "Ole tortoises, I sure appreciate the meals, but you're a low down rotten mu'fucka to had made such deals!"

From inside the shell, the tortoise snickered. "Well, Mr. Lion, I just may be, but all those you ate laughed while the hare showed his speed, while I was forced to take my time! So, a playa had to use my mind to get mine!"

Pimpin' Maxwell concluded and patted Messiah's shoulder. "All things take time, Pimp buddy. As long as you sit back, you can get back. But if you runnin' too fast, you'll bust ya ass! Always keep it playa, Messiah. Some cons are worth the play, and others may cost you everything! Think on it, playa. Go into ya turtle shell and use ya scale of pros and cons," he suggested before leaving Messiah to do just that.

For a moment, he considered the parable. He'd pocketed the diamonds Pimpin' had just dropped on him, but he thought of allowing M's…a ticket. Letting that pot of gold to stay in the leprechaun's midst was unthinkable. As his mind ran wild, his eyes fell upon the book Pimpin' left face down on the desk, and curiously, he rose from his seat. "Henry Box Brown, narrative of the life of Henry Box Brown?" He read aloud before lifting the book. Messiah wasn't intending to read the tale, but as he did, a slow smile spread across his face. Good game is omnipresent! Everywhere!

Chapter 17

After Messiah left Pimpin's spot, his mind was full and he had a lot to do. His first stop being to a man he knew that repaired furniture.

"Can you do it, Poke? I need ya, baby, and if all ends swell, I'ma bless ya mits with somethin' slick!" He swore, and the older man glanced to the large, antique couch he was repairing for one of his best customers.

The couch looked like something that belonged in Buckingham Palace, and he knew the ancient thing cost a fortune. The things Messiah asked him to do with it were absurd, but he'd watched the boy sprout from tragedy to triumph, and looked at him as a nephew. His eyes drifted to Messiah with question marks dancing in his gaze. "You're asking me not only to loan you a hundred-thousand-dollar antique, but also to modify it to outfit your criminal mind, boy."

Messiah said nothing, he merely allowed his stare to speak to his Jewish friend, and after a silent moment, Poke nodded.

"One night, Messiah. One! And I need this back so I can return it to its original state." He relented, all the while, his mental twisted with what he'd just read about why they dubbed Henry Brown as Henry "Box" Brown.

Henry Brown was a slave around 1814 on a plantation in Virginia. When his master died, ole Henry was passed down to a William, his dead owner's son, to work in his tobacco factory in Richmond. In 1836, Henry Brown married a woman name Nancy who was owned by a bank clerk, and with her owner's consent, Henry and Nancy rented a house, and blessed it with three children. Yet, overtime, Henry's beloved was sold twice, and upon the third owner, Samuel Cottrell began charging ole Henry fifty dollars a year to keep his queen from being sold! And how'd Samuel Cottrell compensate this agreement? August of 1848, he sold Nancy, along with her and Henry Brown's three kids!

***

Messiah's second stop after leaving the furniture spot was to another company where he knew the owner. After explaining his plight, Messiah paid for the services he needed and left, full steam ahead, on his way to speak to someone he knew would be the best to share his ideas with.

***

When Nancy was sold, Henry Brown raced to the jail where she and his seeds were held, but it was late! Though he held his wife's hand for four mikes as she, his kids and 350 other slaves were marched on foot, all the way to North Carolina, that was the last time he'd ever set eyes on his family. Henry Brown was crushed! And heartache led him to the only hope the Caucasian's ever offered those in bondage. Prayer! Afterwards, Mr. Henry Brown says an idea suddenly flashed across his mental. The "revelation"; so to speak, was genius.

***

When Messiah made it home, he hurried in, praying that Black Diamond was home. "Mama! Mama?" He shouted, and to his relief, Lady Luck didn't give him the middle finger.

"Boy!" Black rushed into the living room, eyes glossy from a recent dance with the pipe.

As Messiah studied her, his heart cracked at what she was doing to herself. Black Diamond had smoked away all her thickness and her cheeks were sunken, but if only for the moment, Messiah was content with how small she'd become. "Mama, look, I got a plan to get us out the sand, but you have to pay close attention, Baby. I need you!" He pleaded.

"Messiah Ridge, if you don't miss me with all the sugar and give it to me straight, I'm gonna pop you upside the head!" She laughed.

And Messiah did just that! Gave her his spiel straight, no sugar!

Chapter 18

4:25PM

"Thanks for lunch, Calvin, it was delicious!" Kate acknowledged before turning to the man that had just escorted her into the sky scrapper her office was in.

Calvin was a partner at Geilich, Creamer, and Elrich Law Firm, and he had a thing for the beautiful Kate O'Riley. That warm afternoon they'd had lunch at a cozy dig downtown, and as Kate hugged and planted an innocent kiss on both sides of his face, Calvin was already anticipating their next escapade!

As soon as he exited the building, Kate boarded the elevator that would take her up to her fourteenth-floor office. In moments it opened to an open space receptionist area, and her brunette haired receptionist smiled brightly. It was contagious, and Kate smiled uncertainly; not sure why they were smiling in the first place.

Margo was her good friend, and when she shot from her seat and rushed over to her, Margo seemed on the precipice of combustion! "How was it? I know he just swept you off your feet!" She gushed excitedly, and when Kate realized her friend was merely being nosey, she rolled her eyes.

"Ugh! Marge, I thought you had good news about the Simmons case!" She playfully glared, and Margo returned the roll of her eyes.

"Uh, no! Besides, news of Mr. Prince Charming just makes the Simmons case seem sooo nugatory!" She giggled.

"So?" She splayed her hands. "Where'd he take you? What you eat? Did you two kiss?" She was ever excited and Kate laughed before heading for her office.

"No, skank, we did not share a kiss, and—" she was saying when she pushed the door open to her office, but the vision before her was a kidnapper of words. There, spread out around her office, were hundreds of red and white roses.

"Beautiful, right!" Margo exclaimed before rushing into the room and retrieving something. "And here, there's a card too!" She informed as Kate accepted the card and read.

Her jaw dropped and when her eyes reclaimed the assemblage of flowers, her heart fluttered.

"Well?" Margo wanted details. "Prince Charming?"

Kate nodded her confirmation. "Ye-yea, Prince Charming." She whispered.

"Oh!" Margo remembered before rushing to the side of the desk and lifting a basket of green apples. "Apples? Sweet, but different." She giggled.

***

"Ms. Betty?"

The sound of his voice surprised her and made Ms. Betty flinch. "Lord, chile, ya can't be scarin' an ole lady like that." She laughed before closing the Bible she'd been reading. It was the third time Lil Zetti had awaken, but the only time he'd been coherent. "How ya doing, baby? How ya feel?" she asked with a worried expression, and when confusion fell over the boy's face, tears swelled within the old woman's eyes.

"Ms. Betty?" Zetti called for the second time.

Sorrow rose Ms. Betty's voice when she answered. "Yes, chile?" She choked, but before he could voice why he called her, the door to the hospital room opened and Tweety entered.

"I got you some coffee, Ms. Betty, I—"she was saying when she realized her younger her brother was awake. "Zetti!" She cried joyfully. She hurriedly gave Ms. Betty the coffee before rushing over to hug her sibling.

Ms. Betty sat the coffee beside her on the floor, her internal a tropical thunderstorm as she prepared for the inevitable.

"Boy, don't everrrr scare me like that again!" Tweety said as she embraced him, oblivious to the fact he didn't return the love.

"Tweety?" Lil Zetti called when she pulled away, and that's when she noted the dour look on his face. He glared; gritting his teeth as his vision drifted to Ms. Betty. "Mama Betty," he called, and when a slow stream fell from Ms. Betty's left eye, he knew the answer before he even asked. Lil Zetti shook his head in denial. "Why can't I feel my legs? Tweety, I. Can't. Feel. Them!" He shouted, while trying with all he had to will his legs to come back to life.

Ms. Betty rose from her seat, horrified when the boy attempted to crawl out the bed. "Zetti!" She demanded as she moved as fast as her old bones would allow.

Halfway out the bed, Lil Zetti's energy simply vanished; he allowed her and Tweety to help him back into the right position. "I can't walk, Ms. Betty? I-I thought you said God loved me?" He cried, and though he played the streets his entire life, Zetti was only a child; a child trapped within a man's reality.

"He does, baby." Ms. Betty fought for the words sufficient. "He just has to trouble the water sometimes." She tried with tears falling from her eyes.

"Naw." Zetti shook his head vigorously against her claim. "No, he don't, Ms. Betty. God ain't ever loved me! Ever!" He broke.

Standing to the side, Tweety drowned within her pain, and with a hand to her mouth, she agreed with Lil Zetti.

***

6PM

After she'd left her office, Kate rushed over to the penthouse. She'd showered and dressed in record time for the night's exhibit, and after assuring all was fabulous, she made her way to the front, only to walk into the midst of an argument. One of her security men stood glaring at a furious delivery man in a brown uniform, who was attempting to argue his point.

"I'm telling you, dude, I have to deliver this package to ; Ms. O'Riley, for some fancy—"

"Excuse me, is there a problem!" Kate interrupted, and two sets of eyes found her.

"Yes, there is a problem, ma'am. I've been trying to explain to this brute that I have a delivery for a—" The delivery driver glanced down to the clipboard in his hand. "A Ms. O'Riley, but he's giving me a hard time." He huffed, and Kate frowned curiously.

"I'm Kate O'Riley, sir, and you say you have something for me?" She watched the man confer with his paperwork.

"Yes, ma'am, and not to give you any slack, but do you have any identification? I'm sorry, but this thing comes with priority signature."

Kate's brow rose, curiosity full grown. "Sure, just wait here while I go get—"

"Nooo, no." The man cut her off with a quick glimpse at his watch. "My shift was up an hour ago, and I really need to get home." He declined.

Kate frowned in surprise. "But, I thought you just said you need—"

"Yea, yea, but you look like a Kate O'Riley. Just sign here, lady." The man cut her off before thrusting the pen and clipboard into her hands. Kate wanted to argue, but signed, nonetheless. The delivery man nodded before stepping to the entrance of the building and cupping his hands around his

mouth. "Bring her in, boys!" He shouted, and to Kate's astonishment a beautiful, three cushioned, antique couch was brought in. So large that it took four men to bare its weight; the couch was extraordinary!

"I-I think you have the wrong—" Kate began, until a red envelope was thrust. A greeting card, she thought before pulling it from its confines.

"Where do you want this thing, lady, so we can get home to our families?" The deliverer pressed.

Kate read the card:

To you, with love. When I saw this, I knew only beauty could appreciate such opulence. Hopefully you enjoy it as much as I; sorry I won't be there to see your eyes blow, but me and Toya are escaping for a day or two. Chat when I return.

-Don-

With a smile, Kate showed them where to put the couch. Blushing, she said, "Don is so thoughtful. This couch is a beauty!"

***

Two Hours Later

The room was filled with gentle conversations as connoisseurs of the fine arts indulged themselves within the beauty of intricate paintings. It was the second day of Kate's exhibit and she was the perfect host as she smiled at one of her works.

"I call this one A Perfect Death. It's a piece I created with tears in my eyes. It symbolizes the love for my deceased grandmother." Her voice became hoarse with grief.

"Oh, my," a woman murmured as she admired the canvas.

"Just gorgeous!" An older gentleman admired.

The painting had a slash of red, an angry plush of violet, intermingled with a succession of lime green. All of this surrounding a withered white rose placed against a black backdrop.

Nursing a glass of wine, Kate became lost in her own work. That is until an impeccably dressed Messiah slid up beside her.

"Is beauty really in the eyes of the beholder," he asked with the diamonds on his bottom teeth glittering brilliantly.

All eyes drifted to the out of place black man. Messiah's attire was borderline vulgar, but Kate's vision feasted. He wore a fire red two-piece Brunello Cucinelli suit but went naked beneath the jacket; except for the gold rope necklace with a jeweled Jesus piece dangling from it. His sculpted chest was on full display, and the white cocaine hued crocodiles on his feet were a beautiful touch.

Kate smiled nervously before excusing herself from the crowd, and leading Messiah away. "What are you doing here, Milton? Haven't you gotten enough of me being a bad taste in your mouth?" She asked once they were a safe distance away.

Messiah chuckled before nodding toward the far corner of the room. "Nice touch. A new addition?" He was indicating the couch.

Kate's eyes followed. "Yes, and thanks. A gift from Don, but—" She paused as her vision recaptured him. "Why are you here? My brother and your sister are away and—"

"And did you receive my flowers?" Messiah cut in, already knowing of Tutts and Don's whereabouts; he was the culprit who'd advised the getaway.

"Yes." Kate blushed. "And thanks. They were beautiful, and the apples?" Curiosity peeked its head.

Messiah's eyes captured hers as she took a sip from her glass, and to her surprise, he pulled an apple from his pocket. "The apple reminds me of the piece that's stuck in the throats of every man for Adam partaking of the fruit offered by a snake."

"Wha-What?" Kate choked.

Ignoring her, Messiah extended the apple. "Kate, the night is rebellious, mama. Let me whisk you into it and liberate you from what enslaves you."

Kate stared down at the fruit, frowning at his choice of words. "Nothing enslaves me, Milton, and—"

Before she could complete her statement, Messiah had taken her hand and placed the apple within it. "Some people say when Eve partook of the fruit, she cursed us all, but I feel it was the act of partaking that was her sin, but more because she took of it with the wrong mu'fucka. If she would have taken it back to Adam and they ate at the same time, they could've shared the game rather than the blame. Then they would have known that hiding from God was fruitless because even before he told them not to eat of the tree, God knew they'd sin. It was part of His plan to place the tree where all could see, 'cause he knew curiosity is more powerful than discipline. Just as yours is now." He smiled before releasing her. "For once in your life, try the forbidden, ma. You'll see that you've been a slave this entire time. Meet me at Bachman Lake of Northwest Highway. You won't regret it," he offered before making his exit.

***

Four Hours Later
11PM
The night held a humidity promising a summer rain, though the Heavens were starless; a full moon glowed like a Pearl upon velvet. Bachman Lake was a mass of water, surrounded by cypress trees, and beneath the air of the night, the dark waters rippled, shimmering the reflection of the moon. Messiah gazed out at it, finally giving in to resolve— he'd overplayed his hand. Kate wouldn't show! His eyes fell to the pallet he'd made on the grass. Two flames danced upon the candles and illuminated the setting for two. A

chilled bottle of Remy, and a platter of fruits were the spread just as he leaned to blow out the first candle.

"The news predicts rain." Kate's voice drifted from behind him.

Messiah paused, a slow smile spreading across his face. "It's been raining my whole life. A few more drops won't hurt." He whispered.

Kate stepped from the darkness, still wearing the Oscar de la Renta pant suit, her beauty was beautiful. After closing out the showing, she'd wrestled with the idea of the forbidden, but the more she toyed with the apple he'd given her, the more she realized all he'd said about her was absolute. So, she'd bitten the apple. All the while, Messiah's mental recaptured how the tale of Henry "Box" Brown had just secured the bag!

***

In front of the penthouse there was a small area with a TV, and it was there that two off duty officers sat watching an episode of Perry Mason. They were hired to do security for the exhibit, and every thirty minutes they rotated doing security checks on the expensive art on display.

"Hey, Tom, this one's on you, bud." The older officer tapped his partner and though he grumbled, he rose to do his job.

Hurriedly, he made his way to the second level of his place, his eyes sweeping to and fro, and only after he was sure all was well, did he stop to admire a strange painting depicting a design he couldn't distinguish. Shaking his head in disbelief, he chuckled. "The hell folks see in this crap," he mumbled before completing his task and hurrying back to catch his show.

***

Henry "Box" Brown

Henry Brown's revelation was that he'd have himself placed into a wooden box, nailed closed and stamped as dry goods; per the Adams Express Company. Adams Express advertised a one-day trip from Richmond, Virginia to Philadelphia if the package had no glitches or delays. With this in mind, Henry went about the task of finding a box big enough; and being five foot eight, that wasn't easy! Yet, fortune smiled.

A free black man introduced Henry to Samuel Smith, a white man who Henry paid 86 dollars to assist. This came the wooden box created by a black carpenter named John Mattaner. The box— complete with baize lining, air holes, a container of water, and food was ideal for Henry Brown's attempt. In essence, Samuel Smith corresponded with James McKim, a Philadelphia abolitionist, and it was James whom advised that the box to be mailed to a James Johnson at 131 Arch Street, and with "This Side Up, With Care" painted on the box, at 4AM on March 23, 1849, Henry "Box" Brown began his scheme!

***

Just as the security guard completed a security check in the dim corner of the penthouse, one of the three cushions on the antique chair rose almost magically. Yet, there was no magic involved; merely the will of a young playa that was inspired by a runaway slave named Henry "Box" Brown! After a quick peek to ensure the coast was clear, a sounder figure pushed the first and second cushions up and off the couch, before smiling triumphantly.

***

For a moment, the moon peeked from behind the clouds and Kate gazed up at it. The fragrance of the cypress was thick in the night, just as the smell of rain wafted over the lake. Sitting with her arms wrapped around her knees, Kate found a certain intimacy about the late night picnic.

"So, are you going to tell me what all this is about?" She whispered.

Messiah poured glasses of drinks before handing her one. "You," was his sole answer before taking a sip.

Kate's eyes trailed to him. "Me!"

"And what you truly want."

Kate studied him to see if he was serious, and seeing that he was, she laughed in disbelief. Shaking her head, she wet her tongue with the cognac. "What I want? Milton, we hardly know each other enough to gauge each other's wants, and I believe my wants truly doesn't concern you." She shrugged indifferently.

Messiah downed his drink in a gulp, wincing at its smooth burn. "So, you're telling me that you have all you want!"

She took only a moment to consider. "Yes."

"You're a liar!" Messiah demanded, knowing which game was needed to seduce what he wanted from her.

Kate's mouth hung open "You're wron—"

"I'm right." Messiah cut her off before refilling his glass. "Imagine summer without winter, day without night, good without bad. Seems beautiful, huh?" He chuckled before draining his seconds three fingers in width. "Now, imagine each image it in reverse? Some people think they want the days to be all sunny, but—" He took a slice of mango from the platter beside them. "Without night, the sun would scorch us! Without night, romance would be complacent, lacking that nasty freak shit we love when the sun sleeps. Without winter, what would romance be? If shit was all good, what would mu'fuckas appreciate?" He chuckled before suddenly climbing to his feet.

That's when God's tears decided to drip. The first few raindrops were fat and slow, and Kate turned her face up to it. "Milton?"

"Hmm?"

"There's something—" she considered before her vision claimed him. "Strange about you." Then, as if something suddenly dawned on her, her eyes became suspicious. "How'd you know where I worked?"

"Dance with me." Messiah extended his hand, ignoring her.

"Wha-What?" Kate sputtered as lighting struck across the dark skies.

"Will you reject my—" Messiah paused as rain fell harder. "Strangeness?" He completed with a smile.

Already tipsy from the cocktails from the exhibit, Kate drained her glass. Once to her feet, she studied the man before her. His chocolate skin? His mannerisms barely camouflaging his gangsterisms? His handsomeness and his way with words? She found that she was more than intrigued, and as she allowed him to pull her to him, the truth surfaced. "Milton, you are-are..." Speech failed her when Messiah sucked her neck. "Beautiful!" She moaned as he began to sway with her beneath a crying sky, and when she felt his hands cup her ass, her hormones reminded her that she hadn't been fucked in a year!

Then, Messiah began to hum an unfamiliar tune against her collar, and though she'd never heard R. Kelly's hit, the words formed in Messiah's mind as he hummed 🎵 Heyyy Mr. DJ/ why don't you slooow this party down/ The ladies in here are fly/ and it's one whose caught my eye 🎵

***

"It's the painting in the gold frame. The one of the naked white bitch in a garden!" Messiah's words played in her mind as the slim figure moved like a shadow throughout the room. She scanned the paintings on the wall until she found not only one, but two paintings fitting Messiah's description.

Only subtle changes, both were of a white women, naked in the garden.

"Damnit, Messiah." She cursed before deciding on both. It took her a moment to get them off the wall, and to her surprise, she found one screwed into the frame! She shook her head in frustration as she racked her brain for an innovative way to get it out. Glancing down at her watch, she'd timed the guards' rounds, and seeing she only had ten more minutes before their next one, she cursed. "Think girl, think!" She told herself.

***

The two guards sipped coffee as they chuckled at a rerun of I love Lucy, and just as Ricky Ricardo gave Lucy the famous look and said, "Lucy, youuu got some splaining to do," a loud crash came from the second floor of the penthouse, and both officers shot to their feet in alarm.

"Damnit!" The senior man shouted when hot Java spilt down the front of his pants from the sudden action, but his younger partner was already in hot pursuit to investigate.

***

The Heavens had opened up above them, it's downpour pelting the lake in fat drops. It wasn't a storm, but more of a soft summer rain that cried warm tears upon their flesh. Kate was delirious in lust and only had a vague recollection of how they'd wound up nude upon the soaked pallet. On her back with Messiah above her, she could feel his dick thick against her thigh. Water dripped from him as he hovered above her, their eyes seeing, but the night robbing them of a perfect view. Kate inhaled sharply when Messiah guided his knife through her cut, and quivered when he didn't enter her.

"You're killing me. Jus-t do-it!" She demanded before reaching for him, but Messiah caught her wrist and pinned them above her head.

"Do you know how to follow instructions, Kate?" He asked, and though she paused in confusion, the moment was salacious!

"Yesss!" She hissed, unconsciously grinding her hips up towards his strength.

Messiah had recognized the freak in her from the offset. "Prove it! When I release you, I want you to play with this pussy and make yourself cum; you hear me?" He demanded, and it clicked a switch in her.

Kate moaned erotically before nodding her understanding.

Their bodies were slick as Messiah slid down hers until he crouched like a warrior before her southern region. Kate's South America was fuzzy with a newly grown, blonde fuzz, but it was pretty to him. Messiah wouldn't trick his dick on lady; he craved to punish that pussy, but knew being a playa came with rules! So, as he watched Kate's fingers find her clit, he held her ankles to keep her legs open.

"Ms. Pretty Pussy, now I see how that white girl was able to tame the animal in King Kong," he spoke to her kitten. "Beauty has a way of doing that, and your pussy, Kate, is worth the fortune."

"Mil-ton?" Kate cried in ecstasy as her fingers created a hurricane.

"A fortune, mama," Messiah whispered, his meaning pimpish.

"Milll-ton?"

"Cum for me, lady. I can tell you need it. Let me and God watch."

"I-mmmah cum-cum-iing!" Kate's legs trembled and broke the chains of her enslavement to her inhibitions.

When her back arched, Messiah released her before reaching between her legs and massaging her femininity.

After his hand was coated, he slid up her body and smiled down at her. "You're a freak, Kate. Tonight you've shared the fruit with a playa, and I appreciate you for allowing me to enjoy this pleasure."

"Milton—" Kate flushed after ecstasy vanished and she could see through the fog of liquor. "I-I've never done anything like th—" she was saying before Messiah slipped his fingers into her mouth.

He allowed her to taste herself 'cause he would never partake of where a woman bled from once a month. "Taste the fruit of your labor, mama. We never know what morning may bring," he encouraged as she sucked his fingers clean; never thinking his words were a prophecy.

Chapter 19

7AM
Next Morning
"Oh-my-God! Oh my God! This can't be happening to me!" Kate was hysterical as she paced in the vastness of the second floor of the penthouse. She held her hands to her head as if she wanted to yank her blonde locks from her head, and pausing for the millionth time to stare in disbelief at the picture frames, she shook her head. One was still intact, but empty, and the other was in pieces as if the thief had slammed it against the floor to get the painting out.

"I'm sorry, Ms. O'Riley. We searched and searched, but—" the senior guard tried explaining the unexplainable.

Kate's furious gaze captured him. *"What I can't seem to understand is how a thief could somehow break into this place and disappear into thin air! Tell me, Officer Kents, where were you and—"*

"Hey! I told you, you can't go there, pal!" A loud ruckus could be heard from the second floor, and moments later, a group of familiar men in delivery uniform rushed up the steps. Him, the young officer from the night before was on their heels as they went about their business.

Kate's eyes went wild. *"What in the hell are you doing!"* She demanded as three of the men went for the couch.

Yet, the man who'd had her sign for the couch on the day before, stopped before her with an embarrassed expression on his face. *"I'm sorry, ma'am, but this was the wrong couch! Yours is now downstairs, and this one was meant to go to an entirely different area of the city. My humble apologies, ma'am, but if I don't correct this, I'ma be out a job!" He pleaded.*

Kate hated to see the unique couch go but had more dire things to consider than it's wisp of a time in her life.

"Ms. O'Riley, these people shouldn't touch anything. They're contaminating the crime scene!" Tom protested as the men hefted the couch out.

Kate waved a dismissive hand toward them. "The crime isn't the couch, sir, but the stolen art, which was nowhere near those paintings! Furthermore, rather than worrying about that old couch, why don't you focus more on recalling how you and your partner here—" she nodded at the gray haired senior man "—allowed some thief in the night to disappear into thin air with eleven million in art!" She scolded and though he wanted to protest, when Tom's vision captured that of the passing delivery man, the burley mover slapped him on the back.

"She's right, but. Your attentions are in the wrong place!" He shook his head sadly before making his exit.

***

Though the trip was grueling, and he almost died before reaching his twenty-seven-hour destination, after riding upside down for most of his trip— after being loaded from wagon to train in Washington D.C., then from train to steamboat— Henry "Box" Brown had arrived!

His four abolitionists received him, and one tapped on the crate four times. It was code for "All is well."

When the top of the lid was pried off, up rose a disheveled Henry Brown. "How do you do, gentlemen!" He exclaimed before fainting. It's said that when the man was awakened by a glass of water, he sang Psalms 40:13. "Be pleased, O Lord, to deliver me!" This is how "Box" became Henry's self-

chosen legal middle name. *Because of his cleverness, Henry Box Brown became a celebrity amongst abolitionist topics, and after, The Fugitive Slave Act in 1850, which many fugitive slaves fled to England to avoid arrest by slave catchers, Henry spent years lecturing on the British lecture circuit until 1875 when he returned to the USA; again, traveling north and telling his story. Henry Box Brown moved to Toronto where he died June 15, 1897. A free man!*

***

30 Minutes Later
After the couch had been returned to Poke's furniture repair shop, and no one was present but he and Messiah, the older man shook his head in amazement at the story he was just told of a runaway slave. Yet, when the cushions on that old couch popped up and Black Diamond lifted up with a smile, ole Poke could do nothing more than chuckle. Chuckling morphed into full blown laughter as he recalled the reconstruction he'd done to the couch so that the woman could fit comfortably, and live through the ordeal. Forming a casket like box at its base, with breathing holes around its surface, a small tub of water was all she'd been afforded.

"How do you do, gentlemen?" Black repeated the same words Henry Box Brown did two centuries before.

As the two men laughed harder, Messiah's mother's stomach growled, but rather than speak on her hunger, she frowned. "I need a wake up. This shit make a bitch wanna get high," she said before joining them in laughter.

***

"Mane, I know you glad to be leavin' up out this stale mu'fuc—"

"Sunny!" Ms. Betty demanded with a warning glare.

"My fault, G-lady, but my man been laid up in this hospital too long!" He chuckled as he pushed Lil Zetti's wheelchair towards their car.

He'd spent too long laid up recuperating, and though he still wrestled with the idea of never walking again, Lil Zetti was ready to go! The boy was now paralyzed from the waist down, and life as he knew it would never be the same.

Ms. Betty rolled her eyes. "What that gotta do wit ya swearin' and thangs, chile?" She asked, but before Sunjay could respond, a familiar black Crown Victoria eased to a stop before them.

When the window rolled down and Detective Spinx smiled, Sunjay spat at the concrete.

"Good evening, Ms. Betty, Tweety?" He greeted as his eyes found Zetti. "Sorry to hear what happened to you, young man—"

Lil Zetti spat at the ground. "Fuck you, Pig!"

"Zetti!" Ms. Betty's jaw dropped. "Tame ya tongu,e boy!" She admonished. Lil Zetti's glare snapped to her, but softened as she returned on just as fierce.

Detective Spinx chuckled. He'd been working those streets since his patrol days, and he knew all the misfits in them. He'd always known Zetti would be a menace and when the boy's eyes recaptured him, the detective knew that wheelchair was only a pause within the kid's destiny. "Sunjay, we need to talk."

Sunjay gritted his teeth. "Ain't nothin' to talk about, homie."

Again, the detective chuckled. "We can do this your way or my way. But either way, we're gonna do it."

"Now, Spinx, I know you're not threatening my babies, 'cause—"

"I'm good, granny. Take fam n'em to the car." Sunjay surprised everyone.

"Smart man," whispered Spinx. "Smart man."

Chapter 20

"Naw, Zetti, tell me this ain't real, bruh! Fuck this happen? Huh?" Messiah was livid as he paced. Every so often he'd stop and stare at Zetti's condition in wide eyed disbelief before shaking his head and returning to his pacing. It was 10PM and when he'd met up with Sunjay at one of the spots they trapped in, Messiah hadn't expected to find a handicapped Zetti. The sight crushed him, and to add to the stress, Sunjay had schooled him to the squeeze the crooked detective, Spinx, was applying. It was all too much at one time.

"Look, dawg, don't sweat the marks out the Hills. Me and the homies gonna—" Sunjay began.

"See!" Messiah exploded before spinning to face off with him. "That's the problem right there!" He growled as two steps brought them to a foot apart. "You and the homies! Nigga!" He spat before jabbing a finger back at where Zetti sat in his wheelchair as he watched them. "You hit bruh on this gang gang shit, but you foul for not schoolin' him to the truth!" Messiah spat, eyes branding his mans.

Sunjay splayed his arms and shrugged. "What's the truth, Blood?" He smirked.

Messiah shook his head in disappointment. "The truth is, these streets...these niggas in 'em, they don't give a fuck 'bout me, you, not him! Why you pourin' all this gang shit in his tank, fuck you ain't tell him when shit get ugly, all that shit he reppin' gonna leave 'em casket closed! Huh?"

Messiah was fried! *"Why you ain't tell him when the cell doors close on 'em, ain't gone be no mail, and—"*

"Nigga, fuck what you tal'm 'bout!" Sunjay had enough, and turnt up his G. "You ain't out here in these trenches wit' us! Nigga, yo scary ass be so stuck up them hoes' ass that you blinded! I'm the mu'fucka out here puttin' food in these lil nigga's belly when there ain't no love being shown! Where you be at nigga?" He spat, jabbing a finger in Messiah's face. "Pimpin'!" He answered himself. "When the last time you been up in this mu'fucka? Huh, nigga?"

"Sunjay, get ya hand out my face, bruh." Messiah seethed with fire dancing in his eyes.

Sunjay chuckled menacingly before yanking his shirt over his head, preparing for battle, and just as he slung it to the floor, the smoke was up.

Blam! Messiah shot a two-piece that rocked him!

***

The day had wound down, and the sky had become a beautiful bruise of pinks, pale purples, and a shade of soft reds. Sunset! And after Detective Spinx pulled up to his modest brick home in North Dallas, he merely sat there, taking deep pulls from a cigarette as he stared at the ragged appearance of where he called home. Exhaling a cloud of smoke, he wondered where it all went wrong.

He hadn't always been on the jagged edge of the law, but after his third divorce from a woman that took his kids and remarried, things seemed to plunge from there. Before he knew it, he was shaking down D-boys, and sometimes he plucked a lil money from the evidence room. These small sins had tainted the detective's badge, and to his surprise, he came to realize that there was more rotten seeds in the apple than just him! And, with his natural knack for leadership, it didn't take long for Detective Spinx to reach out to a few of those seeds and they formed an unlawful apple tree that was too tainted for Johnny Appleseed to prune.

Detective Spinx exited his car before flicking the cigarette to the ground, and as he made his way toward the house, he was oblivious to the car that pulled to the curb a few houses down. They followed him, and now the hunter had become hunted!

***

Sunjay and Messiah fought like warriors, but in the end, Messiah dipped and slipped a combo from his mans and countered with two jabs, a quick hook, and a wild over hand that closed the casket!

Blam! Sunjay went down, but not out. Landing on his ass, his reflex was auto when he drunkenly fought back to his feet. He reposted his fist, but staggered, he knew he'd been busted. "What's good, nigga? Run-run that shit back, Blood!" Ever the gangsta, pride fed him. Bloody nose and swelling eye, the man wanted more, but Messiah— swollen lips and slit eye— had spent his animosity.

He waved Sunjay off. "We even, nigga, for when you beat me when we were nine," he offered before spitting blood on the floor.

A confused expression blossomed upon Sunjay's face until he remembered their childhood squabble, and then he burst into laughter. He couldn't believe Messiah still held that grudge. Messiah joined him in laughter, and Lil Zetti merely shook his head in amazement. Fuck those boys go from punching to laughin', he was wondering just as Sunjay stumbled to the couch and plopped down.

"We gotta touch them niggas out the Pinks. They drew first blood, Bleed. But before we stretch 'em, we gotta figure out what we gonna do 'bout this pig, Spinx!" He spat.

Messiah nodded his agreement before starting to pace. "Nigga tal'm 'bout thirty percent tax. What you think 'bout givin' him ten?"

Sunjay gawked, mouth ajar in horror. "Wha-What! Ten percent? Messiah—" He paused to get his shirt and dabbed his nose. "I ain't givin' that nigga shit but a closed casket. He won't see a red Lincoln of mine!" He argued.

Messiah paused to see if he was serious, and after noting that he was, he shook his head in disbelief. "Sunjay, we can't kill no law, bruh. That shit will have the whole force at our heels. Naw, we gotta whack him mentally!"

"Mannnn," Sunjay drug doubtfully.

"Deep knowledge and strong action," Messiah mumbled, head down in thought as he paced the floor.

"What?" Sunjay retorted.

Messiah stopped mid stride to look at him. "Taoist says the level of invincibility found within no conflict is deep knowledge and strong action. You gotta learn to spank a nigga without g'tting' physical, Sunjay. That's the only way to last in the game."

"Nigga, fuck all that philosophical shit. We in the trenches. Blood for blood, homie. Bullet for bullet!" Sunjay growled.

"Fam, are you not hearing me? Sunjay, the blood of the police brings the hint of the police! Tags not only bad for business, but it's a guaranteed manhunt!"

"Messiah, them fools blasted me and left me for dead, we gotta get our lick back, Blood!" Lil Zetti broke his silence.

Messiah and Sunjay's eyes connected and Sunjay smirked with an "I told you!" shrug. When they looked to him, the moods temperature dropped as his eyes watered.

"Nigga, I'll never be able to walk again, and you niggas talkin' 'bout this cop. What about them niggas that got at me!" He spat vengefully.

"Lil bro, we gonna step to that, but you gotta forget all this street shi—"

"Fuck that!" Zetti raged, his hands tightening on the wheels of his wheelchair. Tears fell as his resolution became concrete. *"I'm out here, dawg, and on Blood, I'ma kill C-Bo! Look at me, Messiah!"* He shouted, and Messiah did just that. Zetti asked a rhetorical question. *"What would you do?"*

Chapter 21

After leaving the bricks, Messiah's mind was a mad house! The woes of the game had him standing on the ledge of moralities' cliff, and he knew if he jumped, the remaining good portions of self would perish within a blissful suicide. The night was absolute at that hour and as he maneuvered the car onto the street leading to Maxwell's gambling shack, Messiah wondered what he could do to outwit the hands of fate that had dealt him that stinking hand.

"Damn!" He whispered when seeing the numerous cars lined up and down the street. The night life in the triple D was always groovy, but at Maxwell's den of crooks, you could always find a sucka getting his money took, just after getting his hand shook! Messiah found a place to park before checking the clip on his burna—he was sure to shake a few hands, but the only way his money would get took was if his was snatched first!

Maxwell's establishment was lively, and as soon as one entered, his palms would itch with the call of money.

"Hit dice!" Someone shouted from a large dice game, and as Messiah nodded at a few familiar faces, he felt the beckon of the gamble luring him.

The shack was massive with the living room being reserved for the dice, and as he made his way through the throng of hustlas that gambled their rent money, mama's money, and cars, Messiah understood why the mafia invested in Vegas.

He smirked before making his way to the bar and nodding to the old timer behind it. "What's the word?"

"Watch out now, I see ya boy. Still too legit to quit, and talkin' Pimpin' every time you spit!" Big D smiled brightly as they dapped, and already knowing the playas choice, Big D poured him three knuckles of Yac, straight.

Messiah downed it before twisting on his stool to face the action. "The ole man 'round here?" He shouted over his shoulder.

Wiping the bar with a dry towel, Big D glanced up at the dice game in progress. "Yea, he and company been expecting you," he answered as his vision fell to the large parcel Messiah secured beneath his arm. "The pool room."

Messiah nodded. "Pour me another, Big D. It's been a long night."

Big D had noticed the lumps and swollen lip, but minding your business prevents you from knowing too much and making yourself a danger to the next mu'fucka's survival. And Big D knowin' that, hid the key to living just a bit longer, so he didn't ask if one didn't tell.

***

The sound of the pool balls clinking together emitted after Pimpin' Maxwell took his shot, missing the corner pocket by an inch. He cursed when the red ball tethered on the ledge of the pocket, before stilling. The pale skinned man he played against chuckled while cuing his stick. "Shame," was his only sentiments as he took his position.

The game was down to three balls, the white, black and red, with Pimpin' being behind that one shot. Pimpin' Maxwell chuckled when the white man positioned himself for his shot, and with a trained eye, finished the game. Pimpin' shook his head in disgust when his opponent smirked and *collected the money they'd wagered on the game. Three thousand was merely a drop in the bucket for either man to lose, but the taste of defeat is a sour one that no man enjoys. Pimpin' Maxwell chuckled bitterly, but just when he was reracking the balls, his gunman, Bear, opened the door for the man of the hour.*

Messiah strode in with the air of a boss and allowed his eyes to digest his surroundings. Bear, Pimpin', and though the two goons were clearly his bodyguards, Messiah's eyes seemed almost lured to the small man with a big presence. At five foot, six inches tall, Drayton Khrushchev was a powerful Russian that had his hands in many of things; fencing included.

With a smile that fit better on a hyena, the man stepped forward and extended his hand to Messiah, and studying dude, Messiah's grasp connected with his. "You mus be Messiah, ey?" The man's English was strange to him, and Messiah frowned as they shook hands. The fellows hair was cut close to his scalp, and just beyond the expensive suit and the tie he wore, it was the story his clear blue eyes told that revealed the man's dirtiness.

"Yea, yea, and you?" Messiah inquired, and with a quick glance to Pimpin' Maxwell, the older gent chose thy moment to make formalities.

"Messiah, this is an old friend of mine, Drayton, and Drayton, this is a dear young'in to me, Messiah," he intros as the men's hands separated. "Now, don't let the smooth suit and the easy smile fool you, Messiah. This old lion is as slick as a snake." He chuckled before making his way over to slap Drayton on the back. "But he's a sho nuff hood connection to the black market, and that makes him an asset to men of our elk." Pimpin' smiled.

"Which leads us, ey." Drayton clapped his hands and rubbed them together almost greedily. "To the reason for tis... Umm." He glanced to the ceiling in mock thought before recapturing Messiah with his gaze. "Tis business, as

you Amedicans say." His accent was thick as he smirked. Eyes falling to the parcel beneath Messiah's arm, the man waved a hand towards the pool table. "Shall we?"

Messiah had the painting out and spread over the green surface in no time, and Drayton was automatic with accepting a strange optical device from one of his henchmen. Bending over the piece of art, the man studied with a critical eye; Messiah and Pimpin' Maxwell's eyes briefly connected before returning to Drayton. Erecting himself, the man handed the device back to his gunman before his vision captured Messiah within a studious gaze. Seeing the snakishness in his blue orbs, Messiah wondered if he'd have to result to bloodshed before the night was over, but even as he considered it, Drayton smiled big.

"Tis-Tis masterpiece is truly beautiful, and original, but I thought there were two paintings?" He probed, his gaze finding Pimpin' in inquisition before both their eyes drifted to Messiah.

Messiah smirked. "You say this the real deal, right?" He ignored the question as he studied Drayton.

"Yes, but—"

"So," Messiah interrupted before rubbing his hands together greedily. "Let's talk numbers, play boy. I'm thinking two M's."

"Two M's? As in millions? For hot art? Nooo, mi boy, tis won't do—" Drayton shook his head against the absurdity. "I—"

"How do you know it's hot?" Messiah's suspicions rose as his eyes bounced to Pimpin'.

The older man shrugged and only when Drayton laugh did their eyes return to him.

"Amedicans, ey?" He said to one of his henchmen, and though the man chuckled, his smile was noticeably faux. "No, no, Mesi-ah." Drayton's pronunciation of his name came out funny. "Your dear friend didn't give you up. It's just that in my line of work, a man mus keep his ear to the market,

you see. And being a man of my clout, a little birdie whispered in my ear that a very powerful family has been illegally relieved of some very precious art." The Russians chucked at the stunned expressions on the men's faces. "So." He clapped his hands. "With the troubles I'll have to suffer to smuggle such goods out of the country, and with the federal authorities now involved, I think we can negotiate the price a bit more to my liking, ey?" He chuckled. "I'm thinking more like...?"

***

The night was black; like a heart with no love, and in a building in the back of East Dallas Projects, Taco and his squad were getting to the duffle as they trapped out of a dopefiend's apartment. Eight Ball and MJG blasted from a massive boom box as they engaged in their work. Taco and B-Brazy stood over the kitchen counter, chopping and weighing wholesales of that "New Jack City." And as they prepared the different shapes of crack cocaine for distribution in the dining room, and keeping an eye on the four naked felines that counted and rubber banded the week's profits, Block, Deezy, and Nacho kicked the shit.

"Nigga, yo head so big, I bet yo mama still ain't healed after havin' you, and it's been eighteen years since then!" Block capped.

Nacho wasted no time in getting his lick back. "What! Nigga, yo mama so fat, it took her seven days to push you through the birth canal!" He ranked.

"Fool, I seen yo sister yesterday. She still got that lil funny walk! Blood, why every time she walk, it look like she doing the tootsie roll?" Block could tell he touched a nerve, even before Nacho took a threatening step toward him.

"Dawg, keep my sister outta this—"

"Y'all niggas chill. See what all that playin' do?" Deezy tried to extinguish the flame, before passing a half-smoked blunt to Block.

Accepting it, Block chuckled. "What? Blood can't be fucked up with me 'cause his retarded ass sister in Special Ed." He didn't have no quits.

Deezy frowned. "Bleed, you're in Special Ed, too!" He cracked up.

Block hit the blunt. "Naw, Blood, there's Special Ed for the bad kids, and mu'fuckas that's just not tryin' to learn shit, and there is Special Ed for the ones that have funny walks and slur when they talk. All they do in that hoe is make baked potatoes and shit!"

Deezy burst into laughter. "Baked potatoes! Nigga, that's Home Ec., not Special Ed!"

"I'm telling you, Blood, it's two different classes! It's levels to this shit! The one I'm tal'm 'bout is the class where the lil kids walkin' 'round wit the lil helmets on, and bakin' potatoes." Block laughed over a lungful of smoke. "And I was walking by one day when this nigga's sister with the funny walk was askin' the teacher—" He paused to make a strange face and tap his hand against his chest as if he was a special child. "Ms. Tyler, can we bake potatoes!" He mimicked in a goofy voice, and that's when the first slap landed across his face. The blunt fell, and by the time the second slap came, he dipped and a slap box session was on!

"You niggas childish!" Poo, one of the girls counting the money, admonished with a roll of her eyes. And just when Taco rushed out the kitchen to investigate, two things happened.

"That's all you niggas do! Sell dope! Fuck them lil pissy tail hoes! And play all day!" Joann, the fiend who rented the apartment to them, ranted as she stormed from the back room.

Block and Nacho separated, busted lips and bruised up. All eyes shot to Joann, but it was Taco who shook his head in frustration.

"Damn, Joann, a nigga just blessed you with a quarter this morning!" He spat in disgust as her lady fingers combed her dry hair.

Joann was as thin as a broom stick, and still had the nerve to squeeze into a dingy shirt and daisy dukes that only pronounced her deteriorating frame. "Negro," she demanded before placing a hand on her boney hip and attempting a sassy stance. "Quit bringin' up old shit! That lil measly shit gone like the wind, and so will all you lil rotten mu'fuckas if somebody don't hurry up and get a bitch high!" She threatened.

Taco's frown deepened. "You on some bull—"

Blam! The sound of the front door crashing in murdered whatever he was about to say.

"Down! Freeze!"

"Dallas Police Department!"

"Dallas Task Force!"

"Get the hell down!" A multitude of demands and announcements filled the air.

It was madness as the trap stars went for their weapons, but holding court in the streets wouldn't be part of their story that night. Officers swarmed and apprehended efficiently.

"Fuck!" Taco raged as he was tackled in his attempt to make it to the back room. "Y'all trippin, mane, I just came over here to check on my aunt. I don't know nothin' 'bout nothin'," he was saying when a dark-skinned, bald-headed man made his appearance.

"Ole Taco. What ya know good, playa." Spinx smirked as Taco was roughly hauled to his feet.

"Fuck you, pig!" Taco demanded.

Spinx chuckled as his eyes took in the busy he and his men had just made, and knew it was merely the tip of the iceberg. As the arrested was led away, Spinx stopped Taco and his escort before leaning to whisper, "You're going away for a bit, playa, but don't worry." He paused to glance over at the bundles of money scattered across the dining room table. "By the time I'm done here, you'll only get a slap on the wrist." He laughed as Taco was led away kicking screaming.

"Hey, detective, you gotta see this!" An officer waved him to the kitchen, and when he saw the mountains of dope, he salivated with greed. "What should we do?" The cop inquired with a knowing smirk, and Detective Spinx chuckled as his eyes lifted to capture the rogue.

He and his task force were as dirty as a hog pen, and that money and narcotics wouldn't see a second in the evidence room. Operation Sunjay and Messiah was now in full effect, and until they folded to his terms, Spinx planned to hit every one of their traps. Extortion—with a badge!

*** *

"Dam-nnn, nigga, get-thisss-pus-ssy!" Dream cried in ecstasy.

Sunjay had her doggy style on their bed, and was road rage in that kitten. Their bodies glistened from sweat and when he paused his stroke, Dream wasn't hearing it.

"Uh uhh, boy!" She protested before burying her face in the pillow and throwing that ass back at him. The sounds of her cheeks smacking his pelvis fed the fresh in her as she talked her talk. "You-gonna-ta-keee this pussy, nigga!" She growled as her body tingled in anticipation.

Sunjay slapped her ass before spreading her cheeks wide and pushing her passed the point of no return.

"Riiight there, Daddy, right-there!" She cried; fist balling the sheets as her dam broke.

Sunjay didn't ease up until she'd soaked him and his nuts empty. "Fuck!" He growled before collapsing atop her. Both were winded, and when Sunjay rolled to his side of the bed, Dream snuggled up beside him.

"Damn, boy, you be tryin' to kill a bitch." She smiled, satiated as she rested her head on his chest.

Sunjay chuckled, and for a moment silence was bliss. It wasn't to be! In the dead of the night, Sunjay's beeper made Dream groan.

"Ugh! Not tonight, Sunjay, you just got home." She pouted.

Sunjay laughed. "That's this dick talkin'," he capped before kissing the top of her head and slipping out the bed.

"Yea." Dream followed suit with an attitude. *"Well, if you call yourself g'tting' some and bouncin' then this poonanny won't be talkin' for a long time!"* She swore before storming to the bathroom.

Sunjay laughed with a shake of his head before retrieving his pager from the pile of clothes at his feet. "911-415" the code read, and that's all he needed to see to rush to his clothes and grab his strap. The code meant emergency at his East Dallas spot, and Sunjay could only shake his head as he headed for the door.

"Sunjay? I'm tellin' yo black ass, if you leave, you may as well stay wherever you go, 'cause the door will be locked when you return," Dream was saying, but he had already made his exit.

Chapter 21

Next Morning

A million dollars? A million dollars in cold cash! The words wouldn't stop rotating around his mind. Even as the elevator dinged open on the floor of Kate O'Riley's law office, those words were a mantra. He'd barely slept the night before, and though he'd gone from rags to riches overnight, Messiah had one last spin to f his web before he made a grand. "The show's over folks!"

"Excuse me, sir, may I help you?" The receptionist smiled up at him from behind her massive desk, and just beyond her faux smile, Messiah detected the suspicion in her gaze.

Yet, giving her his most charming smile, his eyes barely moved when flickering to the golden name plate on her desk. "Good morning, Mrs. Creamer, I'm here to see Kate."

Marge's vision digested his playerisms; his multicolored Coogi sweater complimented the bark brown Coogi jeans and shoes he wore, but it was more of the eleven white and one red dozen roses he held that piqued her curiosity. "And you are?" She inquired with a raised eyebrow as she recollected the office of roses Kate had received a moment ago in time.

The VVS ones glistening on the bottom row of his teeth made Messiah's smile special. "You can just tell her that a moment in time is here to see her."

"Excuse me?" Marge screeched, smile vanishing. "Sir, do you have an appointment? If not, you need to—"

"Well, we'll be in touch, Ms. O'Riley, and please contact us if you happen to recall anything substantial." The door to Kate's office opened. The speaker was one of the two men in nice suits. Tall, handsome, and Caucasian, and when his arctic blue eyes captured Messiah, both men froze in surprise. Both men's minds ricocheting them back to the night they'd informally met.

"Would you like an hors d'oeuvre, sir?" The waiter had asked, yet it was his eyes; those exact eyes that studied him now! The eyes that told Messiah the waiters uniform didn't quite match a man with such a stare. Nonetheless, Messiah had smirked.

"Appreciate this, my nigga. This shindig y'all kickin' is real jazz; ya dig!" He'd replied. *And as Messiah came back to the present to find the man's gaze swallowing him, he knew the man and himself would create a strange history.*

"Oh my, umm—" Kate's surprise was evident as she stepped forward, "Milton?" Her hand grazed the petals of one of the flowers. "What are you doing here? How do you know where I work? Wait. She paused, frustration taunting her facial as he massaged her temples. "That was insensitive. I'm glad you're here, but—wait? What am I saying?" The woman flustered, and that's when the Caucasian gent intervened.

"Milton, is it?" He smirked while extending his hand. "I'm Agent Barnes with the Federal Bureau, and yes." He chuckled. "I was undercover at the art function the other night. There's been some very intricate heists sprouting here and there, so I was hired to play alliance between the O'Riley's and some very influential folks across the pond, but." He shrugged with a frustrated expression, and the potbellied, black man stepped forward with his notepad and pen poised.

"Mr. Milton, I'm Agent Brown, and you were present at said function, correct?" He asked, and from there, he added Messiah with an onslaught of investigative questions. After

jotting down his every answer, Agent Brown flipped his little notebook closed, and after they'd bade Kate farewell, they'd taken their leave.

Kate stared at Messiah horror stricken. "I'm soooo sorry, Milton. You didn't deserve to be questioned like some common criminal. It's just that something horrible has happened and..." Her words trailed as she sought words sufficient to describe the past twenty-four hours.

"And maybe I can whisk you away for only a moment?" Messiah offered.

Her receptionist's mouth fell open in horror. Kate was white privileged, and Messiah? Black!

Kate flushed; a flash of the fantasy they'd spent in the rain the night before crossing her mind. "Milton." She ran a hand through her hair. "Now's not a good—"

"Time can never be good or bad. Only what happens within it can determine if something is deserving of those titles. So, this isn't a proposition. It's a demand without aggression. Go and get your things, Kate O'Riley." Messiah knew when to stomp down, and turning to Marge, he winked. "Hold all her calls, love. She's taking a thirty-minute lunch." His bossiness was sure nuff and caused the older woman's mouth to fall open further.

"I—" she began.

"Please, Marge." Kaye held up a hand of pause, and without taking her eyes away from Messiah, she submitted to his alpha male. "Hold all calls. I'll be back in thirty minutes."

***

"On Blood, this nigga Spinx gotta die, Damu. I'm tal'm 'bout tonight!" Sunjay raged as he paced. The squad was deep; Sunjay had called an emergency meeting and about twenty gangstas from around the city had shown up at Porsha's spot.

"On gang!" Lil Boosie, a young wild nigga outta Pleasant Grove seconded. *"The pig been on his shake down shit for 'bout a month straight, homie. He hit one of the spots off Jim Miller, too!"*

"Him and them crooked ass swine hit us in North Park, too, dawg!" Another added, and so said most of the other inhabitants as well. *"So, what's the bidness? Why you and Messiah don't just put the nigga on the payroll and—"*

"Fool!" Sunjay spat before rushing over until he and Lil Boosie were face to face. *"You sayin' we should work with the laws?"* He gritted.

Lil Boosie lived for the smoke, but knew Sunjay was big homie. *"Naw, Bleed, I'm just—"*

"Ease off the lil nigga, Blood. I feel what he sayin'." All eyes shot to Murda.

Sunjay chuckled before accepting a blunt from one of the homies. *"Oh yeah?"* He smirked. *"You do, huh? That's bool, but since you're barking your input and all, fuck you been, nigga? You been M.I.A, and it's kinda strange the five-o know where all our spots at."* He glared accusingly, and in a breath, Murda'd drawn his tool.

"Fuck you sayin', homie? Know you not playin' wit my name." He growled.

In moments, eighteen guns were up and trained on him. Sunjay's excluded.

He again chuckled. *"You must've forgot who runs this shit, nigga!"* He declared before sliding up on his man's and searching his soul with his gaze. *"Next time you up ya heat, you better burn somethin', fam. You know the creed."*

"Y'all niggas wiggin' out on each other while the enemy taken us down. This shit whack!" The youngest in the room extinguished the fire. All eyes went to Lil Zetti and he glared back. *"The homie just list his peeps, and we still don't know who did the shit."* He nodded to Murda. *"And this pig, Spinx, ain't playin' with nothin'. We need solutions, Blood, not in-*

house smoke!" He banged a fist against the arm of his wheelchair.

Nods spread throughout the room as Sunjay smirked.

"You right, lil dawg," he agreed before turning to Murda and using his fingers to form a B. "We good or what, Blood?"

It took a moment, but Murda locked up the set. "Watch how you handle me, fam." He declared and pulling Sunjay in for a long hug, he whispered his heart into his ear, "I know Messiah flipped my people, and I'ma answer that."

***

"The Michelangelo, Milton, ten million dollars! Stolen! The Vemeer; one million dollars! Stolen! Stolen from right below our noses! How?" Kate ranted. They were back at the lake, and Kate came unglued! She cried, then ranted; ranted, then cried. "What am I gonna do? My father is so disappointed in me!" She cried and Messiah merely stared out at the dark waters of the lake.

He'd contemplated this last piece of his scheme ever since Kate had proposed the most powerful question he'd ever been asked: "What's worth more, Milton? Something priceless, or something worth millions? Which do you desire to possess?" She'd asked the day they'd met. The question had stayed with him and that's the main reason he'd only sold the Vermeer rather than going for the pot of gold the Russian had offered for both. And seeing the FBI that morning proved him right. A stolen million-dollar painting was a slap in the face, but a ten-million-dollar painting was a punch that would no doubt bring on the type of investing that could not be shaken, so...

"I have a few friends in low places, Kate. I'll check into it, and if these paintings can be recovered, they'll want favors." His voice was low.

Kate's eyes shot to him; hope born, but as if realizing he was just a common thug, hope died. She shook her head. "Whoever committed this terrible thing are not common street hoodlums. No, they—" Her rant was paused by Messiah's hand slipping across her thigh.

"Which do you desire to possess, Kate? Something worth millions or something that is priceless?" He asked, and Kate's mouth began to move, but was void of sound.

For a moment they sat in silence but glancing out at the lake; Kate whispered. "Something that's priceless, Milton. That's all."

Messiah's eyes found her. "I know a few people in low places, but—" Her vision met his. "If they can help, they'll want favors."

The wind blew softly across the lake, and wiping a strand of hair from her face, Kate shook her head in disbelief. "What kind of favors, Milton? Do you know something about this cruelty? Is that what this is? Is this some kind of extor—"

"Bitch!" Messiah exploded, his expression monstrous. "You calling me a thief?"

"I—" she began, and as their eyes wrestled, Kate became her own victim. "No, Milton, I'm not calling you a thief, I'm just distraught; that's all. Forgive me." She swallowed her suspicions, and thirty minutes later, Messiah had her back at her place of business, and anticipating favors for a ten million dollar painting.

***

"All of them in the can, fam. This nigga Spinx on some other shit!" Sunjay ranted as he paced the floor of the trap.

Messiah and Zetti glanced at one another; both minds concluding the same thing: Shit getting crucial!

After he'd left Kate, he'd dipped over to check his mans; only to receive bad news. His eyes recapturing Sunjay, he

253

knew why every man wasn't meant to be kings. "First off, Jay, calm down—"

Sunjay spun on him. "Calm down? Do you not hear what the fuck I'm tellin' you? Nigga, SWAT took down the East Dallas spot! Yea, Taco may stand tall, but I'on know them other boys. They may rat for a Get Outta Jail Free card!" He raged.

Messiah shrugged indifferently. "Then, fuck you let 'em sit at the table if you was skept' 'bout 'em?"

"Say, I ain't got time for all that philosophical shit, nigga. We—"

"Fuck that!" Messiah exploded, before jabbing a finger at him. "We ain't what got them folks on our trail! We ain't panicking 'cause we brought some other side knights to the table! You are, 'cause you did! Nigga, I told you 'bout stretchin' yo hand to pet foreign animal; they'll bite it!"

Sunjay gritted his teeth; furious!

"Bitch ass nigga, you—"

BAM! Messiah's fist clashed with his lips, and for the second time that week, blood was drawn to restore respect.

***

The sun had fallen, and the moon resembled a pearl upon a black cloth as it reigned above the Triple D. And yards away from the apartment where Messiah and Sunjay got 'em up, a black Crown Vic was parked with two occupants devising unlawful behavior.

"Hey, Spinx, ain't that ya boy?" Thor, a dirty narc, smirked with a nod.

Detective Spinx, taking deep drags from a cigarette, watched as Messiah exited the apartment. Spinx noticed a slight limp as the man-child made his way to the trunk of his car and after snatching a duffel bag out, making his way back into the apartment. "Yea, that's him." Spinx chuckled with a exhale of cigarette smoke.

"What ya think in the bag?"

"Oh, there's no need to think. I know what's in that mu'fucka, and that root of all evil is more plentiful where he's taking it."

Within the shadows of the car, Thor nodded. "I hear this is one of their main spots. Should I round up the boys?"

Spinx sucked smoke from the cancer stick before starting the car. "At ease soldier." He chuckled before pulling out of his parking space. "As long as the snakes know where the chicken nests are the eggs." He shrugged with a sinister smirk. "Why rush in for just the eggs when he can slither in and get both them and the chicken?"

***

"I'm gone, Sunjay, and if you're smart, you'll get low, too," Messiah warned, but Sunjay nor Zetti seemed to hear him.

Their eyes were glued to the mountain of dead faces piled atop the coffee table, and beside it was the last of Messiah's work. Two bricks of Columbian flake!

"How much you say this is?" Sunjay wasn't taking heed.

Messiah scoffed before dabbing at his busted lip. Shaking his head in disbelief, he wondered how he and Sunjay came up beneath the exact tutelage but took to the game so differently? "Two-fifty." He confirmed, his eyes falling to what he knew would one day lead to Sunjay's destruction.

"Two hunnid and fifty," Sunjay whispered in awe as his vision lifted to his mans.

"Thousands." Messiah nodded before meeting the gaze. Cuts, bruises, and lumps canvassed both men's faces, but the love within their state contradicted the brutality. "Get outta The D for a while, Sunjay. It's gettin' too hot." Messiah tried again.

Sunjay's eyes drifted to Lil Zetti before falling to the money; seeming to consider it all. "Nigga, Dallas is all we know; it's my bitch, and I ain't lettin' nan nigga, pig, or bullet run me away from her. Ever!" He declared before his vision found Messiah, who frowned; on the verge of argument.

Yet, as if he'd expected nothing less, he chuckled bitterly before his eyes captured Lil Zetti. Making his way I've tried little man, he knelt before the wheelchair. "Remember what I told you 'bout school?"

Lil Zetti nodded but frowned. "Yea, bruh, but that school shit dead. I'm all in now, Messiah. I—"

"I know." Messiah chuckled, sadness in his tone. "But I gotta try, Zetti. This street shit is goofy, lil one, but how can I wipe the lust for it from your eyes when the love of it is in mine?" He shook his head bitterly. Glancing down at the wheelchair, the man's heart ached. "The cost of thuggin' always cost a nigga more than it's worth, fam. Don't believe in trap dreams, Zetti. They're exactly what they sound like. Trapped dreams!" He gave it up.

Lil Zetti's vision was searching, something in his chest wanting that better life Messiah preached about, but when his eyes drifted to Sunjay lifting a stack of money and taking a deep whiff of it, Zetti knew he wanted the same things every other nigga that hails from the slums craves: Ghetto dreams! Money, hoes, clothes and all those fancy things! "Messiah, I'm a dopefiend's son. I gotta eat!"

His words were all Messiah needed to hear to know he couldn't tamper with the hands of fate. He hugged his people before letting them know the work and the fifty bands was to go to Zetti. He then made his exit; leaving behind a chapter of his story in exchange for the next hand life had for him.

Lock Down Publications and Ca$h Presents
Assisted Publishing Packages

BASIC PACKAGE $499 Editing Cover Design Formatting	UPGRADED PACKAGE $800 Typing Editing Cover Design Formatting
ADVANCE PACKAGE $1,200 Typing Editing Cover Design Formatting Copyright registration Proofreading Upload book to Amazon	LDP SUPREME PACKAGE $1,500 Typing Editing Cover Design Formatting Copyright registration Proofreading Set up Amazon account Upload book to Amazon Advertise on LDP, Amazon and Facebook Page

***Other services available upon request.
Additional charges may apply

Lock Down Publications
P.O. Box 944
Stockbridge, GA 30281-9998
Phone: 470 303-9761

Submission Guideline

Submit the first three chapters of your completed manuscript to ldpsubmissions@gmail.com. In the subject line add **Your Book's Title**. The manuscript must be in a Word Doc file and sent as an attachment. Document should be in Times New Roman, double spaced, and in size 12 font. Also, provide your synopsis and full contact information. If sending multiple submissions, they must each be in a separate email.

Have a story but no way to send it electronically? You can still submit to LDP/Ca$h Presents. Send in the first three chapters, written or typed, of your completed manuscript to:

LDP: Submissions Dept
P.O. Box 944
Stockbridge, GA 30281-9998

DO NOT send original manuscript. Must be a duplicate. Provide your synopsis and a cover letter containing your full contact information.

Thanks for considering LDP and Ca$h Presents.

NEW RELEASES

BLOODLINE OF A SAVAGE **BY PRINCE A. TAUHID**

THE MURDER QUEENS 4 **BY MICHAEL GALLON**

THE BUTTERFLY MAFIA **BY FUMIYA PAYNE**

KING KILLA 2 **BY VINCENT "VITTO" HOLLOWAY**

BABY, I'M WINTERTIME COLD 3 **BY MEESHA**

THESE VICIOUS STREETS **BY PRINCE A. TAUHID**

TIL DEATH 2 **BY ARYANNA**

CITY OF SMOKE 2 **BY MOLOTTI**

STEPPERS **BY KING RIO**

THE LANE **BY KEN-KEN SPENCE**

MONEY GAME 2 **BY SMOOVE DOLLA**

THE BLACK DIAMOND CARTEL **BY SAYNOMORE**

CRIME BOSS 2 **BY PLAYA RAY**

THUG OF SPADES **BY COREY ROBINSON**

LOVE IN THE TRENCHES 2 **BY COREY ROBINSON**

TIL DEATH 3 **BY ARYANNA**

THE BIRTH OF A GANGSTER 4 **BY DELMONT PLAYER**

PRODUCT OF THE STREETS **BY DEMOND "MONEY" ANDERSON**

Coming Soon from Lock Down Publications/Ca$h Presents

BLOOD OF A BOSS VI
SHADOWS OF THE GAME II
TRAP BASTARD II
By **Askari**

LOYAL TO THE GAME IV
By **T.J. & Jelissa**

TRUE SAVAGE VIII
MIDNIGHT CARTEL IV
DOPE BOY MAGIC IV
CITY OF KINGZ III
NIGHTMARE ON SILENT AVE II
THE PLUG OF LIL MEXICO II
CLASSIC CITY II
By **Chris Green**

BLAST FOR ME III
A SAVAGE DOPEBOY III
CUTTHROAT MAFIA III
DUFFLE BAG CARTEL VII
HEARTLESS GOON VI
By **Ghost**

A HUSTLER'S DECEIT III
KILL ZONE II
BAE BELONGS TO ME III
TIL DEATH II
By **Aryanna**

KING OF THE TRAP III
By **T.J. Edwards**

GORILLAZ IN THE BAY V
3X KRAZY III
STRAIGHT BEAST MODE III
By **De'Kari**

KINGPIN KILLAZ IV
STREET KINGS III
PAID IN BLOOD III
CARTEL KILLAZ IV
DOPE GODS III
By **Hood Rich**

SINS OF A HUSTLA II
By **ASAD**

YAYO V
BRED IN THE GAME 2
By **S. Allen**

THE STREETS WILL TALK II
By **Yolanda Moore**

SON OF A DOPE FIEND III
HEAVEN GOT A GHETTO III
SKI MASK MONEY III
By **Renta**

LOYALTY AIN'T PROMISED III
By **Keith Williams**

I'M NOTHING WITHOUT HIS LOVE II
SINS OF A THUG II
TO THE THUG I LOVED BEFORE II
IN A HUSTLER I TRUST II
By **Monet Dragun**

QUIET MONEY IV
EXTENDED CLIP III
THUG LIFE IV
By **Trai'Quan**

THE STREETS MADE ME IV
By **Larry D. Wright**

IF YOU CROSS ME ONCE III
ANGEL V
By **Anthony Fields**

THE STREETS WILL NEVER CLOSE IV
By **K'ajji**

HARD AND RUTHLESS III
KILLA KOUNTY IV
By **Khufu**

MONEY GAME III
By **Smoove Dolla**

MURDA WAS THE CASE III
Elijah R. Freeman

AN UNFORESEEN LOVE IV
BABY, I'M WINTERTIME COLD III
By **Meesha**

QUEEN OF THE ZOO III
By **Black Migo**

CONFESSIONS OF A JACKBOY III
By **Nicholas Lock**

JACK BOYS VS DOPE BOYS IV
A GANGSTA'S QUR'AN V
COKE GIRLZ II
COKE BOYS II
LIFE OF A SAVAGE V
CHI'RAQ GANGSTAS V
SOSA GANG III
BRONX SAVAGES II
BODYMORE KINGPINS II
By **Romell Tukes**

KING KILLA II
By **Vincent "Vitto" Holloway**

BETRAYAL OF A THUG III
By **Fre$h**

THE MURDER QUEENS III
By **Michael Gallon**

THE BIRTH OF A GANGSTER III
By **Delmont Player**

TREAL LOVE II
By **Le'Monica Jackson**

FOR THE LOVE OF BLOOD III
By **Jamel Mitchell**

RAN OFF ON DA PLUG II
By **Paper Boi Rari**

HOOD CONSIGLIERE III
By **Keese**

PRETTY GIRLS DO NASTY THINGS II
By **Nicole Goosby**

PROTÉGÉ OF A LEGEND III
LOVE IN THE TRENCHES II
By **Corey Robinson**

IT'S JUST ME AND YOU II
By **Ah'Million**

FOREVER GANGSTA III
By **Adrian Dulan**

GORILLAZ IN THE TRENCHES II
By **SayNoMore**

THE COCAINE PRINCESS VIII
By **King Rio**

CRIME BOSS II
By **Playa Ray**

LOYALTY IS EVERYTHING III
By **Molotti**

HERE TODAY GONE TOMORROW II
By **Fly Rock**

REAL G'S MOVE IN SILENCE II
By **Von Diesel**

GRIMEY WAYS IV
By **Ray Vinci**

Available Now

RESTRAINING ORDER I & II
By **CA$H & Coffee**

LOVE KNOWS NO BOUNDARIES I II & III
By **Coffee**

RAISED AS A GOON I, II, III & IV
BRED BY THE SLUMS I, II, III
BLAST FOR ME I & II
ROTTEN TO THE CORE I II III
A BRONX TALE I, II, III
DUFFLE BAG CARTEL I II III IV V VI
HEARTLESS GOON I II III IV V
A SAVAGE DOPEBOY I II
DRUG LORDS I II III
CUTTHROAT MAFIA I II
KING OF THE TRENCHES
By **Ghost**

LAY IT DOWN I & II
LAST OF A DYING BREED I II
BLOOD STAINS OF A SHOTTA I & II III
By **Jamaica**

LOYAL TO THE GAME I II III
LIFE OF SIN I, II III
By **TJ & Jelissa**

IF LOVING HIM IS WRONG…I & II
LOVE ME EVEN WHEN IT HURTS I II III
By **Jelissa**

BLOODY COMMAS I & II
SKI MASK CARTEL I, II & III
KING OF NEW YORK I II, III IV V
RISE TO POWER I II III
COKE KINGS I II III IV V
BORN HEARTLESS I II III IV
KING OF THE TRAP I II
By **T.J. Edwards**

WHEN THE STREETS CLAP BACK I & II III
THE HEART OF A SAVAGE I II III IV
MONEY MAFIA I II
LOYAL TO THE SOIL I II III
By **Jibril Williams**

A DISTINGUISHED THUG STOLE MY HEART I II &
III
LOVE SHOULDN'T HURT I II III IV
RENEGADE BOYS I II III IV
PAID IN KARMA I II III
SAVAGE STORMS I II III
AN UNFORESEEN LOVE I II III
BABY, I'M WINTERTIME COLD I II
By **Meesha**

A GANGSTER'S CODE I &, II III
A GANGSTER'S SYN I II III
THE SAVAGE LIFE I II III
CHAINED TO THE STREETS I II III
BLOOD ON THE MONEY I II III
A GANGSTA'S PAIN I II III
By **J-Blunt**

PUSH IT TO THE LIMIT
By **Bre' Hayes**

BLOOD OF A BOSS I, II, III, IV, V
SHADOWS OF THE GAME
TRAP BASTARD
By **Askari**

THE STREETS BLEED MURDER I, II & III
THE HEART OF A GANGSTA I II& III
By **Jerry Jackson**

CUM FOR ME I II III IV V VI VII VIII
An **LDP Erotica Collaboration**

BRIDE OF A HUSTLA I II & II
THE FETTI GIRLS I, II& III
CORRUPTED BY A GANGSTA I, II III, IV
BLINDED BY HIS LOVE
THE PRICE YOU PAY FOR LOVE I, II ,III
DOPE GIRL MAGIC I II III
By **Destiny Skai**

WHEN A GOOD GIRL GOES BAD
By **Adrienne**

A GANGSTER'S REVENGE I II III & IV
THE BOSS MAN'S DAUGHTERS I II III IV V
A SAVAGE LOVE I & II
BAE BELONGS TO ME I II
A HUSTLER'S DECEIT I, II, III
WHAT BAD BITCHES DO I, II, III
SOUL OF A MONSTER I II III
KILL ZONE
A DOPE BOY'S QUEEN I II III
TIL DEATH
By **Aryanna**

THE COST OF LOYALTY I II III
By Kweli

A KINGPIN'S AMBITION
A KINGPIN'S AMBITION **II**
I MURDER FOR THE DOUGH
By **Ambitious**

TRUE SAVAGE I II III IV V VI VII
DOPE BOY MAGIC I, II, III
MIDNIGHT CARTEL I II III
CITY OF KINGZ I II
NIGHTMARE ON SILENT AVE
THE PLUG OF LIL MEXICO II
CLASSIC CITY
By **Chris Green**

A DOPEBOY'S PRAYER
By **Eddie "Wolf" Lee**

THE KING CARTEL I, II & III
By **Frank Gresham**

THESE NIGGAS AIN'T LOYAL I, II & III
By **Nikki Tee**

GANGSTA SHYT I II &III
By **CATO**

THE ULTIMATE BETRAYAL
By **Phoenix**

BOSS'N UP I, II & III
By **Royal Nicole**

SON OF A DOPEFIEND 3 | RENTA

I LOVE YOU TO DEATH
By **Destiny J**

I RIDE FOR MY HITTA
I STILL RIDE FOR MY HITTA
By **Misty Holt**

LOVE & CHASIN' PAPER
By **Qay Crockett**

TO DIE IN VAIN
SINS OF A HUSTLA
By **ASAD**

BROOKLYN HUSTLAZ
By **Boogsy Morina**

BROOKLYN ON LOCK I & II
By **Sonovia**

GANGSTA CITY
By **Teddy Duke**

A DRUG KING AND HIS DIAMOND I & II III
A DOPEMAN'S RICHES
HER MAN, MINE'S TOO I, II
CASH MONEY HO'S
THE WIFEY I USED TO BE I II
PRETTY GIRLS DO NASTY THINGS
By Nicole Goosby

LIPSTICK KILLAH I, II, III
CRIME OF PASSION I II & III
FRIEND OR FOE I II III
By **Mimi**

TRAPHOUSE KING I II & III
KINGPIN KILLAZ I II III
STREET KINGS I II
PAID IN BLOOD I II
CARTEL KILLAZ I II III
DOPE GODS I II
By **Hood Rich**

STEADY MOBBN' I, II, III
THE STREETS STAINED MY SOUL I II III
By **Marcellus Allen**

WHO SHOT YA I, II, III
SON OF A DOPE FIEND I II
HEAVEN GOT A GHETTO I II
SKI MASK MONEY I II
By **Renta**

GORILLAZ IN THE BAY I II III IV
TEARS OF A GANGSTA I II
3X KRAZY I II
STRAIGHT BEAST MODE I II
By **DE'KARI**

TRIGGADALE I II III
MURDA WAS THE CASE I II
By **Elijah R. Freeman**

THE STREETS ARE CALLING
By **Duquie Wilson**

SLAUGHTER GANG I II III
RUTHLESS HEART I II III
By **Willie Slaughter**

GOD BLESS THE TRAPPERS I, II, III
THESE SCANDALOUS STREETS I, II, III
FEAR MY GANGSTA I, II, III IV, V
THESE STREETS DON'T LOVE NOBODY I, II
BURY ME A G I, II, III, IV, V
A GANGSTA'S EMPIRE I, II, III, IV
THE DOPEMAN'S BODYGAURD I II
THE REALEST KILLAZ I II III
THE LAST OF THE OGS I II III
By **Tranay Adams**

MARRIED TO A BOSS I II III
By **Destiny Skai & Chris Green**

KINGZ OF THE GAME I II III IV V VI VII
CRIME BOSS
By **Playa Ray**

FUK SHYT
By **Blakk Diamond**

DON'T F#CK WITH MY HEART I II
By **Linnea**

ADDICTED TO THE DRAMA I II III
IN THE ARM OF HIS BOSS II
By **Jamila**

YAYO I II III IV
A SHOOTER'S AMBITION I II
BRED IN THE GAME
By **S. Allen**

LOYALTY AIN'T PROMISED I II
By **Keith Williams**

TRAP GOD I II III
RICH $AVAGE I II III
MONEY IN THE GRAVE I II III
By **Martell Troublesome Bolden**

FOREVER GANGSTA I II
GLOCKS ON SATIN SHEETS I II
By **Adrian Dulan**

TOE TAGZ I II III IV
LEVELS TO THIS SHYT I II
IT'S JUST ME AND YOU
By **Ah'Million**

KINGPIN DREAMS I II III
RAN OFF ON DA PLUG
By **Paper Boi Rari**

CONFESSIONS OF A GANGSTA I II III IV
CONFESSIONS OF A JACKBOY I II
By **Nicholas Lock**

I'M NOTHING WITHOUT HIS LOVE
SINS OF A THUG
TO THE THUG I LOVED BEFORE
A GANGSTA SAVED XMAS
IN A HUSTLER I TRUST
By **Monet Dragun**

QUIET MONEY I II III
THUG LIFE I II III
EXTENDED CLIP I II
A GANGSTA'S PARADISE
By **Trai'Quan**

SON OF A DOPEFIEND 3 | RENTA

CAUGHT UP IN THE LIFE I II III
THE STREETS NEVER LET GO I II III
By **Robert Baptiste**

NEW TO THE GAME I II III
MONEY, MURDER & MEMORIES I II III
By **Malik D. Rice**

CREAM I II III
THE STREETS WILL TALK
By **Yolanda Moore**

LIFE OF A SAVAGE I II III IV
A GANGSTA'S QUR'AN I II III IV
MURDA SEASON I II III
GANGLAND CARTEL I II III
CHI'RAQ GANGSTAS I II III IV
KILLERS ON ELM STREET I II III
JACK BOYZ N DA BRONX I II III
A DOPEBOY'S DREAM I II III
JACK BOYS VS DOPE BOYS I II III
COKE GIRLZ
COKE BOYS
SOSA GANG I II
BRONX SAVAGES
BODYMORE KINGPINS
By **Romell Tukes**

THE STREETS MADE ME I II III
By **Larry D. Wright**

CONCRETE KILLA I II III
VICIOUS LOYALTY I II III
By **Kingpen**

THE ULTIMATE SACRIFICE I, II, III, IV, V, VI
KHADIFI
IF YOU CROSS ME ONCE I II
ANGEL I II III IV
IN THE BLINK OF AN EYE
By **Anthony Fields**

THE LIFE OF A HOOD STAR
By **Ca$h & Rashia Wilson**

THE STREETS WILL NEVER CLOSE I II III
By **K'ajji**

NIGHTMARES OF A HUSTLA I II III
By **King Dream**

HARD AND RUTHLESS I II
MOB TOWN 251
THE BILLIONAIRE BENTLEYS I II III
REAL G'S MOVE IN SILENCE
By **Von Diesel**

GHOST MOB
By **Stilloan Robinson**

MOB TIES I II III IV V VI
SOUL OF A HUSTLER, HEART OF A KILLER I II
GORILLAZ IN THE TRENCHES
By **SayNoMore**

BODYMORE MURDERLAND I II III
THE BIRTH OF A GANGSTER I II
By **Delmont Player**

FOR THE LOVE OF A BOSS
By **C. D. Blue**

KILLA KOUNTY I II III IV
By Khufu

MOBBED UP I II III IV
THE BRICK MAN I II III IV V
THE COCAINE PRINCESS I II III IV V VI VII
By **King Rio**

MONEY GAME I II
By **Smoove Dolla**

A GANGSTA'S KARMA I II III
By **FLAME**

KING OF THE TRENCHES I II III
By **GHOST & TRANAY ADAMS**

QUEEN OF THE ZOO I II
By **Black Migo**

GRIMEY WAYS I II III
By **Ray Vinci**

XMAS WITH AN ATL SHOOTER
By **Ca$h & Destiny Skai**

KING KILLA
By **Vincent "Vitto" Holloway**

BETRAYAL OF A THUG I II
By **Fre$h**

SON OF A DOPEFIEND 3 | RENTA

THE MURDER QUEENS I II
By **Michael Gallon**

TREAL LOVE
By **Le'Monica Jackson**

FOR THE LOVE OF BLOOD I II
By **Jamel Mitchell**

HOOD CONSIGLIERE I II
By **Keese**

PROTÉGÉ OF A LEGEND I II
LOVE IN THE TRENCHES
By **Corey Robinson**

BORN IN THE GRAVE I II III
By **Self Made Tay**

MOAN IN MY MOUTH
By **XTASY**

TORN BETWEEN A GANGSTER AND A
GENTLEMAN
By **J-BLUNT & Miss Kim**

LOYALTY IS EVERYTHING I II
By **Molotti**

HERE TODAY GONE TOMORROW
By **Fly Rock**

PILLOW PRINCESS
By **S. Hawkins**

SON OF A DOPEFIEND 3 | RENTA

SANCTIFIED AND HORNY
by **XTASY**

THE PLUG OF LIL MEXICO 2
by **CHRIS GREEN**

THE BLACK DIAMOND CARTEL
by **SAYNOMORE**

THE BIRTH OF A GANGSTER 3
by **DELMONT PLAYER**

BOOKS BY LDP'S CEO, CA$H

TRUST IN NO MAN
TRUST IN NO MAN 2
TRUST IN NO MAN 3
BONDED BY BLOOD
SHORTY GOT A THUG
THUGS CRY
THUGS CRY 2
THUGS CRY 3
TRUST NO BITCH
TRUST NO BITCH 2
TRUST NO BITCH 3
TIL MY CASKET DROPS
RESTRAINING ORDER
RESTRAINING ORDER 2
IN LOVE WITH A CONVICT
LIFE OF A HOOD STAR
XMAS WITH AN ATL SHOOTER

www.ingramcontent.com/pod-product-compliance
Lightning Source LLC
Chambersburg PA
CBHW051537260626
47170CB00003B/979